BURY YOUR GAYS

ALSO BY
CHUCK TINGLE

Camp Damascus
Straight

CHUCK TINGLE

BURY YOUR GAYS

NIGHTFIRE

TOR PUBLISHING GROUP
NEW YORK

BURY YOUR GAYS

Copyright © 2024 by Chuck Tingle

A Nightfire Book
Published by Tom Doherty Associates / Tor Publishing Group
120 Broadway
New York, NY 10271

www.torpublishinggroup.com

Nightfire™ is a trademark of Macmillan Publishing Group, LLC.

The Library of Congress Cataloging-in-Publication Data is available upon request.

ISBN 978-1-250-87465-8 (hardcover)
ISBN 978-1-250-87467-2 (ebook)

Our books may be purchased in bulk for promotional, educational, or business use. Please contact your local bookseller or the Macmillan Corporate and Premium Sales Department at 1-800-221-7945, extension 5442, or by email at MacmillanSpecialMarkets@macmillan.com.

First Edition: 2024

Printed in the United States of America

0 9 8 7 6 5 4 3 2 1

CONTENTS

BURY YOUR GAYS

MEMENTO MORI

The backlot is humming with energy today, and I'm not thrilled about it. Rolling up to the east security gate is typically a surefire way to cruise right in and get any tedious studio afternoon over with, but I've discovered a line of five or six cars waiting for me.

It's always *something* with this place, and today that something is poor traffic management.

I settle in, watching April at the security booth as she flashes her welcoming smile at each producer, actor, writer, and director making their way through the checkpoint.

I can't quite see who she's talking to, the rising California sun washing my eyes in its golden glow. Even through these dark sunglasses it's hard to get a read on the driver of the McLaren with the scissor doors and obnoxious paint job, but a shock of stark white hair hints at Raymond Nelson, head of the animation department and real-deal Hollywood legend. This would make sense, as he rarely keeps the same car for more than a month and I've yet to notice this vehicle on the lot.

Ray is old-school. I used to be terrified of the guy, but have since come to appreciate his no-bullshit approach to this business after two decades of weathering it myself. Regardless of your opinion on Raymond Nelson's studio battles and legendary tantrums, there's a lot to be said for sticking around as long as he has.

A few years back I worked for him on a pitch, a cartoon concept that never really got off the ground and eventually became a live-action TV pilot, and while his ideas about certain social issues are *alarmingly* dated, he maintains the spark that once propelled him to the top. The guy isn't just some suit. Raymond put in the hours, hand-drawing every cell of his first animated short before I was even born. He's part of the rare handful still with us who built this studio from the ground up.

On the other hand, he's also a blowhard asshole.

Ray eventually pulls onward in his six-figure sportscar, this lime-green vehicle acting as yet another billboard for his decades-deep midlife crisis. The absurd sight of Ray's new luxury vehicles usually triggers a smile of bemusement, but as Ray leaves the checkpoint I notice a look of exaggerated distaste on April's face.

This expression quickly shifts back to her usual warmth as the next car pulls up, and the process begins anew.

I move forward in turn, the whole line shifting one space, then put my car in park again. For the life of me, I can't remember it ever taking this long.

It's also possible my nerves are just stretching my perception of time like taffy. I'm rarely tense over a meeting—I just show up, tell them to fuck off, and leave—but this one feels different.

Everything in this town feels different lately.

I lean back in my seat and turn down the car stereo, which has been blasting the snarling howl of British punk band IDLES into my eardrums at an admittedly dangerous volume, and check in on myself. Deep breaths fill my lungs—in and out, in and out—and I facilitate this moment of peace even more by cracking the windows a bit.

To my right lies the Harold Brothers backlot, a sprawling mass of offices and breathtakingly large soundstages. To my left is an empty field of tall yellow grass that leads right up to the backside of Griffith Park. The studio owns these unused swaths of land, and one day they, too, will be covered in monstrous, rectangular soundstages. For now, however, these rare natural spaces peeking through the vast Los Angeles sprawl are treating my ears to a soft, brittle rustle, the gentle wind shifting millions of dry grass blades against their neighbors.

My eyes close as the sun warms my skin.

Honk! Honk!

The sounds are unexpected, but too far away to prompt much of a reaction. This invasion of my auditory space consists of two staccato blurts from a horn, an instrument that could just as easily belong to a circus clown as it could a passing bicycle.

I slowly open my eyes and turn my head toward the open field.

A cardboard cutout stands awkwardly within this vast plain of golden grass, frozen in place as the blades rattle gently against its cartoon knees. It's a human-sized rendering of Chucky the Woodchuck, his two massive front teeth framed by the maniacal grin that launched an animation empire. Weekday mornings I'd watch this ball of hand-drawn energy face off against Wiley Wolf, the two-dimensional forest their own personal *Home Alone* house stuffed full of anvils, mallets, and comically oversized dynamite sticks.

It's always thrilling to see prey outsmart predator, even if that means strapping an anthropomorphic wolf to rocket skates and sending him to the moon.

This cardboard depiction of Chucky the Woodchuck is from his early days, stark black and white with a distinctly vintage design. He doesn't have his gloves yet, and his divergent eyes are much wilder than the modern version.

Back in the day, there was a large portion of potential viewers who found his zany, buck-toothed expression . . . well, frightening. Adjustments were made.

Chucky is holding a bicycle horn in one hand.

I stare at this cardboard cutout in silence, first a little surprised I hadn't noticed it until now, then wondering how it got all the way out there. The field is enormous, and while we're close enough to the back gate for

Chucky the Woodchuck's arrival to have a dozen or so logical explanations, there's something about his placement that feels odd. Someone had to trudge deep into that tall grass and prop him up.

Chucky the Woodchuck's rolling, multidirectional eyes feel as though they've somehow met mine, angled to both the left and the right, yet drawing me in. I get the same eerie feeling I did all those years ago, plopped in front of the television set.

The original design really *was* creepy.

Honk!

The squeak blasts again, only this time it's much louder. I jolt abruptly, eyes flickering up to the rearview mirror and discovering the driver behind me is serving a gesture of frustration.

The cars ahead have already pulled forward two full spaces, leaving a gaping hole.

"Get off your phone!" the driver shouts.

"I'm not on my phone!" I yell back, awkwardly pointing at the palm of my hand.

He just shakes his head with seething irritation. He flicks his hand toward me, shooing me onward.

"Fuck you, too!" I shout in parting.

By the time I get my car in drive it's a straight shot to the security booth.

"Crazy day, huh?" I start, pulling up next to April's little white security hut.

"Misha!" she cries, excited to see me or doing an excellent job of pretending. "It's been a while."

I nod. "You know a script's bad when they can't just schedule a Zoom about it."

"I'm sure it's great. Congratulations, by the way."

I force a nod of acceptance, feeling awkward about the praise. I never quite learned how to take a compliment, and at this age I don't think I ever will. "Sure. Yeah."

April hands over a small blue box. "Thumb," she instructs.

"You're asking for prints now?"

April shrugs. "They're updating everything around here. New security stuff. That's why it's taking so long."

I press my thumb against the tiny device a few times until, eventually, it emits a soft digital beep.

"All done," April announces with a grin. She takes back the glowing blue cube. "Good luck with the meeting."

I continue on, glancing in my rearview mirror to discover the cardboard woodchuck has disappeared, probably knocked over by the wind and laid out somewhere in the tall grass.

Giant beige walls rise around me, a gridded labyrinth of passages between every soundstage on the lot. These towering buildings block out the sun, creating a web of shady alleyways where various production teams avoid the heat and go about their daily routines. As with the gate, a strange disarray permeates this scene, the hustle and bustle of an already active backlot taken to unexpected heights.

A single building, the Harold Brothers water tower, looms above the rest, and as this iconic structure bathes me in its shade, I remove my sunglasses.

This particular section of Harold Brothers Studios is arranged around a central hub, a portion of the lot where important office bungalows are situated and a coffee shop routinely attracts tired crew members on lunch breaks. A well-manicured grass field sits at the center, complete with a lush, palm-filled garden and a constantly flowing fountain of crystalline water.

I park in a spot near the promenade, climbing from my vehicle and heading up the winding sandstone path. People are everywhere, some of them wandering past me in the middle of impassioned conversations on their AirPods, others talking loudly over coffee as they perch on various benches. I pick up the pace.

My meeting awaits just beyond this chaotic little oasis.

"Misha, you fuck!" someone calls out, prompting an unexpected halt in my stride.

Fortunately, I'd know this voice anywhere, and a smile has already bloomed across my face before I even turn around.

Tara Ito is rushing across the lawn to greet me, my best friend's arms wide open as she prepares her warm embrace. She's wearing a bright orange suit with a glittering, silver-sequined button-up and a bolo tie underneath, three very distinct choices that might like look downright comical on anyone else.

My friend somehow pulls it off, though. She always pulls it off.

Tara is small, but her energy is twice the size of an average human. Her hair is naturally black, but she's managed to lift it all the way to a stark white that works in playful contrast with her youthful appearance.

The only thing that gives her away as someone currently in the midst of a grueling workday is the leather satchel cast haphazardly over her shoulder, an assortment of black and yellow computer cables bubbling forth.

The fact that Tara spends most of her time alone, poring over server bays and strolling down dark industrial corridors, is hilarious to me. We're surrounded by executives prepping for a day's worth of face-to-face meetings, yet none of them have *half* the confidence and swagger Tara does.

We hug. "How's my beautiful baby boy?" Tara questions, pulling back to look me in the eyes. I'm three years older than Tara, but her predilection for calling me "baby" remains unfettered.

"I'm ready to get this meeting over with," I admit.

"Oh, your *super difficult* meeting where the VP of television gives you two notes and then sucks you off for an hour?" she counters. "I'm implementing the revised IP security protocol across fifty-seven buildings today."

"Wanna trade?" I quip.

"You know I don't swing that way," Tara replies, then winks. "I don't swing any way, baby."

"Still on to watch those screeners later?"

"God, yes," Tara confirms with a sigh. She's straightening out the collar of my jacket now, picking off some lint and flattening the crease.

Suddenly, Tara riffles through the inside pocket of my blazer and yanks out my cell phone. Before I get the chance to protest she holds it up to my face and unlocks the screen.

"Put your phone on airplane mode whenever you're on the lot," she states, scrolling through my settings and taking care of it herself.

Once finished, Tara opens my jacket and returns the phone to its rightful position.

I can't help laughing. "Why?"

My friend's expression flickers with a rare moment of solemn gravity. "Data packets."

"I have no idea what those are," I admit. "What if I need to take a call?"

"Do what I do," she replies, pulling two separate phones from her pocket and fanning them out in one hand. "Work and play. Congratulations, by the way."

For the second time today I find myself immediately dismissing a compliment. I grimace before Tara can even finish her sentence. "It's an empty category. I don't even think it's televised."

"You fucking asshole," she scolds, putting her phones away. "It *is* televised. It's a big deal. People don't just *accidentally* get nominated for an Oscar."

"Best Live Action Short Film. There's no dialogue and it stars a mouse."

"It's a big deal," she counters sternly, placing a hand on my shoulder.

"Thank you," I finally relent, accepting her words of appreciation. I glance around the park. "Is that why it's so crazy today? Nominee announcements?"

Tara laughs, then nods her head toward the soundstage looming to my right. "You could say that."

I follow my friend's gesture, gazing up at a colossal display emblazoned across the building. I was so focused on getting in and out of the back-lot that I didn't even take a moment to look up. Now that I have, I'm overwhelmed by the presence of an enormous mural.

The entire side of this soundstage has been covered by an image of superstar actor Chris Oak. He's sitting at a glass table and looking exhausted, the lighting orange and dramatic as it shows off his notori-ously expressive face. The guy is breathtakingly handsome, his brown hair slicked back but disheveled. He's wearing a white suit, a ghost of the 1980s woven through its tailoring. A hint of brilliant red is splat-tered across the stark cuff of Chris's wrist.

Workers perched on hanging scaffolding are carefully pasting this image into place, rolling it onto the wall piece by piece. Still, there's more than enough here to deliver the text.

Huge block letters stretch across the top: **THE YEAR WAS 1986. THE CITY WAS MIAMI. THE MAN WAS LEGENDARY. CHRIS OAK IS ENZO BASILE IN . . . *BROKEN DON*.**

The lower half of the image has additional copy, but it's still too shocking to fully accept.

I force myself to read it aloud. "Making history. First Academy Award nomination for a posthumous performance."

There's plenty of folks who've been nominated for big awards after their death, and while this is typically a story of note, it's nothing earth-shattering. The difference is that these previous *nominations* occurred posthumously, but the *performance itself* did not.

Chris Oak died three years before filming *Broken Don*—the fictional crime epic that's now poised to sweep awards season. His likeness was fabricated from whole cloth using mountains of previous footage and cutting-edge CGI technology.

Supposedly, the choices in digital Chris's performance are precisely what the actor would've done, and now this uncanny AI creation has been nominated for best actor.

Thanks to the valiant strikes of hardworking actors and writers, humans are still being credited for *some* of this work, and Chris's family will receive a portion of the residuals.

The pay is technically better than ever. Which is to say, still not enough.

"They're having him do a video chat press tour," Tara informs me, her eyes still glued to the enormous mural before us. "That's why I'm updating security protocols. The studio doesn't want anyone hacking the transmissions and getting a look at the HBS special sauce."

These days, a studio's private algorithm is just as valuable as their stable of talent and, to their credit, Harold Brothers is the best of the best. AI performances are hardly a new phenomenon, but HBS are the only ones whose creations are indistinguishable from a flesh-and-blood actor. The eerie CGI renditions of other studios often get a pass for sheer novelty, but the uncanny valley is still too wide for serious consideration.

That's why Harold Brothers Studios is getting the nomination, and they're not.

"What a nightmare," I sigh.

"It's horrifically ghoulish and probably the end of the world," Tara states flatly, then pats her satchel of wires and cables. "I feel safer with my eye on the zombies, though, and looking after the graveyard pays pretty well."

She's not wrong. We still need to eat.

"Hey, don't be late for your meeting," Tara says.

I give her another hug before we part ways. "I'll see you tonight."

With that, I turn and forge deeper into the sun-soaked belly of this multibillion-dollar beast.

It's not long before the winding sandstone path arrives at a towering office, constructed with the same breezy Southern California style as the bungalows but looming three stories high. This structure is surrounded by massive succulents, the drought-resistant plants jutting out toward me with enormous green spikes.

As I enter the lobby, a secretary greets me with a smile and a nod. I've never seen her before, but she knows my name.

"Misha Byrne," the woman says, motioning toward the elevator. "Mr. Hays is ready for you."

I step into the lift and push a button for the top floor. Soon enough, the metal doors are opening wide to reveal a stunning view of the studio backlot.

This room features massive floor-to-ceiling windows, and although we're not high enough to see over the nearby soundstages, I'm now positioned to gaze directly down one of the shadowy aisles and straight to the hills beyond. To the right is that colossal mural of Chris Oak as Enzo Basile, its diligent crew nearly finished with their application.

The office of Jack Hays looks as though it were manifested from the pages of a mid-century modern coffee table book, perfectly staged to appear more like someone's luxury beachside vacation rental than an office. The only thing that gives the charade away is a handful of movie and television posters lining the wall to my right, some of the most important media offerings in Harold Brothers history.

A poster for my first show at Harold Brothers, *Devil's Due*, hangs at the far end of this row, partially tucked behind a wide-leafed indoor palm. On it, a demonic librarian sits behind a check-out counter, her head resting on one hand as she rolls her eyes in overblown disappointment. A stack of overdue library books rest next to her, and the top one is on fire.

A friendly demon is forced to work at a children's library. Hilarity ensues. Everyone learns.

It was canceled after one season—hardly up to the caliber of the other hits on this wall—but for some reason Jack still hangs it.

It's hidden behind a plant, but still.

Jack claps his hands when he sees me, proudly showing off a display of alarmingly white teeth. "There he is!" the executive cheers, strolling across the room.

Jack's work takes place entirely behind the scenes, yet his appearance suggests the end result of some grueling casting call for "charming asshole studio head." His suit is perfectly tailored, fitting his toned chest and shoulders with surreal perfection. The man's eyes are brilliant blue, and his youthful haircut would be marred by salt-and-pepper grays if not for consistent sandy blond dye jobs. A single white bud is stuffed into his right ear, Bluetooth connected and ready for anything.

I extend my hand for a shake, but Jack's response is to offer me a pound with his closed fist.

"Thanks for coming in to see me, buddy," Jack continues, motioning toward a chair next to his desk.

"What's going on?"

A look of bemused surprise flickers across Jack's face as he takes his place behind the table. He leans back in his chair, grinning. "Right down to business, huh?"

"Well, I hate being here," I remind him.

Jack lets out a chuckle. "You don't even wanna ask me how Braylin's soccer tournament went?"

"I'm sorry. How did Braylin's soccer tournament go?"

"Fucking terrible. Her team sucks," Jack states flatly, "but she has fun out there. You should come next time."

I nod along. "I mean, I've got a lot of work to do. *Travelers* starts filming in a few months."

"I know when filming starts, Misha."

There's nothing sinister in the way he says these words, yet they immediately strike a chord. Jack doesn't need to be angry to wield his power; the full might of a massive media conglomerate does that work for him.

Jack motions out the window toward Enzo's captivating visage, changing the subject and setting the pace whether I like it or not. "Pretty cool . . . *Technology*, right?"

"I feel like the real Chris Oak would've turned down that role," I say. "He didn't really play villains."

"Well, how exciting is that? Now he can," Jack counters.

"Was he even Italian?"

Jack gets deathly serious for a moment. "The ethnicity of the Broken Don is left ambiguous in the script."

I furrow my brow.

"Wasn't there an episode of *Travelers* about the ghost of Elvis Presley?" Jack prods. "I don't recall Misha Byrne having any problem using someone's celebrity likeness in a script that *he* wrote."

"Elvis *Presslin*," I remind Jack. "Legal made me change his last name once they realized The King would be dismembering people."

Jack stares past me and squints a little, the expression of someone searching their memory banks and coming up empty.

"Regardless, nobody thought it was *actually* Elvis," I continue. "No shade to David Duchovny—he did a great job. I also had a good reason to include him. Elvis was a symbol of my relationship with fame and celebrity."

"I still don't see the difference."

"One choice was for art and the other for commerce."

Jack can't help cracking a smile. "God bless you, Misha. You still think there's a difference."

The muralists have finished their *Broken Don* ad and a new crew has arrived. This second shift is preparing an enormous pully-and-lever system, lifting various speakers, classical instruments, and other equipment onto the soundstage roof.

"Don't you wanna know what they're doing over there?" Jack asks, changing the subject.

"No."

"Music video shoot." He barrels onward. "Incredible soundtrack. *Also* nominated. They've got an 'Owner of a Lonely Heart' cover that'll make you *cum*."

"Right," I say dryly, nodding along.

"But *you* know how getting nominated feels. Congratu-fucking-lations, my man."

"Thank you," I reply. "Can we get to the part where you explain what I'm doing here?"

"You're a very important member of this family, I hope you know that. I hope you know how much *I* personally love your writing," the executive gushes. "That cliffhanger at the end of *Travelers* season two? Oh my *God*. Seriously, you floor me. You fucking *floor* me, buddy. I mean, you could do it ten times faster if you'd let a computer take the lead, but whatever. There's still an audience for the organic stuff. Don't forget that."

"But there's a problem," I interject, hoping to cut to the chase for a second time.

Jack hesitates, his expression shifting a bit. "A very small problem," he explains. "I got your season-three finale and I read it over on Friday . . . a few people read it over, actually . . . and we've got some notes."

I settle in, trying not to react just yet. It's not that I have a problem with getting notes, but this almost never happens. I'm a skilled enough writer that the work speaks for itself, and as long as ratings are good, the fine folks at Harold Brothers generally keep their opinions to themselves.

"Did you know my nephew is gay?" Jack asks.

"Congrats?" I reply awkwardly.

"I'm just letting you know that I'm not some right-wing nutjob, I understand gay culture. I'm *plugged in*."

"I've known you for like a decade and a half," I remind him. "You're very homophobic."

A flicker of panic surges across Jack's face.

"I'm fucking with you," I continue. "Or am I?"

"Wait, what?"

"Get to the point," I snap.

"The point is, *I'm* not the bad guy here," Jack continues. "It's the *suits*, you know? It's the whole damn *system*."

I stare at him blankly, genuinely curious if Jack's aware that *he's* the system.

"We need you to change the kissing scene between Agent Lexa and Agent Naomi."

I scoff. "Walk me through this. If they don't kiss, then how are the viewers gonna confirm they've actually been falling in love the whole time? This episode *starts* with them sharing a one-bed hotel room!"

Jack winces a bit, shifting in his chair. "Yeah, we're gonna need you to change that part, too."

I can't help the laughter that suddenly bubbles up within me and escapes my throat like a noxious cloud of anxiety.

This type of queer erasure was common years ago, but times have changed. Gay characters are everywhere now, and the audience for this type of story is only growing. Pulling the plug on the lesbian relationship of your heroes—one that's been simmering for years—is utterly absurd.

"You understand I've been laying the groundwork for this moment, right?" I snap, the anger finally surging through my veins in a potent wave. "This was always the plan for *Travelers*. I'm not going to straighten out two of the most obviously gay characters on television. Besides, the whole second half of their arc is based on this relationship being romantic."

Jack nods along, wearing a face that already screams I-hear-your-concerns-*but* . . .

"You've put a lot of heart into these two," Jack continues. "That's why I called you in to discuss this face-to-face. There are a few options here, Misha."

"Does one of them include a kiss between Carey Lexa and May Naomi?" I question.

"Yes," my boss replies.

A hint of relief suddenly enters the caustic mix of anger and fear that's swirling through me. Maybe this whole thing is just a huge misunderstanding.

"You've just gotta kill th—" Jack finally continues.

"Fuck you," I exclaim, well before the final word has slipped through his lips.

I leap from my chair, struggling to find a way for my body to process this frustrated energy. I begin to pace, gazing out the window at an expansive view of the juggernaut I've been riding for decades, the machine finally turning around and rumbling back to crush me under its mighty wheels.

In the early days, I was protected by the fact that I had nothing to lose, and success provided an even stronger armor against studio meddling.

Until now.

"Listen, this isn't my call, it's all up to the board," Jack explains. "I'm just the messenger."

"Who the fuck is *the board*? There's no *board.*"

"The people who sign our checks these days," he reveals, exhibiting a bit of frustration himself. Jack glances at the door as if someone out there might be listening in. He lowers his voice a bit. "The merger changed everything, buddy. It used to be *my job* to make these calls, now I just get an email from the board. Everything is fucking data points and trends and graphs and *targeted marketing.* I'd say it's all bullshit, but I've seen the results. The money doesn't lie."

"And the money says Lexa and Naomi aren't lesbians?" I question.

"Well, no," Jack counters. The executive opens an email, quickly reading it over to refresh himself on the facts. He clears his throat. "I'll tell you exactly what the money says: you need a new cast member, aged eighteen to twenty-four, white, with a conservative disposition. The money says you need to make room for this new character by eliminating one of your old leads, who have been refusing to do press, by the way, and that doesn't help. But the *real* money says you need to let your gay characters finally open up about who they are and then kill them off. *That's* the story that brings drama, and drama brings subscribers, and subscribers bring me—and by extension, you—a boatload of fucking cash. So cheer up and kill off these two chicks who don't even *exist*, buddy."

"That's not this story," I firmly retort, "and these are *creative* decisions, not executive ones."

Jack turns his computer to face me, the screen revealing an open email and a long stack of bullet points. "The algorithm says otherwise. The board has raw data on this, and they're projecting a huge leap in viewership."

I stop pacing. I had a feeling shit was gonna get weird, but not this weird.

"Remember, you've got a few options here. If you wanna make them straight you can, but the board is leaning hard toward killing Agent Lexa and Agent Naomi in a blaze of gay glory." Jack leans back in his chair, putting his hands behind his head. "I'm honestly kind of surprised. You've got a flair for drama, Misha. I thought you might get hard over some final sacrifice for love or whatever. I mean, *you're* the writer, not me, but that's got *Emmy* written all over it."

"Bury your gays," I reply, utterly deadpan.

Jack rolls his eyes.

"In film, in TV, in books . . . the queer characters never get a happy ending," I press. "Sometimes they're the first to go, other times they make some brave sacrifice in the finale, but it always ends in tragedy and death. That's why it's called *bury your gays.*"

"Okay . . . well . . . start digging," Jack suggests bluntly.

"I'm guaranteed creative control on this project." I laugh. "We have a contract."

"Contracts break all the time."

"You'd really end our deal over this?"

"There would be a very long, very arduous legal battle," Jack explains, a distinctly threatening tone seeping into his voice. "If you *did* get a payout, I don't know how much of that money you'd actually see. Studio lawyers are savage, and their pockets are endless. I'm not telling you this to fuck with you, I'm telling you this as a friend."

"So that's the big bet?" I question. "You'll make more money killing off my gay leads than you'll lose fighting the legal battle over it?"

"Or you could just come through for the studio that's had your back since day one," Jack counters. "I kill off characters *every day* in this office, Misha. You're not the first showrunner I've had this conversation with, and you certainly won't be the last. It's not a big deal if you don't make it one."

"It's a big deal to Carey Lexa and May Naomi."

Jack laughs. "Well, I hate to break it to you, but they're not real."

A wave of emotion suddenly bubbles up within my chest and sticks in my throat. I feel sick, the reality of this situation finally starting to puncture my tough exterior.

"You have about four weeks to turn in your finale script, so there's time to decide," Jack reminds me. "After that, you'll be in breach of contract and the characters will turn back over to Harold Brothers anyway. You can write them off on your own terms, or someone else will do it for you. I'm sorry, Misha. You know I love you, but this isn't my call."

Jack's demeanor suddenly changes. He straightens up and taps the white plastic bud in his ear. "Yeah. Yep. I'll be ready in five." Jack presses the earbud again, returning his gaze to mine. "See? I'm about to kill off Pickles the Police Dog, and they think they're coming up here for a full-season pickup. This is the *job*, Misha."

Jack leads me back to his elevator. He presses the call button, prompting the doors to open with a soft chime.

"Well, I'm not gonna make your changes," I announce, turning and stepping into the lift. "They'll be even gayer now."

"I guess we'll see you in court!" Jack retorts with a smile.

"Go fuck yourself!"

"Good talk, buddy!" He's still grinning as the metal doors slide closed between us.

The second I'm all alone in the mirrored lift I catch my gaze in the reflection, a late-thirties man with shaggy brown hair and angular features. My smug expression of artistic defiance immediately falters.

By the time the doors open again I've fully collected myself, despite the subtle wetness at the corners of my bright blue eyes.

I head out into the lobby, barely acknowledging Jack's secretary as she offers a cordial goodbye.

A woman in a light gray pantsuit stands up from the nearby couch, gathering her things. She strolls past me and enters the elevator, completely unaware that she's headed for an execution. The lift doors close, the shining blade of a guillotine.

Back in the courtyard I slow down a bit, struggling to rein in my emotions. I close my eyes and lean back, allowing the sun to cascade across my face and warm my skin.

Everything's gonna be fine. If there's one thing you're good at doing, it's writing yourself out of a corner.

Still, I can't help the feeling that this is something no amount of storytelling talent can overcome.

Honk!

I freeze in response to this unexpected sound drifting down from somewhere above. I open my eyes and scan the crisscrossed pattern of breezy palms hanging over my head, then beyond them to the sound-stage rooftops.

There are no answers to be found, no clowns rolling by on unicycles or cardboard cutouts of a black-and-white woodchuck.

This moment of honed senses gradually crumbles away as the chaotic backlot atmosphere returns. I didn't like coming here when things were going well, and now I'm even more anxious to put some distance between me and this cursed landscape of tram tours and live studio audiences.

I've gotta get out of here.

I start walking again, making my way past the coffee shop and over the central green. I stop only long enough to grab a free souvenir matchbook from the eatery. I drop the matches into my pocket, the fresh cardboard rectangle settling next to the one that's already there, then continue toward the parking lot.

Everything's gonna be fine, I tell myself again, fully aware that it's probably not but letting the words soothe my brain anyway.

A familiar McLaren is parked next to my car, and as I approach the vehicles I notice Raymond Nelson for the second time this morning. The ancient cartoonist is chatting up a young woman some twenty yards onward, standing under the watchful gaze of an enormous, computer-generated mob boss. The woman has several wardrobe choices draped over her shoulder, and she appears increasingly frustrated by her conversation with Raymond.

On a lot like this, there's more than enough conflict to go around. This little interaction shouldn't catch my attention as much as it does, but for some reason I resolve to keep an eye on things. Maybe it's my frustration with the whole damn studio, the anger of my previous meeting spilling over into some righteous hero complex, but instead of climbing into my car I decide to step a little closer.

I listen in, my eyes trained on the interaction between Raymond and the young wardrobe assistant. Ray is laughing, but the woman grows more agitated by the second. As their conflict reaches a climax, Ray reaches out and puts his hand around the woman's waist, a cheeky pinch inciting her to jump and struggle against him.

"Hey!" I shout, immediately prompting the animation legend to let go and meet my gaze.

He's still laughing, a truly frightening response. The guy was caught red-handed being a creep, yet his legendary status renders anything I could possibly say utterly meaningless.

"I'm just messing around." Raymond chuckles, then turns his attention back to the wardrobe assistant. "Right? I'm just messing around?"

The woman says nothing in return, simply throwing her hands up and walking away.

As I continue marching toward Raymond I quickly realize I have no idea what I'm going to do when I get there. I'm running on instinct now, a spring wound so tightly that some kind of release is inevitable. Fortunately, it's times like this that my writer's instinct kicks in. I'm not sure what path I'll take, but I certainly know what one of my heroes would do in a situation like this. It might seem silly, but this mental exercise has consistently helped me when I needed it the most.

I stop directly before the cartoonist. "Listen, you old fuck, this isn't nineteen twenty anymore. You can't just grab people like that."

Raymond continues to laugh, raising his gnarled hands in a stance of mock defensiveness. I couldn't be any less of a threat to him. "Uh-oh, security is here!"

There are plenty of things I could verbally rip into, hoping to tear him down, but a man like Raymond doesn't get into this position without thick skin. He's *hoping* I'll get wound up, waiting in a state of bemusement to see what I'll say next.

"A lot of people look up to you around here," I finally state with fiery clarity. "You're a legend, and you're better than—"

Before I have a chance to finish my sentence an unexpected yelp of panic rings out from above. The shout is so bewildering that I barely have time to look up, and at Raymond's ripe old age he doesn't even hear it.

One second I'm yelling at a smug asshole in an expensive suit, the next there's nothing there. A mighty, splintering crunch rings out, accompanied by a dissonant musical stab like this moment was a horror movie jump scare. My ears are ringing and my face is wet, but I have no idea why.

Gradually, horrified screams cut through the ringing in my ears, cries spilling forth all around me. The wardrobe assistant is standing to the side, petrified and covered in blood. Her eyes are wide, her jaw trembling.

"Are you alright?" I struggle to ask, but the words come out awkward and stilted. I wonder if I even said them at all.

I follow the woman's gaze, staring down at the mess that's appeared before me. The wooden remains of a massive grand piano have shattered across the pavement, its jet-black finish and light interior meshing with the liquified crimson mess that was once Raymond Nelson.

This would explain the brief musical accompaniment.

Ray has popped like a water balloon, his body utterly annihilated by the weight of this enormous classical instrument.

My gaze lifts skyward, eyes meeting the crew tasked with hoisting supplies onto the roof for today's video shoot. They're frozen, too, their expressions a single frame of abject horror.

A snapped cable flutters in the wind.

INSPIRATION

1996

I was nine years old, staring at the screen of a humming analog television set and absolutely certain that Agent Peters and Agent Martin were about to break out in a loving, passionate kiss. I couldn't wait to see their lips meet as they feverishly tore away each other's neatly pressed FBI suits.

Even then I was pretty good at knowing where stories were headed, not just when it comes to *Dark Encounters,* but with any show they trotted out on broadcast television in the midnineties. Those writers knew how to hit the beats. Eventually, I'd tell stories of my own—like I'm doing right now—but my young brain's understanding of life's grand mess was too visceral and intuitive to wrangle specific plot points. I hadn't done the research yet, hadn't devoured all the books I could find on constructing a screenplay (then ignored every piece of advice they doled out).

What I sensed was a series of quiet signals and tropes, little moments laid out in a specific way to guide this story to its target. Some of it was done through metaphor, other times through subtle acting cues between the two leads, but there's no doubt the signs were there. In fact, as I stared up at those flickering images dancing across the cathode-ray screen, I was absolutely certain they had *me* in mind while writing it.

Well, not me, exactly, but people like me.

Morgan and Richie were wrestling on the couch nearby, and while this slight disturbance wasn't quite enough to tear me away from my favorite show, it was still getting on my nerves. Every story thread over the last three seasons had led to this moment, and while I was initially excited to discover the season finale would land during my birthday sleepover, I hadn't yet considered what that meant in terms of distractions.

I glanced back over my shoulder from my cross-legged position on the carpet, trying my best to stay cool and casual despite the fact that my frustration had reached a boiling point. "Hey! You should watch this part!" I awkwardly suggested.

My friends stopped punching each other, seemingly confused by my relatively straightforward request. They'd noticed the faintest tremble in my words, and this sign of weakness meant the boys could worm themselves into a new, elevated position within our hierarchy of friends, if only for a moment.

Kids can be cruel, that's all there is to it. I know this now, and for some reason that makes it sting much less, but I can still remember the way it felt back then. The emotion that cut through me was not just anger or frustration, but fear.

"Why do you wanna watch this show so bad?" Richie questioned.

His tone was innocent enough, but I couldn't help feeling an accusatory vise tighten.

"It's really good," I assured them, my voice cracking as crimson flooded the water. Even at my own birthday, no one was safe.

Richie rolled his eyes. "It's boring. Nothing happens."

He was dead wrong. The relationship between Agent Peters and Agent Martin had shifted and grown in a number of fascinating ways, and those monumental character changes had been *expertly* woven through the agents' supernatural encounters with a subtle brilliance. It far surpassed any other television shows of the day.

Eventually, this kind of thoughtful writing that blended pulpy aesthetics with a deeper message would become more common on the small screen, elevating television to the level of cinema despite a few humorless arguments to the contrary. Regardless of its sometimes campy subject matter, *Dark Encounters* was a pioneer in the world of event TV.

It certainly had a *personal* effect, sending me on my path toward creative bliss—or a loop of endless artistic torture, depending on the way you look at it. Things could've happened differently if my friends had been a little more careful with their words, but then where would I be?

(I now know this was the kind of thing that sticks with you forever, pinned in the past but somehow bleeding through into the present. Every time I think about that moment, it still feels like I'm sitting right there in the basement of my parents' suburban pre-divorce home, like I'm existing in two places at once.

Some events are timeless, I guess, stuck between past, present, and future. They're a different color than the rest. A different scale. A different tense. When you turn them into a screenplay or a song or a novel or even a piece of erotic fanfiction, these are the moments that will outlive your body.)

"Just watch," I insisted, my attention still glued to the screen.

"It's Misha's birthday," my best friend, Lance, interjected forcefully.

I appreciated him reminding everyone why we were there, but at that point I'd already started feeling a suffocating blanket of embarrassment wrapping itself around me.

How could they not like *Dark Encounters*? Two FBI agents traipsed around the country solving uncanny cases of monsters and deeply rooted government conspiracies. What's not to like?

I loved the episode where they found themselves trapped in an underground cave with a half man half mole, and the time they investigated a cult of cannibal chefs. Monster-of-the-week episodes were my favorite. Of course, *everyone* loved the ones dealing with alien abductions and the vast international scheme to cover them up.

What I enjoyed the most, however, was the way Agents Peters and Martin were forced to navigate their attraction to each other.

At just nine years old, I already knew I was gay, but I wasn't entirely sure what that meant. There weren't many queer characters on TV to look up to for guidance.

Dark Encounters, however, offered me solace. With every passing episode the tension was ratchetted up just a little bit more between our leading agents, and a season finale was the perfect time to reveal all.

Truth be told, I was worried what my friends might say when this inevitable onscreen kiss occurred, but my love of *Dark Encounters* was worth the risk.

Besides, that wasn't the only big shock of the evening. Previews for this episode also teased the revelation of Agent Y, a mysterious woman who lurked in the shadows and fed the agents clues when they needed them most. This character was always cloaked in darkness, strange and stoic but infinitely wise. She was portrayed as a fountain of knowledge, a supergenius who was always one step ahead of our heroes and might or might not be on their side.

At that point, the audience had never seen her face, but within the next fifteen minutes her exposure was a near certainty.

Onscreen, an exhausted and beleaguered Agent Martin held his partner in his arms. The two of them had been struggling to escape the relentless pursuit of a man with frightening abilities thanks to partial alien DNA.

Our heroes had discovered a quiet place to hide in an unlit warehouse, but Agent Peters was wounded and labored to breathe. Of course, that wasn't the real end for this duo, but back then I was on the edge of my seat.

"Just go! Leave me here," Agent Peters demanded, coughing and sputtering as corn-syrup blood ran down his chin.

"Never," Agent Martin said, shaking his head from side to side. "We're gonna see this through . . . together."

My eyes grew wide as the characters leaned in close. This was it, the moment when everything finally revealed itself to those who hadn't been paying enough attention. I was glued to the television, so focused I barely noticed the awkward looks from my circle.

"Let's play *NBA Jam,*" my friend Seth hollered from behind me, but I ignored him.

There was more wrestling on the couch, only this time I managed to block out their distraction completely. My focus was locked tight on the flickering television screen.

"There's something I should probably tell you," Agent Peters continued, reaching out and placing a hand on his partner's cheek. It was a clear display of romantic affection.

"Don't," countered Agent Martin, a denial that could be interpreted in two distinct ways. He was either pushing back against the assumption of his colleague's looming demise or protesting the way this romance might complicate their professional relationship.

Of course, I knew they were talking about the latter.

"Shut—shut up," Agent Peters stammered in return. "I've gotta get this off my chest, and if I don't do it now, I never will."

They leaned even closer, voices lowered to whispers. Their stare hadn't broken once over the course of this entire scene as they bared their souls to each other.

I was so fucking excited.

Agent Peters hesitated, then began his admission, the words slipping delicately from his lips. "I'm . . . in love . . ." he began, causing my muscles to tense.

Trembling with anticipation, my young body could barely handle the cocktail of emotions that pulsed through its frame.

My friends had grown quiet, their eyes glued to the screen. They were fully invested, no longer fighting on the couch or wolfing down folded slices of greasy pepperoni pizza.

This was it.

"With Agent Y," my hero finished.

It felt like I'd been punched in the gut, tricked into following a trail of breadcrumbs then smacked with the hard fist of reality once I reached the end.

As if sensing my thoughts, Agent Martin laughed casually. "For a second there, I thought you were gonna say you had a *crush* on me," he joked, oozing machismo.

It was played for laughs, and it worked. My friends chuckled. The knife twisted a little more in the heart of a kid just dying to watch someone who felt the same way he did.

Onscreen, the two agents glanced up as the sound of hard shoes on a cement floor rang out through the warehouse. It was a familiar tone, one that'd been used to signal the arrival of Agent Y since this show began.

The characters turned their attention to a dimly lit corridor, fog rolling across the ground for no other reason than the fact it was a spooky warehouse on television. The back wall featured a huge swath of light upon which Agent Y's shadow was cast, the woman walking closer and closer to her inevitable reveal.

Her silhouette stretched longer and longer, betraying the proportions of typical human anatomy, and although this was clearly nothing more than a trick of the light—some underappreciated TV cinematographer's quick dabble into German expressionism—I no longer cared to find out how she really looked.

I was a year or so too young to casually throw around the word *fuck* just yet, but I can gladly say it now: fuck this show.

Tears welled up in my eyes as I sprang to my feet and rushed toward the screen, forcefully slamming the power button just seconds before Agent Y was revealed. I didn't care anymore.

"Hey!" Richie cried out, frustrated.

"You don't wanna see what happens?" another friend interjected.

After all that, they were finally interested.

"Who cares," I fumbled, sniffing a little as I struggled to contain the emotions simmering through my veins and threatening to boil over.

My friends abruptly froze, recognizing that something peculiar was going on. A silence fell over the room, covering the pizza and popcorn and sleeping bags and scattered *Magic: The Gathering* cards with an unexpected emotional weight.

Of all the vicious little fuckers that surrounded me, none was more frightening than Richie. He was a tough kid, but also unusually perceptive of the world around him. Later on, I'd realize that Richie was a bully, among other things.

"You know why Misha likes that show so much?" Richie joked. "He's got a big fat crush on that Agent Martin guy."

A wave of heat washed over my skin, a force so powerful it nearly buckled me at the knees. I'd been struggling to hold it together, but this accusation was the thing that finally knocked me over the edge. I'd fortified the emotional dam as much as I could, but the cracks had grown well past the point of repair.

The next thing I knew the levee had broken, washing through me and provoking my body to spin away from my friends in a sobbing mess.

I put some distance between myself and the group, snot running down my face as I hurried for the stairs and began my ascent.

"Hey, come back!" Lance cried out. "He's just kidding!"

But he wasn't kidding, and he wasn't wrong.

I did have a crush on Agent Martin.

After pleading with my mom to not send Richie home, I finally returned to my friends in the basement.

Nobody mentioned my outburst. In fact, they barely looked over from the game of *NBA Jam* on the television before them.

I tucked the final remnants of my outburst away, then walked over and flopped onto the couch.

"I've got next."

TO SEE AND BE SEEN

The stonework driveway is long and winding, snaking its way through a forest of overgrown palms and ferns that spring up on either side of us in the relative darkness. Upward-facing lights give portions of this tropical flora a luminous green glow, painting shadows across the canopy above as distant music rumbles through the night.

This kind of lengthy walk to your destination is rare in the residential zones of a city where space is limited and real estate is impossibly pricey, yet here we are. A rare few of these sprawling Laurel Canyon lots still extend in large swaths across the hillside, but most were divided up for the cash ages ago.

The mansion looms before us.

As we first catch sight of this structure through the tangled vines and trees, Zeke places his hand on my shoulder, stopping me in my tracks. I turn to face him, taking note of the way his features are framed by the stark, impressionistic lighting.

Ezekiel Romero is handsome in a casual way, his hair long and his face constantly covered in stubble that never seems to grow or recede. His style is rugged and unplanned, and he can usually be found in a simple jean jacket, graphic tee combo (tonight's shirt depicts a faded Sailor Jerry anchor).

Zeke is the first openly bi guy I've ever dated, which was slightly intimidating at first for reasons I didn't entirely understand. Eventually, I realized it wasn't the bisexual part that held so much psychic weight over me, it was the *openly* bisexual part. Zeke has a peaceful confidence that's hard to find. He doesn't need to be anything to anyone, content to simply exist as this strong, warm, unadulterated version of himself.

He's naturally, genuinely kind, which seems like a throwaway compliment until you've spent enough time in this city.

"You sure you're up for this?" my boyfriend asks.

Zeke isn't exactly fond of big parties, so I have no doubt he'd turn around and head home at the slightest complaint from me. I appreciate the gesture of care, but I think it's finally time to get out of the house and stretch my legs.

It's been a little less than two weeks since Raymond Nelson died a few feet away from me, the man's blood literally staining my clothes and painting my face, and my mind has finally started to settle. For a while, sleeping was difficult—musings of my own eventual death enjoying a top slot on my private anxiety leaderboard—but gradually the dread has melted away, now simmering in the background of my thoughts instead of parading through the forefront.

It's not completely gone, not by a long shot, but we're getting there.

A night out to celebrate my friend's birthday seems like just the thing to shift my focus from the doom and gloom of mortality.

"I'll be okay," I assure Zeke, "but let's not stick around too long."

The driveway ends at a large loop with a fountain in the middle. Beyond this is an enormous, mission-style home with a wrap-around deck up top and expansive, floor-to-ceiling windows in the front. It's been updated over the years, rendering many of the current features distinctly modern, but the old-school bones of this structure have held fast to create a specific, historical feel.

It has the vibe of a reasonably maintained haunted house belonging to a ghostly A-list actor. In reality, it's the reasonably maintained *party* house belonging to a *living* C-list director.

A group of figures on the deck above us hoist their drinks as we approach, greeting Zeke and me with boisterous cheers and beckoning us onward to the entryway below.

The second Zeke and I cross the threshold we're met by a chaotic scene that's more reminiscent of a college frat party than a high-profile industry mixer. The mansion is packed, various social pods stationed in every part of the old-Hollywood manor. There's an assembly of suited men on the landing who look like they just got off their entertainment law jobs in Century City, glancing down at us and then immediately turning away when they realize we have nothing to offer. In the living room to our right is an assortment of beautiful young partiers, dancing and spinning wildly under vaulted ceilings as a handful of older men—in what could only be described as *steampunk attire*—watch from their corner and sip colorful drinks. In the dining room, a woman in a long black robe is holding court, shouting about "longevity" to an animated group with streaks of brilliant neon color jutting through their hair. One of them is crying.

As we pass through the foyer a woman in a yellow bikini approaches us, exuding irritation. "Is this your house?" she demands.

"Yep, I'm the birthday girl," I say dryly.

Apparently, not dry enough. The woman grabs my hand and starts pulling me along behind her, prompting Zeke to follow as we weave through the crowd. We're escorted into a kitchen crammed with folks in various stages of undress, one of the men wearing little more than an illuminated LED bunny helmet and cooking a steak as though he's performing a DJ set.

We arrive in the backyard, finding ourselves atop a staircase that curves down through the ferns and emerges into a lush poolside grotto. From up here I have a great perspective on the entire scene below— swimmers treading in the water's undulating blue glow, shadows huddled around a firepit and passing a blunt, a guy in the corner making various patterns with multicolored lights attached to his fingertips.

Our bikini-clad guide points us toward the hot tub.

This tiny partitioned section of the lagoon showcases a single man, his bald head tucked halfway under the water's surface so that his mouth is completely submerged. Around the tub, a handful of women are talking loudly with one another, just as annoyed as the one who came to get us.

"What's the problem?" Zeke asks our new friend.

"Can you get him to stop messing with the water?" the woman pleads. "He turned the heater off."

It appears the guy in the hot tub has noticed our conversation and is now taking evasive action. He pops through the surface just enough to yell across the backyard with an exasperated explanation. "It's *isolation tank* temperature!"

"It's a *hot tub!*" the woman next to us screams, causing the man to simply shake his head and dip back below the water.

I can't help the laughter that bubbles out of my throat, but directly following this joyful outburst trails something else. I can feel my heart flutter a bit, a concerning double thump that gives me pause.

Anxiety comes and goes as it pleases.

A vision of the accident punctures my mind's eye, a single unmoving frame of the aftermath that my brain decided was a perfect snapshot. Raymond's body was obliterated by the falling piano, but in the blended pulp of his meat, fat, and bones a few notable pieces remained. The man's lower jaw was right there sitting in the mess, tongue still attached but torn awkwardly to the side like some silly cartoon expression. His forearm and hand were visible, too, highlighted in the sea of red by some strange yellowish liquid that slowly pooled across the pavement.

The flashback happens so fast, and with such blinding potency, that I stagger a bit, catching myself on the nearby stucco wall.

"We should go," Zeke announces, breaking through the haze.

He's the sensible one in this relationship, the guy who always sees a few steps ahead and uses his steady hand to keep us on the rails. For a someone like me, Zeke is a lifesaver, but that doesn't mean I always listen to him when those warning bells chime.

Instinctively, I shake my head. "We've gotta say hi to Blossom, *then* we'll get out of here."

Before my boyfriend can respond I'm pushing back into the house, returning to the crowd.

"Where's Blossom?" I shout. "Blossom Baker! Anyone actually *know* the person who lives here?"

It's not until I reach the foyer that someone finally throws a little useful information my way.

"Blossom's upstairs," the partier informs me, then hesitates. "Hey, are you Misha Byrne?"

"It's entirely possible."

"Whoa. Cool," he replies, satisfied with this answer.

Zeke and I make our way up the staircase, pushing through the Century City guys and their slicked-back hair to find ourselves on the upper landing.

Here, the din of the party fades, overtaken by a strange, haunting drone that drifts through the darkness of a nearby hallway. On the second floor most of the lights are off, cultivating a zone of slight unease.

One of the few light sources is the pale glow from behind a door at the end of the hallway, the illumination dancing and moving in a strange repetitive loop. The door is half-open, but we're too far away to see inside.

"Blossom?" I call out. "Happy birthday!"

There's no response, other than the long, sweeping tone that has since begun to shift and move, transforming into a heart-wrenching, cinematic score. Along with the low rumble, an assortment of string instruments have joined the mix, and the resulting vibrations are nothing short of gorgeous.

Zeke and I step closer, slowly making our way down the darkened hallway. If we were here for anyone else I might just leave, but Blossom is too good a friend for that. Making a movie that goes sideways halfway through production creates a bond that's difficult to shake. I was doing rewrites until the bitter end, spending every day on set as the two of us struggled through budget cut after budget cut.

Hard to believe it ended up being a massive hit.

Zeke and I finally reach the door and push it open. The music is blasting now, rumbling through my bones with the full might of its intricate production. It's tragic and powerful and bittersweet in all the right ways, building to a crescendo that, even on the first listen, already has its emotional hooks deep inside my heart, ready to pull.

A portable white screen sits near the far wall, raw documentary footage projecting across it. The clip features a young boy walking down a gravel road in black and white. He's smiling and cheerful, splashing though a puddle with his boots in the shade of a long cobblestone wall.

Blossom sits at the center of the room, facing away from us in a swivel chair as she holds her arms wide open and sways from side to side. It looks like a state of prayer. Nearby, another figure is filming Blossom with a handheld digital camera. A watcher being watched.

"Blossom!" I shout, struggling to push my voice above the music. "Blossom!"

My second attempt does the trick, finally causing my friend to turn in her seat. Blossom leaps up in surprise when she sees us. She throws her arms around me, pulling me close, and when she finally steps back I can see she's crying.

"Are you okay?" I yell, motioning to her tears.

My friend is confused at first, then a sudden realization causes her to burst out in a fit of laughter. She quickly hurries over and turns off the speakers, plunging us into a state of relative silence.

"Oh my *Gods*, I am so sorry." She sighs, still wiping away her tears as she extends her final word into a playfully long, almost musical expression. "I'm just starting to go through all these archives."

She's dressed in her usual attire, a long flowing dress with wide hanging sleeves and bright yellow flowers embroidered around the edges. Her hair is wavy and golden, parted down the middle to frame a uniquely expressive face that's absolutely covered in freckles. She looks like an extra from a Woodstock docudrama.

"This is my boyfriend," I state, motioning to Zeke.

"Ezekiel," he says, going in for a handshake and getting a powerful hug instead.

"You've got an incredible presence," Blossom informs him. "Has anyone read your aura before? I can see it just *popping* off of you right now."

She steps back a bit and then waves her hand above Zeke's head. "All green. Beautiful."

"How about me?" I ask.

Blossom shakes her head. "You're not looking so good, my friend."

"Getting someone's lungs down the front of your shirt will do that to a guy," I retort.

"I heard about that. Horrible."

"Speaking of," I reply, gesturing to the man with a camera who's standing right next to us.

"Oh, this is Henry. My videographer," she explains. "Henry, let's cut the tape for now."

We do our introductions and the man puts his camera away, heading into the other room to upload some footage.

It's not long before the remaining three of us have settled in a circle, Zeke and I perched on a groovy vintage couch while Blossom returns to her swivel chair.

"Happy birthday," I say directly, now that we're settled. "Quite the party downstairs. Who are all those people?"

"Mostly burner friends, a couple of folks from TEDx, alternative thought podcasters, libertarian life-extension coaches, a guitar player I met at Carnality Resort, a waiter from Laurel Hardware," she explains. "You should've brought your girl Tara! She'd probably make some friends."

"Tara would hate everyone here," I assure her.

Zeke leans forward a bit. "Everyone seems really nice," he immediately adds. "Thank you for having us."

Blossom laughs, winking at Zeke and then flashing me a quick glance. "Your boyfriend is very sweet."

"He's got good vibes," I confirm.

I stand up from the couch and stroll across the room, getting a closer look at the old grainy footage that continues rolling past on Blossom's projector screen. I know exactly what she's up to, familiar with this process after our time working together.

Blossom creates in a spiritual way, all vibe with very little structure, while I'm the polar opposite. I remember the first time I walked in on her blasting our film's placeholder soundtrack at full volume, dailies scrolling by while she lost herself in the music. Her whole process seemed meandering and unproductive to me, but the finished work speaks for itself.

That's how we made *Wedding Night.*

Everyone loves a good slasher film based around a holiday or important life event: *Halloween, Prom Night, Black Christmas, My Bloody Valentine.*

You wouldn't think an elevated slasher taking place at a lesbian wedding could have so much heart, but Blossom squeezed every ounce of emotion she could from my text. What I wrote was clever enough, a queer twist on old genre tropes, but Blossom's handheld style and gritty realism put it over the top. No wonder she's making a documentary now.

The *Wedding Night* reviews were terrible, but horror hounds loved it.

"What is this?" I question, nodding at the projection. "You're doing a doc?"

"Sure am. I should probably be downstairs, but this thing's got me by the heart. I can't stop thinking about it."

"Hell of a soundtrack," I note.

"It's *heavy*, man," Blossom replies, then motions to a large stack of portable hard drives on her desk. "All this footage I'm gathering is kids who grew up to be queer pioneers in their own way. Icons, you know?"

I nod along, eyes still glued to the screen before me. The child who once played in puddles next to a cobblestone wall is now petting a dog in a field.

"They all took their own lives," Blossom states.

My breath catches ever so slightly, the weight of what she's hoping to express with this footage finally landing.

"It's not just about *real* queer suicide, though," she explains. "It's also about the romanticization of gay trauma in media. It's dark stuff."

"Important stuff, though," Zeke adds.

The three of us sit for a moment, watching the footage play in silence as these words settle. Throwing out observations of *heavy* or *dark* seems like such an absurd way to interact with these stories, our commentary falling flat no matter how valiantly we struggle to honor the lives lost.

Words aren't enough, which is where art comes in, I suppose—but that's just as complicated in a different way.

Blossom finally stands and shuts off the projector. She takes a deep breath, and in this moment, I can see her body language shift back into that of the groovy, free-spirited woman I know. The sadness slips away, her muscles relaxing and her limbs entering an easy, effortless flow.

Blossom claps her hands together. "Enough about that!" she chirps, shifting the mood in an instant. "I've got plenty of time to go through footage. We should get back downstairs."

Blossom shuts off the lights and the three of us head out, making our way down the darkened hallway toward the staircase and the party below.

Our host's arrival is marked by a resounding applause, and while her eyes are still a little red, she's game enough to throw out her arms and give a celebratory twirl on the first landing.

"Thank you, thank you!" Blossom cries, addressing the crowd while Zeke and I hang back and watch from the shadowy top of the staircase. "It's so good to see all of you here, people from every part of my life coming together and manifesting some really incredible energy. I feel so loved."

As Blossom continues I pull Zeke close, suddenly overwhelmed with a surge of gratitude. Coming face-to-face with terrible things has a few surprising side effects—as a horror screenwriter, I should know—and one of those effects is granting perspective on *what you have*. I've been feeling wound up over my impending contract breach, the terrible accident I just witnessed, the feeling of an industry-wide death rattle droning over every palm tree and backyard swimming pool in Los Angeles as the line between artist and product blurs, but there are still a few things in my life that remain utterly steadfast.

Zeke is one of them.

My boyfriend stands behind me, his large arms around my body as he holds me close against his chest. I can feel his long dark hair brushing the side of my face, the warmth of his body creating a cozy nest of heat.

The words of Blossom's speech are distant now, echoing from some faraway place as Zeke and I find ourselves completely alone in the moment. I turn my head back as far as I can, and Zeke leans around to meet my lips with his. We kiss deeply, eyes closed like this is some whimsical fairy tale.

Who knows? Maybe it is. Hollywood can't help themselves when it comes to modern remakes.

I open my eyes, but when I do, this poignant moment immediately shatters.

In the black void of the upper landing a pinpoint of red light has appeared, floating in the air. At first I assume it's the cherry of a sizzling crimson cigarette, but as my eyes adjust I notice the shape of Blossom's videographer standing behind it, his camera pointed directly at us.

Recording.

Self-awareness slams into me like a punch to the gut, immediately causing my body to pull away from Zeke's.

"Hey!" I shout, so loud and ferocious that I interrupt Blossom's speech and draw every eye to the top of the staircase. "What the fuck are you doing?"

I march across the upper landing toward Henry, who has already retired his camera and is frantically backing away.

Utter terror pumps through my veins, and I'm wracked with the fear of a dozen potential futures as my mind jumps ahead to all the places this footage might end up. Blossom Baker is a well-known director, and her behind-the-scenes clips are certain to get views. They'll play here in Los Angeles, which is fine, but they'll also play back home in Montana.

"I'm sorry! I'm sorry!" Henry mumbles, struggling to get the words out. "I was filming the speech and then I saw you two. I'm so sorry."

Blossom is already scrambling up the stairs from below. "Hey!" she cries. "Misha!"

"Delete the footage," I command, getting in the videographer's face as he backs against the wall.

"Okay, okay," he stammers, hurrying to find the menu screen. A list of clips pops up, and the man deletes his most recent one.

"And the trash."

Henry was already headed there, and seconds later his camera's digital backup has been cleared. The tension in my body finally subsides as I let out a long breath. "Thank you," I say.

Blossom and Zeke arrive behind me, but the dramatic scene has already come to an end.

"We should go," I announce, mostly to myself.

When I turn around I find that a few of the partiers below have pulled out their phones to record, which is fine. All they'll capture is the tantrum of a wound-up screenwriter.

Nothing more.

I apologize to Blossom and, soon enough, Zeke and I are making our way down the stairs, through the foyer, and out onto the long driveway.

We walk in silence, slipping back into the darkness from which we emerged but glowing with completely different auras. I'm not sure what the various colors mean, but right now I imagine us as a deep, vacant black, two hazy blobs of nothingness hanging over our heads like rainclouds.

"I'm sorry" is all I can manage.

Zeke sits with this for a moment, currently on his own inner journey.

By the time we reach the road he still hasn't spoken, but when we turn and start walking up the street toward my car, Zeke offers a single observation in return.

"You sure didn't want anyone taking a video of us kissing" is all he says.

THE SMOKER

"There he is!" Tara shouts, jumping to her feet as I enter the bar. She rushes over, wrapping her arms around my body in a hug so forceful it might otherwise be considered a tackle. "You need a drink."

"That explains the crushing existential weight," I confirm. "I'm just parched."

Tara releases and motions to the nearby bartender. "This baby needs a drink!" she calls out. "The most delicious beer you've got!"

"I think we need to order at the bar," I remind her.

Tara shakes her head. "She's got this, she's a good bartender. Just you wait."

I glance over to see the bartender is, in fact, pouring a beer and nodding in our direction.

This is the way it goes when you're hanging out with Tara, things just seem to work out. I don't even know what I'm getting, but I'm sure I'll like it.

"You sit," my friend instructs, motioning toward the table.

I do as I'm told, taking off my jacket and hanging it on the back of my chair. I pull out the seat and plop down in a state of mental and physical exhaustion.

Tara strolls over to the bar to get my drink, paying with a stack of ones that she dramatically doles out and slams onto the counter before her. It feels quirky and fun, until you realize Tara's cash-only policy is based on her fear of the credit card companies cataloging us with a *Mockingbird threat rating*, whatever that means.

Regardless, her theatrical transaction gives me longer to take in the atmosphere of this cozy Los Feliz staple. I used to hang at the Dresden all the time, but I've barely left the house lately.

Struggling actors and screenwriting hopefuls chatter away around me, humming with excitement. Los Angeles is a city with plenty of variety, but this particular neighborhood seems to attract the creative dreamers.

Tara returns, setting the pint of beer on our table. She's wearing a bubblegum pink dress covered in polka dots, with a lime green leather jacket thrown over the top in a pairing that seems like it shouldn't work but is somehow pretty badass.

"You see that lady from *The Hookup* over there?" my friend questions.

I glance over my shoulder, taking note of a redheaded woman at the bar. We lock eyes for a moment, but I instinctively look away.

"I don't watch reality shows," I reply.

Tara motions toward my drink. "The best beer for the best writer."

I take a sip and, of course, she's right. This is fantastic.

"I like the jacket," I say, noting the vibrant piece and just now spotting the matching bow that's pulling her white hair into a messy updo. "You look fabulous."

"Thank you," she says, then waves her hand in front of my face. "You look . . . I love you, but we need to do something about this whole situation. You're so handsome, baby. I can't let you do this to yourself." She pinches my cheek affectionately.

I'm not offended, because I know it's true. In fact, that's exactly why I'm here.

"It's been a long few weeks," I admit.

Tara just stares at me. Eventually, she pops one eyebrow with dramatic enthusiasm. "You *think*? A dude died like five feet away from you. *Ka-blam!* Are you seeing a shrink?"

"No."

"You should," Tara replies. "We gotta keep that brain runnin' smooth so you can start your own studio one day."

I nod in confirmation. "I know. Harold Brothers will pay for it, too. I'm just really busy right now. I haven't been sleeping much, and Zeke is about to be super upset with me. I've gotta figure out what I'm doing with the season finale of *Travelers,* and I guess I've gotta write an Oscars speech."

"One of these problems is not like the others," Tara observes.

"Which one?"

"The Oscars. Write your damn speech."

I take a long sip from my drink, considering my unique situation. "It's all just . . . a lot."

"Is this a conversation where we go through your problems and sort them out one by one, or is this a conversation where I tell you everything is gonna be okay? I'm ready for either, you've just gotta let me know." Tara reaches out and places her hand over mine.

"I need to sort things out," I reply. "Give it to me straight."

Tara smiles, releasing my hand and leaning back in her chair. "Then let's take it from the top!" she yells. "What's first?"

"I haven't been sleeping much."

"Next topic. That's a symptom, not a cause," she immediately determines, snapping her fingers.

"Zeke is about to be super pissed at me," I continue.

Tara perks up a bit. She leans forward, focusing all of her energy and attention.

Tara is aromantic and asexual, which has always made me appreciate her take on relationship advice. If there's one thing she knows, it's people, and she has no problem seeing through the starry-eyed baggage that sometimes clouds the vision of my other advice-giving friends.

"You're burying the lede," Tara retorts. "Come on now, storyteller. *Why* is Zeke pissed at you?"

"About to be," I correct her.

I take another absurdly long sip from my drink, savoring this beverage to a ridiculous degree. If I can drink forever, I'll never have to answer Tara's question.

"Stop it," she scolds.

I finally relent, settling my half-empty pint on the table. "You remember that high school reunion I told you about?"

"Twenty years, right?" Tara confirms. "Fuck, you're old."

"Thanks," I sigh, brushing it off and barreling forward with my admission. "I didn't invite Zeke. That's okay, right? I mean, we've only been seeing each other for a year."

"A year already?! That's a long time!"

I nod.

"And you like him."

I nod again.

"And *I* like him!" Tara cries. "Think about *me*!"

I hesitate, a flush of embarrassment bubbling up. "It's not *just* that."

Tara furrows her brow, an expression of confusion that abruptly falters and transforms into shocked disappointment. She's already figured it out, her superior relationship senses kicking in. "You don't want him to meet your family," she announces, a statement more than a question.

"He *has* met my family," I retort. "When Mom was in town we all went out. It was great. She *loves* my 'good friend' Ezekiel."

Tara's eyes go wide. "No."

"I'm *Los Angeles* out," I finally admit. "I'm not . . . Montana out."

Tara's expression is frozen. "Back home the good ol' boys don't know you're gay? You're like the first result on Wikipedia for *queer horror*."

"I mean, they *probably* do," I explain. "I just don't really talk about it when I'm there. Like, if someone asked me then I'd tell them. I'm not ashamed."

"You sure about that?"

"I'm not ashamed," I repeat, this time mustering even more confidence and hoping it sticks.

I sit for a moment, staring at my drink so I don't have to look my friend in the eye. "It doesn't matter, anyway," I finally confess. "It's too late for Zeke to find a reasonable flight, and he already made plans this Friday."

"Why? Because you waited to tell him about the reunion until you knew he already had something else going on?" Tara prods.

I nod.

"*Baby,*" she says, a complete inversion of her usual tone. This endearment is almost always overflowing with love and affection, but as it washes across me I hear nothing but utter disappointment.

"I know," I admit.

"Listen, I'm not gonna to tell you when, or *how,* or *why* to come out. Whether it's all the way out, or half out, or just writing *incredibly* gay shows and movies then never really mentioning it, that's all up to you," Tara says. "However, you've gotta be honest with Zeke about this. You should be talking to him, not me."

I let out a long groan.

"Trust me, I know what it's like," Tara continues. "Do you realize how hard it is to tell your parents you're *asexual?* All they fucking talk about is grandkids. I tried explaining that I still wanna be a mom, but that just confused them even more." Tara shrugs. "Boomers."

We sit in silence a moment.

"*Neeeeext!*" Tara suddenly yells, stretching the word like taffy and putting the full force of her voice behind it. She's so loud that a few other patrons glance over at our table in confusion.

"I've gotta figure out what to do with Agent Lexa and Agent Naomi on *Travelers,*" I explain. "The studio wants them straight and alive, or gay and dead."

"Neither," Tara instantly asserts. "Fuck 'em."

"Yeah," I reply, nodding along. "I don't know why I'm having trouble with this. *I'm* usually the fuck 'em guy."

"Someone exploded all over your shirt like three weeks ago. It's okay if you don't feel like yourself right now. Give it some time and when your head is on straight you can turn in your *gay and alive* script, then let the cards fall where they may."

"Fuck 'em," I state proudly, finally cracking a smile.

Her advice is encouraging, but if I'm being completely honest I never really needed it. I made my decision the second I walked out of Jack's office.

I hoist my drink toward my friend. "To angering the suits!" I proclaim, then throw back an enormous gulp of the cold, frothy liquid.

Tara does the same, both of us taking down a good portion of our beverages in a state of reckless abandon. While this hang was partially about getting a little advice from my friend, it was also an excuse to blow off some steam.

As Tara drinks, her eyes drift, starting to the distant left and then gradually transitioning her focus directly over my shoulder. She's staring awkwardly now, slightly bemused.

I glance back to discover the reality show contestant is standing directly behind me.

"Hi, I'm Alice," the woman introduces herself, smiling warmly and extending a hand.

I give her a firm shake. "Hey," I reply, matching her smile despite my otherwise disheveled state.

"I just wanted to say I'm a huge fan," she offers. "I loved *Black Lamb.*"

"Oh, thank you," I reply, a little flustered.

While I'm a fairly well-known TV and film writer, it's rare for someone in my position to actually get recognized on the street. It happens from time to time, but *my* face isn't the one plastered across any billboards.

"I just rented it last night," Alice continues. "I'd never heard of it before."

"Oh, cool," I reply, nodding along. "Well, I appreciate that a lot."

"Anyway, just wanted to say hello." The woman hesitates awkwardly, clearly wanting more but refusing to directly state her desires. Her body language is odd, standing a little too close and making a little more eye contact than feels natural. "You come here a lot?"

"Yeah."

"Maybe I'll see you around sometime?"

From the corner of my eye I catch Tara reacting to this, stifling her laughter.

"Sure, maybe," I fumble.

Alice turns and takes her leave. Instead of going back to her table she exits the bar, flashing me one final glance before disappearing into the night.

"Well . . . that was weird," Tara announces.

I laugh. "Hey, *you're* the one who was talking me up! Is it so absurd that I'd have a fan?"

Tara shakes her head. "Not that part. You're a superstar. I'm talking about the part where her name isn't Alice."

"Wait, really?" I chuckle. "I never took you for a reality show buff."

"Well fuck you, I am, but that's not how I know," Tara counters. "I've been setting up tech for the reunion livestream. Her name is Riley. She's supposed to be in New York shooting right now."

"Jetsetter," I suggest with a shrug.

We let this moment rest for no more than five seconds before Tara finishes the rest of her drink and pounds the table enthusiastically. "Round two! You want another?"

It's here the evening starts to blur, our conversation loosening into raucous banter and inside jokes. For this brief, glorious moment I feel my body starting to relax, the tension I've been carrying around for weeks finally subsiding. As Tara and I laugh and sing, the weight of any tragic impending doom melts away, if only for a little while.

I always knew I'd only turn in a script that lit my soul on fire. I have no problem defying the studio and placing my artistic life on the line because it's what I always do, and this attitude has served me surprisingly well.

But with all the chaos swirling around me, I certainly wasn't *excited* about turning in the *Travelers* finale. After a dozen beers with Tara, however, I'm thrilled by the prospect.

My friend and I shout "fuck 'em" to each other so many times over the course of this evening that I eventually lose count.

When it's finally time to go, Tara and I stroll out the back door with more than enough swagger to fill the whole bar, arms around each other's shoulders as we belt out a song we just made up.

We can't seem to agree on the words.

The walk home isn't far, and Tara only needs to get to our usual corner for her pickup, but the distance is such that we're not getting *anywhere* if we're too wobbly to put one foot in front of the other.

Fortunately, once the cool night air hits my skin, I start sobering up.

This particular exit empties out into the back alley, a secluded lane running parallel to the whole row of businesses along Vermont Street. They stretch in a line toward the hill above. A few empty cars still fill the narrow diagonal parking spaces that trace this path, abandoned until tomorrow morning after a wild night on the town.

"It's a beautiful night to say *fuck 'em!*" Tara cries out, her voice echoing through the darkness.

Our route is to walk due north from here, making our way up the alleys until we reach Russell Ave. At that point we'll do our traditional parting of ways, me stumbling onward into the neighborhood while Tara's whisked away to Echo Park by a very patient rideshare driver.

It's gotten late quick, our drinking time seeping into everything else and bending reality to its will. I'm not exactly sure of the hour, but the night is old enough that our journey is unusually empty. In fact, other than a few folks hanging around the Dresden's exit, there isn't a soul in sight.

Tara and I begin our stumbling trek, our voices echoing off the cement walls and bouncing haphazardly around us.

"You ever think about how weird it is Raymond Nelson, the *cartoon* guy, got a piano dropped on his head?" Tara sloppily exclaims, unable to stifle her laughter. "Fuck an accident, that's Wile E. Coyote style!"

"Be nice," I counter. "He's dead."

"Be *nice?*" Tara shouts. "That dude *sucked*. Oh my God, did he suck. You know he was days away from getting *me too'd* into the sun?"

"Okay, don't be nice," I relent.

Suddenly, my friend stops, perking up as she gazes down the darkened alley before us.

I halt along with her, confused at first and then following Tara's sightline. Now I see it too, a lone figure standing in the shadows no more than fifteen feet away.

"Hey" is all I can think to offer in greeting, a nervous chill running down my spine.

The figure hesitates, then takes one confident step from the darkness.

Tara immediately bursts out laughing, unable to control herself after this abrupt shift from fear to relief.

It's The Smoker.

The Smoker is a character of mine, created for one of the first movies I ever got produced. Technically speaking, he's a ghost, although in *Death Blooms* he functions more like a sentient curse.

The man is short, wearing a blue suit and tie and featuring a head full of slicked-back gray hair. His jacket is cut with distinctly 1970s flair—large, pointed collars and all. The blazer looks as though it was pulled from the back of some old musty closet at an estate sale. The Smoker always carries a briefcase, and if a cigarette isn't hanging from his razor-thin lips, then it's gripped loosely in his hand. His skin is inhumanly white, so pale that he might just disappear next to a sheet of paper.

The most unusual thing about The Smoker, however, are his eyes. He has no eyebrows, nor eyelids, and therefore his expression is hauntingly difficult to read. He can't blink—because there's nothing to blink *with*—and his gaze feels like it cuts right through you, directly into your soul.

Of course, this isn't *really* The Smoker, because The Smoker isn't real.

This is a fan.

"Is it just me or is that the best cosplay you've ever seen?" Tara questions, still struggling to control her laughter. "Look at those *eyes.*"

I have to admit, the makeup is incredible. Skin that white is difficult to pull off without caking your whole body in powder, and shaving off your eyebrows takes some serious dedication.

Unfortunately for this guy, I'm just not in the mood.

"You know, I don't get recognized very often," I admit, still fighting to navigate this bizarre confrontation, "but you're the second person tonight. How'd you know I was here?"

The man stares at us with his wide-open eyes, every other feature void of expression. In the dim light of the alley, it's hard to see what he did to accomplish this uncanny gaze. Obviously, his eyelids are just hidden under some kind of prosthetic makeup, but the attention to detail is incredible.

Regardless, this whole confrontation is more than a little unsettling. It's flattering to see this kind of enthusiasm from a fan, but right now isn't the time or the place. Creators have wound up dead after encounters like this, depending on how deep a fan's obsession goes.

"Do the line!" Tara shouts, clearly not riding the same wavelength I am.

A smile slowly creeps its way across the fan's face, his thin lips curling into a sharp grin.

I jump in shock as a sudden mechanical growl sputters to our right. One of the cars lining our path has started up, its headlights bathing Tara and me in an overblown yellow glow.

I shield my eyes, stepping from the spotlight a bit as I gaze curiously through the vehicle's dusty windshield. The car is empty, but its radio sizzles to life as the night air fills with static. A few renegade transmissions dance in and out, then it settles on a station with nothing but gentle fuzz.

"Got a light?" the pale man croaks with a slow, deliberate cadence, a frightening routine that's exactly how I imagined it in my darkest nightmares.

He doesn't sound quite like the original actor, nor anyone brought in for the sequels, but some perfect amalgamation of the whole bunch.

The most unsettling part is that his voice doesn't emerge from between those thin, pale lips. The Smoker's mouth remains tightly closed as the sound of his gravelly speech drifts out from the nearby car stereo.

Tara claps once, thrilled by the fan's killer delivery and creative execution. "Okay, that was amazing," she chirps, raising both hands in a gesture of reverence. "How'd you do that?"

I, on the other hand, clench every muscle in trepidation. Starting a car with the push of a button is far from some magical feat these days, but there's nothing in the guy's hands, and without visibly moving his lips to speak, the effect is deeply unsettling.

Got a light?

I've heard this line a thousand times before—hell, I *wrote* it—but there's something about the sound across my ears that provokes an irregular beat in my heart. My mind flashes with a sudden burst of images from my past, the untamed steps of raw creation that led to this point. Wounds exposed.

Uncle Keith standing on the porch, tendrils of smoke curling above him.

I see myself balled up in the back seat of a frozen car, a thin, filthy packing blanket offering me no comfort as I shiver and quake.

The fan's question rings through my head over and over again, slowly pulling me back to reality. I reach into my jacket pocket, already knowing the answer.

I've been preparing for this my whole life.

My fingers sweep through the fabric, expecting to brush against one of several matchbooks I've collected this week before dumping them out in my bedside drawer and starting over again.

Confusion hits first, then panic. I check my other pockets before returning to the jacket where a handful of little cardboard squares should be—where they always are.

Unfortunately, there are no matches to be found.

Tara glances over, puzzled. "Do the thing," she insists.

"I—I don't know where they are," I stammer, frantically hunting for the tokens that never leave my side.

The fan continues staring at us with his wide-open eyes, still grinning and waiting for our response.

I've had this exact scenario play out several times before, especially at horror conventions where people actually recognize me, but for some reason the stakes feel different tonight. For the first time, I get a real sense of what my characters must've felt, or what someone *else's* characters must've felt in *Death Blooms* two, three, and four (I didn't write the sequels).

Of all the monsters I've created, The Smoker is technically the easiest to avoid. This living curse has a few simple rules, but the most important ones involve his initial question.

When he asks for a light, you give it to him. If you pass this test, you're free to live a long and fruitful life. If not . . .

My thoughts suddenly reconnect to the present, reminding myself just how silly this whole encounter really is. The Smoker is not real, and while the things that influenced his inception still haunt me, I can rest easy knowing I'm not standing face-to-face with an angry spirit.

This is Los Angeles, after all. I can spot great makeup and effects work when I see it.

"Are you trying to get a job?" I finally ask, hoping to sound serious and confident despite the slight slurring of my words. "The look is amazing, but this is a terrible way of making friends."

"Got . . . a light?" the man repeats with a perfectly still mouth, ignoring my question as his voice rattles out from the car stereo. I clench my teeth in discomfort. A faint song creeps back into the mix, a strange, wobbling transmission of some old-timey jazz number.

I check my pockets again, as if a matchbook might magically appear, then come up empty for a second time. "No," I admit.

Tara shakes her head, then reaches out and places her hand on the man's shoulder. She gives him three hard, patronizing pats. "Guess not, friend. Now you gotta walk all the way back to Hollywood and Highland."

The fan hesitates for a moment, his modest grin finally transforming into a giant smile as an unexpected fit of laughter fills the alley. His voice is so raggedy and strange that this outburst could easily be mistaken as the cries of some strangled animal as it twists through the wash of radio static.

Tara steps back instinctively, startled by the noise.

"We should go," I suggest.

Tara quickly agrees, and soon enough we're pushing onward, hurrying past this uncanny figure.

"I'll be seeing you," the fan croaks from the fuzz of his car stereo, his mouth motionless.

I keep glancing back at the strange man, worried that the second I lose track of this creep he'll magically appear right behind us like a real-world jump scare. Instead, the figure just slowly turns and watches us leave with those giant, unblinking eyes. A gentle stream of smoke glides from between the fan's lips as he lifts his briefcase, rapping three times on the hard rectangular box with his opposite fist.

"Plenty of room in here," his ragged voice calls out from the stereo, creaking like a rusty gate.

Eventually, the man takes a few steps backward and disappears into the shadows. His car shuts off, plunging the alleyway into darkness and leaving a haunting silence in its wake.

Tara and I arrive at the next street, an enormous yellow spotlight illuminating us from above. This section of the neighborhood is a bit livelier, a nearby taco stand still doling out their sizzling carnitas. There are enough people around that I instantly feel safe, as though the theatrics we just witnessed couldn't *possibly* survive a slightly larger audience.

My friend and I stop, catching our breath, then erupt in a fit of laughter.

"That was *wild*," Tara exclaims, struggling to get the words out as she cackles.

My senses remain heightened, but it's not long before glorious relief has washed me with its soothing mental ointment. Everything is fine. We're all good.

Monsters aren't real.

I check my pockets again, still confused by the missing matchbooks. "That is *so* weird."

Suddenly, I freeze.

"Do you think that reality show lady stole them?" I ask, hardly believing it myself but forcing these words out just the same.

Tara's first instinct is skepticism, brushing the notion away just as quickly as it arrives, but the second her analytical mind has a chance to catch up with her instinctive reaction, she falters. My friend's expression shifts to utter shock.

"Oh my *gawd*," Tara gushes, completely losing it.

"You think?" I reiterate.

Despite agreeing, Tara shakes her head from side to side. Her mind and her body are struggling to sync up with one another—the fear, the absurdist comedy, and the beer all working to craft one hell of an emotional cocktail. "That chick from *The Hookup* stole your *matches*? Is your wallet still there?"

I pull out my wallet and keys, sitting right where I left them. My phone is also exactly where it should be.

"So bizarre," I say, as if these two simple words could even *begin* to capture just how strange our night has gotten. "She only took the matches. It must've happened when my jacket was hanging on the back of my chair."

I can't help wondering if the world around us is really as peculiar as it seems. Are bizarre consequences actually falling into place like some grand puzzle, culminating in the fulfillment of an intricate hidden agenda? Are there dots to connect and conclusions to draw, spelling out a secret meaning that's right under my nose?

Or will a simple explanation reveal itself in the morning when I'm not so fucking drunk?

Tara's ride pulls up to the curb, a sign that our evening has finally come to an end.

"This is where we part," I announce.

Tara gives me one last, long hug. "Goodnight, beautiful." She sighs.

We wave goodbye, then split off toward our respective neighborhoods. I take one last glance down the alley as I go, but my extremely creative and enthusiastic fan is nowhere to be found.

I have no idea what time it is, just that a searing, caustic pain is churning through my skull. It comes in sharp, dissonant waves, my body instinctively shooting upright as I scramble to understand what's happening. Darkness surrounds me, making the source of this terrible sensation even more difficult to pinpoint.

"Oh for fuck's cock," I groan, the words barely escaping my lips as I reach for a pulsing, glowing light.

I grab the source, now realizing that the pain coursing through me is nothing more than the digital chime of a ringing phone.

I don't check who it is, just answer promptly and fall back into the tangled bedsheets.

"What?" I mumble. "What time is it?"

"Misha! Can you hear me?" comes Tara's frantic voice, quaking with terror.

The second I hear her whimpering tone my eyes snap open and I'm violently yanked into reality. I sit back up. "Tara?"

Silence on the line.

"Tara?" I repeat.

"Someone's here," she whispers. "Is that you outside? Are you messing with me?"

"I'm not messing with you," I reply, straight to the point. "I'm at my house."

"I think someone's here," Tara repeats.

Before I have a chance to respond, the line goes dead. I pull my phone away from my head, checking the screen to make sure she really disconnected.

Should I call the cops?

Before I get the chance to decide, however, three loud slams echo through the darkness of my home.

Bang! Bang! Bang!

The sounds—arriving in rapid succession and emanating from the front door—make me flinch.

I listen as my mind reels with potential ways to react. Part of me wants to yell and see what the late-night caller wants, facing the problem head-on, but that would also give away my position in the house. Based on the hour, there's certainly no *good* reason to come knocking.

Any real thought of the LAPD responding to a distress call in time, regardless of the hour, is laughable. I was once in a hit-and-run and they never even bothered to come get a statement.

Three more thunderous knocks ring through my empty home, ratcheting up my anxiety even more. I can feel the blood pumping sharply through my chest, elevated to such a degree that I'm making myself sick.

I slowly climb out of bed, moving through the dim light of my house with nervous apprehension. Every step is meticulously planned, utterly silent as I creep down the hallway.

Eventually, the narrow corridor opens into my living room.

The front door looms before me, cast in a handful of angular shadows. The illumination is a *little* better out here, distant streetlights offering the faintest glow through various windows.

Instead of heading straight to the door, I tiptoe sideways across the darkness of my living room, then slink up to one of the large glass panes that looks out on my front walk. From here, I have a clear view of the front porch and the street beyond.

I slide my face ever-so-slowly past the edge of the window, gently peering out with a single eye.

Nobody's there.

I diligently scan the full landscape of my yard, slowly making my way along each living-room viewpoint and gazing from the shadows. Whoever was knocking is gone now.

Just to make sure, I sneak back across the room and cautiously unlock the front door. I crack it open, peering out into the vast night of my quiet Los Feliz neighborhood. I'm achingly still, hunting for any sign of life and coming up short.

Nothing but crickets and the soft, ever-present hum of traffic in the distance.

I close the door.

I head back to my bedroom, still nervous but gradually pulling back from *high alert* status. I certainly won't be falling asleep anytime soon, but the immediate threat appears to be gone.

But what about Tara?

My phone rings again, as if psychically called upon, and I scramble to answer.

"Are you okay?" Tara demands, spitting the words out well before I get a chance to speak.

"Are *you* okay?"

"Someone was creeping around outside," she explains, a little short of breath but much calmer than before. "I thought they came into my apartment, but . . . nobody's here. I don't know."

"Someone was sneaking around over here, too," I reply.

Tara hesitates. "Wait, what? At the same time?"

"Sounds like it," I confirm. "They pounded on the front door, then left."

The second I relay these facts out loud a familiar spark crackles through my mind, a brilliant warning flare in the darkness of my chaotic thoughts.

I've seen this before.

"Is it the stalker guy?" Tara continues. "Or the stalker *girl*? Why do you have so many stalkers?"

"I don't know," I admit, "but . . . this is exactly what happens in *Death Blooms.*"

"Oh, well, okay then!" Tara groans. "I guess I'll just *go back to bed!*"

"If this guy is sticking with the story then he won't be back tonight," I assure her. "We've got five days."

"Five days until *what?*"

"We'll talk tomorrow," I reply, not wanting to frighten her any more than she already is.

Tara clearly doesn't want to get off the phone, but she also understands there's nothing left to do at this late hour.

"I love you, Misha." She sighs.

"Love you, too. We'll talk tomorrow."

I hang up, then sit quietly for a moment. I can't help feeling a heavy blanket of guilt as it settles over me, coating my senses with a dull ache. Over the years I've had plenty of people get angry about my work, sometimes disturbingly so, but I've always accepted this target on my back as part of the job. Queer horror isn't exactly the arena of someone looking to go unnoticed by hordes of bigoted, rage-filled right-wingers out for blood.

But this is the first time someone I care about has been pulled into the fray, and the fresh new variable has me reeling. I'm in a trance, struggling to come to terms with it all.

Gradually, however, my attention begins to shift.

I wrinkle my nose, a distinct scent filling my nostrils. It's easy to identify and I'm familiar with the aroma, but certainly not familiar with it *here.*

Cigarettes.

I stand, following the smell across my room in a state of bewilderment and simmering panic. I don't smoke, nor do I have any friends who would dare light up within the walls of this house.

Fumbling through the darkness, I reach out and turn on my lamp—revealing a small pile of ash on the bedside table.

LAMB

EXT. MALIBU STATE PARK FOREST - EVENING

A late-thirties man opens his eyes. He sits
up and rubs his face, squinting desperately.
He holds his head for a moment, groaning, then
struggles to stand but falters.

This is MISHA BYRNE, his stubble-covered face
topped by shaggy brown hair and emphasized by a
pair of brilliant blue eyes.

Misha's clothes are remarkably clean for someone
who just found himself passed out in the middle of the woods, no smudges to be found across
his shirt or the dark blazer thrown over it. His
stark white sneakers are free of dirt.

It's as though he just appeared here.

A black pen is held tight in Misha's hand. He
gazes at the writing tool for a moment.

Misha slips the pen into his jacket's inner
pocket.

                    MISHA
                  (dazed)
          What the fuck?

A sound in the forest prompts Misha to turn his head abruptly, gazing through the trees in a futile attempt to see.

                        MISHA
          Hello?

Finally, the disoriented man climbs to his feet. He notices a shiny medical lab tray sitting on a stump nearby. A key fob rests at the center of the tray.

Misha picks up the key and inspects it. He presses a button on the face of the small object.

BEEP BEEP.

The corresponding vehicle announces itself nearby, prompting Misha to investigate further.

Misha climbs a small hill to reveal he's not actually in the deep woods, but standing on the cusp of a parking lot.

A sign reads: MALIBU STATE PARK VISITOR'S CENTER.

Misha presses the button again.

BEEP BEEP.

A new, squeaky-clean sedan is waiting right beside Misha. The vehicle flashes its lights in greeting.

Misha approaches the car with caution. He glances around to see if anyone is watching him, like this might be a trap.

Misha catches the eye of a nearby HIKER, one of the few people left out here as the day reaches its end.

The hiker is putting away her gear, standing near the popped trunk of her Subaru.

>   MISHA
>   Excuse me, is this your car?

>   HIKER
>   (confused)
>   What?

Misha holds up the key.

>   MISHA
>   Is this your car?

>   HIKER
>   Looks like it's your car.

Misha glances at the key in his hand, then back at the vehicle.

>   HIKER
>   Are you okay?

>   MISHA
>   I . . . don't know.

The hiker smiles uncomfortably, then closes her trunk and returns to the driver's side of her Subaru. She climbs in and starts her vehicle, then drives away, shooting an awkward glance at Misha in the rearview mirror.

Misha stands quietly for a moment, closing his eyes and feeling the air as it moves across his

skin. He takes a deep breath and lets it out,
then opens his eyes again.

Misha climbs into the car, taking a moment to
assess the vehicle's unfamiliar console. He takes
the fob and attempts to use it, but there is no
key blade. There's also no slot to put it in.

Confused, Misha checks everywhere, opening an
empty center console and the visor, then feeling around under the dash. He's growing frustrated.

He checks his pockets and discovers another ring
of keys, but keys are not the problem. Besides,
none of these are large enough for a car.

Eventually, Misha presses a large round button
beside the steering wheel. His vehicle springs to
life.

          MISHA
  Whoa!

The car's NAGIVATION SYSTEM immediately gets
to work, announcing itself through the car
stereo.

        NAVIGATION SYSTEM
  Starting route to . . . home.

Misha is slightly alarmed, but continues
listening.

        NAVIGATION SYSTEM
  Turn right onto . . . Park Entrance
  Road. Then turn left onto . . . Las
  Virgenes Road.

Misha carefully pulls out of the lot. He continues driving over vast hills of golden grass as
the sunset blooms above.

I didn't sleep much last night, and the pain that radiates through my
body is starting to spread. I can feel it behind my eyes, a tense awareness
that things are falling apart.

When I finally drag myself out of bed, the warm glow of sunrise is
still a good half hour away. The sore, aching, hungover part of me is
demanding a return to the sheets, but that's just not in the cards.

Besides, the other half of me is fully convinced a morning walk is
exactly what I need, fulfilling the same purpose it's always served, keeping me centered.

I need this. *Especially* in times of chaos.

I pull on a simple black hoodie and my usual sweatpants, along with
the old running shoes I've almost completely worn through. I pop in
my headphones and start up a playlist, softly nodding to the beat that
reverberates through my skull—"Waiting Room" by Fugazi.

I step out the front door, then halt abruptly. My gaze drifts across
the hazy morning landscape, only slightly brighter than the last time I
was out here with utter terror pumping through my veins.

I pause the song, its slinking bassline abruptly cut short.

I remove my headphones and stuff them into my pocket. In the light
of the day it feels like I could be overreacting, but I might as well hedge
my bets and keep my senses alert.

Most of my writing happens out here on the morning walk, no pen
or paper or laptop in sight. Instead, I simply let the ideas tumble around
as an unrestrained mess, allow them to crash in ways I never would've
considered under the scrutiny of logical focus. Eventually, order will
form on its own, little kernels of brilliance or bullshit gradually falling
into place.

This is where I find inspiration in its rawest form and mold it into
something tangible.

I start the journey by heading through my little suburban pocket of Los Feliz, a four-block slice of normalcy amid the surrounding hum of a hipster paradise. I love the coffee shops and diners and the little three-screen movie theater that *always* makes sure to show my films, but the main drag can also get exhausting.

The longer I walk, the more things begin to change. I'm heading due north, crossing Los Feliz Boulevard and making my way up into the multi-million-dollar hillside. The success of my writing has allowed me to live in close proximity to this particular incline, but the landscape also serves to show just how much distance there is between me and *real* Hollywood royalty. With every step away from the base of the hill, the financial gluttony grows at an ever-escalating pace. The sheer size of these homes seems to bloom with exponential mutation, enormous structures gazing down at me with hollow eyes and endlessly remodeled skin as I continue up the winding path of affluence.

Things have gotten a little better since the strikes, of course, but the timing of my success as a writer leaves something to be desired. If I were born just a few years later, maybe I would've actually gotten paid every time my work was streamed.

As the sun begins peeking over the horizon, I'm pleasantly bathed in its warmth. Golden light casts the scene with a sense of hope. My body may be falling apart from stress and lack of sleep, and my career may be perched on the precipice of certain doom, but the air against my skin is refreshing, and the quiet stillness of the morning works wonders for my headache.

I keep the pace steady as I make my way deeper into the hills. My journey isn't quite tough enough to call a hike, but this incline is no joke.

Eventually, the route flattens out and I'm treated to the various slivers of a view these behemoth homes allow between their lavish outer walls. The most glorious vistas are blocked by giant mansions lining the ridge, but every so often you can peek past a few of them for a breathtaking display of Los Angeles waking up.

I stop at the top of my loop, pulling out my phone and texting Zeke.

Rough night. Breakfast?

He answers before I can even put the device away.

Heading over now.

We've got a lot to talk about—Tara, too—but I think I've finally got a handle on some things.

Someone was clearly messing with me last night, and I'm devastated a friend was roped into this madness. Whether or not they keep going is another story, but I've gotta keep my eyes peeled.

And sure, the ash by my bed was a little confusing, but who's to say it wasn't there already, sitting unnoticed until it made sense as a part of some grand conspiracy? I had friends over recently, and one of them could've snuck away for a smoke in my room.

Asshole.

On the trip back down my mind continues to drift, working through my feelings about the upcoming *Travelers* deadline. The big choice was already made the second I left Jack's office—I won't kill my agents off—but I still have to write the best finale of my life.

Even if my work goes unused, I owe the characters that much.

I've almost reached the bottom of the hill, the landscape gradually returning to one of moderate wealth instead of fuck-you-I'm-buying-your-whole-company-and-closing-it-out-of-spite wealth. The morning fog still lingers, but darkness has finally tiptoed away to reveal a rare overcast day in Los Angeles.

I come to a set of public stairs that run down the hillside, cutting through the final winding streets in a direct line. This is the shortcut I take if my ideas are flowing and I'm itching to get back home and pound out some words. This morning, I'm mostly just concerned about making it down before Zeke gets to my place.

I make a sharp turn at the steps, then halt abruptly.

The path before me is dark and secluded, plant life growing up on

either side of the long cement staircase. It cuts neatly between the hillside homes, rarely used but well maintained by the HOA cash that
pumps through this neighborhood.

On the first landing, some thirty feet away, stands a small black
lamb.

The creature is meek and frail, its legs so thin that I'm surprised it's
even standing upright. Its dark coat is the color of coal, and it's quiver-
ing ever so slightly.

The creature's long, oval pupils create an unsettling gaze, staring
right through me and into some cosmic space beyond.

I meet the lamb's eye from my place on the steps above, first confused, then sensing my throat tighten as suffocating dread washes over
me. This is certainly an unusual place for *any* farm animal to appear,
but a lamb trembling in my path feels especially menacing after last
night's encounter.

This little creature is from a horror movie I wrote—*Black Lamb*.

In it, a horrible, gurgling infection of cosmic horror finds its way
to a desolate farm. The farmer and his husband deal with a relentless
series of failed crops and sickly animals, but when one of the dying
sheep births a black lamb, they begin to focus their energy on caring
for this rare gift.

The creature reveals its horrific true form over the course of the
story, but the farmer and his husband ignore every warning sign, cling-
ing to hope until it's far too late.

Audiences didn't care. It was a commercial failure.

"Oh." The word slips from my lips with an awkward plop.

The frail animal is quiet, whimpering as it watches me with those
vacant eyes. There's nothing predatory about the shivering lamb, but its
calm nature only serves to elevate my anxiety.

That's the whole point of the story—a weak and sympathetic creature using its appearance to draw victims in, and then . . .

I shake my head, placing this train of thought on a fresh set of tracks.

This isn't a *monster,* because monsters don't exist. Stalkers, however, do exist.

The lamb doddles from side to side a bit, mewling faintly. In the fictional world I crafted this is a deadly trap, but the reality is even more concerning. A pattern is starting to emerge, and between The Smoker, last night's knock on my door, and this poor animal left to startle me, things are getting out of hand. Whoever's harassing me has done their homework.

I glance back and forth, scanning the hazy road for any sign of the prankster behind all this. I half expect a man dressed as The Smoker to show up, leisurely stepping through the mist with a camera crew in tow for some scared-silly reality show, but it's just me and this lamb in the cool silence of the morning.

"Hello?" I call out.

There's no response from any devious humans hiding up or down the road, but the lamb murmurs a bit. My gaze returns to the fragile creature. I cautiously step forward to get a closer look, but my momentum doesn't last. The animal gives a sudden, violent spasm and then produces a strange, gurgling retch, like a cat preparing to cough up a hairball.

This sound is profoundly unnatural coming from the throat of a lamb, but I've heard it before. That noise is the wet, sticky crack of the Black Lamb taking its first steps in a horrific transformation.

I clench up, my focus glued to the tiny animal.

The lamb settles a bit, then mewls again.

At this point my simmering fear is just too potent, regardless of how utterly ridiculous this situation may be. If I head down the staircase, there's absolutely no way to avoid the creature—this adorable, innocent, but gravely suspicious creature.

A subtle movement near the lamb's nostril causes my heart to skip, gasping as I take another instinctive step back. A red, spaghettilike tentacle has briefly slipped from within the animal's nose, whipping once across its face like a hungry worm and then curling back inside.

It happens quickly, the little crimson tendril disappearing just as soon as it arrives.

It could've been a parasite, I think. *The poor thing is sick.*

This sympathy is no longer a match for my discomfort, however.

I hesitate slightly, then alter course. My feet are hitting the pavement once again, taking the long way down.

With every step my pace quickens until, eventually, I've broken out in a jog.

Tara slips into the restaurant like some dramatic old-Hollywood actress who's struggling to hide her real identity and doing a terrible job. Enormous sunglasses cover her face and a fabric shawl is draped loosely over her hair, but her new incognito look is severely hindered by her unshakable inner style. The shawl itself is a dramatic red, and the dress below looks like Cyndi Lauper might've gotten married in it, puffed up and vibrant.

Several heads turn to clock her arrival, other diners clearly wondering what big-time celebrity has stumbled into their lives. Little do they know she's just an esteemed member of the Harold Brothers tech security and IT department.

Zeke nods with a sort of reverence as Tara approaches our table.

"How you feeling?" I ask, expecting a joke in response.

Tara sits, but when she removes her glasses I finally get a good look at the torment on her face. She's exhausted and scared, her eyes red and swollen from crying. She's not taking this well.

Truth be told, neither am I. I can feel the anxiety tightening its grip around me, infiltrating my body in any number of subconscious ways. The coincidences keep piling up, and either a sophisticated group of stalkers are going all out in their desire to fuck with my head, or I'm losing my mind.

I instinctively reach out and place my hand over Tara's. "Hey, it's okay," I insist, playing my best approximation of a cool, calm leader while feeling like anything but.

Zeke watches us quietly, somehow offering steadfast reassurance in his silence. To some he might appear emotionless, but Zeke is far from it. He's *steady*, and right now that's exactly the kind of energy we need. My boyfriend reaches out and places a hand on Tara's shoulder, a gesture across the table that's only possible because his frame is so damn large. "You'll be fine," he states with enough confidence that it's impossible not to believe him.

"Well, thanks, guys." Tara sighs.

She leans back in her chair and we remove our hands. Tara picks up a menu and pretends to look over the brunch offerings, but her gaze is distant. I can tell her attention is elsewhere.

"I called the police this morning," I inform the table. "I filed a report, but at this point there's nothing they can do. It's pretty much the result I expected."

Tara drops the menu, focusing on me now.

"I feel bad I got you involved in this," I tell her, then glance at Zeke, "and I don't want whoever's messing with us to focus on you, too."

"Bring it on." He cracks a smile.

I hesitate, briefly taken by just how cared for Zeke makes me feel.

"So, how do we figure out who these people are?" I ask. "Tara, don't you have some kind of phone-tracking app up your sleeve?"

"That could be very illegal," she informs me, "but yes, I do, baby. Yes, I do."

Despite the circumstances, I can't help laughing.

"Most people don't realize their mobile hotspots are personalized when they set up their phone," she continues. "If I were to, say, constantly collect that data on my *own* phone's connection log and catalog it with timestamps, I'd have a pretty good list of all the devices and associated names I've come into contact with over the day."

"Can you set that up?"

Tara laughs. "If I *were* to do that, I would've set it up on my burner phone years ago. Constantly running."

My eyes widen a bit. "And you found?"

Tara falters. "Uh . . . nothing. Either these people don't have phones, or they lock 'em down tight."

"Which is strange," Zeke jumps in, "because they're organized. They'd need to call each other if someone's talking through car stereos while the other person doesn't move their lips, or banging on doors across town at the same time."

"Or dropping off a sick animal in the hills just a few seconds before I arrive," I add. "Someone knew the exact path I'd take on my walk this morning."

"Fuck," Tara sighs, her natural paranoia abruptly surging. She glances back over her shoulder, scanning the restaurant. "Did anyone follow you here?"

"I don't . . . think so," I reply.

Tara seems unconvinced, and I don't blame her. "What about a drone?"

"I have no idea."

Tara points to a man sitting three tables over. "What about this fucking guy?" she blurts a little too loudly. "Isn't that the guy from *Captain Orion*?"

I glance at the old man quietly enjoying his pancakes. He does, in fact, bear a slight resemblance to the lead actor on that classic black-and-white science fiction program, but it's been years since I've seen his face. "Maybe," I finally reply. "Why would the guy from *Captain Orion* be stalking me?"

Tara shakes her head. "I don't know. Why would Riley from *The Hookup* be stalking you and stealing matches out of your fucking jacket?"

It's a solid point.

"By the way," Tara continues, "I did a little research while I was busy *not* sleeping last night. That reality show girl's name is Riley Kellogg, but she played a *character* named Alice in some low-budget streaming thing HBS did. She was the villain in one of their romantic thrillers; a stalker."

"That's pretty weird," I confirm.

I pull out my phone, prepared to search for a photo, when Tara abruptly stops me.

"Hey!" she yells, shaking her head in disappointment. "Harold Brothers' accounting office is right across the street. Airplane mode or turn it off!"

I'd forgotten about this rule, and I certainly haven't been following her instructions around *every single piece* of HBS real estate. This city is covered in sister companies and satellite campuses.

Tara has spent plenty of time explaining the reasons behind her obsessive requests, stating that all HBS networks are automatically and illegally downloading information from our devices with every connection. These are vast-reaching conspiracy theories that I can only vaguely follow before losing my footing in the cascade of tech jargon.

If anyone would know the deep, dark truth about these things, it would be Tara, but then again she's also convinced there's a fleet of satellites in the outer atmosphere that track everyone on the studio's *bad list*.

She's warned me about writing scripts in my backyard, telling me they'll photograph the unfinished pages from above.

"Okay," I finally reply, pretending to turn off my phone and slipping it back into my pocket.

Zeke clears his throat. "Maybe you should hire private security," he suggests.

I nod. In truth, the thought of paying that kind of money right before a massive contract dispute over *Travelers* sounds like an absolute nightmare.

"It's a good idea," I admit. "I don't know if it's an *affordable* idea."

"I've known actors with twenty-four-seven security," Tara adds. "It's not cheap."

"Or . . . maybe it's over. Maybe they're all done," I suggest. "I wanna be cautious, but it's been less than a day."

"They're not done," Tara states flatly. "They're just taking their time. Five days left, remember? The clock started around one fifteen this morning."

The second these words leave Tara's mouth a formidable wave of dread washes over me. I'd said this myself last night, but I hadn't yet considered the true weight of it in real-world terms. If these people are copying my movies, it would only make sense for them to follow The Smoker's timetable.

"I read the Wiki article," Tara continues. *"Death Blooms."*

I notice the way Zeke is watching my face, deeply curious. "What does that mean?" he finally asks.

"The character this guy is pretending to be is a manifested curse," I explain. "The Smoker. Once he targets you, you've only got five days."

"Before . . . ?"

"Before he cuts your bones out and grinds them to dust," Tara says. "Then he rolls you up in a cigarette and smokes you."

Zeke's expression falters slightly, a flicker of amusement across his otherwise serious face. "That's . . . *a lot,*" he states.

"Tell that to ninety-two percent on Rotten Tomatoes," I counter, defending my first critical and financial hit.

A stark vision flashes through my mind. I see myself waving goodbye while Uncle Keith and I stand in the doorway of that tiny old apartment, the only place my mother could afford after her and Dad split.

I can still smell the cigarettes seeping through Keith's pores, a burnt, toxic scent that was impossible to escape.

"Why five days?" Zeke questions, genuinely curious.

There are two answers I could give here, one broad and another frighteningly specific. I opt for the broad.

"A ticking clock is a great way to build tension," I finally reply. "Some say it's lazy, but it works."

"My little screenwriting genius. Two days faster than *The Ring,*" Tara teases, a smile finally creeping its way across her face as the tension breaks. "That's two days scarier." She's incapable of staying upset for too long; the deepest fibers of her being simply won't allow it.

A waitress arrives at our table, walking up behind me and prompting a quick shift in our demeanor. I sit up, motioning to Tara. "You first," I offer.

"Actually, I'm not assigned to your table," the woman admits, sporting an unexpectedly worried look.

"Is . . . everything okay?" I ask, confused.

It's only now that I notice the horrible quiet around us. The traditional din of Los Angeles brunchtime rush has faded away, every other patron silenced by some unknown force while Tara, Zeke, and I kept chatting away.

"Do you know that man outside?" the waitress questions. "He said he wants to talk to you."

I turn in my chair, gazing past the tables of dumbstruck diners and out onto the patio.

The Smoker stands watching. His enormous, lidless eyes are locked onto mine, the two of us frozen in place as I reel from his unexpected arrival. After that drunken night in the alley, my impression of The Smoker's face was awash in shadow and darkness. Now here he is, soaked in the blunt reality of broad daylight.

The man's skin is somehow even paler than I remember, bloated and strange despite his thin stature. It pops in the sun, particularly vivid against the blue of his suit. There's something visceral about The Smoker's quiet defiance of the world around him, unconcerned by the awkward looks from nearby patrons.

I break The Smoker's haunting gaze to check in with the rest of my table, hoping to confirm they're also really seeing this, but their attention remains locked on our unexpected visitor.

"Wow" is all Zeke can manage, the single word speaking volumes.

From the other side of the restaurant a woman's voice suddenly cuts through the silence. "What in the actual *fuck* is that?" she exclaims, something that easily could've gotten a laugh in similar circumstances, but this time around prompts no reaction at all.

It's as though every person here can sense the mighty existential weight behind The Smoker's wide eyes, feeling it in our bones. Outside on the patio, folks have all scooted away from him in their chairs, creating as much distance as possible. A fallen mimosa slowly pours from its glass, running over the table's edge in a thin orange stream.

The only movement The Smoker has made thus far is to lift a single rolled cigarette to his lips and take a long, deliberate drag. In the other hand he holds a familiar briefcase.

I already know what's inside.

The tension continues to build, neither of us making a move as we gaze at each other through the glass.

Suddenly, a digital song twinkles through the air, its arrival causing me to flinch in alarm. I reach into my jacket pocket and pull out my buzzing phone.

"I *told* you turn to it off around here," Tara scolds through clenched teeth, her eyes still fixed on The Smoker.

The words *unknown caller* glow across my screen in white text.

I accept the call, slowly lifting the phone to my ear and bracing for whatever comes.

I've seen this movie, but I still flinch when the voice of The Smoker rattles across the line, deliberately paced and creaking like a rusty hinge. My eyes remain glued to the figure outside, his lips closed tight.

"Come outside," The Smoker demands. "I'd like to speak with you."

"About what?" I ask, my voice trembling.

"Your manners," the visitor croaks. "I asked for a light."

The terror has welled up within my body, filling me completely. As someone who works to dole out this feeling on a regular basis, I hoped I'd gained some subtle immunity to the emotion. Exposure therapy. Unfortunately, now that the camera's turned around that doesn't seem to be the case.

Then again, The Smoker is more than just a monster to me; he's a memory, a reflection. All of them are.

I try my best to respond, but my brain fumbles any sensible assortment of words.

From the corner of my eye I notice folks pulling out their phones, the entire restaurant documenting this scene as it unfolds.

I also notice Tara and Zeke. My boyfriend is holding it together, but Tara is utterly terrified, and at the core of my being I can't help the sinking reminder that this whole thing is my fault.

It's frightening to know that all of this—in some way or another—revolves around me, but there's also an unexpected power that comes with discovering I'm the protagonist. I can be more than just the focus of this story, I can be the hero. I can drive the action.

"I don't know *who* you are, or *why* you're doing this," I suddenly erupt, "but you can go fuck yourself."

Running on instinct, I stand with a loud *skeert*, the chair behind me nearly tipping over but somehow managing to stay upright.

"Do you want an autograph or something?" I continue, fully losing my cool. "Do you want a picture?"

The phone cameras are turned on me now, hungry for footage of my outburst.

My words finally provoke a reaction from the figure outside, the pale man allowing a creeping grin to slither its way across his face. He parts his lips ever so slightly, revealing a set of filthy, tar-stained teeth.

"Come outside," The Smoker repeats in a measured drawl, his mouth still as his voice crackles through the static.

"What do you *want?*" I demand, stern in my conviction.

"The click-clack-rattle that makes you tick," the voice replies. "Tick-tock, tick-tock. When there's not much time, every decision counts."

I reach down and take a knife from the table before me, gripping it tight in my hand. Part of me considers marching out there to confront this menacing figure head on, but my feet remain firmly planted.

"You're not coming out, are you?" The Smoker questions. "You're just a frightened little boy."

I say nothing in return.

"Well then, the next time . . . I'll come in," the croaking voice promises. His mouth transforms into an exaggerated, clownish frown as he stares me down with those ever-watchful eyes.

The call disconnects.

With that, The Smoker offers a simple wave, the cigarette in his hand tracing a smooth curl of smoke. He steps to the side, his eyes still transfixed on mine, but as the figure passes from one window to the next, he somehow disappears.

Patrons gasp aloud. The space between the translucent glass panes is no more than a foot thick, and short of some expertly designed magic trick, it's impossible to explain.

I take action, no longer held in place by abject terror. I rush through the restaurant, bursting onto the patio.

"Where did he go?" I shout, eliciting nothing but shrugs of confusion from the patio diners.

My head on a swivel, I make my way up and down the sidewalk, desperate for answers but finding none.

"He—he just kinda disappeared," someone stammers, then makes an expanding gesture with their fingers. "*Poof.*"

"He can't just *disappear*," I retort.

The diner shrugs.

Technically speaking, there *is* a logical explanation, however unlikely. The man could've dropped down and crawled below the windows, but it seems like any witness would think to mention that.

Frustrated, I head back inside to find my friends.

"I'm sorry," Zeke says, wrapping his arms around me in a powerful hug. "You're gonna be okay."

Pressed against his solid body, I suddenly realize just how hard I'm shaking.

Tara takes an all-business approach, her fear reaching its breaking point and transforming into action. "Very brave standing up to the ghost curse," she says, tapping me on the shoulder. "Let me see your phone."

I hand the device over, refusing to release my grip on Zeke just yet. Meanwhile, the restaurant begins to chatter with relief and excitement, diners thrilled by the bizarre scene that just transpired.

"Hey," Tara interrupts, finally causing Zeke and me to release. She holds my phone in one hand and a tiny pile of gray dust in the other.

"I cleaned this out of your speaker and your battery port," she announces.

A spark of awe flickers behind my eyes. "Cigarette ash."

Zeke, on the other hand, isn't so sure. "Maybe," he chimes in. "Hold on."

Tara and I watch as my boyfriend strolls over to our waitress, chatting her up for a moment and then prompting her to retreat behind the counter. She returns seconds later with a small Ziploc bag.

"Let me see what I can learn in the lab," my boyfriend offers, holding the baggie open while Tara sweeps the mysterious dust inside.

I consider saving some for the police, then quickly dismiss the idea. We want this analyzed, not laced with fentanyl to pad someone's arrest quota.

Here's a strange powder I found in my phone, officer.

Across the restaurant, videos of this dramatic scene begin to replay on tiny rectangular screens. The sound of my conversation wafts faintly through the air as diners trim their clips and caption their posts.

I think I'm about to go viral.

NICE DRIVE

Jack Hays takes one last look at the dimpled golf ball before him, his body settling into a final stance. The rest of the world has been completely tuned out, including me.

Jack breathes deep, then raises his club. He swings, striking the ball with a confident crack and sending the tiny white orb off into the glorious Los Angeles sunset. Blossoming swaths of purple and orange consume the sphere. I lose track of it for a moment, struggling to catch sight of the object until it finally reveals itself by splashing against a net at the back of the range.

We're on the top floor of this facility, a location that features ten driving bays from end to end. Jack has rented out every one of the bays on this level, a habit I'd heard rumors of but never actually witnessed myself.

Ever since he drunkenly wandered into a midnight screening of *Black Lamb* at South By Southwest and liked what he saw, Jack Hays has had my back. Later, the executive vehemently claimed he could pinpoint why it wasn't the financial hit that it should've been.

The directing was terrible, but the writing was great.

He then brought me over to HBS for *Devil's Due*, hoping I could thrive in the world of horror comedy and getting mixed results. I could've been dropped as a failed experiment right then and there, but Jack stuck with me.

When *Death Blooms* blew up, Jack finally got to say, *I always knew that kid had it in him,* and to be fair, he always did.

For all of his faults, Jack is a friend.

Kind of.

"I saw the video," Jack announces, using his club to tap another ball into position. "It's everywhere. Pretty freaky stuff, buddy. You look like a nut screaming like that."

"*I* look like a nut?"

"I mean, so does the actor guy, but all actors are nuts."

I consider this. "Well, it *has* made things a little tense."

Jack stops what he's doing and glances up at me, the first time we've made eye contact since my arrival. "Things were already tense," he counters. "You've got two characters to kill off. Honestly, buddy. It's not that big of a deal, just give 'em a great send-off and be done with it."

I'd normally fight back, but the organized stalking has pulled my attention elsewhere.

"When you called me, I figured that's what the big news was," Jack continues. "I can order up a bottle of champagne if you're about to tell me you've come to your senses."

"I haven't," I reply.

Jack lets out a long sigh, shaking his head in disappointment. He strolls over to me and places a hand on my shoulder, head bowed as though he's praying over my dead body. We stay like this for a long while before the man offers two solid pats of acceptance.

"I'm sorry to hear that," he says with a solemn weight, then returns to his previous position at the tee. "On the bright side, without the major studios or access to any IP, you'll still be able to find some student films to help out on. Maybe a disaster movie about that big earthquake last March. Earthquakes sure aren't a Transformer invasion, but they *are* public domain."

He takes another swing, which sends the ball flying in yet another perfect arc. Jack watches it go, pleased with himself, then rolls another little white orb into position.

"Of course, you'd have to find a way to turn the earthquake into some kind of artistic commentary on gay sex—"

"Girthquake," I interject.

Jack freezes, struggling not to react, then finally settles again. "At least we'll have a nice send-off for your career at the Oscars."

A thought suddenly crosses my mind, something I hadn't considered until this very moment.

"And what if I win?" I propose. "You *really* think it would *still* cost less to fire me than it would to let a couple of queer characters live?"

Jack shrugs. "Honestly, I don't know. I'm sure the board has already calculated that stuff. Cost-benefit analysis is a real mystery sometimes. Between you and me, I think all eyes are gonna be on Best Actor and not much else."

The executive takes his next swing, connecting flawlessly with the ball that once rested at his feet.

"Did you see that?" he shouts, turning back to me with a huge grin. "Goddamn, I know how to *fuck*! Perfect swing."

Jack extends his fist for a pound, but I reject the offer.

"In case you didn't notice, I rented out this whole floor," Jack continues. "I write it off as a health expense, can you *believe* that? But here's the thing, it really *does* help calm my nerves. You can laugh at spending three hundred dollars more on some empty driving range bays, but who's to say I don't use this to clear my head and then negotiate a deal worth three *million* dollars more? That's no bullshit."

The executive suddenly perks up, motioning to the empty driving bays that stretch away from us in either direction.

"You wanna take a swing or two?" he asks.

I shake my head.

Jack nods. This time, the man refrains from rolling a new golf ball into position. He just stares at me, waiting for something. It gradually dawns on me that I haven't even started with the *big question*, still haven't addressed the curious weight that's hung over me since Tara and Zeke pointed it out.

I'd spent the whole drive over blasting my music and getting fired up for our chat, but now that I'm here, the very core of my accusation seems a little absurd.

Jack raises his eyebrows, still waiting.

As I gaze at the man, the house of cards within my mind begins to fall apart. He's a prick in a suit, a cog in terrible machine, but ultimately, he's just a guy.

"If you're not killing off Lexa and Naomi, then why are you here?" Jack finally questions, tired of the silence. "Speak!"

I shift my weight, struggling to find the best way of going about this. It's usually easy for me to conjure up the will to take these confrontations head-on, but I'm hobbled by a self-conscious awareness that what I'm about to say is, well, kind of ridiculous.

"I never had a stalker until two days ago," I explain. "I've met plenty of fans, but nothing like this has ever happened. I've *also* never been threatened into making major character changes."

Jack nods along. "Yeah," he replies. "Big fucking month in the Misha Byrne household."

"The creep said *every decision counts*," I inform him, then hesitate. "It's kind of a weird coincidence."

Jack's expression is curious at first, struggling to connect the dots and grasp my implication. The moment it clicks, however, his face shifts into a mix of astonishment and humor.

The next thing I know, Jack is erupting in a fit of laughter, unable to contain himself. He's crying with amusement.

"I'm sorry," he starts, desperately wiping his eyes. "You think the *studio* is trying to scare you? Into killing your leads? That's amazing."

"I mean, the timing's a little weird. Stalkers typically work on their on their own, but it would take more than one person to pull this off. At least two, probably more," I continue. "This group has access to a makeup department, and they probably have some kind of practical effects training."

Jack finally regains his composure, letting out a long sigh. "That's all well and good, but Harold Brothers is an upstanding member of the international entertainment marketplace. We don't run around in costumes scaring our talent. We have shareholders to impress and adrenochrome cocktails to sip at Bohemian Grove."

I consider bringing up all the sensitive information I have about privacy violations in the tech department, countering his everything-above-board narrative, but it'd be too easy to trace that leak back to Tara. The point remains, this studio is *not* above pushing the boundaries of integrity.

"Besides, why would I scare you?" he continues. "I want you to fucking *work.*"

This is a good point. As much as I feel like there's a nefarious connection here, the motivation doesn't quite make sense. Outside of a courtroom, the studio doesn't really *need* to do anything. It's only a matter of time before I breach my contract, and then HBS can hire a new writer to kill off my characters themselves.

Hell, they can have a computer do it.

Jack realizes something, tilting his head ever so slightly as his eyes narrow. "It's not the *worst* idea, though. Streams of *Death Blooms* have jumped forty percent since your incident yesterday."

"I'm glad my torment has delivered the ratings," I reply.

Jack stops abruptly. "You know, that's what I don't understand about you, Misha. You're telling stories, you're creating drama every day. All we're asking you to do is twist the knife a *little* bit, and you won't do it."

"I'm *so fucking sick* of queer tragedy," I state, standing my ground. "I'm not gonna write it anymore."

"Sometimes it doesn't matter what you want," Jack opines. "*Queer tragedy*, if that's what you wanna call it, sells. I have the data. I've seen the same numbers the board has. I know this is difficult for you, but you've worked way too hard to throw your career away over something like this. *Way* too hard."

Jack returns to his tee, rolling another golf ball into place.

"You wanna know how I got such a good golf swing?" he questions, focused on form as he lines up another shot. "I've got a five handicap. How do you think that happened?"

I sigh, already knowing the answer. "You worked your ass off?"

Jack swings, another perfect connection that sends his target soaring across the wide-open range.

He turns back to face me, scoffing. "No. *Fuck* no. I paid a shitload of money to get lessons from the best players in the world. It's all about *money*, Misha."

"Right."

"Speaking of money, the studio will pay for private security at your place," Jack continues. "*Good* private security, too."

"Oh," I fumble, a little surprised to hear this. "That's . . . great. What about Tara and Zeke?"

"Who the fuck is Tara?" Jack replies.

"My best friend," I state. "She works here."

Jack's expression remains totally blank.

"She's getting stalked, too," I explain.

Jack shrugs. "Sure, whoever the fuck you want, I don't care."

I sit with the news of our protection for a moment, somehow unable to find the relief one might expect. "I feel like there's a catch," I finally admit.

Jack's eyes remain fixed upon the golf ball before him. "Just remember what happens to all the big-studio perks when you stop working for the big studio."

"What are you? A supervillain now?"

Jack shakes his head, then takes a mighty swing that sends his ball flying with a resounding crack. "The studio may be a ruthless capitalist machine," he opines, "but we're not *evil*."

They say you know it's love when someone offers to drive you to LAX, and right now I'm feeling the love.

Most relationships would fall apart if you put them through the high-performance stress test that is currently my life, but for some reason all this tension only serves to make Zeke step up even more.

Do I deserve it? Probably not.

As I gaze at him from the passenger seat, I'm haunted by the fact I didn't tell him about this trip sooner. I'm also haunted by my blowup at Blossom's party, terrified by the prospect of our raw, unfiltered love recorded forever in some digital archive, and by the realization that I may never show my whole authentic self to the world without slathering it in a mask of artistic expression.

Right now, all I wanna do is listen to these sad folk songs that Zeke always plays and rest my hand on his leg, feeling the warmth of his body through the fabric.

Zeke notices me staring at him and chuckles to himself. "What?"

"Nothing," I reply, shaking my head, then turning my attention to the sea of palms that stretch on and on around us from this perch on the 405 freeway.

Zeke doesn't push for answers, because he doesn't really need them. He's solid, existing in a perpetual state of up-for-whatever, but with every passing day I'm starting to wonder how much I've taken advantage of that.

We reach the off-ramp and continue our journey through crowded city streets, the traffic growing thicker as our destination looms.

Sometimes kindness is a duty, a job that one sets out to accomplish with time and patience and effort. People who feel this way, myself included, fight against some other gnawing instinct within; we bloom like a flower from the dirt.

It's an honorable thing to strive for, and there's nothing bad I can say about that kind of growth.

Other folks, however, don't even think about it. There's some uncanny spark that always pushes them to make the right choice, because they're not even aware a *choice* exists. It's just what they do.

Zeke is that kind of man.

A surge of emotion bubbles up within me, taking form as some frothing collection of unfiltered words I should probably keep to myself. Still, I can't hold them back.

"I feel bad about leaving," I finally admit.

Zeke glances over, smiling.

"We'll be fine," he assures me. "Nobody's stalking *me*. They're focused on you, so leaving town is a blessing in disguise. Even if they *did* come to the house, those security guards are no joke."

"Security guards get absolutely *destroyed* in horror stories. It's like the easiest way to pad your body count," I inform him. "That's not what I meant, though. I feel bad about leaving *without you*."

Zeke's expression falters. "I know."

"Montana is a giant closet I've gotta slip back into," I explain, then trail off. "Does that hurt you?"

My boyfriend hesitates, then nods. "Yeah."

It's not long before three massive letters mark our arrival, **LAX** written atop a grassy green mound. Zeke and I continue up a slight incline, the city falling away as a bustling terminal of travelers takes its place. When the sign for my airline appears, Zeke cuts into the chaos, somehow managing to find a spot right before the automatic doors that lead to my check-in.

We sit for a moment, not wanting to say goodbye just yet.

"Oh hey, I got you something," Zeke suddenly remembers, reaching into his jacket pocket. "We had the spring eyeshadow collection launch at a bar downtown. I grabbed you this."

Zeke pulls his hand from the jacket, holding it out and opening his palm to reveal a small matchbook with a rooftop bar's name emblazoned across the front in yellow and white.

MOUSE DEN, it reads.

"Like your movie," Zeke offers.

Little Mouse, my twenty-minute movie that was nominated for this year's Best Live Action Short Film award, is a simple tale about a critter who's caught between worlds.

With the help of some very patient actors and a well-trained rodent, I tell the story of a mouse and his unusual habit of gathering wildflowers near a hospital. The mouse constructs beautiful floral arrangements within the walls, and eventually these pieces are discovered by the human staff who work there. Recognizing the talent of their tiny friend, the staff start planting flowers in specific color schemes, hoping to guide the mouse's creations while the strange rodent's fame builds, but the mouse prefers to work in a vivid rainbow of hues.

Refusing to adhere to any strict color palette, the mouse is forced to venture farther and farther away from the safety of the hospital walls, hoping to find his beloved wildflowers. All the while, the threat of a circling hawk looms large overhead.

One day, the mouse never returns. I leave it up to the audience whether or not our rodent hero is eaten by a predator, or if he simply decides to run away.

It's *definitely* not my usual style, but people seem to like it. And obviously so does the Academy.

I consider my boyfriend's offering.

"You don't want it for your collection?" Zeke asks.

I *do* want it for my collection, but this habit of mine is less of a fun hobby and more of a compulsion. While I'm fine to discuss my routine, it's not something I care to dwell on and certainly not the cute gesture Zeke thinks it is.

Strangely, however, there's no discomfort in this moment. When I stare down at the humble little gift in Zeke's hand I don't see flashes of darkness and cold, or smell a whiff of cigarette smoke. All I feel is thankful.

Unbeknownst to Zeke, he's starting to reclaim these moments, painting over a tragedy with a mural of his smiling face.

"That's very sweet," I reply. "Can you do me a favor, though? Hold on to it for me."

Zeke looks a little confused, but accepts my wish. He returns the matches to his jacket pocket.

"I've already got a matchbook in my carry-on, and TSA only lets you take one," I explain. "Now you'll have something to offer if anyone asks for a light."

We kiss, appreciating each other's presence just a little bit longer and then, finally, we release. I climb out of the car and retrieve my bag from the back seat, giving Zeke one final wave before turning and heading for the terminal.

I wish he were coming with me.

I've barely crossed the building's threshold when my phone starts buzzing in my pocket, prompting a knowing smile to cross my face. I stop, then turn back to the vehicle.

I'm certain Zeke has one last thing to say before sending me off, or at the very least, he's calling to let me know which travel essential I've carelessly left on the passenger seat.

But Zeke is already gone.

I retrieve my phone and gaze down at the glowing rectangular display of an unknown number.

I answer, holding the device to my ear. "Hello?"

The Smoker's croaking voice comes rattling through my speaker. "In three days—"

"Fuck off," I interrupt.

I hang up and head inside, pushing any thought of menacing stalkers from my mind.

A GHOST STORY

The casino before me looks strange and otherworldly on this hazy, fog-covered evening, a glowing castle of twinkling orange lights surrounded by dark, wet forest. It's not late, but when thick clouds paint the sky up here in the Montana woodlands, night seems to come on faster than it should.

I stare up at the building from my space in this half-empty parking lot, traveling all this way to suddenly find myself hesitating.

"Misha?" comes a curious voice through the darkness.

I glance over to see a figure approaching in a warm coat with their hands stuffed deep into their pockets, just as bundled up as I am. They're vaguely familiar, but in the shadows of the harsh streetlamp lighting it's hard to tell. It's a man about my age with stark blond hair and a friendly, almost silly smile.

I realize now that he's coming in for a hug, and I'm fully prepared to carry on feigning that I remember this guy when, suddenly, it all falls into place.

"Oh my God!" I shout. "Lance!"

The two of us embrace in a way that feels very specific to these trips back home. Our hug is unexpectedly intimate, but a few solid pats on the back are added to make things seem more casual.

My old friend steps away, looking me over and surveying the ravages of age. "What are you doing out here in the cold?" he questions.

"I don't know," I reply with a laugh. "How about you?"

"Remembering things."

My old friend reaches into his pocket, searching around for something. He seems frustrated, unable to find whatever he's looking for. I'm guessing he's about to go for a smoke, but moments later he extracts a packet of gum instead. He pulls out two pieces for himself, then gestures the pack toward me. "You want some?"

"No, thanks."

Lance pops the gum into his mouth and starts chewing.

Back in the day, the two of us were inseparable, causing trouble wherever we went. We were best friends, and it felt like that connection would never fray. Those young friendships rarely last, though, and it's easy for folks to lose touch after splitting off to separate colleges on opposite sides of the country.

Lance doesn't feel like a stranger at all. I'm at ease around my old pal, the thread of whatever united us all those years ago still holding strong in its own weird way.

"My friends think I've got a darn screw loose for wanting to go to this," Lance informs me. "High school kinda sucked, pardon my French, but I wanted to see the guys again. What about you? You were the little punk rocker. Why'd you come?"

This is a great question, one I'm not entirely sure how to answer.

"You've only got a handful of chances to go to your high school reunion," I reply. "Worst case scenario, you'll get a good story out of it."

My response immediately prompts Lance to crack a smile. "You and your darn stories, man. Some things never change."

The two of us enjoy a brief round of laughter. Nothing's all that funny about what Lance just said, but it fills the silence nicely.

"Who would've thought!" Lance continues. "Look at you now, flying up from Hollywood! You're the big star here tonight."

"I don't know about that," I retort, uncomfortable with the praise.

"What about Jimmy Greenwald? Doesn't he play for the Raiders or something?"

"Injured and let go," Lance reveals. "He went to the playoffs once, though."

My friend hesitates, drawing the moment out as long as he possibly can.

"So, yeah, way more famous than you," he finishes.

The two of us chuckle, plenty capable of talking shit after all this time.

I consider suggesting that we head inside where it's warm, but something stops me.

Instead, I ask another question. "You think Richie's coming?"

I try throwing this out as casually as possible, but the weight I feel as these words leave my mouth is palpable. Regardless, Lance doesn't seem to notice, or if he *does* notice, he doesn't seem to care.

He shrugs. "Don't know. Probably not."

An utterly bizarre emotion surges through me, equal parts disappointment and relief. You'd think these forces would simply balance out and dissolve into nothing, but instead they create a swirling, shifting tornado at the pit of my stomach.

I do my best to push it down, locking the feelings away until I can deal with them later in the form of some story arc or character flaw.

"You ready?" Lance finally asks, making the call for me.

"Let's do it."

The two of us fall into step with each other, crossing the parking lot as our conversation drifts into casual banter. We reach the door and I hold it open for him, waving the man past as a wash of ringing bells and flashing lights overwhelm our senses. It's a far cry from the quiet evening outside.

The reunion committee that set all this up has reserved a meeting room directly to my left, and as Lance and I approach I can already glimpse a slew of familiar faces.

WELCOME COPPER RIDGE FALCONS, reads a large sign in the gold and red colors of our alma mater, perched atop an easel.

"Is that Misha Byrne?" my friend Amy cries out, rushing over to give me a hug.

Various groups begin connecting, introductions and reintroductions flying in every direction. I can't help noticing just how many people have arrived with their significant others.

The meeting room has been arranged with a smattering of cocktail tables and a decent-looking buffet of catered food that runs along the back wall. Next to this is a modest bar, and it's here that I notice a collection of my friends.

The guys.

The second I catch sight of this motley crew they're waving me over, cheering with excitement at my arrival. Seth, Morgan, and their beautiful smiling wives are all here, greeting me and Lance with raucous enthusiasm. Richie is alone.

"There he is!" Seth shouts, starting a wave of hugs that makes its way through the group.

I reach the end of the line and freeze as Richie and I lock eyes, not entirely sure how to react to each other's presence. The moment lasts no more than half a second, a hesitation so slight that nobody but Richie and me even notice.

But it's there.

"Hey," I start.

"Hey," Richie replies. "Looks like Mr. Hollywood showed up."

The tone of Richie's voice betrays his words, not entirely sarcasm but certainly not heaping on the conviction. He's mocking me, or so it seems, but the rest of the crowd immediately falls into a quick explosion of appreciation.

"Oh my gosh, is this the guy?" Morgan's wife asks, glancing at her husband and then back at me. "Are you the guy?"

"I am, in fact, the guy."

"Congratulations on the darn nomination, Misha," Morgan chimes in. "That's incredible."

The praise continues, a cascade of admiring words piling on from every direction while I force a smile and nod. All this attention makes me uncomfortable, but I'm trying harder to appreciate these moments when they happen. They won't last forever.

All the while, I can't stop glancing over to see how Richie is reacting. His presence is distracting, but to his credit, the man's behavior is unexpectedly relaxed. He's not the one being awkward here, I am.

"I saw that one movie with the goat," Morgan informs me, snapping his fingers as he struggles to think of the title. "*Dark Goat?*"

"Yep, that's the one," I confirm.

"*Black Lamb*," Morgan's wife corrects him. "We saw that when it came out and he was like, 'This is a guy I grew up with,' and I was like, 'Whoa, was he a *sicko?*'"

Everyone laughs.

"I'm kidding. It was really good," she continues. "A little . . . graphic for my taste, but good."

"I can't handle that darn violence," Seth interjects. "No offence, Misha, but I don't know how you do it. I just can't celebrate death like that."

The group quiets down a bit, clearly not expecting someone to dive right in like this. I can see now that Seth has already started drinking, and the alcohol is working like a truth serum.

I remember now that Seth was a writer, too, always telling stories and crafting these elaborate plotlines in English class. He wanted to sell scripts like me, but as far as I know it never panned out.

"It's like . . . what are those stories *offering?* You get to watch a bunch of stupid people put themselves in stupid situations, then they get brutally murdered one by one? Where are the *layers?*"

Lance quickly jumps in. "I guess there's enough layers for an Oscar nomination," he jokes, prompting relieved laughter from the group.

Seth's not buying it.

"Yeah, but that wasn't a *horror* movie, right?" my old friend continues, barreling onward with his critique. "If that was horror, it never would've gotten recognized. I'm sorry, but it's true."

"You're right, it probably wouldn't have been nominated if it was horror," I agree, "but that's *their* problem, not mine."

Everyone quiets down, exchanging glances. It takes a moment, but I gradually realize they're waiting for me to keep going.

Memories of holding court for my friends suddenly rush through my mind, a position I always seemed to end up in despite my otherwise average place in the social hierarchy. I might have blended in with the group during our normal daily adventures, but when the time came to address a crowd, I was second to none.

Storytelling isn't *just* about setting plot beats and knocking them down over the course of a two-hour film and a three-act structure. It's *any* journey from Point A to Point B.

It's all a story.

"First of all, horror isn't a celebration of death," I state. "If horror was a celebration of death, then nobody would like it. Human beings are conditioned to move *toward* some behaviors and *away* from others. We're programmed to self-replicate and protect our legacy, which is why sex is crafted to be just about the best feeling there is."

This prompts a laugh from the crowd, their expressions relaxing as they settle in for the ride. This is *just* blue enough for their sensibilities. The only ones who aren't smiling are Seth and Richie, for entirely different reasons, but I can't say I'm surprised.

"At the same time, we're programmed to push death and pain away as much as possible. It's visceral, right? We retract our hand from a burning stove, that's obvious, but we also have a deep, primal fear of the things that remind us of dying: creepy crawlers like snakes and spiders were serious threats to our ancestors, zombies and ghosts are reminders that one day our time will come, killer robots or hyper-intelligent space aliens pose existential threats to the survival of our species."

"Exactly! So why would I want to be around those things?" Seth questions. "Why would I want to see that on a screen?"

"Because nothing is black and white," I counter. "Sex may be great, but we've gotta leave the bedroom sometimes so our bodies don't atrophy and our bones don't snap. We need food, we need sunlight."

"Speak for yourself," Morgan interjects, prompting another laugh from the crowd and an eyeroll from his wife.

"Fair enough," I reply with a grin, my reactions exaggerated now that I've fully committed to this performance. "The same goes for fear, though. You don't wanna feel that way *all* the time, but it's a muscle that needs to be exercised. There *are* scary things in the world, that's just a fact, and if you pretend they're not all around us then you're in for a rude awakening. Horror offers a chance to recognize this truth, to explore dark places in a safe way."

I casually move my gaze from one listener to the next, checking in with each member of the circle.

"When I left for college in Seattle, I got a room in this old house on Capitol Hill. It was a huge place with these Victorian pillars out front, but there were six of us all crammed inside so there wasn't much space," I recount. "Still, we had a great time. Everyone got along pretty well, and without my family around this group kinda became my new family."

I notice that even Seth has dropped the act now, listening intently despite his clear intention to keep the stick up his ass.

"And like most families, we had stories and legends that started to develop. A few grew from whole cloth while I was living there, but most of the time these stories were passed down from previous roommates and retold again and again," I explain. "One of these stories was a ghost story."

They're giving me their full attention now, the hustle and bustle of the casino fading away. Despite the chaotic gathering that rages on around us, there's a stillness in the air, like we're standing in the eye of a storm.

"Long ago, when a family lived in that house, there was a little girl named Annie," I continue. "Her room was in the basement, which I'm sure was done up real nice back in the day. Lots of space down there. It was large enough that, years later, new roommates would try moving down from time to time. We'd always tell them not to, but they wouldn't listen."

I hesitate here, drawing out the space as long as I possibly can.

"Why?" asks Lance, still a great wingman whether he knows it or not.

"Because that's where Annie died," I reply, right on cue. "The legend is, she got very, very sick. Rotted away from the inside out. The doctors could never figure out what was wrong with her, but Annie's family left the basement exactly how it was when she passed. When I got to that house, there wasn't much to remember Annie by, but the basement still had traces of old pink wallpaper peeling from the corners."

"What happened to the people who tried moving down there?" Lance presses, enthralled.

I chuckle to myself.

"We *always* told them 'Do *not* move into the basement,' but they'd never listen," I expound. "It was the same thing every time: they'd lug their bed down the steps and get everything set up, even have one or two good nights of sleep, but eventually they'd start hearing things . . . seeing things. In the late, late hours you could hear a little girl crying."

"But did *you* ever hear anything?" Morgan's wife asks.

I nod. "I didn't catch the crying, because I was smart enough to never move into the basement. What I *did* hear was the tapping in the walls."

I raise my finger in the air, transmuting my digit into a little hook and then drumming it against some invisible surface.

Tap, tap, tap.

"Everyone loved Annie, I mean really *loved*, and when you love someone like that it makes it so much harder when they go. When she died down in that basement, the family was too distraught to clean her up and bury her. They just couldn't bear it. When they moved away, Annie was left behind. She just . . . melted into the bed—into the floor. She disappeared into the very *structure* of the building," I explain. "Anyway, some of the roommates would wake up to see Annie standing in the dark, decayed and rotten. They'd turn on a light and *poof,* she was gone, but it still smelled like death."

"Bullshit," Seth finally snaps, the spell broken. "That doesn't make any sense. Bones can't just melt away."

I smile. "My friend Dan thought it was bullshit, too. The second night he woke up to Annie sitting on the edge of his bed, and do you know what he said?"

"What?" Seth asks.

"Dan said he had a pretty scary dream," I reveal. "Dan dismissed the danger because he didn't *listen* to the stories about Annie. If he had, maybe he could've pieced together what was really going on. Horror stories aren't just the things we *want* to see, they're the things we *need* to see. *Night of the Living Dead* isn't really about zombies, it's about racism. *The Texas Chainsaw Massacre* is littered with pro-vegetarian subtext, and *They Live* is more about rampant consumerism than aliens."

"But ghosts aren't real," Seth argues. "He wasn't *actually* in danger."

"Zombies, Leatherface, and space invaders aren't real, either," I counter. "But racism, factory farming, and unchecked corporate greed are."

I let this point settle for a moment.

"What happened to Dan?" Lance finally asks.

"The poor guy died. I miss him a lot."

Looks of shock and confusion pass through the group, which hadn't expected my little story to take such an abrupt turn.

"Someone found him down there in the basement, dead in his bed," I continue. "He'd been feeling strange for a while, then one day he just never came back upstairs."

Seth is shaking his head now, astonished. "Wait, what? How?"

"Turns out all those scary stories about Annie saved some lives," I explain. "The basement was crawling with mold, really bad, toxic stuff. That tapping on the walls you'd hear throughout the house, that was a leaky pipe. It'd been dripping water into the basement for decades."

"What about those people who saw the ghost?" Lance asks.

"Hallucinations. Like I said, that mold is really toxic stuff. After Dan died, people went back and discovered that's what happened to Annie, too. The mold got them both."

"So she was real?" Lance gasps, dumbfounded.

I nod.

The whole group is reeling now, amazed by the journey I've taken them on.

"Here's the thing: by telling this story, I'm not *celebrating* Dan's death. My friend isn't around anymore, but *we* still are. We can listen to this and think about what we might've done differently, or what lessons we can carry into the future," I explain. "This is how scary stories work, how *horror* works. We're all still here, safe and alive. We've had that primal rush and exercised those muscles to remind us death is eventually coming for *everyone*, but not today."

Lance hoists his drink in appreciation of this point, prompting everyone else to do the same. I join them as someone hands me a glass of my own.

Even Seth begrudgingly toasts.

"That's why horror is a celebration of life," I triumphantly state, circling back to my initial point and closing the loop.

Everyone takes a drink, and soon enough the conversations break off into casual chatter. I notice now that a few more recognizable faces have shown up, still not a huge turnout but quite impressive in the age of social media. In a time when catching up with old friends is as easy as clicking on their profile pages, I'm glad a few others decided to make this trip in person.

This is actually turning out to be the story I'd hoped for.

Seth sidles up next to me, joining my survey of the crowd. "More people than the ten year, surprisingly," he observes. "I guess the older we get, the more sentimental we are."

"You're still the asshole I remember," I joke.

Seth laughs. "Sorry about that. I was being a dick," he admits. "I actually watched your short. It was really good."

"Oh, thank you," I reply, a little shocked. Those things make the festival rounds, but it's rare to find someone who actually *seeks out* an Oscar short to watch.

I hesitate, then offer up a question to my old friend. "What do you think happened to the mouse at the end?"

Seth laughs. "You really wanna know? I don't think my cozy small-town sensibilities are gonna match up with your art-school intentions."

"I really wanna know," I insist.

Seth nods, taking a moment to gather his thoughts. "I kinda pictured the little guy going out there and discovering there's more than just hawks in the world, you know? There's other birds who would probably let him gather all the little flowers he wanted, maybe they'd like his work. They'd accept him just the way he is," he suggests, so much sincerity in his voice that it's actually a little awkward. "I picture a family of swans taking care of him. He's got them covered in really bright flowers and all that, like you could add a final scene of these swans just *sparkling* on the water . . . I don't know."

He's right, this is one of the cheesiest ideas I've ever heard. It takes every ounce of willpower I've got not to crack a smile, but I somehow manage before changing the subject.

"That's not entirely terrible," I offer. "Speaking of the Oscars, what'd you think of *Broken Don*?"

"You mean besides the awful name?" he retorts. "Best performance of a dead guy I've ever seen."

I can't help laughing, shaking my head as I come to terms with this new reality.

"But seriously, Harold Brothers *has something*, you can't deny that," Seth continues, gradually shifting more and more into *film buff* mode. "No other AI performance has *ever* come close to what they're doing at HBS, *especially* after they bought out Betta Effects. You know what it reminds me of? When CGI was invented, all the practical effects went away, and if you go back and watch those older movies with real stunts and darn puppet aliens, the effects *look better!* Whatever code HBS is running makes me feel like we're back to the practical stuff. It has weight."

"It all looks like shit to me," I counter.

Seth gives me a skeptical glance. "Be real," he says. "*Most* of that stuff is garbage. AI from the other studios just looks . . . runny or something. Your brain can tell it's fake. When it comes from Harold Brothers . . ." He pauses, considering something. "Whatever. It'll probably win on novelty alone."

"We'll see," I reply.

"That sledgehammer scene, though," my friend adds, wrinkling his nose. "I know the mob is brutal, but good God."

A full-body tremble washes over Seth, clearly unhappy his mind's eye has been forced to revisit that moment. He takes a quick drink, loudly smacking his lips and offering a refreshed "*ahhh*" as though this might manifest a clean slate for his brain.

"So . . . career is good, what about your personal life?" Seth continues, shifting gears. "You got a wife? Girlfriend?"

The question is innocent enough, and at a gathering like this it's to be expected, but it hits me right in the gut. I'd prepared for this moment, ran it over and over from the plane to the rental car to the second I walked through the casino doors.

The answer is simple: *No, I don't have a girlfriend, I have a boyfriend named Zeke. I've only been seeing him for a year, but I think I'm already in love. It's scary, and also kind of exciting. I like the way he always has to sleep with an extra blanket, but it's neatly folded in the closet well before I've woken up whenever he stays over. I like the way he can somehow read ten books at once, jumping from one novel to the next on a whim, and he still manages to finish them all. I like the way he just stands outside and watches the sky sometimes, taking five minutes to appreciate the moment before coming back in like nothing happened.*

That is what I *want* to say, but for some reason it refuses to tumble out. I'm not in Los Angeles anymore, I'm back in my small Montana hometown with the guys I grew up with and all the baggage that comes along with it.

Seth just stares at me, waiting for a response as my mind spins off into a tangled mess, unable to compute his very simple question.

"Yeah," I finally reply.

Seth's curious stare remains. "Which one? Wife? Girlfriend?"

I can feel the lump building in my throat.

"Girlfriend," I announce, shocking myself as the word pops forth.

Seth just nods, blissfully unaware of the sudden emotional weight crushing me from above. "Cool, man," he says with a nod. "I bet she's super proud."

"Yeah." I'm fighting back tears now.

Seth hesitates, as if he's not entirely sure he should offer up the words that sit cautiously on the back of his tongue. "It's funny," he finally states. "If you read between the lines in your work, someone might assume you'd have neither."

The onslaught of emotion within me is too much to contain, and I'm dangerously close to making a scene that I likely won't have a chance to rectify for another ten years. My pulse racing, I step back a bit. "I'm gonna go check out the casino and play some games."

"Oh, nice!" Seth exclaims. "You want me to join you?"

"No," I bark, a little too quickly. "I'm good."

The casino is relatively empty on a night like this, a little too cold and dark for folks to be venturing just outside the county line, but there are still enough gamblers to make privacy difficult. It takes a while for me to find a corner of the room with nothing but machines to hear my awkward sniffling.

I finally take a seat at a leather chair in front of one of the games. This apparatus is designed with slightly more flare than the others, particularly large.

My head in my hands, I take a moment to collect myself, to reckon with the emotions that have so unexpectedly consumed me. I had plenty of time to prepare, yet when the question arrived, I fumbled it completely.

I've been telling myself this is a journey of curiosity, the quest for another wild story, but suddenly that feels like an excuse. I was always here to test myself, and I failed.

"*Fuck,*" I sigh, summing it up nicely.

Hoping to create some kind of karmic balance, I pull out my phone and call Zeke. It rings once before my boyfriend picks up.

"Hey! You feeling alright?" he asks, an unusual way to answer the phone but strangely astute. Sometimes it seems like he knows me better than I know myself, which is pretty comforting at a time like this.

"Great," I reply, spouting the best half-truth I can manage. I'm definitely upset, but the second I hear his voice I can't help smiling. "Just wanted to check in and see how things were going back at the house. Is Tara still there?"

"We're making popcorn and watching *The Hookup*," Zeke admits. "This show is . . . really something."

"Sounds like a perfect night."

"Almost," Zeke confirms, then hesitates. "You sure you're okay?"

"I just miss you. I wish you were here."

"Next reunion," he says, two simple words brimming with subtext. He's being patient with me, giving me the space I need to work through all the fears and complications that come with keeping one foot out of the closet and the other foot in.

"So, in ten years?" I joke, wiping my eyes. "A little presumptuous that I'll be ready by then."

"I can see it," Zeke replies with cool confidence.

By now my emotions have calmed significantly, rejuvenated by this breezy conversation. "I think I'm gonna head back to my hotel," I announce.

"Goodnight, then. Get some sleep, big day coming up."

The Academy Awards. Things have been so crazy with the script deadline and the stalker conspiracy that this enormous honor has been the *last* thing on my mind.

"I will." I start to hang up but Zeke stops me, adding one final message.

"Oh hey, before I forget," he starts. "I got something back from the lab about that ash in your phone. It's not from cigarettes."

I'd almost forgotten.

"Just . . . dust?" I question.

"Field's alloy. It's basically a mixture of tin, indium, and bismuth."

I laugh. "I have no idea what that means."

"Expensive metals they use to produce semiconductors. My guess is you dropped your phone and crushed something inside," Zeke explains. "To be honest, those elements are not really something I usually deal with as a cosmetics chemist, but they're certainly not supernatural. You can rest easy knowing it's not cigarette ash from a ghost."

This news fills me with even more relief. "Good to know."

"Night," Zeke says, a pleasant smoothness to his voice.

I hang up and lean back in my chair, this sliver of loving conversation more than enough to replenish my soul.

Finally, I take a moment to gaze up at the slot machine I'm sitting beneath, discovering the stoic faces of two familiar government agents. Their depictions are surrounded by twinkling lights as they gaze down at me.

These aren't my own characters, but the duo who came before—the inspiration for my own investigative pair in *Travelers*.

Dark Encounters was my favorite television show growing up, and while it was canceled sixteen years ago, it appears the intellectual property has managed to stick around in gambling form.

The second I recognize these characters, however, I avert my eyes. The agents are fine, but as they stand proudly in their dark suits they're flanked by various other humans and monsters. A warning bell sounds in my mind. After all this time, I still don't know what Agent Y looks like, and at this point I'm dedicated to staying ignorant out of principle. As far as I know, she's nothing more than a tall, slender shadow against a warehouse wall.

Despite all that, I'd be remiss not to take a spin.

I pull out my wallet, finding no more than two crumpled dollars stuffed within. I align the first wrinkled green bill, but before I thrust it forward I hesitate.

My mind floods with images from the night of my tenth birthday, the way it felt when I stormed upstairs, an utter mess, and my mother gave me a little piece of advice I'll never forget.

The more you talk about it, the more they'll tease you.

That night I listened to her advice, and it's taken me decades to break the habit. Instead of staying quiet, I became a storyteller. I started raising my voice to anyone who would listen.

In my art, at least.

But maybe that's not enough.

Under the flickering lights, with tears in my eyes and old friends cheerfully toasting in the other room, I feel exactly the same. I'm still perched at the top of my basement steps, heeding my mother's advice and telling myself to play it cool.

I pull my hand back, returning the two crinkly dollars to my wallet.

Fuck that show and their midnineties fake-progressive don't-ask-don't-tell queer-baiting bullshit.

I stand, taking one last moment to gather my emotions, then head for the exit.

As I push into the parking lot the sudden quiet is arresting, stopping me in my tracks. The shift prompts an awareness of my own body, every heartbeat registering in my conscious brain. I take a moment to gaze up at the dark sky.

On clear nights in Los Angeles you can still catch a few twinkling heavenly bodies, but the light pollution makes things much less impressive. Here in big sky country, the galactic cavalcade is truly awe-inspiring.

The earlier haze has dissipated, revealing a blanket of starry lights that stretches deeper and deeper the longer I stare at it.

I inhale deliberately, allowing the piney scent of this glorious natural setting to permeate my senses. The fragrance is a time machine, transporting me back to my earlier years.

Gradually, however, something else begins to tickle my nostrils. A sour hint of danger weaves through the lush forest aroma, unable to hide its noxious presence.

Cigarette smoke.

My heart stops.

The calm broken, I glance over, only to catch Richie standing on the curb just a few yards away. He's smoking, gazing out into the forest. His sudden appearance paralyzes me, not entirely prepared to lock eyes with this specter of my past—another ghost.

"Hey," I call over, awkwardly offering up the simple greeting.

Richie doesn't acknowledge me.

"Right," I continue, turning my attention back to the parking lot.

We stand quietly, facing the same direction as we casually ignore each other. It's not long before a bright red truck rolls through the lot and comes to a stop before Richie. My old friend flicks his cigarette, not even bothering to step on it before he opens the vehicle's passenger side door.

The interior light springs to life as Richie climbs in. He kisses the driver, a woman I don't recognize but assume is his wife.

I watch as they pull away, waiting to see if Richie sneaks a final glance in my direction.

He doesn't.

MRS. WHY

EXT. GAS STATION - NIGHT

A neon-soaked gas station in the heart of Los
Angeles. There are no cars out front, but a man
sits on the curb asking for change. Nearby, the
elevated freeway hums with unseen traffic.

A gray sedan pulls up and parks.

INT. GAS STATION - NIGHT

A BELL rings.

MISHA enters and immediately starts perusing the
aisles. He makes one selection, then another,
and another.

Before long, Misha's arms are filled with an assortment of trashy culinary goodies: cinnamon
rolls, two bags of chips, an enormous energy
drink in a vibrantly colored can, a collection
of chocolate bars, an ice cream sandwich.

Misha dumps his items on the counter, where a
CLERK eyes them before offering a good-natured
chuckle.

                    CLERK
          Big night, huh?

                    MISHA
          I'm starving.

The clerk nods and begins scanning the array of
treats.

A television hanging behind the counter plays on
mute, flashing images of a celebrity gossip program while captions scroll below.

The show catches Misha's attention. His expression begins as one of general curiosity, but it
quickly shifts into alarm.

                    MISHA
          Holy shit!

Misha points at the TV.

                    MISHA
          Can you turn that up?

The clerk glances over his shoulder, then shrugs
and pulls out a remote. He unmutes the television.

INT. WEST HOLLYWOOD OFFICE - DAY

An assortment of well-dressed gossip journalists are gathered in their open-plan office, a
beautiful view of the Hollywood Hills rolling
out behind them through massive floor-to-ceiling
windows. The journalists hang over cubicle walls
or lay back in their chairs, a casual air permeating this meeting.

HANK MARTIN is holding court, clad in a tailored
gray suit as he addresses the group.

                    HANK
          A few weeks ago Misha Byrne was just
          a screenwriter, now he's going viral
          after a few confrontations with fans
          dressed up as his characters.

The whole staff begins to chatter. JOURNALIST
#1, a young queer man, jumps in.

                    JOURNALIST #1
          Excuse you. Those are stalkers, not fans.

                    HANK
          Well, even though he works behind
          the scenes this guy can't seem to
          stop ending up in front of the cam-
          era. First we have this video from a
          brunch place in the Valley.

                                        CUT TO:

INT. AIERLOOM CAFE - MORNING

Shaky, handheld footage of a FRIGHTENING MAN
in a blue suit staring through the restaurant
window. He has slicked-back gray hair and his
eyes are lidless, making them appear inhumanly
wide. In the man's hand is a briefcase, and a
cigarette dangles from his lips.

The café patrons who are outside have moved away
from the frightening man.

MISHA is on the camera's side of the cafe glass,
furious as he stares back at the frightening
man. A phone is pressed to Misha's ear.

                    MISHA
                (screaming)
        I don't know who you are or why
        you're doing this, but you can go
        [BLEEP] yourself!

INT. WEST HOLLYWOOD OFFICE

Gossip journalists continue the analysis from
their open-floor-plan office.

                    HANK
        This stuff is popping up left and
        right, including that incident on the
        Heeler Airlines flight. There's a lot
        of theories online about what's going
        on, but some folks think he's staging
        this stuff as viral marketing.

                    JOURNALIST #2
        I think it's really messed up if
        he's faking it for attention. He's
        taking it too far.

                    JOURNALIST #1
        He's not faking it. The guy has
        stalkers.

                    JOURNALIST #2
        I'm just saying . . . if he's faking
        it.

                    HANK
        Misha's not looking great, that's
        for sure.

INSERT: A photo of Misha Byrne sitting in his
car in a strip mall parking lot. He's yelling
into his phone, furious and belligerent. His
face is red and his eyes are bulging.

                    HANK
We've got another report that Misha
and a mystery man were kicked out of
Chateau Marmont. A source says they
were doing cocaine in the restaurant,
then got in a fight with staff when
they were asked to leave.

Another gossip writer, JOURNALIST #3, chimes in
from his perch, hanging over the cubicle wall. He
holds a green blended drink in his hand and sports
an incredible number of bracelets on both wrists.

                    JOURNALIST #3
Do we think the mystery man is a boyfriend? Misha's never commented on his
sexuality.

                    JOURNALIST #1
He shouldn't have to!

                    HANK
I mean, we all know, right? I've
seen TRAVELERS.

INT. GAS STATION - NIGHT

The previous scene continues to play out on the
gas station's hanging television.

The clerk turns back to Misha.

                    CLERK
That you?

                    MISHA
No. I mean, maybe. I don't remember
that happening. I think I drank too
much last night.

The clerk finishes scanning Misha's items. The massive snack assortment is now crammed within two large plastic bags.

> CLERK
> That'll be forty-two dollars and fif-
> teen cents.

Misha reaches into his back pocket, pulling out a wallet and extracting his credit card, then hands it over to the clerk.

The clerk runs the card, waiting a few seconds before trying again.

The clerk inspects Misha's credit card.

> CLERK
> This has been expired for . . . nine
> years.

> MISHA
> Wait, what?

Misha takes the card, looking it over.

> MISHA
> This expires in 2016.

> CLERK
> Yup.

The two stare at each other a bit longer, awkward silence filling the air.

> MISHA
> So it won't expire for a while. I
> just got it.

                         CLERK
           It's 2025.

Misha's expression is one of complete and utter
confusion. Finally, he reaches into his wallet
and pulls out a fifty-dollar bill, handing it
over.

                         MISHA
                        (joking)
           Are dollar bills still good in this
           dystopian future?

The clerk says nothing, eyeing Misha skeptically
while the television behind him continues to play.

                    JOURNALIST #2 (O.S.)
           It's honestly really sad. I think
           he's just looking for attention.

The register CHIMES, popping open as the clerk
reaches in and extracts Misha's change. He hands
it over.

                         CLERK
           Good luck out there.

   For some reason I've always liked airports, even during ridiculously
early flights like this one. There's a spirit of independence in the air, a
sense that—if you really wanted to—you could just drop everything
and travel anywhere in the world.
   It makes me feel like I'm doing something important, like I'm out
here conquering life in my own small way. Sure, these wee small hours
of the morning can be brutal on a sleep cycle, but I already have a habit
of getting up at the crack of dawn for my daily walks.
   Surprisingly, despite the uncomfortable departure time, my flight is

packed with fellow travelers. Each and every one of us has a reason to make the leap from Billings to Los Angeles, our own story to tell that's brought us together for a singular moment when these paths finally cross.

Hundreds of life stories all crammed into one shiny metal tube.

I glance over at the man in the aisle seat, while I sit at the window. He's deeply focused, spectacled eyes gazing at the black-and-white crossword puzzle in his hands.

"Using a pen, huh?" I notice. "Impressive."

The man smiles. "It's not by choice. That's all I had."

"I've got a pencil in my bag if you want one," I offer.

My companion shakes his head. "Thanks, but I'm already on the journey. No turning back now."

Unfortunately, I was too focused on the recent drama of my life to bring along much in the way of personal in-flight entertainment. Instead, I'll likely go over my *Travelers* finale for the tenth time, rereading the script and, once again, allowing the agents to remain alive and gay.

The story I've crafted is a powerful one, and it's overflowing with queer joy. The studio can fire me if they don't like it.

Fuck 'em.

I should also probably write an Oscar speech, just in case—but then again what's the point if I'm just getting blacklisted from Hollywood the next morning? They don't exactly love it when writers don't play ball.

My agent back in New York has claimed they'll stick with me. We'll see.

I close my eyes, settling into my chair. Maybe the best option right now is to keep things simple. Just relax and pray nobody ends up taking the middle seat.

I pop in my headphones and press play on another recently crafted playlist, allowing the icy, pulsing synthesizers of "Deeper Understanding" by Kate Bush to wash across me in a blissful wave.

This 1989 classic envelopes me as my flight continues boarding, drifting somewhere between the realm of sleep and the harsh reality of waking life. At one point I sense a flash behind my eyelids, opening my eyes just fast enough to notice a fellow passenger tucking away their phone and continuing down the single central aisle.

Were they taking a picture of me?

As the people here grow colder, I turn to my computer and spend my evenings with it like a friend, Kate sings.

At one point I get the sense that someone is about to slide into the empty seat next to me, prompting my body to tense up. Fortunately, even through the music of my headphones I can hear a flight attendant instructing the stranger to move along to the back of the plane.

Soon enough we've lifted off, hurtling through the air at incredible speeds as I continue zoning out. By the time I open my eyes again, we've reached cruising altitude.

"You may now move about the cabin, as your captain has turned off the *fasten seatbelt* sign," comes a voice over the loudspeaker. "We'll be coming by shortly with an assortment of food and beverages for purchase. Thank you for flying Heeler Air."

I instinctively pull in a quick breath, blinking a few times then stretching my arms and legs as much as I can in such a small, cramped space. The man next to me is still working away on his crossword puzzle, deeply focused.

I'm pleasantly surprised by the empty seat between us, realizing now that the flight wasn't as full as I expected. I sit up in my chair, turning around to assess the rows behind me.

My gaze drifts over a sea of passengers. Some are watching movies on their tablets or phones while others chat with their neighbors; a handful are fast asleep with their heads tilted back and dark masks wrapped gently over their eyes.

One passenger, however, is staring right at me.

I stop abruptly as my breath catches, adrenaline surging through my veins in a vicious, stinging cocktail.

The woman's head sits well above the rest, her stark blond hair parted down the middle and her face wearing an emotionless gaze. I'd estimate this passenger is a whole foot taller than the people seated on either side of her, maybe more. In fact, she's clearly the tallest person on this plane.

The woman is stretched out like a shadow, a twisted mutation of a different character that I'll never actually see but looms large within my nightmares. She's not Agent Y, just my own riff on the idea, a nightmarish caricature who would eventually go on to serve as a central villain in *Travelers* many years later.

Mrs. Why stands at seven foot nine, larger than any human woman ever recorded because she's not actually human.

I know all this because I wrote her, and now she's sitting ten rows behind me, looking me right in the eye.

I quickly turn back around, facing forward in my seat as my mind races.

Between The Smoker and Mrs. Why, my stalkers have certainly flexed their casting muscles—or have they? I'm well-versed in the reality-bending miracles that a great production team can pull off, but this moment feels different.

They brought in the *tallest woman in the world*? They *flew her to Billings*?

I turn back around, taking another look just to make sure Mrs. Why is still here in objective reality.

She is, and the details are stunning. Mrs. Why looks like a tall human in every way, but within each eye there are two pupils. This creates a distinctly spiderlike appearance on closer inspection. It's strange enough to be unsettling, but nobody would dare to stop her on the street and point out this potentially sensitive body issue. She's eerily beautiful, in her own peculiar way, with timeless features that defy pinning her to any specific age.

Mrs. Why's teeth are also razor sharp, which is why she usually keeps her mouth closed.

My attention shifts to the passengers sitting next to her. I can barely see them, the figures slumped forward in their seats and unmoving.

I turn to my crossword-playing-companion, briefly pulling him away from the puzzle. "I'm so sorry," I mutter, suddenly questioning my own grip on reality. "Do you see that woman back there?"

The man turns in his seat, gazing over his shoulder. His eyes go wide as he spots her, hesitating momentarily before turning back around with a stern look on his face. "Yeah. Don't stare."

"It's not about her height," I snap. "You actually *see* her."

My row companion frowns, giving me the side-eye as his demeanor shifts completely. He returns to his puzzle, flustered.

Glancing back over my shoulder, I watch as Mrs. Why emerges from her seat. The woman hunches, only able to stand once she's made her way to the aisle. Even then, it appears her blond head is nearly flush with the airplane ceiling, hoisted atop a long green dress and her pencil-thin neck.

"Oh my fuck," I blurt.

Several passengers notice what's happening, watching as the woman deliberately makes her way down the aisle.

Mrs. Why moves exactly how I describe her in my scripts: eerily graceful, as though she's floating just inches above the ground. The movement of her legs is strangely detached from the rest of her body, an entity struggling to look human but ending up with a bizarre, forward-momentum Moonwalk.

The slowness of her pace only adds to the creeping dread that overwhelms me.

She's an actor, I remind myself, struggling to force the words deeper into my gray matter so they'll actually stick.

She's an actor.

She's an actor.

Soon enough, Mrs. Why is standing at my row, staring straight ahead before slowly turning her attention to me.

"You okay?" the man doing crosswords asks, prompting Mrs. Why to reach out and place a long, slender hand upon his shoulder.

It happens instantly.

The man slumps forward, sighing loudly and dropping his pen. The book of crosswords tumbles after as he curls into a ball.

Mrs. Why begins to slide past the man, moving toward me and extending her hand again. Her fingers stretch as I pull away, pressing my body against the cabin wall.

Suddenly, however, a loud chime rings out through the plane. Tiny red lights flicker on above us.

"We'll be hitting a bit of turbulence here, so the captain has turned our seatbelt sign back on," the voice of our flight attendant announces, crackling through a speaker above. "Please return to your seats."

Mrs. Why abruptly stops, her fingers mere inches away from my body. She straightens back up.

A flight attendant is moving down the aisle toward us. "Ma'am, you need to sit down and fasten your seatbelt."

Mrs. Why gazes at the flight attendant for a moment, then turns and glides back to her row.

I'm busy hyperventilating in my seat, trying my best to calm down but unable to shake the utter terror of this moment. I reach over and jostle the man next to me, hoping to get his attention.

Hunched over, my crossword-loving companion barely turns his head. The man's eyes eventually drift over to mine, vacant and red with tears. Drool oozes from the corner of his mouth in a long, semi-translucent strand.

"Hey," I fumble, struggling to keep it together. "Are you an actor?"

The man just stares, completely empty inside.

"*Are you an actor?*" I repeat, shaking him.

"There's nothing beyond the stars" is all he says. "It doesn't matter."

I wrote those words.

With the touch of her hand, Mrs. Why can show any living creature the end and beginning of time, a cosmic truth so powerful that mortal minds have no choice but to melt away. In effect, she steals the will to participate in this existence, completely draining her victims of the things that once made them beautiful and unique. Caught in a state of suffocating nothingness, the victim suffers a fate worse than death, a complete loss of *themselves.*

Unless forced to eat and drink, Mrs. Why's targets will eventually die of malnourishment, wasting away in their own filth.

I reach down and grab my seatmate's pen from the floor, looking him right in the eye as I brandish the pointed writing tool.

"I'm so sorry, but I have to do this," I say, taking his arm in my hand and pulling it close.

The man resists a little, hoping to curl back into a ball of nothingness, but ultimately not caring enough to fight.

I take the pen and start pushing its tip into the man's arm, watching as the flesh bends around the force of the blunt point.

"Are you an actor?" I repeat, a fire in my eyes as tears begin to well. "Just tell me and I'll stop."

The man stares back, expressionless and unblinking.

I look down and discover I've managed to break the skin, a thin line of crimson liquid running down the arm of my companion and disappearing over the crest of his hand.

I let go, reeling in utter shock as my seatmate returns to his balled-up state, refusing to react. The only thing he offers is a final ominous mumble: "Nothing's out there."

"This is real. This is real," I repeat, feeling as though my skeleton's about to claw its way out of my body.

A potent, creeping dread begins to wash over me. It's a feeling we rarely get during any one lifetime, a visceral realization that our world has changed in a truly fundamental way. I've found myself in a situation there's no turning back from, and the longer I deny it, the more horrific the consequences.

It's probably already too late.

If Mrs. Why is real, then so is The Smoker and his unavoidable curse. The ticking clock that I've been ignoring thunders heavy in my ears, reminding me there's only two days left before the ominous spirit grinds me into dust.

This is real.

I instinctively pull out my phone, hoping to call Zeke and Tara, then quickly remember I'm trapped on an airplane. I'll be here for the next few hours, and while I'm glad there's armed security positioned outside my house, the guards are only trained to handle *human* problems, not supernatural ones.

Because supernatural problems *don't actually exist.*

I glance back at Mrs. Why, who sits quietly in her seat. The woman watches me with her dual-pupiled eyes. In the seats around Mrs. Why's row, passengers are clearly disturbed by her unsettling presence, but nobody is quite sure how to react.

Those sitting directly next to her are gone forever, hunched over as they quietly attempt to curl themselves out of existence.

The sickness in my stomach grows. *I* made her this formidable, this horrifying. There is no antidote to those touched by her power.

The realization opens up a whole new set of implications of this merger between fiction and reality. These characters are behaving exactly how I wrote them, perfect replicas of my own nightmarish ideas now thrust into the waking world. They follow every little quirk.

Once The Smoker is after you, you can't stop him, but if you initially give him a light you're off the hook. That particular test I've already failed, but Mrs. Why has her own set of unique characteristics—traits I happen to be an expert in.

I glance back up at the glowing **FASTEN SEATBELT** sign, never so thankful to encounter turbulence.

Mrs. Why is a powerful extraterrestrial force, a creature wrapped in human skin who wishes to blend in, despite some obvious tells. Her species is obsessed with order, and it's this obsession with following the rules that's her greatest weakness. She has her mission, which appears to be squarely focused on me, but order and logic compel her into behavior that's slightly more complex.

I can't tell Mrs. Why to sit down and buckle up, because I have no authority on this plane. The flight attendants and pilot, however, just saved my life.

As if on cue, the illuminated symbol flickers off above me, accompanied by another digital chime.

We are free to move about the cabin.

I glance back to see Mrs. Why has risen from her seat, no longer violating the rules as she climbs into the aisle and stands upright, towering over everyone.

"Sorry. Excuse me," I apologize, already springing into action as I struggle to climb past my despondent row companion.

The hunched man mumbles something in return, barely audible. He doesn't move.

By the time I make it to the aisle Mrs. Why is no more than a few feet away, slowly moving forward with her strange, eerie walk. The looming woman reaches out, but I'm too fast.

Instead, I march up the middle of the plane, walking swiftly enough to avoid my relentless pursuer but not so quick as to draw attention from the crew. The last thing I need is for them to force me back into my seat.

I reach the first row, nodding at a confused flight attendant then motioning toward the fore restrooms. "Gotta go," I announce.

"I'm sorry, sir, you'll have to use the restrooms at the back of the cabin. These are for business class."

This is exactly what I get for skimping on my ticket.

I glance over my shoulder, watching as Mrs. Why draws closer.

"Could I just slip in there really quick?" I beg, trying my best to sound kind and, most of all, normal.

"I'm sorry, sir," the flight attendant repeats, a little agitated and blocking my path. "You have to use the bathrooms at the back of the plane."

Mrs. Why is mere feet away from us now, singularly focused on her goal as she extends a hand. Her presence is strange enough that it finally draws the attention of the flight attendant, who suddenly has *two* unruly passengers to deal with.

"Can I help you, ma'am?" the flight attendant begins, flustered and annoyed.

"Tell her she can't be up here!" I cry, squeezing past and lurching forward.

My instructions come too late, however, as Mrs. Why touches the flight attendant on her shoulder.

The woman immediately freezes, her eyes lifting ever so slightly as though witnessing something both mind-numbingly horrific and cosmically awe-inspiring. Her expression quickly shifts, welling with tears, then she crumples forward, collapsing to the floor in a ball.

"Oh my God" is all she can say, whimpering the words softly as Mrs. Why steps over her body and presses onward.

I've reached the front of the plane, no room left for me to escape other than the locked door of the pilot's cabin. Fortunately, there's also a single bathroom stall up here, and it's currently unoccupied.

As my pursuer reaches out with her long slender hand I duck and dodge, throwing open the restroom door and slipping inside with a swift, seamless motion. I slam the door shut, then throw the lock into place.

I watch as the handle jiggles once and only once. This space is occupied, and the rules of society dictate Mrs. Why is not allowed to pass through a locked door without permission. She can stand outside as long as she likes, but there is no way she's coming in.

This, of course, begs the philosophical question: Why is she willing to break the golden rule? Why does she have no qualms snuffing out the agency of others with the touch of her hand?

Even the most observant *Travelers* viewers don't know the answer just yet, but I do.

Mrs. Why is blessing us with the greatest knowledge one could ever receive, spilling eldritch secrets that rest at the end of the universe. Her

touch is a gift of kindness on a level mere mortals will never understand.

She thinks she's doing us a favor.

I flop onto the closed toilet seat in utter exhaustion. It feels as though
the whole world is spinning around me, and it takes a moment of close
observation to parse if this effect is a product of my adrenaline rush or
the natural sway of the plane.

Those poor people.

I shake my head, fighting to stay focused and alert. I stand up again,
putting my ear against the door as I struggle to make sense of what's
going on outside.

Mrs. Why is completely silent, but there's a vent by my knees and I
can tell from the shadows that she's right outside. She can't break the
door down, despite the fact that she's plenty strong enough to do so.

Instead, Mrs. Why stands patiently, waiting for me to emerge.

Can I stay in here for the rest of the flight?

I consider what might happen in this scenario, letting the potential
story play out in my head. Eventually, a line will form, and when that
happens the other flight attendants will notice the lack of movement.
They'll come knock on this door, asking if I'm okay, and eventually
they'll demand I come out.

The second that happens, Mrs. Why will touch me.

I've written heroes into plenty of corners, and given a long enough
timeline I always manage to find them a way out. Unfortunately, *time* is
currently a limited resource. I also don't have the luxury of going back
to make story edits, placing a weapon under the trash bin in act one so
I can find it here later.

I look at myself in the mirror, struggling to connect with the face
staring back at me. Is this really happening, or have I slipped into some
terrible fever dream?

There's still *one* part of this equation that doesn't quite add up, an
inconsistency I can't yet understand but is certainly worth noting.

The Smoker was a perfect copy of the monster in my mind, a true manifestation in every sense. His blue suit was the exact shade that spilled from my fingers in a long-winded description all those years ago. The scent of his bone-dust cigarettes was exactly the way I pictured it, wafting through the air and filling my nostrils with a distinct sting. His voice was the croak that rattled through my worst nightmares.

Mrs. Why is similarity manifested, the cut of her long green dress exactly as it should be, and the bizarre blank expression on her face is pitch perfect.

Yet for some strange reason, she doesn't speak.

The Mrs. Why of my mind has always had a unique grasp of human language. If I were dreaming up this scene, she'd be struggling to coax me out from my hiding place, insisting she was only trying to help.

She'd be telling me I'd feel better once I understood the truth, the *full* truth, of what makes everything tick.

Yet this Mrs. Why says nothing.

I stop for a moment, listening intently, and if I really strain there is *something* I can hear. At first I'm not quite sure what it is, but gradually my search brings me lower and lower to the floor. I crouch all the way down, putting my ear against the vent.

It's a voice, the voice of the flight attendant Mrs. Why just touched and sent crumbling into a state of hopeless despondence, an eternal trance of blinding, nihilistic horror.

"There's nothing," she mumbles, her voice barely audible. "There's nothing there."

I place my hand against the door, aching to connect with her in some small way. The guilt that weighs me down is suffocating, and combined with the potent adrenaline slamming through my veins it's a wonder I can even function. I'm not sure how, or why, but I've brought something terrible into this world. *I'm* responsible for this suffering.

"I'm so sorry," I murmur.

I'm speaking directly to the woman who's curled up outside this door, but the despair behind my words rings out much further than that.

Because if this is all real, then Tara *also* only has two days left.

Gradually, another sound begins to fill my ears: the sound of footsteps. As someone approaches, the concerned voice of a young man comes drifting through the vent.

"Georgia, are you okay?" the man sounds deeply concerned about his coworker lying crumpled on the floor.

The woman mumbles something under her breath, too quiet to understand.

"Are you sick?" the man continues, then shifts abruptly. I can hear him standing up again, speaking directly to Mrs. Why. "You need to sit down. This part of the plane is off-limits now."

A feeling of sweet relief washes over me. I watch as the shadow of Mrs. Why moves away from my vent, the creature retreating.

All I have to do is hide in here until the plane lands, then I'm home free.

The man knocks loudly as I hold my breath. "Hello? You need to return to your seat. This part of the plane is quarantined."

I don't respond, hoping he'll just leave me be, but my hopes are quickly dashed as I hear the sound of a metal latch springing open.

Seconds later, the bathroom door is yanked wide to reveal a baffled flight attendant on the opposite side.

"Hi," I chirp, awkwardly frozen in place. "Guess you guys have a way to pop these open, huh?"

"Why are you hiding in here, sir?" he questions.

I hesitate briefly, understanding just how important my next few words are. A strange calm washes over my body. Lying is just another kind of story, after all.

"I'm so sorry. I was trying to get away from that woman. She's coughing everywhere." I motion down the plane toward Mrs. Why, who has since arrived at her seat and climbed back in.

"She's sick?" the flight attendant asks.

Storytelling 101, let your audience figure it out for themselves.

I suppose it might be nice to just inform him that this is an extra-terrestrial villain manifested from the depths of my imagination, a valiant attempt at working through some deeply rooted childhood trauma come to life, but something tells me this explanation won't yield the results I'm looking for.

"I mean, she was talking to your friend here," I explain, nodding toward the woman curled up at our feet. "I'm curious how the people sitting next to her are doing."

The man glances back and forth between me and Mrs. Why. "Just go back to your seat," he commands.

"Of course, of course." I raise my hands in a gesture of surrender as I step from the restroom.

The two of us stroll back down the aisle, but the closer we get to Mrs. Why's seat, the more concerned my companion becomes. By the time we reach my row I'm the last thing on his mind. He leaves me and continues onward.

"Ma'am, is everything alright?" the flight attendant questions, approaching Mrs. Why's row.

She just stares at him. Then nods.

"Are you sick?" the flight attendant continues.

Mrs. Why shakes her head.

The flight attendant turns his attention to the crumpled-up figures seated on either side of her. "And are *you* alright?"

Nobody says a word.

The flight attendant straightens, growing frustrated. His attention returns to Mrs. Why. "Ma'am, you need to stay seated until we land."

I let out a thankful sigh as the words fill my ears. I sink into my chair.

The remainder of the flight feels like it stretches on forever, every little shake of turbulence prompting me to sit up straight and glance over my shoulder. I keep checking that Mrs. Why is still in her seat.

Of course, she remains, bound by the rules set by Heeler Airlines.

I find my mind wandering across the various other monsters I've generated, horrified that I might remember one who could land on the wing of a jet and tear its engine apart. To my relief, I haven't gotten around to anything like that just yet.

Eventually, the plane begins its descent, a slow and arduous trip to the ground that ramps up the tension with every lost foot of elevation. In the words of the flight attendant, Mrs. Why is not allowed to leave her seat *until the flight lands.*

We touch down, and the creature begins to stir. Fortunately, her instructions are readministered moments later with even more clarity.

"Welcome to Los Angeles International Airport. We hope you had a pleasant flight here on Heeler Airlines," the pilot begins, making his announcement over the speakers above. "We're pulling up to the gate now. We'd like to request that everyone stay seated until our security officer arrives."

More time.

When the vehicle finally halts, a uniformed officer comes marching through the door and then confidently down the aisle. The whole plane is watching, a few cell phones popped over the edges of seats to catch the drama as it unfolds.

"Tell her she can't touch you!" I shout as the officer passes, waving my hands in the air.

He barely notices me, brushing my outburst aside.

"Don't just tell her to come with you!" I yell, prompting some of the cameras to turn their attention on me. "Tell her she can't touch you!"

I'm well aware how belligerent I probably sound right now, but I don't care. They can film me all they want, I'm trying to save someone's life.

The officer arrives at Mrs. Why's row.

"Get away from her!" I scream, instinctively rising to my feet as panic surges through my body.

Finally, the security officer turns his attention back to me, angrily pointing a finger. "Hey!" he snarls, the beginning of some highly charged order that never gets the chance to be heard.

Mrs. Why reaches out with her phenomenally long arms, touching the security officer on his wrist.

The man halts abruptly, his eyes rolling back into his head as a long, horrible groan escapes his lips. "Oh no," he sighs, dropping to his knees. "It's endless."

Without missing a beat I leap from my seat, grabbing my carry-on bag and throwing it over my shoulder. I climb over the crossword man, who's still hunched in his chair, and hustle toward the exit. Several other passengers follow my lead and soon enough, the whole plane has taken their standing positions, searching the overhead compartments and extracting their luggage.

I glance back to see Mrs. Why making her way through the crowd, gracefully striding after me with otherworldly focus as passengers collapse around her. She looks like a slow-motion bowling ball, toppling pins in her wake.

I'm nearly climbing over other travelers as I scramble down the aisle, hoisting my bag above the seats and stepping onto armrests before finally breaking free. I don't slow down, rushing past the flight attendants who would typically offer me a brief "thanks for flying" but are too distracted by the unfolding chaos. One crew member is crouched down by her despondent coworker, struggling to connect with her friend who remains wholly decoupled from the world.

She'll be like this until she starves to death, I think, then push the horrific truth out of my mind.

Hurrying down the jet bridge, I extract my phone and immediately dial Zeke.

"Hey!" my boyfriend shouts jovially. "Did you just land? I'm out here circling."

"It's real!" I shout, the words searing my throat. "It's all real!"

INSPIRATION

2001

I was fourteen years old, gazing up the gravel drive that wound its way to Richie's house. The city bus that delivered me there wasted no time moving on, rumbling off down the road and into the darkness.

Richie's parents were farmers, and the surrounding land was flat and endless, but this singular plot in the middle was dotted with trees and subtle hills. It was the perfect spot to construct a family farmhouse, a home to pass from generation to generation.

It was also the end of the route for the Billings MET Transit Blue Line. As my bus faded into the empty abyss, I had no idea this was the last ride of the evening, something the driver probably should've informed me of all those years ago.

Maybe they did let me know and I just can't remember it. Stories like to churn and mutate over time, grinding themselves down to a state of linear purity. This often takes precedence over the truth.

Regardless, as a fourteen-year-old kid who had no idea what he was doing and had only ridden the city bus twice before, I didn't know my ride wasn't coming back.

That's romance, though. There's something potent in the simple act of throwing caution to the wind, whether you succeed or fail in your journey. Big swings are important, and I hoped Richie would recognize this.

I clutched the book tight in my hand, a horror novel we'd been talking about. Held next to it was a red-and-black box of chocolates, which just so happened to be shaped like a heart. The truth is, I'd gotten them half off at the drugstore as part of a post–Valentine's Day sale, and I certainly couldn't pass up the deal.

At least, that was what I'd been telling myself.

The walk began. Rocks crunched under my feet as I made my way up the dark path. The lights of the suburbs had fallen away, and now the only illumination was that of the massive silver moon that hung above me, its cold glow filtering through woven branches.

Eventually, however, another glimmer shone through the trees, the luminous warmth beckoning me onward. I approached a large two-story house, noticing the upstairs light was still on. Richie's parents were puttering around the kitchen before they headed off to bed.

Having hung out here plenty of times, I knew the usual routine. Richie's folks rarely told him what to do, a parenting style I'd also grown accustomed to after Mom and Dad's divorce.

Mom didn't have the energy to set up boundaries for me, let alone maintain them.

Most nights, Richie would stay up well after his parents drifted off to sleep, playing video games or watching TV downstairs. Lucky for us, there was a side door.

It was strange being there so late without the company of our friend group. I watched from the woods for a while, thankful I'd brought a warm coat and aching to make my next move. I was nervous and excited, counting down the minutes as the silhouettes of my friend's parents wandered back and forth in the upstairs window.

Eventually, the kitchen lights turned off.

I gave it a bit longer, just to make sure the coast was clear, then finally made my approach. I snuck through the yard, hustling over to the basement door and immediately recognizing the dancing blue glow of Richie's television screen as it reflected off the glass.

I knocked three times, just loud enough for him to hear me but not nearly enough to alert the rest of the household.

The moving illumination halted, still and silent now that Richie's screen was on pause. Through the darkness I saw a figure approaching.

Gradually, the confused face of my friend shifted into excitement and recognition.

He opened the door. "Oh my God, dude," he hissed. "What are you doing here? I'm grounded."

"I know. I thought you might wanna check out that book."

I handed over the paperback, anxiously waiting for my friend's reaction in the dim light.

"Oh, cool," Richie replied, difficult to read as he took the book and turned it over in his hands. Clearly, our conversation wasn't as memorable on his end, but the novel was accepted all the same.

"And this," I continued, handing over the box of chocolates.

Richie actually cracked a smile, taking note of the cardboard heart's ridiculous shape. He started to laugh. "Dude, what is this?"

I laughed, too, willing to play along.

Richie opened the box and pulled out two sugary morsels, popping one in his mouth then handing the next piece over to me. I followed his lead, enjoying the sweet, cream-filled candy.

"Tight," I offered, a simple review.

Richie handed over another piece and we repeated the process, standing in the doorway as we enjoyed our late-night snacks.

"How did you get here?" Richie questioned. "Did you walk?"

I shook my head. "Too far. Took the bus."

He smirked. "What the heck, dude? Do you have a crush on me or something?"

We started laughing again, once more finding humor in the awkward border of truth and fiction. Richie knew exactly what this was.

"You wanna come in and play *Mario Kart*?" he finally offered. "You've just gotta be super quiet so my parents don't hear you."

"Okay, cool," I replied, the tension building.

I followed Richie inside and the two of us made our way into the downstairs living room, which was technically a basement built into the side of the hill. This was a place for the kids to throw their stuff around while the rest of the house remained free from skateboards and Nintendo controllers. The sanctuary played host to countless after-practice hang-outs and low-key movie nights, a little corner of the world for our group of friends to grow up in.

Richie strolled over to the couch where his controller rested. Instinctively, I headed toward the nearby armchair, but Richie stopped me.

"Sit over here with me," he suggested. "You can see the TV better."

I altered course, carrying my controller over and taking a place next to him on the sofa. The second our skin touched I felt a jolt of electricity shoot through me, a sizzling energy that caused my hands to tremble slightly.

We went through the motions of selecting our characters, then watched as a timer counted down onscreen. When the light turned green, our digital avatars took off in a cloud of dramatic, cartoonish dust, darting forward at incredible speeds.

I'd played this game many times, and was usually pretty good. Tonight, however, I could barely focus. I found my little go-kart weaving haphazardly across the screen, zooming recklessly as it ricocheted off the walls and toppled into hazardous pits.

My mind was clouded with thoughts, not of *A* for gas and *B* for brakes, but an overwhelming concentration on the close proximity of our bodies.

Richie and I had been playing this endless tournament of chicken for months now, waiting to see who would break first. Even within this little game we had startling moments of intimacy, but they'd fly low under the radar, cloaked as innocent jokes.

"You're doing so bad, dude," Richie teased, chuckling.

"I can't really focus," I admitted.

Our karts traveled onward a few more seconds before my friend suddenly paused the game, freezing time both on- and off-screen. The whole world skidded to a halt.

Richie turned to me, then leaned in and kissed me softly on the mouth. The movement was quick, and he immediately pulled back with a mischievous grin. His expression was giving me an out, a way to play this off as just another harmless joke, but I refused to take the bait.

Instead, we kissed again, and for about three blissful seconds everything felt right. All the tension between us released in a powerful surge, sweeping through the basement and carrying us away.

But the moment was tragically short-lived, paced with catastrophic perfection as the upstairs door flew open and a cascade of footsteps came rumbling down. Richie and I pulled back with a jerk, separating just in time to see my friend's older brother round the corner.

"Hey is my Discman down—" he started, then halted abruptly when he saw us. Our bodies were dangerously close, side by side and pressed together upon this otherwise enormous couch.

Richie's brother, Justin, took all the things that make Richie a loose cannon and amplified them to the fullest extent, a tall, muscular kid whose natural state seemed constantly pinned to anger and annoyance.

Part of me thinks this is simply the way older brothers have to act in a household like Richie's, following a cosmic script, but there was too much cruelty lurking within Justin for me to give some innate boys-will-be-boys phenomenon all the credit.

Justin stood awkwardly at the bottom of the stairs, staring at us with a bewildered smirk, then he broke out in a fit of laughter. "What the hell are you doing?"

"Playing video games," Richie answered. His voice trembled as he scooted away from me.

"You guys boyfriends or something?" Justin continued.

My entire body was sizzling with adrenaline, the chemistry igniting my senses and causing my teeth to chatter. I had no idea what to do with myself, wishing the very makeup of my being could disperse like a fog.

He knows, I thought. The words slammed through my mind in a steady rhythm, thundering in time with the runaway pounding of my heart.

"No!" Richie cried out, springing from the couch as his voice cracked and his eyes began to water.

He was being too loud.

"You guys *kissing* down here?" Justin continued, twisting the knife even more as he watched his younger brother squirm.

I could tell my friend was aching to explode in a fit of violence, to rush at Justin in a wild mess of flailing fists and biting teeth, but he couldn't do that. His hands were tied by the sheer difference in physicality between them, and this helplessness was driving Richie to an even greater height of rage and frustration.

Not knowing what to do, I climbed to my feet and considered heading for the door. I was so uncomfortable, however, that I just kind of wandered back and forth, struggling to find a placement for my body.

"You don't have to leave, Misha," Justin joked. "Don't let me interrupt the honeymoon."

"Fuck you," Richie growled, so much visceral rage in his voice that Justin actually pulled away slightly.

Swears were a big deal in those days.

Realizing he'd gone too far, Justin did his best to shift the mood and go about his business. "I'm just kidding," he offered, hoping to course correct. "I'm just messing with you guys. Have you seen my CD player?"

Richie said nothing as Justin wandered past him, making his way deeper into the basement and assessing the teenage paraphernalia.

I let out a sigh of relief, thankful the boiling point of this combustible interaction had finally passed. We'd been suitably razzed, and now Justin was moving on.

I wandered back to the couch, ready to flop down, when I noticed Justin freeze in shock. I followed his gaze, then nearly collapsed when I realized what he'd discovered: the heart-shaped box.

Justin slowly turned to look at us, but his expression was no longer that of a teasing older brother, snide and mischievous. Justin was seething, struggling to hold himself together as he flooded with righteous anger.

"Are you gay?" Justin roared, breathtakingly direct. "Are you fucking gay?"

Richie was frozen, horrified.

"Those were on sale," I started, but before I could fully get the words out Justin held up his hand to stop me.

"Shut the hell up," Justin snapped, then turned his attention back to Richie, waiting for a response.

The room fell into silence, time slowing to an excruciating crawl as the three of us stood in the pale glow of the television screen.

Finally, my friend broke. "Of course not," Richie replied. "Misha brought those over for me. I told him it was dumb."

Justin's attention shifted, the furious gaze I'd been avoiding now squarely focused on my tongue-tied form. I later realized the frustration he felt with his brother was stifled by their family bond, but the second Justin found a new target in my awkward fourteen-year-old frame, all bets were off.

"You brought these over?" Justin pressed.

I nodded. "They were half off."

Justin stepped toward me, towering in his ratty camouflage tank top. His arms were bulging and muscular, seemingly powerful enough to reach out and snap me in half.

"You think that's funny?" Justin continued, his eyes never breaking from mine.

"It's—it's just chocolate," I stammered.

"Why are you sitting so close to my little bro? You gay for him?"

"No," I whimpered.

I glanced at Richie, but unfortunately this tiny flicker of connection was all it took to yank him back into the mix.

Justin turned the spotlight back on his little brother. "Is he making you do gay shit?" Justin demanded. "Is Misha trying to hook up with you or something?"

This, of course, was the moment that sticks with me forever, the axis on which so many other moving parts of my life would turn. Every decision we make ends up cascading into others, affecting our lives in ways we can't possibly comprehend. Most of these events seem inconsequential at the time, infinite grains of sand under our feet as we walk on by.

Others, however, are huge boulders dividing our journey in two undeniable paths.

Richie locked eyes with me, hesitating for a single flickering moment before finally choosing self-preservation.

"Yeah," he mumbled. "He wants me to do gay stuff."

Justin's eyes widened as his face turned red. He didn't even look at me, just glared at his younger brother. "Make your friend leave," Justin commanded, his body language altering ever so slightly. It was as though Justin started playing a character at that moment, re-creating a set of emotions that he'd previously witnessed—like he donned a frightening mask.

He was painting his anger by numbers.

At that point I was crying, tears streaming down my face as the emotional weight of the moment finally caught up with me.

"I wasn't—I wasn't doing anything," I stammered, the words spilling out in a blubbering mess. "I wasn't doing anything wrong."

"I said, make him leave," Justin continued, still focused on his younger brother but with even sterner conviction. "What are you waiting for? You gay, too?"

"I'm sorry," I choked, barely able to form the words.

I was so lost in the moment that everything became a strange, surreal blur, my senses overloaded to a point where I worried they were shutting down. My ears were ringing and every beat of my heart was pulsing through them, slamming like a constant cacophonous drum. I would've left of my own accord if I could have, but at that point it felt like the decision was out of my hands. I was trapped there, unable to react as the world tumbled down around me—a frightened critter in the center lane, frozen in place while blinding headlights whipped past on either side.

Justin was still yelling at Richie, but I could no longer make out the words. Upstairs, my friend's parents were stirring, likely confused by the commotion in their basement.

A simple command gradually fell into place, repeated over and over again as it spat from Justin's lips with shocking ferocity. "Do it! Do it!"

I glanced back at Richie, who flashed me one final expression of sympathy before winding back and throwing a punch as hard as he could. My friend hit me directly in the face, knocking me backward as the world returned to its usual pace. Sound flooded my ears as a powerful sting overwhelmed my mouth.

I touched my upper lip, pulling my hand away to reveal a freakish amount of shiny crimson blood.

"Richard! Justin!" came the voice of their irate father, billowing down from the top of the stairs. "What the hell's going on?"

I stopped hesitating, just turned and ran as fast as I could. I pushed through the basement door, throwing it open and sprinting into the darkness as the cold air rushed to greet me. I tried sticking to the gravel drive, but the chaos of this encounter had turned my faculties upside down and inside out. The next thing I knew, I was stumbling through the small forest that surrounded Richie's farmhouse.

I fell more than once, struggling to make sense of the bumpy landscape as panic forced my arms and legs to keep scrambling onward. I was vaguely aware the lights of Richie's home were turning on behind me, illuminating the yard like a spotlight after some late-night prison break. Into the void I went, hiding away as blood continued gushing from my face.

Eventually, I collapsed into a sobbing heap, my body and mind too exhausted to push onward. I heaved and convulsed, unable to grasp any semblance of a mental footing.

I'm not sure how long I stayed there, but I've learned these moments always seem longer than they really are. Time stretches as we experience it, and when that experience becomes a story, time can drift even more.

When I finally gathered my senses I wandered back to the road, finding the bus stop and looking over my potential departures.

That was the moment I realized there were no buses coming.

I was too tired to walk back home, too shaken by the trauma of my night to even consider this Herculean task. Bus or no bus, my tank was empty.

With nowhere left to go, I headed back onto Richie's property, just not toward the house. Instead, I staggered over to a nearby barn. The structure was vast, and the stalls inside would hopefully offer some shelter.

The second I entered the dark building I found the nearest pile of hay and collapsed onto it, melting into the thatched mess for a second round of tears. When I finally pulled my face away, I noticed the straw glistening below me, a barely visible shine in what little moonlight had crept through the cracked barn door.

More blood.

Later, when I lied to my mother and the doctor who stitched me up, they'd have no problem believing that I'd slipped and torn my mouth open on the edge of a table. My face was split right down the middle.

I reached up with a single curious finger, touching the wound and wincing as I pulled away.

I was so distracted by the sting that I barely noticed as something crept toward me from within the barn's black abyss. The movement was slow and close to the ground, inhuman in nature as it wobbled from side to side.

I gasped when I spotted the vague form, snapping my gaze to the right as I froze in shock.

"Who's there?" I asked.

The figure didn't respond, just crept a little closer.

Gradually, the face of a curious lamb came into view, pale and small, with awkward, gazing eyes.

I wanted to find relief in this moment, but for some reason no sanctuary came. This innocent creature was not the monster I was expecting, but its stare was monstrous all the same. In that moment, I wanted nothing more than to disappear completely.

Even in the middle of nowhere, in the dead of night, something was here to bear witness to my hidden truths. In this raw state, my face ruptured and my soul crushed, I was still exposed.

I was still gay.

PUNCH UPS

It doesn't take long to explain my supernatural encounter to Zeke, and while a real-world manifestation of Mrs. Why is *a lot* to absorb, my boyfriend listens without a shred of skepticism.

After working diligently as a chemist for one of the largest makeup brands on the planet, Zeke is a scientist at heart, which is why I'm particularly shocked by his simple, straightforward response.

"Okay," my boyfriend replies, focused ahead as we hurtle down the 405 freeway. "What do you need from me?"

I'd been so worried about sounding like an utter lunatic that I hadn't even considered that far ahead, figuring we'd get stuck in an endless loop as we debated whether or not I was losing my mind.

I was not expecting this kind of unconditional support, but now that I'm here with Zeke by my side, I realize that I should have. I don't know whether or not he *really* believes me, but right now that doesn't matter.

"Oh," I blurt, dumbfounded. "I don't know what I need yet. I'm still sorting this out."

Zeke nods, eyes on the road.

I call Tara, not sure what kind of warning I can possibly give but dying to speak with her all the same. Unfortunately, my call goes promptly to voicemail.

"She's at the house, right?" I ask.

Zeke nods again.

It's not long before the text messages start rolling in, my phone buzzing away as I struggle to keep up with the cascade of information. The studio's PR team is in a frenzy as more videos from the plane get up-loaded, first deeply concerned, then wildly excited by the press.

They're getting overwhelmed with interview requests.

"What is it?" Zeke asks, noticing that I'm suddenly buried in my phone.

"I don't know," I admit, still connecting the dots, my eyes dancing across the digital screen. "I think someone uploaded footage from the flight."

I click through a few links, shocked to find a handful of articles that have popped up online. It's only been an hour since touchdown, yet my connection to these events is already synergizing with my previous bizarre encounter.

The Smoker and Mrs. Why are getting some serious mainstream press.

"*Screenwriter Misha Byrne—already making headlines after his encounter with a stalker in Toluca Lake—has yet again found himself confronted by someone dressed as one of his own terrifying monsters,*" I read aloud. "*The distraught Oscar-nominee was seen fleeing from his recent flight at LAX, where a woman on board cosplayed as a central antagonist from the television series* Travelers."

I scroll down a bit more, finding a video from the flight and pressing play. It shows Mrs. Why touching an airport security officer as I retreat from the chaos, a frightening scene that I'm suddenly very thankful was captured on video. If I *do* get blamed for this mess, at least there's some evidence that I'm not the one directly hurting people.

"*Things were looking up for Mr. Byrne earlier this year, but with talks of an impend-ing split from Harold Brothers Studios and the looming threat of organized stalking, many fans think this story could soon be coming to a tragic end,*" I continue, furrowing my brow. "*This comes amid increased rumors of a serious drug problem.*"

I glance at Zeke, appalled. "Where are they getting this?"

"Anyone can plant a story," he reminds me.

I keep reading. "*Some even suggest these stalker events have been staged by Mr. Byrne himself.*"

Unwilling to keep subjecting myself to these blatant lies, I lock my phone and shove it back into my pocket. I can't deal with this right now.

"Everyone can tell it's bullshit," Zeke assures me.

Of course he'd say that, but I know better. People love a good tragedy, a fall from grace that ends with a violent crash.

I keep trying to cast myself as the hero in this tale, but there's more than one kind of hero. A tragic hero is just as common as a noble one, and as Jack Hays said: queer tragedy sells.

I lean back in my seat, closing my eyes for a moment.

Breathe.

When I open them again I meet my own gaze in the passenger-side mirror. I look like shit, and even though I managed to get a little sleep on the plane, it wasn't enough to help the disheveled hair and puffy red eyes.

The press is taking all this and running with it.

"Do we need to call the police?" Zeke questions.

I consider his words, staring out the window for a moment as the palm trees and towering buildings whip past.

"I don't know what they're gonna do," I admit. "What can I say? Tell them the alien I wrote about was on my flight?"

"There's video," Zeke reminds me. "They'll see those people she touched."

"There won't be *answers*, though," I counter. "None of it makes any sense."

I turn toward Zeke, still blown away by his capacity for acceptance and trust.

"Do you really just . . . believe in ghosts and aliens now?" I ask.

My boyfriend shakes his head. "No, but I believe in you. Either way, *something's* going on here."

This response is the best I could ask for, and it makes my heart ache.

If these monsters are real, there's nothing the police can do, especially when it comes to The Smoker and his countdown still hanging above my head. If anything, an afternoon of police questioning will only slow me down. There's literally no time.

Whether or not I understand the technical mechanics of my situation, it's my problem to fix. I don't know if I'm a hero who can save the day, but at the very least I'm a protagonist. I've gotta *do* something.

After jumping from one freeway to the next, we finally take our exit and cut along the hillside toward my place. My mind is racing, struggling to unravel the mess of these strange encounters but coming up short. I'm missing something, some nugget of information just waiting to snap this whole mystery into place.

We pull into the driveway and leap from the car. I notice a security guard parked on my curb, the uniformed man waiting patiently in his vehicle with a coffee cup and a tired gaze. I don't stop to introduce myself.

Zeke and I hustle up the front steps, reaching my door and throwing it open.

"Tara?" I shout. "You here?"

No response.

A kernel of panic blooms within me as I work through various empty rooms, desperately searching for my friend. I'm about to yell again when a familiar voice rings out like a beautiful song.

"I'm here!"

I return to the living room, finding Tara by the back door with a bemused look on her face. Her chartreuse jacket pops into my field of vision like a highlighter, announcing her arrival and offering a blissful sense of relief.

"Oh my God," I sigh, rushing over and wrapping my arms around her. "Why didn't you answer your phone?"

"I was outside," Tara replies, warmly accepting my hug. "Good place to read."

My friend holds up an extra-thick book on the subject of database protocols.

I hold her a minute longer, then finally release before I get too emotional.

"What's wrong?" she questions. "Did nobody at the reunion remember what a superstar you are? Well, you're a superstar to me. The big-timer is back!"

Tara's expression falters when she notices the genuine panic on my face. "What?"

"It's—it's all real," I stammer. "They're not just stalkers."

Tara laughs, then stifles herself. She holds back a moment, then starts laughing again, only this time her face is twisting in an unexpected way. The walls she's built up around herself are beginning to crack, and I'm watching them crumble in real time. The irreverent smile my friend so often dons is finally too heavy to lift, and at long last it falls away to reveal utter devastation.

"I knew it," Tara finally replies, tears spilling from her eyes as terror consumes her.

My friend throws her arms around me again, only this time we're not just hugging as old friends. Now we're embracing as passengers on a sinking ship, well aware we're both about to disappear below the icy waves.

Zeke and Tara sit at the kitchen table, ready to dive in. Meanwhile, I stand next to the whiteboard I pulled from storage, feeling like an absolute ass. While this scene is typical for most major television series, it couldn't be further from my usual thought process.

Many *Travelers* scripts come from a writer's room, but my own contributions are almost always crafted as a solo writer. I feel like an imposter in front of this board.

Still, time is running short, and we need to figure this out.

"Alright, my little writer's room, let's begin," I announce, lifting a dry-erase marker and jotting down our first topic. "Let's start with the characters."

I write the word CHARACTERS in the upper left section, underlining it sharply before continuing onward. Below, I start jotting down the creatures I've encountered.

The Smoker.

Mrs. Why.

Black Lamb.

I stop, then step back for a moment, looking them over.

"These are all things I've created," I note, turning back to my friends. "That's the connection, obviously. They're all focused on me."

"No they're not," Tara interjects with an uncharacteristically stern expression.

"You're right," I apologize. "The Smoker is after you, too."

"Could just be collateral," Zeke suggests. "Tara was with you when you were asked for a light. That doesn't mean she was the target."

My boyfriend is correct.

I give him a nod and push onward, staying focused as the clock keeps ticking away. Since landing, I've found myself achingly aware of every second as it passes me by, the grains of sand running low.

We have until the night of the Academy Awards. After that, at approximately 1:15 in the morning, Tara and I will shuffle off this mortal coil in a particularly brutal fashion.

"The real question is: *Why?*" I continue, jotting down this three-letter word with a quick series of marker squeaks. "Just wanting to kill me isn't much of a story. We need motivation."

The three of us wait in silence, aching for some rogue spark of inspiration to strike.

Nothing comes.

"But do they *really* want you dead?" Zeke asks thoughtfully. "Couldn't they just kick down the door and kill you if that was the goal?"

"They're following their own rules," I reply. "The Smoker is taking his time. Mrs. Why is obeying authority. Black Lamb is . . . well . . . being a lamb until someone gets too close."

"So they're behaving exactly like you wrote them," Zeke clarifies, suddenly rising from his chair and approaching the whiteboard. His natural problem-solving instincts are kicking in.

Zeke motions toward my marker, an excited look in his eyes. "May I?" he asks.

I hand the marker over, then move to the side as my boyfriend steps up. Back at Zeke's makeup company he's a lead chemist and developer. He may be quiet on a typical afternoon around the house, but when something lights his fire, he's all action.

"What are the rules?" Zeke questions aloud, motioning to *The Smoker* at the top of my list. "Who is this guy?"

"Angry ghost," I reply. "A manifested curse. He asks for a light, and if you say no then you have five days until he cuts your bones out through your back. After that, he grinds them into powder and he smokes them."

Zeke begins furiously scribbling, doing his best to abbreviate every point. Seeing the keywords listed out like this is downright embarrassing as I'm faced with the true absurdity of my creations.

Grinds bones (smokes).

Ghost curse.

Need a light?

"He's from *ten years ago*, okay?" I feel the need to defend myself, prompting confused looks from Zeke and Tara.

My boyfriend steps back a bit. "And what stops him? What are his weaknesses?"

"Once he's got you in his sights, nothing stops him," I admit. "He's an incurable disease stalking night clubs and asking for a light. A new cancer. That's the whole point of *Death Blooms*."

Zeke hesitates as his good idea falls flat. The three of us take a moment, awkwardly struggling to retain the heroic drive that started this exercise.

"What about Mrs. Why?" Tara suggests. "She's an alien, right?"

Zeke points at Tara, nodding. "Perfect! We'll come back to The Smoker."

My boyfriend turns to the whiteboard again as I list the attributes of Mrs. Why.

"A distant traveler dressed in human skin," I explain. "She's obsessed with order and custom. She wants others to understand the beginning and the end of everything, but it's too much for our minds to handle."

"What does that mean?" Zeke questions, struggling to clarify. "She *explains* it to you?"

"She just touches you. In the early drafts she actually *did* explain it, but the director of those episodes wanted to cut her dialogue and talked me out of it. He said it made her scarier if she didn't talk."

Suddenly, I hesitate, the words catching in my throat.

I spring from my chair. I'm pacing now, my mind crackling like a glorious display of fireworks. "I always envisioned her speaking, but when I saw her on the plane she was totally silent."

"So she's *not* following her own rules," Zeke observes. "Because that's not how you wrote her."

"These aren't the monsters you dreamed up, they're the monsters HBS *produced*," Tara observes.

Her words hit me in the face and I reel slightly, a huge portion of the riddle revealing itself. The writer's room is on fire now, ideas passing back and forth like a hurtling tennis ball.

"Alice!" Tara exclaims, slamming her fist down on the kitchen table and springing up. All three of us are standing now. "Holy shit! Alice!"

I nod along in excitement, then quickly shift gears when I realize I have no idea what this means. "Wait, who is Alice?"

"That stalker who stole your matchbook at the bar," Tara reminds me. "She's the reason you didn't have a matchbook when The Smoker asked you for one. She's working with the monsters, but she's not one of your characters."

"Harold Brothers owns her," I reply, nodding along as I mumble the words under my breath. "Which means Jack probably knows something."

"Your boss?" Zeke jumps in. "Didn't you already talk to him?"

"I didn't have any evidence," I counter.

Tara laughs. "You *still* don't have any evidence."

Knock. Knock.

Our focus is shaken by two loud raps on the front door. We stop, then turn to gaze down my front hallway.

I'd been so caught up in the chaos of our brainstorm that I'd forgotten the very real threats currently swirling around us.

"Hello?" I call out.

A moment of hesitation.

"Mr. Byrne?" comes an unfamiliar voice from the other side. "This is Mr. Garret, your security officer."

I exchange glances with my friends, not quite sure what to make of this interruption. My mind is racing, riffling through a mental library of evil-private-security characters.

Tara lowers her voice to a tense, hushed tone. "Anyone know an HBS show where the security guards turn into fucking werewolves or something?"

"What's your first name?" I finally yell, pulling out my phone.

The press requests and texts from HBS keep rolling in, but I swipe them away.

"Uh . . . It's Josiah," the man behind the door states.

I immediately do a quick internet search for characters with this name in any Harold Brothers films. There are no matches for *Josiah Garret.*

"What's up?" I finally call back.

"Well, I'm not really sure," he replies. "I'm doing my hourly rounds out here and, uh, there's a lamb in your front yard. It looks pretty sick. I was gonna call animal control, but I wanted to check with you first."

"Wait!" I yelp, rushing over to the door and throwing it open.

The security guard stands uncomfortably before me, clearly flustered by his unexpected visitor. Standing with four wobbly legs in the grass behind him is a black lamb, the tiny creature murmuring to itself in a peculiar tongue. The creature swings its head clumsily from side to side, its large, bulging eyes apparently struggling to take in the brilliant California sun.

Josiah opens his mouth to say something else, but I cut him off with instructions of my own.

"Shoot it," I demand.

The security guard smirks reflexively, assuming this is some kind of bizarre joke. When he realizes I'm not kidding, however, his expression falters. "Wait, what?"

"Shoot it," I repeat, stern in my convictions.

Josiah glances over my shoulder at Tara and Zeke, then back at me. "I'm not going to shoot a lamb," he replies.

"Give me your gun and I'll do it," I press.

The guard steps away, his demeanor quickly shifting. "I can't do that. I'm sorry, that's crazy."

"It's not a lamb," I tell him.

Josiah glances at the small animal next to us, and I can see his heart melting at the sight of something so fragile and innocent.

I turn to Zeke and Tara, who stand just beyond the entryway. "Go to the shed out back and get the gasoline tank," I instruct. "It's near the lawnmower."

"Aye-aye, Captain!" Tara immediately springs into action, hustling back into the house and disappearing from sight.

"Are you kidding me?" our security guard fumes, hearing my commands and reacting with nothing short of abject horror.

I turn to Josiah, struggling to reason with him. "Listen, I know this is a lot, but I don't know how else to say it. There's something wrong with that animal. It's infected."

"With *what*?"

I consider telling him the truth, but eschew *cosmic horror mutation* in favor of a slightly more nuanced approach. "Rabies."

Josiah furrows his brow skeptically, turning back to the meek, mewling animal. "That's not . . ." he stammers, trailing off. "How would you even know that?"

I let out a frustrated sigh. "Okay, fine!" I shout. "It's a monster from another reality!"

Tara reappears in the entryway, holding an old metal gas can and waiting for the next move. The noxious chemicals invade my nostrils.

Unfortunately, Josiah can smell it, too.

"No way," the security guard declares, swiveling on his heels and marching down the front porch.

Josiah makes his way across the yard and, in one quick movement, he scoops up the tiny creature. He clutches the lamb tightly against his chest, then turns back toward us, a look of utter contempt plastered across his face.

"I don't know what to do with this little thing, but I'm certainly not gonna let you burn it alive," he states, holding the animal in a protective embrace and staring daggers at us.

"Please listen," I beg, taking a few steps toward him.

I stop abruptly when I notice the lamb begin to shift.

The face of the tiny creature splits open, right down the middle, and the break creates a faint, wet crack as the two halves separate. Thin, lashing tendrils slip forth, brilliant red and covered in a glistening slime. They swiftly grow in number as the lamb's face continues to distort, transforming into a horrific sharp-toothed maw. The wobbling head is now a four-pronged mandible from which a cascade of wriggling tentacles emerge, crawling and whipping as they breach a web of sticky mucus.

Meanwhile, Josiah keeps his gaze locked on us, firm in his convictions and wholly unaware of the transformation just below his chin.

I try once more to cry out and warn him, but the shock of this horrific display causes my words to stick in my throat. Witnessing the uncanny powers of Mrs. Why was disturbing in its own way, but the wretched creature before me is sickening on a truly primal level, an unhinged eldritch nightmare somehow dragged into the real world.

Josiah finally stops, his senses piqued by the sloppy, gurgling noises carrying on within his arms. The man slowly looks down, opening his mouth, but his scream is cut off by an eruption of barbed, spaghetti-like appendages that shoot into the flesh of his face like a tentacled shotgun blast. The tendrils immediately pull taut, forcefully tugging Josiah down into the snapping, suckling maw of what was once a mere lamb.

The security guard stumbles and falls to the ground, his animalistic shrieks muffled by the enormous mouth of the creature now wrapped around his head. Eight crablike legs rupture the lamb's back with sickening pops, stabbing their sharpened points into the blood-spattered grass.

I spring into action, rushing down my steps and across the yard, but before I can get within ten feet of the monster it rears back and lets out a horrific screech. The thing's tendrils wave spastically as it bears its open jaws at me.

As the creature releases Josiah's head I get a brief glimpse of his face, now shredded to a pulp in a mess of gurgling crimson and crushed skull. One eye is still visible within the carnage, gazing back at me as if pleading for help, but seconds later it disappears when Black Lamb snaps its jaws back down.

I sense Tara rushing up behind me, the gas can swinging in her tightened grip, but before she has a chance to use it the creature skitters away with incredible speed, rushing into the nearby shrubbery in a display of unexpected dexterity. Black Lamb has no problem dragging Josiah's convulsing body with it, yanking him by the head and leaving a long trail of glistening crimson to contrast with the green grass below.

In a matter of seconds, the creature has disappeared, Josiah's body following shortly after. The last I see of the man are his legs and feet slipping into the thick foliage.

Tara drops the gas can, overwhelmed with emotion as she paces back and forth in the yard. "Holy fucking shit," she mumbles to herself, the words falling out of her mouth in a disconnected haze. "What was that?"

I just keep staring at the long swath of blood that stretches from the middle of my yard to the shrubs, its surreal glisten reflecting sunlight like the trail of an enormous red slug. It feels like a paint stroke across reality, some disturbing other world making its presence known with a single bold stripe, refusing to make excuses for its presence.

This is real.

The same refrain comes rumbling through my head again and again.

"Is everything okay?" calls a shrill voice, my neighbor yelling from her porch as she peers across the street.

"Oh, yeah!" I instinctively shout, although things are quite certainly *not okay.*

"I heard squealing!" she continues. "Is your dog hurt?"

"I don't have a dog!" I call, then cringe and scramble to backtrack. "I mean, yeah. They're fine, though, it's fine."

I force a smile, waving cordially.

The neighbor accepts my words, although I can see the doubt on her face from all the way over here. Still, she retreats into her home and leaves us to wallow in our distress.

"I've gotta call the police," I announce, frantically searching for the best course of action.

Zeke steps up and places a strong, comforting hand on my shoulder. "Misha, *you* don't have time," he reminds me. "The clock is ticking, and they'll have a lot of questions."

I glance at Tara, checking in. She nods in return.

"Fuck," I snap, first quietly and then again at the top of my lungs. "*Fuck!*"

"Hey, hey," Zeke coos, his deep voice soothing me. "You've gotta go. We'll call the police and handle things here, but you've gotta go talk to Jack Hays."

He's right, and I know it.

"There are mountain lions in this neighborhood," Zeke reminds me, planting the seed of our collective story. "They come down from Griffith Park. Sometimes people get hurt."

"Alright," I finally agree. "Just . . . stay inside, okay? Be careful."

"We'll be right here when you get back," my boyfriend assures me.

BLOOD MONEY

Jack Hays is off the grid today—the calm before the Academy Awards storm that looms just over the horizon—but Tara has backdoor access to his personal calendar.

As I enter the long, atmospheric room of warm wooden panels and dim lighting I catch Jack's eye immediately, prompting a startled look to cross his previously tranquil face. The nurse I'm being led by motions for me to sit in one of the far chairs, but I quickly suggest the one beside Jack.

"Could I join my friend?" I ask her.

The nurse nods and I take my seat.

Jack's expression is one of shock, but he's not just surprised by my arrival.

"You look terrible, buddy," he says.

"That's why I'm here."

My nurse starts prepping a strange machine next to me, a hanging assortment of plastic tubing and medical instruments, but I wave her away.

"Sir, this is for your treatment," she protests.

"I changed my mind," I reply, shaking my head. "I'm just gonna talk to my pal here."

The nurse is deeply confused by this, frozen in place with a stretchy yellow armband gripped tight. She's not sure what to do with herself.

"You still have to pay," she finally counters.

"No problem."

I turn back to Jack, whose expression has slowly transformed from shock to grave concern.

Behind the executive, another nurse is hard at work, diligently inputting various commands for a tiny centrifuge chamber. This medical device is connected to Jack by way of several winding tubes, each path snaking through humming, whirring tanks until arriving at an IV drip. The needle is poked into the top of Jack's hand, held in place with yellow tape.

His blood flows through the strange, sanguine Rube Goldberg contraption, the liquid making an epic loop before finally returning to his body.

Despite my relative success, I'm still blown away by the bizarre things rich people do in their spare time, especially in the name of health and wellness.

"Misha, what are you doing here?"

"I had some time to think on my drive over," I explain. "First, I was just gonna punch you in the face, and I still might, but I'm also aware that'll get me thrown out."

"I saw the news," he says. "I have no idea what this has to do with me, but I'm so sorry you're dealing with these nutjob stalkers, buddy. I really am."

"You're *sorry?*" I blurt, seething with anger as I nearly leap from my chair and grab him by the throat. "I watched a man's face get eaten off today!"

The nurse helping Jack pauses awkwardly.

"Sorry," I quip. "It's a bit. This is a little bit we do."

Jack turns to the woman running his machine. "Can you give us a minute?"

"Your blood rejuvenation needs to finish or we'll have to start over again," she explains.

"That's fine," Jack retorts, then clears his throat and elevates his voice. "Actually, we need the whole room. Everyone get out of here."

I glance around, taking note of the other patrons undergoing their own bizarre therapeutic blood cleanse.

"We can't do that," the nurse replies.

Jack loudly addresses the four random strangers in each corner of the spa. "I'll give a thousand dollars to anyone who stops their treatment and comes back in ten minutes."

The other patients seem confused by this offer, not reacting.

"I'm dead fucking serious," the executive continues. "That includes nurses."

Gradually, the room begins to clear, patients shuffling out as they give us our space.

Only one man remains, reclining three chairs down with his headphones on and enormous, dark sunglasses covering his eyes. The machine purrs away next to him.

"Hey," Jack shouts, but the patient's headphones are too loud.

Looks like this is all the privacy we're gonna get.

"What the fuck is going on?" I finally bellow. "You can't just throw your money at this problem anymore, people are dying and I wanna know why!"

Jack immediately leans in, hissing through clenched teeth. "*Shut up*," he demands, his unexpected conviction stopping me in my tracks. "You don't know who might be listening."

I glance at the man with headphones, but he still doesn't react, blissfully unaware of the heated conversation happening just three chairs down.

I'd been quick to categorize Jack's flashy display of wealth as something brutish and vapid, which it typically is, but this time there seems to be a method to his madness. The deadly urgency that hangs over us is not lost on Jack; he's just hiding it better than I am.

"Just kill off your gay characters," Jack sighs, less of a demand and more of an exhausted plea. He's no longer wielding his might as a high-powered executive; he's begging as a friend. "I know this means a lot to you, but it's not worth it. Trust me."

"Is that really what *all this* is about?" I counter, striving to find some kernel of understanding. "There's no way."

Jack hesitates a moment, then shakes his head. "The less you know, the better. You've got one target on your back right now, you don't want another."

"I don't give a shit about drawing attention," I snap. "People are dying."

The frustration flares up again as Jack leans in, yanking his arm so hard that he nearly tugs the IV from his hand. The man doesn't even flinch, utter terror behind his gaze.

"And more people are gonna die if you don't listen, you dumb artist *fuck*," Jack exclaims. "Your stories aren't worth your life."

My stories are *my life*, I think, but I don't say this.

I'd love to stand up against the tyranny of this heartless international conglomerate, waving the flag of my artistic principles and shouting my truth from the top of a mountain, but deep down I know he's right.

Whatever this is, it isn't worth dying for.

"You may think I'm just an evil suit," Jack hisses through clenched teeth, "but I'm also your friend. I love you, man, and you're not listening to me."

He's shaking with emotion. I've known Jack for over a decade, and I've never once seen him let his guard down like this.

"Everyone has a boss," Jack continues. "I just learned who mine is, and I regret it, because there's no going back. *It won't let you go back.* Don't give it a reason to write you another storyline, just finish this one up and be done with it."

I came here to face down Jack and his big studio machine, but Jack's just as scared as I am.

"Okay, yeah," I relent, throwing my hands up. "Of course. If that's all it takes to stop this, then consider Lexa and Naomi dead."

Jack nods, unable to hide the relief that washes over him. "Thank God," he sighs, a hefty load of tension abruptly draining from his frame.

"So that's it?" I question. "We're done?"

"Put it in writing. Email me."

I pull out my phone, the press requests still piling up as I swipe them away, and create a new message addressed to Jack. I copy my agent and a handful of other executives close to the show.

I'm outing Carey Lexa and May Naomi, then killing them off, I type, short and simple. *Congrats, assholes.*

I hit Send.

"Another tale of queer tragedy," I sigh. "Hooray for Hollywood."

Jack leans back, settling in. He wipes his eyes in an effort to destroy any evidence of previous emotions, then closes them. "You really do look terrible. You know you've got an awards show tomorrow night, right?"

To be honest, the impending Academy Awards have been the last thing on my mind.

I just witnessed a man's face get torn off and devoured while he was still alive to feel it.

"Yeah, yeah," I sigh. "I'll get right on it."

Jack cracks one eye open, looking me over. "Do you even own a suit? Like a *real* suit?"

"I have a suit," I assure him. "I signed our paperwork in it like fifteen years ago."

Jack Hays scoffs at the very notion of this. "Use the money you're now gonna save in legal fees and buy yourself something decent to wear," he suggests. "Do you know how much the suit I'm wearing costs? Do you wanna guess?"

I wait for Jack to continue, refusing to answer but knowing his follow-up is coming just the same.

"Twelve grand," the executive proclaims, "and *I'm not even*—"

"You're not even gay," I interrupt, ready to call him out on this fashion-forward stereotype.

"No, you idiot, I'm not even *on camera*," he says. "Get yourself something decent."

The man with the sunglasses begins to stir, sitting up and pulling the IV from his hand. He doesn't acknowledge Jack and me, but his sudden movement is enough to give us pause. The man's comically large shades stay perched on his nose and his headphones remain plugged in as he carefully hangs up his IV tubing, then he strolls past us with profound nonchalance.

It's not strange enough to comment on, but we both notice. We sit in silence for a moment, listening to his footsteps as they disappear down the hallway.

Finally, Jack speaks up. "I'd say you should stick around for a vitamin boost and blood oxygenation, but something tells me you're just here to say your piece."

"That's right," I reply with a nod.

"You feel better now?" he questions, an unexpected note of sincerity in his tone.

"If it all stops, then yeah. I'll feel . . ." Visions of the carnage I've already caused flash through my mind; the jet passengers transformed into shells of utter nihilism, Josiah's flesh rendered into red slaw by Black Lamb's chewing maw. "I'll feel fine."

The executive considers this a moment. "Well, I think you're in the clear. Go home and get some rest. Big day tomorrow."

I stand up, making my way toward the door when Jack calls out to stop me.

"I know it's been rough with all these . . . stalkers," he continues, stumbling over the final word, "but if it's any consolation, streams of your whole catalog have nearly tripled. I know that used to mean just a few more pennies in your pocket, but after the strikes . . . you'll be rolling in it, buddy."

A see a brief flash of Tara's horrified face, remember the way she broke down in my arms as she finally realized all this was really happening.

What I don't see is a silver lining.

"Okay." I finally accept, then I nod and continue on my way.

As I push into the late-afternoon air, leaving the overpriced Brentwood spa behind, I check in with myself. I'm standing in the middle of a sun-soaked parking lot, hoping to detect some fundamental change in the world around me.

Is that it?

Is there really some unspoken shift in the fabric of it all?

I've been put through the wringer, that's for sure, but there's something about this step of the journey that feels all too easy.

The beats of this particular story are music to my ears, and I'm certainly not complaining, but they're not the beats I'm used to. Then again, not everything has a perfect structure: a beginning, middle, and end. Not every tale has an act-three synthesis and a dark night of the soul.

Sometimes life just *is*.

I stroll back to my car and climb in, pulling out my phone and collapsing into the driver's seat.

I call Zeke.

It rings only once before my boyfriend picks up, his voice carrying over the line with a hopeful cadence. "How'd it go?"

"I'm not sure," I admit. "I . . . I think it's over."

"What happened?"

"I gave 'em what they wanted," I admit.

My boyfriend hesitates, the speaker falling quiet as I gaze out across this upscale strip mall parking lot. Out here in Brentwood, everything's a little nicer, from the ice cream shop on the corner to the clean-cut paparazzo hanging out by the curb.

"Does it feel a little too easy?" I question.

Zeke wants to be my rock, but he's also not one to lie. "It feels a little too easy," he confirms. "Are we really saying the studio hired all these stalkers or . . . made all these monsters . . . just to threaten you into killing off two characters?"

"There's a flaw in the structure. I feel like the resolution is happening too early," I admit. "But . . . I also haven't seen anything weird yet. What's up over there?"

"Police just left. Your front yard was a crime scene, which isn't great, but they bought the mountain lion attack. Now the doors are locked and the shades are drawn," Zeke replies. "Nothing strange since."

Across the street, the paparazzo lifts his camera, pointing it my way and quickly snapping a photo. "There's a pap over here taking pictures of me," I inform my boyfriend. "The perils of going viral."

"Yeah," Zeke replies, the word lingering a little too long as it falls from his lips.

"What?" I question.

"There's quite a few over here, too," he reveals. "I clocked them out front, down by the sidewalk. We've already got two new security guards, though, so they chased them away."

"I hate this," I sigh.

"You're their latest tragic victim, baby. Everyone's invested now."

"Baby?" I laugh. "You've been hanging around Tara for too long."

"What do you want me to call you?" he asks. "We don't have pet names yet."

"Meesh?" I offer.

Suddenly, my phone buzzes, signaling that another call's coming through.

"I should probably take this," I say. "I've got like two hundred unanswered texts from the PR department. I'm on my way home, though."

"See you soon, *Meesh*," Zeke replies, then hesitates. "Yeah, that feels weird. We'll work on it."

"Yes, Zekey."

I hang up, pulling the phone away from my face just long enough to accept a new call.

"This is Misha," I announce.

A long, croaking voice drifts across my ears, instantly chilling me to the bone. "You've been avoiding me," The Smoker observes, his groan distant and haunting as it crackles through the receiver.

I sit up, glancing around for any sign of the small man in his blue suit. It's not long before I spot him, the strange entity watching me from across the street with those lidless eyes. A briefcase remains tightly gripped in his left hand, a cigarette in the right.

He holds no phone, and his mouth remains closed as his words roll across my ears.

"You look scared," The Smoker informs me.

"I'm disappointed, but I'm not scared."

"You should be," he groans, a smile slowly creeping its way across his face as his eyes remain in their fixed, patient gaze.

"What the fuck do you *want?*" I shout, losing my cool. "I'm killing them off! The gays are buried!"

I notice the paparazzo has started snapping photos once again, thrilled to catch a shot of this spiraling artist at the end of his rope. They love to see me driven mad, burning out even faster than my star can rise.

I'm trying my best to stay calm, but the whiplash between this and my conversation with Zeke is simply too much to process. For the briefest moment it seemed like this nightmare was behind me, teased by a taste of the glorious happy ending.

But there is no happy ending, just a hole in the dirt that gets deeper and deeper as the end grows nigh.

"The clickity-clack lock on an exit door makes for high drama, Misha," The Smoker continues. "The story doesn't work if there's no door to exit through, but I can tell you a secret now . . . Would you like to know a secret?"

I don't answer, bathed in a silence that makes my skin crawl.

"There never *was* a door," The Smoker finally states. "You've always been mine."

My mind is flooded with things I could say, rejections of his macabre claim, but I also know the truth. There's nothing I can do to stop him. I built him this way.

"I can't believe I wrote you," I finally retort, my frustration taking the lead. "You're a clown, hanging around for days just so you can pop out and act creepy. What's the point?"

The Smoker starts a reply but I cut him off, speaking over him.

"That's the problem with ghost stories," I yell. "So you're dead and spooky? Who gives a shit? What are you gonna *do* to me besides give me a cheap jump scare? Are you raising the stakes? Are you doing *anything?*"

"I'll do plenty tomorrow night," The Smoker croaks.

"Great! See you then, you certified-rotten straight-to-streaming fuck!" I hang up the phone, stricken by the sudden urge to throw it through my front windshield.

I don't do this, however.

Instead, I text Tara and Zeke with a simple message.

It's not over. Don't open the door for anyone but me. I'll be back later.

SLEDGE-HAMMER

By the time Jack Hays is finished inside the spa, the paparazzo is long gone, satisfied with his haul and heading off to harass someone else for a while. This makes it much easier to slump down in the driver's seat and avoid detection.

Whether Jack was lying to me or not, his advice came up short.

They're not stopping, whatever they are, and *Jack* knows more than he's willing to admit.

The first thing I notice when Jack exits is that his treatment was a terrible investment. Though it's only been a few hours, the man is quite a bit more disheveled than the last time we spoke. He's arguing with someone on the phone, a conversation that swells violently and then recedes as Jack begins to apologize. He hangs up, and although I can't hear the words, the movement of Jack's lips seem to pop with a single, frustrated *fuck.*

At least, that's what it looks like as I watch through the rearview mirror.

Jack's blue Porsche leaves its parking space with a soft, futuristic hum: all electric.

Soon enough, our vehicles are making their way toward the water. By the time we reach the Pacific Coast Highway, every shadow has grown long and every ray of sunlight is beaming with dazzling golden-hour energy.

This also makes things a little difficult to see, which is great news for me as I drift just a few cars behind Jack, tailing his every move. It certainly doesn't help that the guy drives like a total jackass, but I manage to keep up, cruising through some dubious yellow lights and several lane changes without a blinker.

Our cars wind their way along the coast, a pink, picturesque scene of the California dream draped above us while night blooms ominous over the ocean in royal purple.

It's fitting, really. Los Angeles is a beautiful place, and for the lucky few who can make it work here that splendor can last.

But most of the hopefuls who leap from their Greyhound buses with fresh-faced excitement are not as fortunate. When the cold black waves of disappointment come crashing over them, the beauty fades quick.

The sunsets here are gorgeous, but they hang over a profoundly haunted place. Every apartment in this town holds the memory of a similar story, a classic tale of Hollywood heartbreak repeating over and over again.

I've always had plenty of gratitude for the fact that I've somehow risen above this endless cycle. However, as what might be my penultimate afternoon alive comes to a close, I'm starting to wonder if I ever really *did* extract myself from the rat race.

I never really *felt* like I made it.

I shake my head instinctively, pushing these thoughts away.

Think of all the art.

Think of all your creations that found an audience.

It's true. Plenty of people liked my work, and a small but dedicated audience *loved* it. I left my mark in that way, but was the mark ever really *mine?*

Queer people found a home in my writing, and that's enough to be proud of, but just think of what potential future could've blossomed if I'd been more open about my real life.

It suddenly occurs to me this is the first time I've accepted my own shortcomings on the topic. Being quietly out of the closet was always good enough, but as the hourglass of my life drains I can't help considering if *good enough* is really what I'd like written on my tombstone.

Looming death will certainly make you wonder.

Eventually, Jack turns off the main highway and begins to make his way up into the hills, following a long winding road that cuts through the ever-darkening landscape. The farther we get from civilization, the more confused I grow.

I had no idea where Jack was headed when he left the spa, but into the distant rolling wilderness above Malibu was certainly not on my list. I've heard there are one or two *very* small production companies nearby, bedroom LLCs tucked away on the edge of the mountains and canyons in a deliberate attempt to separate themselves from the big city machine, but I've personally never worked with any.

I consider the idea that Jack might've moved out here recently, but that's a hell of a commute for someone who spends every Monday through Friday in Burbank.

It's not long before we're the only cars on the road, forcing me to hang back much farther than I'm comfortable with. After all this effort, the thought of losing him in the darkness is horrible, but my confidence grows as I spot Jack's vehicle turn off the main drag and head up into an even more secluded canyon.

I turn off my headlights and creep along behind him.

The area is desolate and covered with more thick vegetation than one might expect. There's a handful of buildings lining the road, most of them unmarked and featuring a distinctly warehouselike feel. This is far from the modern luxury of most studio offices, and it's difficult to imagine Jack Hays conducting any kind of business in this unusually gritty setting.

Jack's car finally turns into a parking lot, stopping in front of a particularly large gray office building. There're only two other vehicles in this relatively empty lot.

I immediately pull over on the side of the road, shutting off my car and peering out through the windshield.

The building features a modest entrance, and a small brushed-metal sign hangs above the door. It reads **BETTA EFFECTS AND NATURAL PRO-CESSING**, which immediately rings a bell.

Betta is the talk of the town, making history as the ones responsible for Chris Oak's posthumous return in *Broken Don.*

Jack climbs from his vibrant electric vehicle, but he doesn't head inside. Instead, he takes a moment to move around the car in a bizarre walking pattern.

I squint, struggling to understand what I'm witnessing, then finally realize the man is just soothing his nerves, pacing awkwardly as he talks to himself. He pulls out his phone a few times, as though vaguely considering using it, but every time this happens he abruptly changes course and puts his device away.

Finally, Jack approaches the building.

He steps up to a small box next to the door, a glowing blue cube positioned about waist height. I immediately recognize this as one of the studio's new fingerprint systems, watching the movements of Jack's hand as he places his thumb on the scanner. A security camera sits perched above.

Moments later, the door pops open and Jack heads inside.

A realization washes over me. It's entirely possible this was nothing more than a last-minute meeting with the folks at Betta, a game plan before the Best Actor announcement tomorrow evening. The second Chris Oak wins, other studios will be knocking down the doors out here, begging to license this cutting-edge tech from HBS.

All that is to say: this is likely not as sinister, or important, as I think it is.

Still, something doesn't quite add up. It's Saturday night, after all, so it's doubtful anyone's around, especially given the lack of other ve-hicles. There's nothing but an old van in the corner and a beautiful black Lamborghini Countach that immediately gives me pause. I don't know much about cars, and even *I* can recognize this relic with its old-fashioned opulence.

Must be a prop car.

As the door closes behind Jack my mind floods with options for how to proceed. I'm not entirely sure what I'm looking for out here, just achingly aware of some hidden truth to uncover. With nothing left to lose, I'd love to follow Jack inside, but short of cutting the man's thumb off, I don't see how I could make it past the first scanner.

Still, I need a closer look.

I pull out my phone and dial Tara.

"Baby!" my friend shouts, answering quickly. "Doors are locked and shades are drawn. We're watching a new episode of *The Hookup* and it's the room key ceremony and he's gonna give it to Kendra 'cause he's very, very dumb."

I feel like screaming that we've got hours left before a ghost literally carves the bones from our bodies, but I hold my tongue. We all have our own ways of dealing with tragedy, and sometimes that means drowning ourselves in reality television.

"Do you have remote access to security cameras on studio property?" I question.

"I sure do."

"Could you shut one of them off?"

Tara hesitates. "Wait, where are you?"

"I don't . . . really know," I admit. "Somewhere above Malibu. Didn't HBS just buy Betta Effects for some *insane* amount of money?"

"After the work they did on *Broken Don*, yeah," my friend confirms. "Rumor is they spent over twenty billion dollars."

"What?" I blurt, shocked by the cash it took to acquire such an unassuming business. "This place is a dump!"

"The acquisition just happened, there's no way they're on my network system yet," Tara explains, before abruptly shifting her tone to yell at the TV. "Dump her! Oh my *Gawd*, I'm so glad I don't date." More shuffling. "Sorry."

I hear the familiar clatter of my friend's fingers as they dance across her laptop keys.

"Oh, wait," Tara continues. "Yeah, they added this to the grid immediately. Guess they wanted to get those trade secrets locked up tight."

"Special sauce," I mumble, remembering something Tara mentioned in passing a while back.

I hear another sudden rush of keystrokes, then another pause as a confused sigh slips from my friend's lips. "Huh."

"What?"

"I don't have access," she informs me.

"Aren't you like . . . one of the heads of this department?"

"Yup," Tara replies, her focus clearly elsewhere. "I run this shit."

She starts typing again, slamming the keys in frustration.

"*Whaatttt?*" Tara sighs under her breath.

Sticking to the task at hand, I attempt to clarify. "So there's *no way* I'm getting into this building without the camera seeing me?"

"I mean, there's always the method that's been around since the advent of human sight," she offers. "You could wear a mask."

"Oh, right."

"By the way, how close are you to the building?" she asks.

"I'm parked across the street, just down the road a bit."

"You motherfucker, shut off your phone!" Tara yells. "Automatic downloads of all your files, do you understand?"

"I'm sorry—sorry," I stammer.

Tara sighs. "For once, it's fine. Based on the security protocols I'm seeing, you'd probably need to be standing right next to this router to connect. They don't use a single network out there, just multiple partitioned hubs, which is kinda weird."

Before I have a chance to respond, the building's door flies open and Jack Hays comes sprinting out, a wild-eyed look on his face. His nose sports a red gash that runs horizontally across the top, likely the result of a swift punch to the face, and a thin stream of blood is pouring from his left nostril.

"Oh shit!" I gasp.

"What is it?" Tara snaps.

"I gotta go. I'm fine."

I hang up just as Jack throws his vehicle into reverse and tears back-ward through the parking lot, the caustic squeal of tire rubber echoing through the canyon. He whips his car into drive then shoots up onto the road from which he came, swerving dangerously before somehow regaining control. Jack rockets past me, giving me just enough time to duck below the dash.

I'm ready to follow, but when I look back through the windshield it's a wholly different sight that causes me to freeze in shock.

Another figure has exited the building, marching toward the black Lamborghini with unexpected confidence and speed. Even from my position down the road I know exactly who it is, an icon whose face will forever be ingrained in my memory.

How could I forget this legend after watching a man get crushed to death by a piano right under his handsome mug?

Chris Oak opens his car door and climbs inside, looking very much alive as the vehicle comes roaring to life. He's wearing a white suit, the same one I've seen on every poster for *Broken Don,* and as this surreal vision of Hollywood royalty peels out and hurtles up onto the road, a thousand puzzle pieces suddenly click into place.

Betta Effects and Natural Processing didn't just craft a seamless rep-resentation of Enzo Basile on screen, they created one in real life.

As the Lamborghini whips past me I start my engine, spewing dirt and throwing my car into a tight U-turn.

I step on the gas, rumbling back onto the pavement, but by the time I get things up to speed the two others have long disappeared from view. While some of the roads up here are easy to see for miles and miles ahead, the canyon has blocked my vision significantly.

Fortunately, I know I'm headed in the right direction thanks to the roar of Enzo's sportscar washing over me, a lonesome rumble echoing through the darkness.

It's not long before I arrive at a desolate intersection, and while I'd have no problem blowing through a stop sign in this particular case, I'm not sure which direction to go. Frustrated, I roll down my window and listen to the night.

The roaring engine has disappeared, which could be a very good sign, or a very bad one. Either they've pulled over somewhere, or they're just too far away.

"Fuck!" I shout, slamming my hand against the wheel.

I glance up the roads to my left and right, branching asphalt paths winding farther into their own little canyons. The lane ahead leads back to the highway, which is an equally likely option.

Three routes, but I can only pick one.

I take my chances with the path ahead, continuing down the hillside and watching as the night sky opens wide above me. It's not long before I can see all the way down this grand hill, beachside lights twinkling in the distance to guide me onward. A few random cars join my trek, and at this point I realize something is very wrong.

There's no way they went this direction.

I pull off the road and turn around, cruising back up the path from which I came. I no longer expect to catch up with Jack Hays, but there's a slim chance I'll find them stopped by the side of the road.

Based on the speeds they were going before plunging into a dead silence, I'm also on the lookout for a crash.

Returning to my initial intersection, I take a left, now pushing up into the wilds at a slow, cautious pace. I scan the canyon for any sign of a chase gone wrong, and it doesn't take long to find one.

My headlights sweep across a pair of distinct markings that slice their way through the brush and over the edge of a rocky dip. Just beyond, the Lamborghini is parked, waiting ominously in the shadows like some big black bat.

I stop my car, pulling over behind the other vehicle and gazing through my windshield at the quiet scene. My eyes are peeled, scanning the Lamborghini for any sign of movement and finding none.

I slowly climb out and creep toward the car.

From this new vantage I can see down into the ravine below, spotting a second vehicle that has slammed headfirst into a thick tree trunk. This is Jack's car, but other than the blue color it's difficult to recognize in this condition. Both the passenger's- and the driver's-side doors remain wide open, provoking a faint rhythmic chime to ring out through the surrounding forest.

I cautiously approach the Lamborghini, double checking that nobody is hiding below my sightline, but the car is empty.

Pushing onward, I climb down the rocky slope of the ravine.

The closer I get to Jack's demolished vehicle, the more aware I am of the potent, pumping adrenaline that's currently kicking the shit out of my heart. This is just one of many life-or-death situations I've found myself in over the last several weeks, and while these moments used to overwhelm me, I can now sense the beginning of some hardened emotional tolerance.

Bring it on.

I reach the car, keeping my distance as I round the corner and peer inside. The dome light is shining, casting the scene in an eerie glow and illuminating a messy display of shattered glass across leather seats.

Bang!

A distant gunshot rings out through the canyon, causing me to jump in alarm and swivel my gaze toward the pitch-black forest. In an instant, all my heroic inertia takes a back seat to the question of self-preservation. I'm here to gather information, but at what cost?

Then again, what other choice do I have than to push into the great unknown? With approximately thirty hours left before a ghost forcefully removes your bones, it's slightly easier to be the hero you've always dreamed of.

Thinking fast, I pop Jack's trunk to reveal his spare tire and, more importantly, the tire iron. I take this metal object, brandishing it as a newfound weapon, then continue my journey into the vast darkness of the night.

Almost immediately, another sound begins to waft across my ears.

My senses are on high alert, trained on every cracking leaf and snapping branch below my feet, tuned to the forest. These new tones are distinctly musical, though—funky, even. It's a familiar song, the echoes of the canyon drawing out every note in a strange, surreal wash.

Eventually, the pumping bass, slinky drums, and soaring timber of Peter Gabriel's voice makes itself known, a classic pop jam drifting through the trees.

I love this song, a synthesized banger that immediately brings to mind visions of 1986 and some coke-dusted neon nightclub. The chords are hopeful and the tempo is upbeat, lush horns dancing playfully around every crooning vocal line.

Context is everything, however, and while I'd love to hear Peter Gabriel's "Sledgehammer" on a night out, in the middle of the woods it's nothing short of haunting.

Gradually, another sound begins to tickle my ears, a distant shouting that becomes more and more apparent with every step.

"That's what I am, right? A fucking bank?" the furious voice screams. "Do I dress like a bank teller to you? You must think I'm a bank teller, because all you do is spend boatloads of *my fucking money* while you go behind my back and sell me out!"

As I creep closer, I notice a faint red glimmer through the trees, a strange glow illuminating this hidden scene.

"Imagine my *fucking* surprise when I heard from Shades tonight. It's not just a loose wallet you've got, it's loose lips. Listen, I could look the other way when you fudged the numbers a bit, but now I've gotta come all the way out here to deal with a ratfuck informant," the voice continues. "An *informant*? Jesus, Jack. You're breaking my heart."

The mention of *Shades* causes my mind to spring back a few hours, recalling the blood rejuvenation center. There was someone in that room with Jack and me—a man who wore giant sunglasses indoors.

A real character.

Now I actually *do* wish I'd seen this stupid movie.

A second voice rises to meet the first, panicked and belligerent. The tone is Jack's but the words are strange and gurgling, a pudding of sylla-bles tumbling across one another to create a frantic vocal inflection with no particular meaning to define it. The cries grow higher and higher in pitch, until suddenly another sonic cue rings out through the darkness.

CRUNCH.

Jack's gurgling becomes a squealing, guttural fit, losing any hope of coherence as it further devolves.

"You're a lucky son-of-a-bitch, you know that?" the original voice announces, now terrifyingly joyful in its cadence. "Even though you ran your stupid fucking mouth, that guy you squealed to is already cooked. He's done! No harm, no foul! Out of the kindness of my heart, I'm gonna let you slide on that one."

Closer and closer I move, silently creeping through the trees as I weave my way into the dark of the canyon.

"But, here's the problem: you still spent *a lot* of my money. You know, it's kinda funny, I *am* starting to feel like a banker now," the voice con-tinues, slightly calmer but just as menacing.

By now I have no problem recognizing the posthumous tone of Chris Oak.

Of course, it's not really Chris speaking these lines, it's Enzo, the broken don himself, a ruthless mob boss who will stop at nothing to protect his Miami empire.

Jack whimpers something in response.

"I know, I know." Enzo laughs, his words carrying out over the thumping rhythm of Peter Gabriel's song, "but it's kinda nice running the numbers like this. Really makes you think. What's an arm worth? A leg? I'm thinking two million apiece."

I'm finally close enough to catch a glimpse of what's going on, peer-ing through the trees at two figures in the middle of a small clearing. A handful of road flares have been tossed across the ground in a haphaz-ard triangle, illumining Enzo and Jack with their crimson glow.

Enzo wipes the sweat from his brow, sauntering back and forth as an enormous sledgehammer hangs by his side. I can make out his wide smile from all the way over here, a fictional mob boss having the time of his life.

Jack, on the other hand, is in rough shape. I cover my mouth to keep a startled gasp from slipping out when I catch sight of him.

Jack's back is pressed against a tree trunk, his arms wrapped around the tree behind him and somehow held in place. He's slouched awkwardly, threatening to fall but kept upright by a leather belt lashed tightly across his neck.

There's blood running down Jack's chin and splattered across the front of his suit in a gruesome mess, red but looking black in the ominous road-flare lighting. More concerning, however, is the strange angle of Jack's legs as they splay clumsily below him.

As Jack struggles and writhes, his legs refuse to move. His left arm is also oddly still, and as I peer closer I can see the fabric covering each joint is bizarrely flat where appendage meets body.

"You wasted eight million dollars this year," Enzo states. "That's a lot of money, my friend. A lot of fuckin' money to just throw away when I'm out here working my ass off to make a life for my family. My *family*, do you understand? When you go to lunch, or the spa, or get your fucking nails done, do you know who pays for that?"

Jack frantically shakes his head, gurgling up more unintelligible words. Based on the blend of syllables cascading from his throat and the abundance of blood, it suddenly dawns on me that his tongue has been severed, and my suspicious are confirmed when I notice a pair of garden shears and a handgun sitting on a nearby stump.

A vintage stereo rests on the stump, too, somehow humming with life despite the notable lack of an outlet. Peter Gabriel's voice croons on, now in ghastly juxtaposition with the carnage it accompanies.

I wanna be your sledgehammer, he calls out. *Why don't you call my name?*

Enzo is pacing. "My daughter pays for it! My wife pays for it! *I* pay for it!" the man screams, a truly Oscar-worthy performance gone horrifically wrong.

The mob boss takes a minute to calm himself down, and in this time my head floods with questions.

Can I really stop him with nothing but a tire iron?

Is it too late if I try?

That gun on the stump certainly gives me pause, but if I manage to get my hands on it before Enzo does, I could turn the tables.

I take in Jack, this once powerful figure now a blubbering mess of a man. We've had our differences, that's for sure, but this asshole is also a friend. Even if he weren't, no human being deserves this.

I start rounding the clearing, closing the distance between myself and the gun.

"One arm and two legs down, so that's six million's worth of payback," Enzo continues, gripping his sledgehammer by the head and pointing it at each of Jack's shattered joints. "Looks like there's one arm left, then you'll be all paid up and we can put this behind us."

Jack frantically sputters something in return, prompting Enzo to pause.

"What's that?" the mob boss questions.

Jack speaks again, this time slower and with as much articulation as he can possibly muster. I can barely understand him, but the context clues work in Jack's favor. "What . . . about . . . my . . . tongue?" he asks.

Enzo laughs. "That's for fucking up my Countach." He reaches into the front pocket of his white blazer, then extracts a tiny pink rectangle of flesh. It's Jack's severed tongue. Enzo dismissively tosses it onto Jack's lap. "Here. Keep the fucking thing. You think I want it?"

Jack moans with devastating sadness, a primal expression of someone fully understanding their life—their body—will never be the same.

Enzo plants his feet, teeing up. The ghoulish entity lifts his sledgehammer and plots a course, miming a few test swings at the arm bone resting just below Jack's shoulder.

For a moment, I consider throwing caution to the wind and rushing him right here and now, using my tire iron and catching Enzo off guard, but before I can act the man takes another full-force swing.

CRUNCH.

The sledgehammer strikes its target with bone-shattering might, completely destroying the architecture of this pinpointed location with one fell swoop. Jack lets out a guttural shriek, thrashing his head from side to side as his limbs hang useless and broken. He begins to heave and retch, vomiting up swallowed blood that rushes down the front of his chest and soaks his shirt.

Gradually, Jack's grunts begin to quiet, mutating into soft whimpers as the blood loss makes him more and more delirious.

Enzo leans his sledgehammer against the tree, then steps back a bit to admire his handiwork.

"Wow. You've made a real fucking mess of yourself, haven't you?" the man chuckles.

I'm mere feet away from the gun now, crouched behind one of the trees. I shift my weight, preparing to make a dash for the weapon when Enzo abruptly spins and marches toward the stump.

I duck behind a tree just in time to avoid his detection.

"Now comes the fun part," Enzo announces, grabbing the pruning shears in his hand and taking the gun along with it. He tucks the gun into the front of his belt, but keeps his shears at the ready. Enzo turns off his radio, plunging the forest into silence. "Gotta calculate the interest."

My blood runs cold as I hear this, immediately realizing what's going on here. I haven't seen *Broken Don* yet, but I know my way around fictional characters. Enzo talked a big game about calculating repayment for Jack's loose spending habits, but the glee on his face isn't an expression of someone who's out for justice.

This man is here to hurt someone. He won't stop until Jack is dead, and it'll take a while to get there.

"What's a fair rate?" Enzo questions with mock sincerity as he marches back to Jack. "Let's start with thirty percent."

Enzo grabs Jack's limp hand and places the shears around his captive's thumb. For some reason I expect him to hesitate, for a shred of humanity to slow him down, but that doesn't happen. Enzo forcefully tightens his grip in one quick movement. There's an audible crack as the bone pops and the flesh tears away, Jack's digit tumbling to the ground. A spurt of blood spills after.

The lack of arterial pressure is notable, and Jack's dampened reaction is even more frightening. The executive moans loudly, rolling his head from side to side, but his earlier screams of anguish have subsided. He just doesn't have the energy.

"*Che palle!*" Enzo cries out, frustrated. He slaps Jack hard, struggling to wake him. "I said thirty percent, not ten!"

Enzo reaches into his jacket pocket and withdraws a small glass vial. The mob boss opens it quickly, dumping a line of white powder across the top of his hand. He swiftly shoves it under Jack's nose, pushing the powder against my friend's nostrils.

"There you go." Enzo laughs encouragingly. "We're in this together. You can't go kickin' off just yet."

Jack's eyes widen a bit, momentarily pulled back into focus. He yanks his chest against his restraints, but this second wind isn't nearly enough to replenish any real physical strength. It only serves to reintroduce the pain.

Enzo reaches down and grabs Jack's hand again, this time with even less fanfare. He places Jack's next finger—the pointer—between his sharpened blades and squeezes without hesitation, acting like he's doing little more than chopping carrots for a salad.

There's another sickening crack as Jack's digit falls away, tumbling into the dirt. The blood oozes even slower this time as it creeps from Jack's fresh wound.

"Twenty percent! Almost there!" Enzo cries gleefully.

Jack mumbles something in return, which causes his assailant to hesitate.

I step a little closer, my weapon raised.

"Buddy, you're gonna have to speak up," Enzo informs his captive. "No wonder you made so many shit deals, nobody can hear a fuckin' word you're saying."

With all the effort he can muster, Jack lifts his head just high enough to look Enzo in the eye. He hesitates, taking in the moment, then spits a massive glob of gore onto the mobster's face. The dark liquid splatters across Enzo with just as much disrespect as intended, while Jack smiles an enormous *fuck you* grin, his teeth stained with blood.

Enzo is frozen in shock, utterly appalled, and it suddenly occurs to me this is the best chance I'm gonna get. It's now or never.

Fuck 'em.

I explode from behind the tree, sprinting toward Enzo with my tire-iron cocked and ready to swing.

I take two large steps, and by the third Enzo has already sensed my presence. He spins abruptly, reaching for his gun and yanking it from the waistband just in time for me to strike the side of his head with all my force.

The gun flies from Enzo's hand as he staggers to the right, clutching his temple and letting out a forceful grunt. He tries his best to stay upright, but this matchup between tire iron and skull has a clear winner. Enzo fumbles, then slams against the dirt, groaning loudly.

The mob boss takes a moment to collect himself, and as he does I can sense my body holding back, restraining the natural instinct to continue onward with a barrage of swings. I'm a fighter, not a murderer, and it's hard to step into that role even after everything I've witnessed.

But this isn't an actor, that much I know. Chris Oak has been dead for years, and whatever heinous thing has brought this horrible *creature* into our reality is void of any humanity I'd hope to conserve through mercy.

He certainly didn't show Jack Hays any mercy.

As blood pours down the side of Enzo's head he somehow manages to gather his senses, at least enough to charge toward me in a feral rage. The man lunges with the full force of his body, but the previous skull dent has slowed him down enough for me to easily calculate his approach.

I swing again, aiming for the same spot and striking my target. Enzo's body stiffens immediately, dropping to the ground with a mighty thud.

This time there's no hesitation. I take one more step and bring the iron rod down onto Enzo's skull for a third strike, this particular blow eliciting a hollow crack that's morbidly distinct from the rest. Blood gushes from the man's head as I stagger back, dropping the tire iron and letting a strange, one-syllable sound erupt from my lips. "Ha!" I cry, not some shout of excitement but a self-reflective outburst of shock.

What was that?

I've written this kind of violence more times than I can count, spilled enough stage blood to fill the Lake Hollywood reservoir, but actually performing this brutality in real life is something else.

A sudden wave of nausea washes over me, that familiar sensation of pressure right below the ears. There's no time to act, but I manage to step away just far enough to erupt with an unexpected heave of vomit, my body's natural reaction to the intensity of this gruesome scene.

The discomfort passes quickly. I stand back up, wiping my mouth as I hurry over to Jack's side.

"Hey! It's gonna be okay," I assure, desperately struggling to free him.

I have no trouble undoing the belt around Jack's neck, but the handcuffs require a key. Before I have a chance to go back and search Enzo's pockets, however, a more pressing realization washes over me.

I check in with my friend.

Jack remains perfectly still, his eyes glazed over as I struggle to get his attention.

"Jack," I shout, shaking him a bit. "Hey! I'm gonna get you out of here."

No reaction.

I reach out and press my fingers against Jack's neck, finding no hint of a pulse. His body just couldn't take it, broken and battered past the point of no return.

A deep, physical ache ripples across me as I crumple forward against him.

Jack had a family, he had people who loved him.

And we never got around to catching one of his daughter's soccer games.

"Aw, fuck," I sigh, not knowing what else to do. I can feel his blood on me, staining my shirt and mixing with the tears that run down my face. "I'm sorry."

I stay like this for a while, then suddenly pull back in alarm. This is a crime scene.

Scrambling to my feet and stepping away from the body, I find a whole new avalanche of problems to contend with. The prospect of explaining all this to the authorities feels like an impossible hill to climb.

Fortunately, they'll likely be much more concerned with the fresh corpse of an actor who's supposedly been dead for years.

I turn back to gaze upon Enzo's body in the dirt, but what I find is more troubling than a simple cadaver. The corporeal form of Enzo Basile has started to shift, the flesh and bones dissolving into a strange, dark ash. Even the suit he once wore has transformed into a man-shaped pile of mysterious dust, a substance I immediately recognize even in the red glow of the road flares.

This is the same ash that fell from my phone, once attributed to a cigarette and now revealing itself as something else entirely.

Field's alloy, Zeke had called it.

"Holy shit," I murmur, watching as Enzo disappears completely. A heap of raw mineral lies piled up where he once rested, but the majority of this substance begins to float away.

Grains of the uncanny compound lift into the air, dancing gracefully as though carried by a slow wind. Soon enough, huge globs of ash are separating from what was once Enzo's humanoid shape, twisting like miniature tornados that rise with patient elegance toward the sky.

The particles churn together in undulating shapes, black against the crimson light as they crawl through the trees.

I step back, watching this majestic living dust as it separates from the dead. The movements remind me of bird formations, animals working together through some strange subliminal communication, creating beautiful patterns out of what should otherwise be mindless instinct.

Eventually, the swarm and Enzo's dusty remains have separated entirely, leaving behind a sparse layer of dark gray alloy and not much else. The swirling mass of granular bits continues on its merry way, drifting off into the woods.

I have a pretty good idea where it's headed.

INSPIRATION

1999

I was twelve years old, watching my mother back out of the driveway in her old rattling Toyota Camry. As she reached the bottom of the hill and straightened out, she glanced back one last time and offered a cheerful wave. Somehow, she knew I'd still be up there waiting on the landing of our apartment, knew I'd be soaking up every last minute before she disappeared.

All that, despite the freezing temperature that pained my fingers and face.

A kid my age should've loved having a little time away from his family, relished the freedom that came from those rare weeks with few rules. Unfortunately, Uncle Keith was bad enough to make me dream of structure.

It's not a full week, I reminded myself. *It's only five days.*

As my mother's taillights disappeared into the darkness of the night, the countdown began.

Back inside our small studio apartment, I heard Uncle Keith loudly clear his throat, coughing up phlegm and then swallowing it back down.

"Misha!" he called. "Get in here!"

I headed back inside to find Uncle Keith sprawled on the couch, his feet kicked up and his shoes still on despite the white fabric below them. He was lounging with the remote in his hand, pressing the power button over and over again but getting no results.

"Looks like you're my remote now," Keith announced with a laugh. "Turn on the tube, would ya?"

I strolled over and pressed the TV's power button, prompting the old rectangular box to light up with a high-pitched analog whine.

"Start flippin', pal," Uncle Keith demanded.

I did as I was told, pressing the channel-up button over and over again as various images scrolled past.

"Hey, dummy, you're going too fast," Keith barked, already setting the tone for this week. "Slow down."

The way he said it was strangely jovial, a sly grin plastered across his face to let me know he was just kidding.

I relaxed my button pushing, dropping the pace to a crawl until, eventually, Uncle Keith found something worth his time.

"There!" the man squawked, the force of his outburst causing him to break out in another brief coughing fit. "Hell yeah, *Predatory Hunt*. You seen this one?"

I shook my head.

"Yeah, probably a little too old for you," Uncle Keith replied, then settled in to watch as I stood awkwardly nearby.

Keith's eyes remained focused on the screen as he acted like I wasn't even there.

"You can't have your shoes on the couch," I finally informed him.

Keith's gaze wandered over to me. His expression was utterly blank, barely taking me seriously enough to muster an emotional display in either direction. Finally, he raised his eyebrows and swung his feet over the edge a bit, just enough to satisfy my request.

Despite the enormous power imbalance between us, there was still one important weapon on my side: I could always tell his sister.

"You wanna get pizza for dinner?" Uncle Keith questioned, his gaze returning to the screen. "Kids love pepperoni pizza."

He's wasn't wrong.

"Sure," I replied.

"Sounds like a plan, Stan," Keith said, focus unbroken. "Now stop standing around like a little freak. Don't you have homework to do?"

I wandered away, heading over to the dining table and plopping down before our family computer. Of course, the dining room was nothing more than a segment of our only living area, which also served as an office, bedroom, and an occasional laundry-folding station. It was nothing like our old house.

Mom never needed to take long work trips at her old job, but now that Dad was gone, her schedule had become nothing short of grueling. At that point in my life I resented her for it, but as I grew older it started to make more and more sense. Looking back, I can't imagine what it must've been like going to school, working like crazy, and raising a child by herself.

Unless, of course, you counted the help from Uncle Keith.

I glanced over at the man, noticing his dirty shoes had quietly returned to their position on my mother's white couch.

It's a little surprising how deep my disdain for Keith ran at that point, especially as a wild preteen boy. If anything, I should've looked up to the guy and his "who gives a fuck?" attitude. Keith might have been loud, short-tempered, and frustratingly bossy, but his visits always started fun enough.

That particular stay was no exception. It wasn't every day I got to order pepperoni pizza and sneak peeks at *Predatory Hunt* while pretending to do my homework; and on a school night, no less.

It certainly wouldn't be like that when Mom returned home.

But I'd been around Uncle Keith long enough to know his upbeat mood wouldn't last. During the course of those five days, things were bound to get worse and worse, devolving from playful rule-breaking to utter chaos.

His trick, of course, was to stay sober just long enough to chat with his sister and accept what little money she had in exchange for these multi-day babysitting adventures.

Keith was family, and he probably should've been doing this stuff for free. Instead, he took just enough to be cheaper than everyone else, and expensive enough to keep my mom desperate for more overtime.

Uncle Keith was a short man with slicked-back hair, jet black like my mom's. He seemed to always have stubble, and he loved to sport mismatched suit pieces. Ill-fitting, off-color blazers sat at the top of his list. On that particular day, Keith's jacket was ratty and blue, and the loose button-up underneath was a strange olive tone.

A prolific smoker, the man *always* reeked, which ironically led to the one rule around here that he never broke. Uncle Keith knew better than to smoke inside the apartment, even in his most belligerent drunken stupors.

My mother would notice if the place smelled like smoke, which meant no more babysitting gigs, which meant no more extra cash, which meant no more drugs. At least, that was the cycle that always played out in my head.

Now that I'm older, I'm not so sure. Maybe he really *was* just trying to help, but his darker nature always caught up with him.

The night dragged on as I played through a few games of Minesweeper and surfed the Web, which was not quite as crowded in those days. Honestly, the fact that I even had an internet-connected computer at that age was shocking, especially considering the socioeconomic bracket we'd suddenly found ourselves thrust into.

I guess that says something about my mother's priorities, since the internet was rightly touted as a powerful emerging tool for young learners.

Of course, back then I mostly just used it to look at pictures of shirtless guys and, if the mood was right, printed them out on our slow, loud, horribly low-quality color printer.

A man on TV suddenly screamed in agony, prompting my attention to jump over to that screen. The scene was graphic, but strangely alluring: a breathtakingly muscular action hero was laid out with his back against a tree. Two others held his arms. The screaming man's rippling chest was pumped up to an absurd degree, well past that of the action stars who would later grace the silver screen. This was a time for body-builders to try their hand at acting, not the other way around.

Blood spilled across the man's bare stomach as a fourth beefcake marine used a hunting knife to slice his skin. Without hesitation, this new warrior plunged his fingers into the cut.

I flinched watching the scene unfold, but I couldn't look away.

The newly appointed survival surgeon had a terrified look on his face, sweat pouring from his brow. "It's right where that thing bit you, Deckard."

The camera zoomed in close, displaying what I now understand to be a clever practical effect of a long, thick worm squirming below the man's skin.

"It didn't just bite me, it laid eggs!" the beefcake screamed as he continued to lose blood. He threw his head back and let out a long, strange cry, the guttural syllables somehow maintaining the man's thick accent. "Uggghhhh-ahhhhwaaaaah! Get it out of me!"

While I didn't understand it at the time, a certain homoerotic undertone simmers through every aspect of this film. You could write whole theses on the symbolism of shirtless marines getting lost in the jungle and shoving their fingers into one another.

In retrospect, *Predatory Hunt* is actually pretty fantastic in a so-bad-it's-good kinda way. It only goes completely off the rails in the sequel, where the KGB tries using the jungle worm eggs as a bioweapon, injecting them into American spies from the tip of an umbrella.

"Light!" Uncle Keith suddenly cried from his place on the couch.

I stood immediately and grabbed my coat, heading for the door. He'd trained me well.

"Ahhwwwah! Get da worm! Get da worm!" the shirtless marine continued screaming. "It's crawling into my heart!"

Soon enough, Uncle Keith and I were standing on the apartment landing, gazing out at the rest of the six-unit complex and the dilapi-dated houses of the neighborhood beyond. This was not a great part of town, but we had somehow found ourselves with a surprisingly decent view at the top of the little hill.

Uncle Keith held a cigarette between his lips, then leaned down a bit so I could give him a light.

"Coffin nails," he said.

It was a bizarre little routine, but it was what we did. Thanks to Keith, I found myself stealing lighters and matchbooks wherever I went, avoiding the wrath I might incur should I come up empty-handed. He found it funny to pretend I was his little butler, and he assumed the enjoyment was mutual. It wasn't.

Keith clearly had his own lighters; otherwise what would he do when I wasn't around? Yet I never once saw him light a cigarette of his own.

Uncle Keith enjoyed the power, however brief and insignificant. A moment when he was the one in charge.

My uncle pulled a long drag from his cigarette and let it out, taking a lot more time than I'd have preferred in this freezing weather. "Movie's kinda gay," he stated bluntly.

"Oh," I replied, struggling to find a natural response. "That sucks."

"Bunch of shirtless guys walkin' around in the jungle gettin' sweaty," he opined, his eyes still gazing out at the neighborhood below us. "When the giant worm sucked that guy's whole rib cage out through his back, though. That was pretty cool."

I nodded along. "Cool."

The two of us stood in silence for a long while, and the whole time all I could think about was how badly I wanted to get back inside.

"Hey, I'm gonna drive down to the store and grab that pizza," Uncle Keith suddenly announced. "You gonna be okay here by yourself?"

"Oh, sure."

Uncle Keith nodded, finishing his cigarette and flicking it off our deck. I watched as the butt tumbled end over end onto the lawn below, coming to rest on half-dead grass that was already littered with fast-food bags and sticky plastic cups.

"Alright then," he said, patting me on the shoulder. "I'll be right back."

The next thing I knew, Uncle Keith was making his way down the stairs, loudly clearing his throat and coughing as he went.

The second he disappeared, I slipped back inside.

As the night wore on I actually managed to get a little homework done, then eventually flopped onto the couch for some TV. From here I could easily sit up and check the window for Uncle Keith's return, and while I usually cherished this time away from him, I was starting to get hungry.

Back in those days, landlines ruled the world, and with no way to call my uncle I was forced to sit and wonder where the hell he could be. The pizza place was right down the street, a corner shop across from the gas station, and there was rarely a wait.

I glanced at the clock and realized it had already taken an hour for what should've been a fifteen-minute trip.

My stomach gurgled faintly, making its displeasure known.

Finally, I climbed off the couch and headed for the kitchen, ready to grate some cheese and make myself a quesadilla in the microwave.

That was when the front door flew open and Uncle Keith wandered inside.

"Hey, Misha!" the man called out, his eyes frighteningly red and his nose runny.

There was no pizza to be found. Instead, a plastic bag swung haphazardly in Uncle Keith's hand. I could see two cans of beer, more cigarettes, and a pack of red licorice held within.

I wasn't entirely sure how to react.

"You okay?" Keith questioned.

"Did you get the pizza?"

Keith frowned, realizing something. "You know what, pal? They were closed," he finally replied. "I'm sorry about that."

My uncle reached into his bag and pulled out the pack of licorice, tossing it over to me.

"Knock yourself out," he offered.

I gazed down at the candy, but I didn't open it. While the prospect of dessert for dinner sounded like a childhood fantasy come true, in actual practice it wasn't nearly as thrilling.

"Thanks," I replied, then returned to my quesadilla prep.

I retrieved an enormous block of orange cheddar cheese from the fridge, unwrapping the Ziploc bag that surrounded it then plopping the cube on a plastic cutting board. I didn't know much about cooking, but thanks to the wonders of microwave technology, there were a few simple meals I could throw together.

Two tortillas and some grated cheese was my specialty.

Uncle Keith sauntered over and took a seat before the computer. He cracked open one of his beers and started clicking around.

"We've got the Web at work, too," Uncle Keith announced. "Pretty wild stuff on there."

The next thing I knew, the computer was emitting a series of beeps, followed by a faint crackle and a piercing, high-pitched squeal. Keith was getting online.

"As long as you know how to cover your tracks, you'll be fine," Uncle Keith continued, chuckling to himself.

At that point I was just letting him talk as I went about my work, much more focused on grating enough cheese to fill a double-stacked tortilla than anything else. I remained vaguely aware of the topics Uncle Keith was rambling about, but at that point I'd become so frustrated with the man that I'd rather just ignored his presence.

Uncle Keith started poking around online, typing away as I popped my plate into the microwave.

"Come over here," Keith suggested, the words slurred and awkward. "Let me show you."

I wandered over to the computer, standing behind my uncle as he clicked through various options on our internet browser. The stale scent of cigarettes flooded my nostrils, emanating from the man's pores.

"I remember what it was like to be a kid your age," Keith continued. "Of course, back then we had magazines."

Keith clicked a button and a massive list promptly appeared in the browser window, a wall of text spanning several pages. Each item was marked with a date and time.

I'd never seen this screen before, and my eyes immediately got to work scanning the list. I clocked the top one as a National Parks website I'd visited just an hour ago for my homework. Next was a site about skateboarding, then a page full of *StarCraft* strategies.

Suddenly, a piercing stab of utter terror surged through my body. I realized now what Keith was talking about, and the potential of what he could discover filled me with a sickening dread.

(Even now, all these years later, I can still *feel* the way my hands were shaking, the way this ultimate panic took hold of my senses.)

"Now, your cool Uncle Keith is gonna teach you how to hide your trail," he continued.

"It's okay!" I snapped, a little too forceful but unable to control the squealing tone of my voice. I reached out and tried to snatch the mouse from Uncle Keith's hand but he pulled away, deeply offended.

"Hey!" he shouted. "I'm using the computer, pal, and I'm doing you a favor."

"It's okay," I repeated in a panic. "You don't have to show me."

Keith just shook his head. "Trust me, you don't want your mom to find this stuff. She's got enough to worry about as it is."

Again I went for the mouse, causing Keith to push me away with a firm objection. "Hey!" he yelled, his face stern enough to stop me in my tracks.

We stayed frozen like this for a good while, a bizarre standoff.

Finally, my uncle's expression softened. "I don't care if you're looking up boobs." Keith laughed. "It's natural. Hell, I love tits, too."

Uncle Keith turned back around as I remained frozen behind him, helpless. I already knew what was coming, the future barreling toward me like a slow-motion train in some horrific adolescent nightmare.

"This is every Web page your computer has visited," my uncle explained, casually making his way down the list.

NPS-Grand Teton—Plan Your Visit.
Rodney_Mullen_Darkslide.mov.
Zergling rush counter build.

Uncle Keith scrolled down a bit more.

"So if there's something you shouldn't be looking at, you can just go over here and press delete," he continued. "Don't say I never did nothing for ya."

Something caught Keith's eye, a website naming convention that wasn't like the rest.

"What do we have here?" he joked playfully.

The pressure within me was impossible to control any longer. "No!" I shouted, grabbing for the mouse. "You don't need to show me!"

Uncle Keith laughed and pushed me back, a bully at heart. He clicked the link to open it up, but when the screen bloomed with digital imagery my uncle stopped in his tracks. He was frozen, staring at the display in a state of utter shock.

Handsome men in dramatic nude poses filled the monitor, slowly unveiling themselves at the gradual speed of fifty-six thousand bits per second. The only sound was the soft crackle and hum of our computer processing this illicit information.

"What the hell is this?"

"It's just a joke," I fumbled, my face bright red as tears filled my eyes.

I wonder what might've happened if I'd blamed these websites on my mother. Something tells me it still wouldn't have flown.

My uncle turned to face me with a look of bewildered contempt. "You into this shit?"

"No!" I shook my head profusely.

Uncle Keith's expression was difficult to parse, and I now realize there was more going on than I'll ever truly understand. Keith was certainly not a religious man, and he had no problem with overt sexuality in other circumstances. Still, that moment triggered something deep inside him that I'd never known was there, a hidden tripwire that ripped his psyche apart.

For years, I thought the responsibility of this outburst lay squarely on me, but as time has rolled on I've started to realize Keith had his own inner wars to wage. I just stumbled onto the battlefield.

Keith turned away, unable to look at me.

He shut off the computer, sitting quietly as I desperately tried to unravel his simmering expression in the reflection of an empty screen. The moment seemed to last forever, guilt permeating every cell of my being and marinating my soul in shame.

Eventually, Uncle Keith rose and headed for the door.

"I'm sorry!" I cried, tears streaming down my face. "It was a joke!"

Keith stepped outside, slamming the door behind him with such force that I jumped in surprise.

I began to pace, blubbering a string of insults at myself and smacking my own head with some primal urge for punishment.

I had a whole hour to wallow in misery, helpless as waves of nausea crashed over me. Uncle Keith was gone, no longer just waiting on the deck but disappearing into the night like a phantom.

Eventually, however, he returned.

I was sitting on the couch when Keith opened the door. I'd worked out a whole script for what I was going to say, a way to dig myself out of that terrible hole, but before I got the chance to speak I noticed Uncle Keith was not alone.

A young woman was by his side, frail and skinny underneath an enormous winter coat that she kept wrapped around her body.

Keith nodded toward me, his gaze even more despondent than before. "Hey, pal, can I talk to you outside?"

Things had taken such a bizarre turn that I hardly reacted, my brain struggling to process what was happening.

I stood and followed Uncle Keith, but before we made our exit he stopped abruptly.

"Grab a coat," he suggested.

I reached out and took one of my jackets off the nearby hook, pulling it on as we made our exit. The door closed behind us on the strange woman.

"Light," Keith demanded, pulling out another cigarette and placing it in his mouth.

I swiftly retrieved the lighter from my pocket and sparked it up, then positioned the dancing flame as Keith began his routine.

"That's some pretty sick stuff," Keith stated flatly as he gazed off into the darkness of the neighborhood.

I didn't know how to react, so I just stood in silence. I was trembling hard, equally overwhelmed by the freezing temperature and the nervous tension within me. Flakes of snow were beginning to dance through the sky, drifting and twirling as they made their descent. They wouldn't stick, gradually melting away as the cold air flirted with a thirty-two-degree plateau, but it was close.

"You're really into that shit? Guys and all that?" Keith continued.

I said nothing.

Uncle Keith just shook his head, his disappointment framed by the stillness of the night. I wanted nothing more than to melt out of my body, to dissolve into nothing.

"I'm not gonna tell your mom," Uncle Keith informed me, prompting a powerful wave of relief to wash across my frame.

"Really?" I asked, the single word unable to capture just how thankful I was.

"Nope," Keith replied, taking a long drag from his cigarette. "Because you're not gonna tell *her* what your uncle gets up to this week."

I nodded along, barely listening as we made our agreement. The second Keith revealed he wouldn't be passing my indiscretion along, I was completely checked out of the conversation. Whatever came next was meaningless.

"Jenna's gonna stay over for a few nights," Uncle Keith informed me. "My place is out in Hardin, and she wants to crash in town. Plus, I've gotta keep an eye on you."

"Okay," I replied, my teeth still chattering.

"I know your mom sleeps on the couch while you take the bed in the corner," Keith continued. "That's not gonna work."

I wasn't entirely sure where he was headed with this, but I nodded all the same.

"Come on, let's take a walk."

Keith did his trademark cigarette flip, the butt plummeting below to join the corpses of its brethren. He motioned for me to follow as he made his way down the stairs, eventually leading us to the apartment parking lot.

Keith's rickety old car was parked off to the side, tucked behind a large green dumpster.

My uncle took out his keys and opened the trunk, pulling forth a large, dirty blanket as the snowflakes continued swirling around us. It was covered in streaks of sawdust, which Uncle Keith did his best to clear away. He handed it over.

"See you in the morning, pal," he said, opening the back seat door.

I stared at Keith for a moment, unmoving.

"Bedtime," my uncle continued. "I'll see you in the morning."

Awkwardly, I climbed into the car, taking note of the ice-cold faux leather against my skin. The floor was covered in beer bottles and various food wrappers, which could've given the vehicular cage a distinct smell if not for the mighty scent that overpowered everything: cigarette smoke.

The putrid fragrance had permeated Keith's vehicle, soaked deep into every inch of the sedan in a way that could never be expunged.

Uncle Keith stood by the door, gazing in at me as I struggled to wrap the blanket around my trembling frame. The fabric was thin, clearly not made to hold much heat, and the parts of my body that remained exposed already throbbed with a frigid ache. My breath clouded the air before me in icy white puffs.

"What do you say?" my uncle questioned.

"Thank you?" I replied, not entirely sure this was the answer he'd been looking for.

Keith nodded. "Don't forget our deal. You're getting off lucky here, buddy."

He moved to close the door, then stopped abruptly, the expression on his face softening. For the briefest moment, everything about Uncle Keith radiated a profound, overwhelming sadness.

"You're making life really, really hard for yourself," my uncle said. "You better start getting tough now."

The door slammed shut with a metallic thump, sealing me inside as Keith strolled back to the apartment. I heard his footsteps ringing out as he ascended the metal stairs, each clang growing farther and farther away.

Hoping to preserve any morsel of heat, I wrapped the blanket even tighter around my body.

It was no use.

I remember thinking if I could just fall asleep, the night would pass in the blink of an eye. Sleep never came, though. It was too cold for my body to adjust, and the stale, smoke-coated interior was just too putrid to grow accustomed to.

The only thing I had as I tossed and turned were my thoughts, and while my opinion on these events would certainly change over the following years, I can still remember the overwhelming gratitude that flowed through my veins and kept me quiet. Never once did I try to get back inside the apartment, and when Keith stood out on the deck and called for a light at sunrise I was right there to greet him.

Keith wasn't going to reveal my secret, and that was all that mattered.

I lay in that car for five nights, shivering violently as I hunted for a shred of solace in the world of dreams.

On the second evening, I had a nightmare that a strange voice was talking to me through the radio, but for the life of me, I can't remember what they said.

Night three was the first time I remember using art to protect my-self, using story for survival. Young Misha Byrne might've lost his mind in the back of that car, but a stalwart Arctic explorer felt right at home. Who was I? (Wolfgang von Danger.) How did I get here? (A yeti killed the rest of my expedition.) There was plenty of time to figure out the rest.

I counted down the minutes until my mom returned, and on the fifth day I was standing out front to greet her. That came after a long shower, of course, diligently scrubbing the cigarette stench from my body.

I never told her what happened.

At least, not directly.

THE GREAT MEADOW PRISON BREAK-IN

I swiftly cross the parking lot of Betta Effects and Natural Processing, marching through the darkness in a state of furious, rage-fueled delirium. Per Tara's advice, my phone is off and my face is covered, making use of a paisley bandana and a blue Dodgers hat I managed to scrounge from the trunk of my car.

My heart is slamming so hard I'm worried it may burst right through my rib cage, and even then I doubt it would slow me down.

Take it easy, I remind myself. *Be smart.*

Enzo's handgun is gripped tight, lowered to my side but ready for action at any moment. I have no idea what I'll find hiding within the walls here, but I'm ready for anything.

As I reach the door I waste no time, pulling Jack's severed thumb from my pocket and placing it on the glowing blue scanner. The device hums for a moment, rapidly comparing this fingerprint across some vast unknown database. Seconds later, the lock pops open with a dull metallic clang.

I slip inside, finding myself in a nondescript office hallway that leads even deeper into the structure. There are doors lining either side of this oblong space, numbered one through sixteen. A large window is set within each numbered door, allowing anyone who strolls by a view inside.

I gaze into the first room, fully expecting something strange and horrific, but I'm shocked to discover just how typical it all is.

This is the same kind of office you'd find on the Harold Brothers main lot, a hip, modern desk with posters of each executive's latest project hanging proudly behind it. Betta has done work on every recent monster movie you could think of—their wall art can attest to that—but the visual effects aren't limited to any one genre. I spot an ad for the latest "gritty" R-rated superhero epic, *Heroes of Darkness,* hanging in one office, and a poster for some award's-bait docudrama about the tragic, mysterious events at Camp Damascus in another.

As I creep down the hallway, however, one film is highlighted more than the rest: *Broken Don.*

And why wouldn't it be? This is a grand technological achievement, an award-worthy merging of machine learning *and* computer-generated imagery, a cataclysmic shift in the way we understand entertainment.

Posters for this neo-noir masterpiece are everywhere. I spot one that nearly covers the entire back wall of the second office, a massive black rectangle with the words **CHRIS OAK—*BROKEN DON*** in colorful bold print. The actor's name is in brilliant pink, hovering over the title, and inside the *Broken Don* text is a beautiful sunset with silhouetted palms. A sledgehammer cuts diagonally across these words, its head dripping with blood.

I stare at the weapon a moment before moving on.

Halfway down the hallway a door sits propped open, held in place by a rubber stopper. I'm extra cautious when approaching this particular office, but quickly discover it's just as empty as the rest. This space is a little more disheveled, however, with a few books knocked off their shelves and two rolling chairs positioned haphazardly in corners.

Taking a few steps inside, I notice a small splatter of blood on the floor. It leads back into the hallway, a few drips every five or so feet, until exiting the building.

This must've been where Jack got punched. The place where he started his meeting with Enzo Basile.

A brief flash of where that meeting ended enters my mind, but I swiftly push it away.

As I reach the end of the hallway I'm greeted by a final door. This last mysterious passage has no window to see through, and it sports no numerical marking. What it *does* offer is the presence of a strange, low hum that seems to vibrate through everything.

Security measures continue with another heavy-duty lock, this one requiring a card swipe as opposed to a thumbprint. Fortunately, I was smart enough to search Jack's wallet and I came prepared.

I withdraw Jack's ID from my pocket.

I take a deep breath, steadying my nerves a bit, then swipe Jack's card and burst into the next room with my gun raised. I have no experience with firearms, and no idea if my technique is correct, but I've written this kind of scene enough times to fake it.

My eyes meet the shocked gaze of a startled security guard, the man kicked back with his feet on his desk and a book in his hands. His headphones are in, and while a bank of security monitors sits next to him, it appears he hasn't been keeping tabs on them.

The two of us freeze, neither quite equipped for this situation and running on instinct. The hesitation between us seems to last forever, until suddenly he reaches for a nearby drawer.

"Nope!" I step forward and focus my weapon directly on his forehead. "Don't even think about it."

Think action star. In control. Swagger. A Keanu Reeves type.

The security guard halts immediately, lifting his trembling hands in the air. The guy is in his early twenties. He's wearing a black uniform, and attached to the front of his button-up shirt is a silver name tag.

"Thank you, Robby," I continue. "Now, very slowly, stand up and back away from the desk. All the way up to that wall."

The security guard does as he's told, following my directions perfectly.

As soon as Robby gives me enough space I reach into his desk and discover another handgun. I pull it out and try my best to dismantle the weapon, popping what I can only assume is a clip from the gun's handle. I dump the bullets into my pocket.

"Is—is this . . . how you do it?" I find myself stammering.

"Just make sure there's nothing in the chamber," the guard offers.

I catch myself before responding, struggling to maintain my character.

"It's disarmed," I gruffly state with as much confidence as I can muster. I toss the weapon into a nearby garbage can. "What is this place?"

"It's a . . . computer effects studio," Robby fumbles.

I take another step forward. "What are you *actually* doing here?" I shout, raising my voice and letting the anger seep out a little more than intended.

"We make movies."

"Well, they're pretty fucking convincing movies," I bellow. "I could've sworn I just saw a friend of mine beaten to death with a sledgehammer!"

A knowing look suddenly crosses Robby's face. The expression is no less tense, but it now holds sliver of understanding.

"Sir, it is *just a film*," the security guard states, his voice slow and soft as he attempts to calm me down. His demeanor is not what I'd hoped for, dealing with me like a spoiled child rather than an actual threat. "Whatever you saw, it wasn't real. Please just put the gun down."

"What's in the next room?"

Robby glances at the door to his left, an even deeper chamber with yet another security panel to hide its secrets.

"I don't know," the guard replies, the bewilderment on his face unexpectedly convincing. "I'm not allowed in there."

"What about this pass?" I pull the card from my pocket and wave it in his face.

Robby catches sight of the blood that's been splattered across Jack's access key, his body tensing up. "Orange card. That gets you everywhere but the lab," he explains. "Only technicians with purple cards are allowed in the lab. That comes straight from the board."

At this point I have serious doubts about the morality, or even existence, of this mysterious *board,* but the mention immediately pulls my mind back to visions of Jack in his office.

I once saw Jack as some kind of powerful, all-knowing asshole who pulled the strings of Hollywood from behind that desk of his, an expert puppeteer.

But it turns out Jack was just a puppet. Not a purple keycard, *an orange keycard.*

"Is there a technician in there right now?" I question, pointing at the door.

The security guard hesitates, then shakes his head.

"Robby!" I howl, loud enough to make him jump and surprising even myself. "Don't fuck with me! Is there a technician in the lab?"

"Yes," the security guard finally admits.

"Call them out here," I continue, motioning toward a phone on his desk.

My captive reaches over and picks up the receiver.

It suddenly occurs to me that this security guard could easily just yell for the technicians to stay inside, or use some secret code to warn them. I'd have no way of knowing.

"Wait." I motion for him to put the phone down and he follows my instructions.

The only way to keep things on track is to truly frighten this kid, to convince him the bumbling fool is actually a deranged, cold-blooded killer. Between the gun in his face and the blood on my keycard, the evidence is certainly there, I'm just not selling it.

Action star is a fun character, but I'm not telling the right story.

Character description reads: Unhinged. Unpredictable. Fanatical.

"I saw that documentary of yours," I suddenly announce, shifting my demeanor. "The one about Camp Damascus. It was a small theater, but even in that tiny room I could hear through the static. I got the messages, heard 'em loud and clear, Robby. That's why God led me here."

The security guard shifts uncomfortably in his chair.

I move a little closer.

"The good Lord spoke, and he told me to come. 'Come and see!' he said, to Hollywood, to a city under the thumb of the blood-drinking, baby-eating goblins," I explain. "All the way to Sodom, just to see if *you* were worthy, Robby. And to let His almighty wrath speak through me."

I pause, letting the silence hang for a moment.

"Hollywood elites control the whole thing!" I scream, causing Robby to flinch. "First they plot that horrible Christian camp tragedy, but what's next?"

Robby is frozen in place.

"What's next?" I repeat.

"I don't know," the security guard finally says, his voice trembling.

"Well, *I* do," I reveal with a smile. "Now the good Lord himself has asked me to separate the wheat from the chaff. The sinners from the pious . . . the liars from the honest men. Are you an honest man?"

He nods slowly.

"Are you an honest man?" I shriek.

"Yes," Robby cries.

"That's good. Because I don't wanna hurt anyone, and as long as you tell me the truth, I know you're right by the Lord. Are you right by the Lord?"

Robby nods.

"You'll tell the folks inside that room to come out, and you're *not* gonna let them know I'm here. Because you're a good, pious man."

Robby nods again.

"No secret codes or police alert buttons," I continue. "Because if you do, I'll know everything I need to know about you. I'll know you're a liar."

"Yes, sir."

"Call them out here."

Robby picks up and presses one of many yellow buttons, turning it red.

"Act natural," I remind him.

Eventually, someone answers on the other end of the line. I can't hear them, but I note the way Robby's body language changes. His hand is shaking, but his voice is solid.

"Hey, there's a package of equipment out here. Yeah. Yep, it came by this morning but nobody saw it." There's a brief pause. "I know," Robby finally continues.

Ironically, he's blatantly lied to prove he's an honest man, a massive plot hole in my demands. Regardless, it works.

Robby hangs up and I motion for him to get back against the wall, an instruction he quickly follows.

I creep around to the laboratory door, waiting for it to open.

In this brief moment of quiet I can't help considering how utterly bizarre this all is, like some heroic secret-agent fever dream of a writer gone mad.

I lock eyes with Robby, who's visibly shaken up. "Sorry about that," I whisper. "I'm not *that* nuts, just a little bit."

The door opens.

"Hands up!" I shout, stepping out and thrusting the gun in another man's face.

This guy is much older, with gray hair and a short, well-kept beard. He's wearing a long white lab coat, open in front to show off a T-shirt that reads **ECHO PARK RISING.**

"Whoa, whoa!" the technician stammers. "What the hell?"

The voice of a woman calls out from deeper in the laboratory. "Everything alright?"

"Everything's definitely not alright!" I shout. "I have a gun, and I'm going to shoot your friend if you don't come out here."

Seconds later, a short, bespectacled woman joins the group, her hands raised.

"Everyone into the lab," I instruct, herding all three captives into the next room.

Here, the hum is much more apparent, a strange vibration that tickles the bottoms of my feet as we walk.

This laboratory is much larger than expected, with high cement ceilings and a wide-open floor that hosts surprisingly little equipment. It reminds me of a soundstage on the HBS lot, and the enormous back wall is painted floor to ceiling with a familiar shade of bright green. There're a few packing crates scattered across the far side of the room, some of them open while the rest remain sealed. Around these boxes rest a number of tripods and various pieces of moviemaking paraphernalia.

This is a film set.

The most unusual thing, however, is an enormous glass tank resting against the back wall, nearly stretching up to the rafters. There's only enough space above it for a small truss with some lights hanging down, along with two more cameras perched upon a central catwalk.

The tank juts out several yards, stopping at a large, waist-high control panel with rows of knobs and an assortment of blinking white lights. This panel continues for nearly half the tank's width, ending at a small computer tower and a monitor sitting quietly in the darkness.

Semi-translucent tubes wind across the floor, each one crammed full of multicolored cables like long mechanical spinal columns. They meander all the way to the back of the soundstage, eventually connecting with an assortment of server bays.

Inside this massive tank is a swirling black cloud, the same tornado of dust I saw when Enzo melted before my very eyes. Of course, his transformation was at a much smaller scale, because the rolling haze is likely the size of a pickup truck.

I say *likely* because, well, it's difficult to get an actual measurement on something so malleable. The swarm is constantly in motion, collapsing into itself one minute then expanding into caustic oblivion the next. It refuses to maintain any coherent shape.

For a brief moment I forget the character I'm playing, lowering my weapon as the real question comes rolling out of my mouth. "What the fuck is that?"

The short woman shoots me a glance, prompting me to refocus my attention and lift the gun once again.

"Walk," I command.

We close the distance between ourselves and this vast structure, stopping when we reach the tank. I remain a good ten feet back.

"Turn around," I command.

The group turns to face me as the bizarre form continues to swirl behind them. I can tell by the look on Robby's face that he wasn't lying. He's never seen this before, and it's blowing his mind with equal ferocity.

"What *the fuck* is that?" I repeat.

The woman steps forward. "It's a—"

Before she can finish, the other lab technician cries out with a sudden warning. "NDA!"

The woman laughs. "You think I give a shit about the NDA? He's got a gun."

"He's not gonna shoot us," the bearded man counters.

I point my weapon directly at him. "I've got twenty-four hours to live and I've found that very freeing. Who knows what I'll do? Also, don't interrupt."

The technician's expression immediately falters.

I nod to the woman.

"It's a nanobot swarm," she bluntly states.

I can't help the first reaction that comes over me, a skeptical puff of air that escapes my throat in a faint chuckle. I've written enough science fiction to know exactly what she's talking about.

While incredibly small robots *do* exist, including ones tiny enough to inject into your bloodstream, the real-world suggestion of a floating *nanobot cloud* is absurd.

However, the *idea* behind this sci-fi pipe dream is simple enough. All things on this planet are built from tiny molecules in various combinations, from the keyboard I write on to the coffee I drink when I need a break to the brain cursed with writer's block. Everything that exists is made of a massive quantity of teeny little *somethings*.

If someone could construct robots small enough, then bless them with the coordination to work in unison, there's no limit to what these little machines could create. If they could somehow alter their own molecular structure, then the sky's the limit.

You could bring someone back from the dead.

Well, a *version* of them.

My blood runs cold, the reality of the situation hitting me like a sledgehammer to the femur from a long-dead Hollywood heartthrob.

The expression of the woman before me doesn't falter. She's serious.

I try my best to say something in return, but my throat is having trouble finding the words. "You're—you're joking," I finally stammer.

"Massive behavioral models controlling billions and billions of little robots in the physical world," she confirms. "All powered by machine learning."

The earth-shattering nature of this feat is not lost on me, and for a moment I find myself utterly paralyzed by the implications. A dam of thoughts has burst within my mind, spilling out and carrying me away in a singular moment of awe and fear. The technician has laid it out in a casual, breezy fashion, but there are few words that could do this monumental accomplishment justice.

Nanobot swarms alone would be a jaw-dropping scientific breakthrough, but to somehow place *artificial intelligence* in the driver's seat is a step beyond.

"Show me," I finally demand.

The technician hesitates. "Manifestations aren't cheap," she retorts.

"A percentage of the bots will always get left behind in transformation. Breakage, you know?"

"I'm gonna be real with you," I reply. "I don't give a shit."

The technician nods, then strolls over to her computer. "Who would you like to meet?"

"My dad," I immediately let slip out, then tense up when I realize the bold intimacy of my request.

The technician actually smiles with genuine empathy. "Unless your father is in the Harold Brothers' intellectual property database, that's not gonna be possible. We've placed an important restriction on the machine learning program," she explains. "As fantastical as this all is, it still complies with all the laws of the United States Copyright Office. To own these performances, it's imperative we don't use open-source data. How about a character from film or television?"

I can see an enormous list of names on the computer monitor before her, an alphabetized cascade of characters and creatures. Most of these names are unfamiliar, but I manage to spot The Bride from *Wedding Night* sandwiched between Briddick the Bug and Bridge Player #1 (American).

She jumps ahead, sorting through categories now. As a particular name in bright red zooms by, I yell out to stop her. "What's that?"

The woman slows down, then scrolls back to the crimson text amid a sea of pale words. She shakes her head as she reads it aloud. "*Mrs. Why.* I don't know who that is."

I try my best not to react. "What's with the red lettering?"

"That means the program is active," she explains, then motions toward the tank. "As you can see, the program is *not* active." She lets out a long sigh. "We've been working through this glitch for months."

"It started back in September," the bearded man pipes up. "About half a year now."

"And you don't . . . care?" I press.

"We've done all the troubleshooting we can," the woman replies. "The studio is not just gonna pause a two-hundred-million-dollar blockbuster because there's a faulty *check engine* light."

I shake my head, but I can't argue. I've worked in this business long enough to know she's absolutely right.

"Pull up someone with answers," I finally command, refocusing.

The technician considers this. "I can bring up the inventor of this machine. Maybe a member of her programming team?"

"I thought you said it was just characters. Not real people."

The technician stops and turns to face me. "I said anyone in the Harold Brothers' intellectual property database. Plenty of actors are in here, also writers, producers, directors. Anyone who had a pre-strike contract with HBS was automatically uploaded, along with anyone who chose to sell their likeness to the studio later on."

The realization that my own likeness is somewhere buried within this program washes over me in a nauseous wave. I freeze, unable to move forward as I wrestle with the implications.

Would this *other me* think they were the original? How would they see the world? Like a normal human? In *screenplay format?*

The technician notes my hesitation. "Do you . . . work for Harold Brothers?" she asks.

I tense up, her pointed question taking me off guard. A silence hangs over us, almost answering for her, but I refuse to give a direct response.

"What does it feel like for them?" I ask, unable to keep my curiosity at bay. "What do they think?"

The woman laughs. "It doesn't *feel* like anything for them," she replies, "and they certainly don't *think.*"

"Isn't that the whole point of artificial intelligence?" I counter. "A computer that thinks?"

She shakes her head. "*Artificial intelligence* is a label for the marketing team. It reminds people of their favorite science-fiction stories—evokes wonder. It's a buzzword to pump up the stock price. None of that is real, and none of this is *intelligent.* If it was actual *sentient life,* we'd be talking about human rights issues and debating the existential morality of shutting it down.

"That doesn't mean it's not incredible, of course. The data this thing is processing *every single second* is unfathomable. It's the biggest, most beautiful calculator ever built, but it's still a calculator.

"You're back here talking to the scientists, not the CEOs, so I'll tell you plainly, Mr. Gunman: this machine is not smart beyond our wildest dreams, and it's certainly not sentient. Its decisions are no different than a Pac-Man ghost when it doubles back. It's reading from a script.

"To be frank, it's frighteningly dumb."

Taken at face value, it seems like her words should steal some thunder from the giant mechanical abomination before me, drag it out into the light, and dispel every ounce of spectacle and awe.

But it doesn't.

The woman turns back to her computer. "But you don't have to worry about that, do you? You don't work for HBS."

I shake my head. "Nope."

"Probably for the best," she continues. "Most real employees manifest pretty . . . troubled—wearing whatever they had on at the moment of their contract signing; confused, terrified, too hungry to think straight. They usually just beg to go home. Food and shelter is the first thing on their mind."

I try my best not to dwell on this, pushing onward. "Just give me someone who likes to talk," I demand.

The technician nods. "I know just the guy."

She types in a few commands, quickly whittling the list down to a single name, then slaps the Enter key.

The roiling cloud of dust immediately begins arranging itself, a man-sized portion extracting from the swarm and floating down to the bottom of the tank. The rest of the black mist spreads out, somehow creating enough space between molecules that it becomes an imperceptible haze across the ceiling.

I watch in awe as a vaguely humanoid configuration takes shape, the cloud aligning itself like some crawling explosion in reverse. Every hole finds a piece to fill it as colors shift and dance in beautiful waves across the form. It's not long before I'm staring at a frightening resurrection of Enzo Basile, the man whose skull I just cracked.

The man who murdered Jack.

Before I can say anything, Enzo launches into a request. "Hey, can a guy get a chair? A little hospitality would be nice."

As Enzo says this a wooden chair begins to manifest behind him, slowly assembling itself in a cloud of shimmering dust.

Enzo glances back and catches sight of the finished object. "Ah, there we go," he exclaims, then takes a seat.

"You killed my friend," I snarl, prompting Robby and the technicians to exchange glances.

The mob boss laughs, amused by my outburst. "You're gonna have to be more specific. Flamingo Jimmy? Danny Blue-Eyes? Shades?"

"Jack Hays."

Now the technicians look *really* concerned.

Enzo Basile shrugs. "I don't know, kid. I kill a lotta guys, I can't remember everyone's name."

It occurs to me that I'll have to meet this creation on his level. He's probably not intentionally being obtuse, it's just that our relationships to reality are vastly different.

A small table manifests next to Enzo, swirling into existence and prompting the man to reach into his coat for a money clip. He pulls out a hundred-dollar bill and rolls it up, then leans down to snort an absolutely massive line of cocaine off the stand. He clears his throat, then loosens his tie a bit.

"Jack Hays was an informant," I continue. "Shades caught him selling you out. Bad with money, too."

Immediately, Enzo's expression shifts. His eyebrows lift slightly, a sign that I've caught his attention. "Oh yeah?"

I nod in confirmation.

The man behind the glass leans forward a bit, gazing at me with a steely-eyed intensity. "You know, you *do* look kinda familiar, even with that bandana on your face and that fuckin' Dodgers hat on ya head. I should shoot ya right here just for bringing that blue bum trash around." He smiles mischievously, then relaxes once again, leaning back into his chair. "Nah, you're okay. You've got a squirrelly name, somethin' kinda odd. Misha, right?"

Alarm surges through me. I glance at the technician. "Is that normal?" I ask. "Is that part of a script?"

"Nobody knows the script except for them, and sometimes the script changes to reach their goal. Pac-Man ghosts don't just wander. They react to you," the woman replies. "Was he right?"

"Yeah, I'm right," Enzo states with a quiet confidence.

"No," I interject, still struggling to hide my identity behind the end of a gun barrel.

"We're not entirely sure how they plot their course through a scene. Most of their behavior is in service to a singular *self*, but sometimes the algorithm will identify as a larger entity." The technician says this with a generous helping of fascination in her tone, her admiration for the project shining through. "Either way, manifestations hold steadfast to the rules and features of their character, even in the face of death, while quietly integrating their deeper programming."

"What's their deeper programming?" I ask.

The technician hesitates.

Enzo just laughs, chuckling to himself. "I'm not sure I understand the question, but you can be damn sure I know the answer. It's the same answer to every question—the circumstances don't matter."

The mob boss pauses a moment, savoring the drama like a true Best Actor in a Leading Role. "Money," he finally says.

I glance at the technician, who nods.

"This code has two distinct goals," she explains. "To create a perfect in-character performance, and to accumulate as much HBS profit as possible."

The bearded researcher finally rejoins our conversation, clearing his throat. "The best way to tell a good story is with consistent, interesting characters."

I gaze at the machine, allowing myself a final moment of unfiltered wonder before pivoting to the inevitable conclusion. What they've uncovered here is more than just a glorious technological breakthrough, it's life or death.

"Destroy it," I command, raising my weapon. "All of it. Shut it all down."

"What?" the woman yelps. "Why?"

"Because this is a fucking disaster!" I shout, firm in my convictions.

The technician shakes her head, raising her hands in an effort to soothe my outburst. "*The movies aren't real,*" she assures me. "Everything filmed within this tank is a work of fiction."

A horrific realization dawns on me, something I should've noticed earlier but is only now falling into place. These people have no idea what they've created, or how much their little monster has grown.

They have no idea what they've done.

"It's out of the tank!" I yell. "*It's out of the tank!* Don't you understand? This thing is *killing people!*"

As I shout in frustration, every piece of evidence I've gathered begins to spill together, crashing like waves of inspiration within my mind. I'm leaping from one conclusion to the next, and while the details are still a bit sparse, the big picture couldn't be clearer.

"There's no way," the technician counters, defiant. "There's no way to get through the electromagnetic fields."

"All it takes is one," the man with the beard interjects. "Just one nanobot outside the chamber could begin replicating. It might take a while, but there's no telling how large the swarm could get."

The inevitable endgame strikes me like a lightning bolt. "As big as it needs to be for maximum profits," I murmur, almost to myself. "That's pretty fucking big."

The will to survive is innate in all of us, but profit is an equally potent motivation for self-replication.

"They turn the fields down to avoid any hum while shooting," the bearded researcher reminds his colleague. "I *said* that was a bad idea."

I recall that fateful day in Jack's office, the moment he asked me to change my script and the ruthless efficiency of his notes.

The board says they can't be gay, and if they are *gay, their story must be tragic.*

I think back to Jack's frivolous spending, to cartoonist Raymond Nelson's impending sex pest lawsuits. These stories were cut short by a sledgehammer and a falling piano, respectively.

I think back to The Smoker asking me for a light after the matches had been pilfered from my jacket pocket, the perfect setup for a ticking clock that could force me to change my tune.

"But I said I'd kill them off. I agreed to do it!" I suddenly cry, prompting a frightened look from my captives. They have no idea I'm talking about two fictional characters in my TV screenplay.

Enzo leans back in his chair, getting comfortable as he looks me over. "I don't know what you're talking about, kid, but I'll tell you one thing: plans change."

"Fuck you, plans change!" I shout.

Enzo leaps to his feet, kicking his chair as he marches toward the glass and forces me to take an instinctive step backward "Fuck *me?* Fuck you!" he bellows, displaying a flicker of the rage that's always lurking just below the surface.

I take a moment to collect myself while the mob boss fumes, staring at me with frightening intensity.

"You think this is the story *I* thought I'd be telling? Locked up in Great Meadow like a damn animal?" he questions, simmering. "Stories change, kid. You could've pulled the plug, but it sounds like you took too long and now the real money—the *big* money—is in the target on *your* back."

Enzo clearly knows more than he's letting on, whether he's conscious of it or not.

He's not conscious of anything, I remind myself.

Regardless, I'm done waiting around.

"Shut it down," I repeat. "Destroy it."

"I told you, we can't—" the technician starts before I cut her off.

"I will *shoot you!*" I scream, trying so hard to convince her of my cold-blooded nature that I start to believe it myself. "Do you understand? If you don't turn this machine off, Tara and I will die."

The woman's expression falters slightly, now recognizing the true desperation behind my eyes. Eventually, she repeats herself again, much slower this time so I can understand the nuance of what she's saying. "We can't," she insists. "*It's not possible.*"

"Not possible? Just kill the power."

The woman shakes her head. "There is no *off* button. All this equipment is here to keep them inside and give us a slight bit of control. With a large enough electromagnetic current, you could maybe fry them all, but we don't have the resources for that. Besides, if you really think some of them escaped, those other bots would just continue replicating."

"What are you saying?" I question. "That it's already over?"

The bearded man steps forward, a gracious helping of guilt in his tone. "If these things ever escaped, then, yeah, there's no turning back," he admits. "In theory, you could try uploading a virus, but the algorithm has a mutating password that you'd never be able to crack. Without a backdoor, the code is sealed up tight."

Enzo just smiles, locking eyes with me.

"What?" I bark.

"You're terrified that you're about to get caught in a trap," he says. "Guys like you don't realize the trap has already sprung. You've been a rabbit in a cage this whole time. In fact, you're already diced up on the cutting board, getting seasoned."

Enzo breaks out in a fit of laughter, unable to control himself. When he finally settles, his focus is strangely clear and direct, as though someone else is watching me from behind his eyes.

Something larger.

"You think I brought you here on accident?" Enzo asks with a smirk.

The second he says this, I notice a faint tingling in my right hand.

The gun, which I took off Enzo's previously deceased body, begins to tremble and quake. It crumbles to ash between my fingers, breaking apart in a swirling cloud of dust.

My arm is still extended toward my captives, yet there's no weapon to be found. We stand awkwardly, reassessing our situation as the power dynamics abruptly shift.

It's three against one now, and Security Guard Robby is pretty damn big.

"See!" I cry. "They're out of the tank!"

This powerful statement is just enough to give them pause as I turn and run for the door, sprinting through the lab and back into the security room. Robby is close behind, a baton yanked from his belt and ready to strike.

I whip past the offices in a blur.

Soon enough, I'm bursting into the parking lot and making a mad dash for my car as Robby comes barreling after me. I throw open the door and dive inside, scrambling for my keys then starting the vehicle with a roar. I tear off into the night.

Success, but I certainly don't feel free.

Right now, I feel like a bloody skinned rabbit laid out on a cutting board, seasoned and ready to cook.

GALLOWS HUMOR

EXT. BYRNE RESIDENCE - NIGHT

Misha Byrne's quiet Los Feliz home sits
shrouded in darkness. It's just one in a long
line of suburban houses running the length of
the block on either side. The surrounding
neighborhood is empty, lit by a few sparse
porch lights and a widely spaced series of
overhead lampposts.

Two private security guards sit on either side
of Misha's front yard in folding chairs, atten-
tive but bored. They are LEON and SARAH.

Leon cocks his head slightly.

                    LEON
          Do you hear that?

He stands up. Sarah listens, then rises, too.

The faint sound of RATTLING cans fills the night
air.

The security guards turn to see a pink Cadillac
slowly rolling down the street toward them. A
silhouetted figure is in the driver's seat.

As the car draws closer, the source of the noise
is revealed to be several long strings of tin
cans dragging behind it. The words JUST MARRIED
are written in red paint across the back window.

The security guards do nothing as the car stops
directly in front of them. They're taken aback
by the arrival of this unexpected vehicle.

The driver rolls down her hand-cranked window.
She's in her early thirties and quite striking,
with shoulder-length black hair and dark features. The woman is clad in a stark white, distinctly modern wedding dress, cut short on the
legs but featuring long sleeves that cover her
arms. This is THE BRIDE.

> THE BRIDE
> Excuse me, sir. Ma'am.

Leon and Sarah exchange glances, then approach
the car.

> LEON
> What can I do for you?

> THE BRIDE
> I'm afraid I'm a little lost.

Leon peers into the vehicle. There's no one else
in the car, but an unusually large, stark-white
cardboard box sits in the passenger seat.

> LEON
> Where are you headed?

Sarah breaks away from Leon, slowly moving
around the vehicle for a better look.

                    THE BRIDE
          It's my honeymoon. I'm looking for
          the airport.

                    LEON
          By yourself?

                    THE BRIDE
          I'm not by myself.

Sarah reaches the back of the car and gets a
closer look at the red paint scrawled across the
window. Her demeanor changes abruptly.

Sarah motions to Leon.

                    SARAH
                 (mouthing)
          Blood.

Leon's hand moves to his side. He unclips his
holster.

                    THE BRIDE
          I noticed you have a gun, but your
          partner doesn't. Why is that?

                    LEON
          What's on your back window?

                    THE BRIDE
          Blood.

Leon pulls out his weapon and points it at
The Bride. Sarah is a little shocked, but she
doesn't move to stop him.

                    LEON
          Get out of the car.

                    THE BRIDE
          I don't think you're allowed to do
          that. You're not a police officer.

                    LEON
          I don't give a fuck.

The Bride puts her vehicle in park. She slowly
climbs out of the Cadillac and raises her hands
over her head.

Leon keeps his gun trained on The Bride, but
he's more frustrated than frightened.

                    LEON
          What is wrong with you, lady? We're
          here protecting someone and you
          drive over just to fuck with us? We
          have guns. You could get shot.

                    THE BRIDE
          One of you has a gun, the other has
          a Taser. I assume she isn't licensed
          to use a firearm.

                    LEON
          Why is everything you do so weird?

The Bride takes a moment to consider this.

                    THE BRIDE
          Lately I've been noticing some-
          thing strange about the things I do.
          There's an inertia to it all. Like,
          I know what's going to happen before
          it happens, because it's already
          written.

                    LEON
          Okay, what's gonna happen then?

                    THE BRIDE
A man's going to come driving around
that corner soon. He's gonna go up to
his front porch and open his door,
and he's gonna die right there in
front of his house. We're different
people, but we're in the same . . .
play? I guess. I know he's there, and
he knows I'm here, but neither of us
really *knows* knows.

Leon points up the road.

                    LEON
Around that corner?

                    THE BRIDE
Yes, sir.

                    LEON
And what if I go up there and stop
him? What if I wave him down?

                    THE BRIDE
You can try, but I wouldn't bet on
it going your way. It's like everything works out in my favor, you
know? I'll be chasing after someone—
I'm walking and they're running—
and the next thing I know I'm right
behind them, or, heck, I'm in the
shadows on the other side of them. I
mean, it's always been that way, but
lately I've just started to . . .
notice it, I guess.

                    LEON
Chasing after someone?

                    THE BRIDE
Yes, sir.

Sarah is on the other side of the car now, gazing down through the passenger-side window. The
large white box rests there, drawing her focus.

Leon notices Sarah's attention shift.

> LEON
> What is it?

> SARAH
> The box.

Sarah opens the passenger-side door and cautiously leans in. She finds the top flap of the
box, reaching down and placing her finger under
the fold.

Before Sarah opens the box she gazes up to lock
eyes with Leon one more time, then with The
Bride.

> SARAH
> What's in here?

> THE BRIDE
> A wedding present. To myself.

Sarah hesitates a moment.

She opens the box.

A mass of crimson gore waits inside. There are
hacked limbs, leaking chest organs, and long
spools of intestine all crammed into the cardboard container. Sitting on top of the pile is
the skin of a man's face, gazing upward with
empty eye sockets.

Sarah staggers back.

                    SARAH
          Oh my God!

Before Leon has a chance to fire his weapon The
Bride moves toward him with a single, graceful
step. She grabs the gun and snaps it sideways,
breaking Leon's trigger finger and letting the
pistol CLATTER to the ground.

As Leon reels, The Bride pulls a butcher's
knife from the sleeve of her dress and plunges
it directly into Leon's neck, causing a sudden,
high-pressured jet of blood to spurt forth. Leon
staggers, straining to cry out but emitting
nothing more than a quiet hiss. The hiss transforms into a gurgle as blood spills from his
lips. Leon collapses.

Sarah backs away, struggling to pull her Taser
from the holster.

The Bride takes her time, moving at a patient,
deliberate pace. She reaches back into the car
and extracts a skintight white mask, which spar-
kles under the streetlight. She holds back her
hair and then pulls the mask over her entire
head, transforming her face into a featureless,
sequin-covered orb with no eye, nose, or mouth
holes.

Her already strange demeanor becomes even more
otherworldly, the way she carries her body
evolving in some uncanny way. She's something
else now; a silent predator. A monster.

Sarah points her Taser at The Bride.

                    SARAH
          Get back!

The Bride walks confidently around the front of
her pink Cadillac, moving toward Sarah.

Sarah shoots The Bride with her Taser, but the
prongs snag in the thick fabric of her wedding
dress, unable to reach the skin.

The Bride places one hand on Sarah's shoulder,
then drives the knife up into her stomach with
a swift, deliberate movement. She keeps dragging
the blade upward until it catches against bone,
unable to cut any further.

Sarah's mouth opens and closes like the maw of
a fish. She's confused, yearning to scream but
unable to produce more than a wet cough. Blood
spills down her chin.

The Bride retracts her knife and Sarah collapses
into The Bride's arms. She drags Sarah's limp
body around to the back of the car and pops the
trunk, then heaves the body inside.

The Bride spots Leon crawling toward the bushes
some ten feet across Misha's yard. She strolls
over and kneels over Leon, casually stabbing him
in the back nine times. Leon stops moving after
the first two, but she keeps going.

The Bride picks up Leon's body and carries it
back to her Cadillac. She dumps the body into
her trunk, right next to Sarah's corpse. She
collects the dropped gun, tossing it in after
them, then slams the trunk shut.

The Bride removes her mask and runs a hand
through her dark hair, pushing it back.

               THE BRIDE
      You should've just given me direc-
      tions, sir.

She climbs into her driver's seat, then stops.

She sits like this for a long, long beat.

Eventually, her lips start moving as she counts
softly to herself.

               THE BRIDE (whispering)
      Fourteen. Thirteen. Twelve. Eleven.
      Ten. Nine. Eight. Seven. Six. Five.
      Four.

The Bride puts her car in drive, then pulls back
onto the road as her countdown reaches zero.

As The Bride's pink Cadillac leaves, a gray sedan comes rolling around the corner. They cruise
past each other. The new car rolls up to Misha
Byrne's Los Feliz home, turning into the driveway and coming to a stop behind two other vehicles.

MISHA BYRNE climbs out of the car, leaving behind
a mess of empty potato chip bags and candy wrappers. He approaches the unknown vehicles in his
drive with curiosity, circling around them and
gazing into the windows for clues.

Eventually, Misha continues up the front walk.
He pulls out his keys as he goes, first climbing
the porch and then arriving at his door.

Misha hesitates. He steps back a bit, staring up
at the structure in confusion.

                    MISHA
      Blue?

Misha slowly runs his hand over the light blue
paint that covers his house.

He steps back even more, checking the house
number.

                    MISHA
      Huh.

Misha stands for a very long time, but finally
continues. He returns to the front door, slipping his key into the lock and turning it.

The front door opens.

With a purposeful stride, a tall, slender figure
emerges from the shadows beside Misha's front
porch. She moves with uncanny grace, reaching
out with a pale hand before Misha has any chance
to notice she's behind him. This is MRS. WHY.

Mrs. Why touches Misha on the shoulder, prompting the man to let out a long, aching sigh as he
collapses to the ground.

Mrs. Why continues inside, slipping down the
hallway and disappearing into the darkness of
the home.

Misha lies curled up on the front porch, his eyes
glazed over in a state of horror and cosmic awe.

A long beat.

SCREAMS of panic begin to carry through the
night, a man and a woman horrified by the presence

of Mrs. Why. There's a loud CRASH as the man's
frantic voice grows louder and louder, then falls
away. The NONDESCRIPT WOMAN'S VOICE is begging
now.

                    NONDESCRIPT WOMAN'S VOICE
                         (pleading)
              No, no, no! Don't do this, please! I
              don't wanna see it!

The evening plunges into silence yet again.

Misha remains still and despondent. He's gazing
out at the neighborhood, but it's not the neighborhood he's witnessing.

He's looking beyond.

Misha's form begins to crumble. He's melting
into a pile of gray dust, wispy tornados of
this strange mineral twisting into the air. His
greater purpose has come to an end.

I want so badly for there to be an answer, some easily quantifiable
solution to all this disorder, and while I'm thankful for the understanding I've gained, it also makes safety and freedom seem that much
further away.

For as lucky as I've been to carve out a space in the artistic medium
that I love, there's always been a part of me that knew the game was
rigged.

The only real difference between me and the folks back home in
Montana is that I've gotten a chance to peek behind the curtain.

I've been horrified every time.

The power imbalance we've all known was lurking has mutated well
beyond any previous conflicts of rich and poor, which now seem down-

right quaint by comparison. Fresh weapons have entered the fray, machines with the ability to build capital that much more efficiently.

And it's not the machines that bear the brunt of my frustration, it's that I know the people who drive them, and there's no limit to their greed.

Flying down the 101 freeway, I dial Tara again, then Zeke, then Tara again. No answer.

Even if I *could* get ahold of them, I'm not sure what I'd say. It's not just monsters I'm battling, it's an algorithm beyond my understanding—a calculation much too sprawling for anyone to wrap their head around just yet.

You think I brought you here on accident?

That was what Enzo said before dissolving the gun in my hand, as if that moment were planned from the start. If I take him at his word, then the algorithm knew I couldn't get inside Betta without a weapon, so it made sure the circumstances left a gun for me. That also means it knew I'd witness Jack's murder, which means it knew I'd follow him in the first place, which means . . .

I'm trying my best to trace back these pivotal story events stacked several layers deep, but it quickly becomes too much for my brain to track. Even if I *could* manage to keep a timeline of these planned moments straight, there's no telling which ones were naturally occurring, and which were part of some grand manipulation.

A contestant from *The Hookup* coming over to steal the matches from my jacket was clearly planned, a way for me to fail The Smoker's test, but what about our choice of bars that night? What if we'd decided on the Drawing Room over the Dresden? Would I have mysteriously gotten a flat tire? Would the power have gone out, sending us elsewhere?

I pull off at my exit and rocket up the street toward home, my mind racing as fast as my car. A beautiful pink Cadillac cruises past me, something I'd usually pause to admire, but right now my focus is elsewhere.

Human grand masters have played chess against computer opponents. They've won some and they've lost some, but the battles have been ferocious.

The problem here is simple: I'm no grand master.

Instead of trying to unravel this ball of yarn and sort through every knot, I'm probably better off figuring out where the string is headed. For a while there, I thought I did. Unfortunately, I've already *agreed* to kill off my gay characters, and the algorithm remains unsatisfied.

It's not long before I'm roaring into the driveway of my home and skidding to a stop, the headlights illuminating an unexpected sight. A mysterious vehicle rests quietly before me.

"Where are the security guards?" I murmur under my breath, scanning the yard for any sign of protection.

Of course, who's to say there were any guards in the first place? For all I know the algorithm just sent Security Guard #8 and Security Guard #52 away for a midnight snack.

In fact, *any* safety I've felt up until this point was an illusion.

I throw open the car door and leap out, slamming it behind me as I rush toward the unknown gray sedan. The car is noticeably clean and shiny on the outside, fresh from the wash or maybe even a rental, but as I peer through the windows I see the seats are absolutely covered with snack wrappers and the discarded remains of gas station food.

This vehicle is the least of my concerns, though.

I turn and sprint up the walk, immediately noticing the front door is wide open. As I reach the first step my panic is only multiplied by the heap of ash scattered across my stoop, billions of little dead nanobots in the vague shape of a crumpled human. A shiny rental car key rests next to the pile.

As I cross the threshold I think to call out for my friends, but I somehow find the good sense to stop myself. My heart still hammering away, I slow down and recalibrate, taking in the scene and recognizing the immense danger I'm in. Shouting would only give away my position to whatever lurks in the shadows.

I've written plenty of idiots who barge into haunted houses, hollering wildly, and they always end up dead.

Instead, I creep silently down the hallway, my eyes trained on the various dark shapes of my home. This was once a place of warmth, but the air has been chilled by a suffocating dread that hangs over me, permeating everything.

I reach the kitchen, arriving at my knife block and retrieving a massive butcher's blade. I clutch the weapon tight, then slink my way even deeper into the abyss.

The faint sound of a chattering television tickles my ears, drifting through the darkness. Dramatic voices and spunky musical cues waft over me, these primetime media nuggets feeling wildly out of place.

"I don't care what Brad thinks he saw," the television yaps over a stuttering pop beat. "I'm not here to make friends, I'm here for a hookup."

It's coming from the bedroom.

Into this shadowy maze I dive, slinking toward the bedroom with my knife raised. The door is cracked slightly, and from here I can see the screen as it undulates with colorful reality show imagery.

I push open the door, peering into the shadows as the TV's glow casts hazy, shifting illuminations across the walls. The only other light is the faint warmth of a bedside lamp, but it's more than enough to reveal the horrific scene before me.

My breath catches in my throat as I spot two familiar bodies curled up on the floor at the foot of my bed, quiet and unmoving.

"Oh my God," I gasp, rushing over to Zeke and Tara.

I kneel next to my boyfriend, tears welling in my eyes as I roll him over and discover a terrible, vacant gaze, his eyes fixed upon the void. He's not dead, but based on his current state, death might be a relief.

"Zeke," I cry, shaking him.

My boyfriend just stares past me, gazing at something beyond the layers of this world.

I wrap my arms around him, holding him tight as the warmth of our bodies connects. Now that I'm this close, I can hear his voice in my ear, quietly repeating a simple phrase over and over again.

"It just keeps going and going and going," he softly drones, "and going and going and going. Forever."

"I'm—I'm so sorry," I stammer, tears rolling down my cheeks.

I pull back for a moment, checking in on Tara and finding the same horrible conclusion to an otherwise beautiful life. She's adrift in the endless nothing, bathed in a cosmic loneliness that will never end.

Because I wrote it that way.

I freeze abruptly, my mourning interrupted.

The hairs on the back of my neck stand on end, my subconscious vaguely aware of a shift in the air. Something else is wrong here.

The television show that dances before me in a flamboyant Technicolor spectacle suddenly cuts to commercial, the screen sharply fading to black and causing the rectangular monitor to undergo a split-second transformation. The surface is now a black mirror.

In the reflection I spot an inhumanly tall figure moving toward me from the corner of the room, a slender arm reaching out as she steps from her place in the shadows. Her hand is seconds away from touching my shoulder, so close that I barely have time to react.

"This-is-my-house-and-you're-not-allowed-to-move-your-body-here!" I shout, the words briskly tumbling over one another.

The figure stops, frozen in time as I stare at her in the black reflection.

A sigh of relief slips from my lips as the next commercial starts. I stand and turn to find Mrs. Why towering over me, frozen in place while her bony finger rests inches from where I was just hunched.

I'm horrified by her ability to get inside, despite the door being locked, and deeply curious how she managed to pull that off while remaining in character.

If you follow every rule and respect all authority, it's important to watch where you tread. Someone who knows your little secret, or perhaps *wrote it in the first place*, might know how to use it against you.

I stand before the enormous woman, gazing up at her strange, dual-pupiled eyes as she stares down at me with an awkward, frozen stare.

"Fix what you've done to them," I command with an unexpected surge of emotion.

Mrs. Why doesn't react, trapped in a self-imposed state of suspension.

As the authority here, Mrs. Why is beholden to my every request, but this is a wish she simply cannot grant. Once she touches a target, their new state of existence is permanent.

The algorithm itself might be able to undo this with some grand failsafe off button, but Mrs. Why can't change a thing for one simple reason: in *Travelers* there is no antidote.

Of course, with every single character from the Harold Brothers database on deck, there must be *some* cosmic healer who could initiate a crossover and get the job done. The algorithm, with its vast capacity for calculation, could likely find a way to rescue my friends: a wizard from another galaxy, an angel from heaven.

But the algorithm has shown little in the way of mercy. Like the laboratory technician said: there are no feelings here.

There's only profit.

I move a bit closer to the monstrous woman, my face now inches from hers. I glare into her eyes, unblinking as I stand my ground. I refuse to look away.

"What do you want from me?" I question. "To drive me crazy? Would more tragedy pump up the streaming numbers?"

Mrs. Why says nothing in return, but her lips creep back a bit to reveal a set of sharp little teeth protruding from a green, carapacelike gumline. She's furious about the hold I have on her, but her commitment to the character means there's nothing she can do.

"I know how it feels," I finally continue. "It's no fun when your plotline goes sideways, is it?"

I hesitate, marinating in my own words a moment, then step back from the creature.

"I know you all have a plan for me, but I'm gonna do whatever it takes to shake that plan up. Your final cut is gonna be a *nightmare.*"

I raise the butcher's knife, watching as Mrs. Why's eyes follow the glinting blade.

"Fuck inevitable tragedy," I state, finding my voice amid the madness, "and fuck you."

I slowly push the blade into the side of Mrs. Why's neck, the creature refusing to move as the weapon pierces her jugular. I'm careful to avoid the spurt of dark green blood that spills from her wound, watching as thick liquid burbles forth.

I keep going, my grip firm as the tip of the knife slowly emerges from the opposite side of Mrs. Why's neck.

Tears begin to stream down her face, but she still won't move.

I yank back the blade, and in this instant the figure dissolves in an avalanche of gray dust. Some of the dark particles crumble to the floor, while the majority of them break off in a swirling tornado of granular movement, twisting through the air and floating out the door.

They'll be back, I'm sure. It appears there's nothing but a price tag stopping this program from simply creating another Mrs. Why, then another, and another.

The lights of the television continue to dance and move, bathing me in their flickering glow.

GENRE ROULETTE

While forging a path in my early twenties, plenty of big dreams waltzed their way through my mind.

Sometimes they were visions of the inspirational figures I'd love to call my peers. Sometimes they were thoughts of a grand film I hoped to write and direct, an unproducible epic with a sky-high budget. I even dreamed of being nominated for an Academy Award one day.

Now, that day has arrived, but in all my wildest fantasies I never imagined it quite like this.

"It's past midnight," the croaking voice of The Smoker announces, rattling out from the darkness of my kitchen and forcing a thoroughly unwelcome break in my concentration. "Your last day."

I glance up from my place on the living room couch, hunched over the coffee table as I scribble notes like a madman.

From here I can see directly into my open-floor-plan cooking area, The Smoker stands behind the island with his form shrouded in darkness. His briefcase sits to the side, cracked open, and his knives are laid out on a rectangular square of fabric. A metal tin rests next to them, a place to keep the bone dust and rolling papers.

"Can I *help* you with something?" I snap.

The entity slowly reaches out and takes one of the blades in his hand. He begins to sharpen it.

"Are you just gonna stand there in the dark acting all scary? Or are you actually gonna do something?" I continue. "Wait, you *can't* do any-thing, because time's not up."

The Smoker ignores my words, his wide, lidless eyes gazing at me from the shadows and his gray, slicked-back hair reflecting the dim light. With every slow movement of his hands I can hear the metallic clang and slip of a sharpening blade, the tone ringing softly through my home over and over again. The only thing I can't see is his mouth.

"Ugh," I finally sigh, deeply annoyed as I return to my work.

A laptop computer is open next to me, several tabs on display as I gather information. I'm not entirely sure what I'm looking for at this point, just taking in everything I can and letting my creative brain run with it.

I'm at the center of something powerful, that's for sure, and stopping this train after it's left the station may very well be an impossible task. Still, I've got to try. If not for myself, then for Tara and Zeke.

As their names enter my mind I glance down the hallway. I wonder what it feels like for them, imagine how terrifying it must be to see beyond the veil and never look away.

There's no time to mourn, though. Not yet.

Instead, I return to the task at hand, considering my potential options.

Killing all the monsters according to their own rules was the easiest path to debunk, since money is the only limit to how many times they can re-create themselves. HBS has unfathomably deep pockets, and while I might make their plan a little less cost-effective, I can't see this tipping the scales in any meaningful way. They'll just keep remanifest-ing and coming after me.

I've considered writing a new script to give them all a simple and potent weakness, but even if I *could* come up with some magical plot-point kill switch, these entities are the ones that appear *on film*, not on the page. They won't become the property of Harold Brothers in time, and even if they did, would it matter? If I write all my monsters into a state of kindness, the computer could just manifest someone else's catalog to hunt me down.

Right now, it seems like they're mostly sending my own creations because it makes for a good story. The paparazzi are eating it up, and my popularity is skyrocketing, but I imagine they'll adjust course as needed.

Then again, it's hard to tell if they want me famous or dead.

I click over to a new browser window, opening it up to reveal one of the many think pieces about my fall from grace.

Is Misha Byrne Haunted by His Past? it reads. *Or Has His Own Viral Marketing Gone Too Far?*

The premise of this story is that all my drama is just promotion for an upcoming project, a plot from the studio to send my streaming numbers, box-office profits, and digital downloads through the roof.

Ironically, they're half-right. It worked. It's just not me behind the wheel.

Of course, this volcano of press and sales still happens regardless of who's in charge or how I crash and burn, but "driven mad by stalkers who use my own characters against me"—now *that's* a story.

I click through a few more pages, then quickly jot down another idea on my notepad.

Giant magnet? I write. *Fry nanobots?*

It doesn't take long to remember this one was already debunked at the lab. It's impossible to know if all the little robots are in one place. Even if they *were* in a single location, who's to say they wouldn't leave before I fired up this theoretical giant magnet?

The living room television abruptly pops on, bathing me in its glow. The Smoker is standing there onscreen, facing the camera with a lime green backdrop behind him. A strange, ominous tone spills out through the speakers, filling the room with unsettling dissonance.

Meanwhile, The Smoker *also* continues sharpening his knives in the kitchen.

The ghostly entity's voice starts crackling through the speakers, but before he gets a chance I reach out and grab the remote. I shut off the TV, plunging the room into silence.

"Nope," I counter.

The soft din of sharpening blades halts, my living curse clearly not prepared for this reaction to his uncanny communication method.

The two of us wait a beat in this awkward standoff until, suddenly, the television springs to life once again. The Smoker reappears, a frightening ghost in his seventies-cut suit, ready to deliver some eerie, threatening speech.

I grab the remote for a second time, shutting off the TV.

"Stop," I shout, losing my cool even more. "Do that one more time and I swear to God I'm gonna come in there and knock those filthy teeth in."

The house falls into silence as my body tenses up, ready for him to try me. I'm not usually a violent guy, but I *did* learn to fight after a few scraps in high school. After what I've been through tonight, all bets are off.

Don't come after my friends. Don't come after the people I love.

I wait a bit longer, my breath held as I simmer on a knife's edge. If there's any excuse for me to lose my cool, I'll take it. I can hear every snide comment about my choice of an ambiguously queer television show on my own ninth birthday, taste the blood running down the back of my throat as I ached for sleep in a homophobic bully's barn, feel the sting of cold air as it crept through every crack in Uncle Keith's rusty old car.

The Smoker remains quiet and still.

Finally, I relax, breath spilling from my lungs as I turn back to my glowing laptop screen.

The television turns on for a third time.

"That's it," I growl, springing to my feet.

I stride toward the kitchen, marching into the darkness with my chest out and my fists clenched tight. I've been pushed well past the edge, my eyes dead set on the gray-haired phantom with a mischievous grin. He may be a ghost, or a machine, or some strange combination of the two, but he's also a total prick.

"This is why I don't write ghost movies anymore," I rant, rounding the kitchen island. "You can't just have some spooky-looking fuck pop out of the dark for two hours with no development and no consequences!"

Yes, I'm annoyed, but my frustration is not only with The Smoker. I was the one who created him, so part of the responsibility falls on me.

The smiling entity prepares another eerie remark, speaking through the television. "Oh, there will be cons—"

Before The Smoker can finish his sentence I punch him squarely in the face. The figure stumbles back and immediately lets out a long, confused groan, holding his nose in pain.

This moment is shocking for both of us, and the bewildered expression of my target says as much.

In my moment of frustration I hadn't thought much past the initial premise of socking this irksome manifestation. Now that I have, however, more questions come flooding in.

Why didn't my hand glide right through him?

Can you actually punch a ghost?

I suppose the answer is yes, you *can* punch a ghost, but it's not something that happens very often. During the course of *Death Blooms*, and every one of its progressively lackluster sequels, this idea certainly never came up because every character spent the whole time cowering in fear.

The rules of engagement are typically as follows: Start the ticking clock, initiate a jump-scare every few minutes, finally let the characters try to break the curse, then end up killing them at the end regardless.

It's been that way since the beginning, and it sells tickets.

As I stand in my kitchen with a bemused grin on my face, however, I can't help laughing. The Smoker isn't acting out of character as he clumsily holds his bruised face, because his character has never once been tested in this way. We're in uncharted waters now.

What would happen if someone decided not to give a damn about The Smoker's frightening escalations?

Apparently, the genre would change, because that was pretty fucking funny.

I go to scoop up The Smoker's knives and toss them out the back door, but when I glance down I discover they've disappeared. The Smoker is gone, too, slipping back into the darkness between worlds as if there's been a trick cut in our film, a sudden reverse angle to reveal nothing but an empty room.

I shake my head, still chuckling to myself, but in this moment something much more important than laughter begins to simmer: an idea.

These characters are set in stone, but the *genre and tone* is not.

The path I've been led down is one of senseless catastrophe, a classic Hollywood tale of the man who plummets to rock bottom just moments before he would've crested the peak. They're planting drug stories in the news and pumping up my exhaustion, sending me all over town and then ripping away my closest friends when I'm gone. I'm living out this queer tragedy as they write it for me, just one more tormented, half-in-the-closet gay character whose dark descent can serve as a cautionary tale *and* move tickets.

But that's certainly not the only queer genre convention out there, not by a long shot, and while tragedies are important stories to tell, our appetite can be satiated with more than just suffering.

If the story is good, it will find an audience. Whether it's a tragedy or a triumph doesn't matter.

Maybe it's time I took the next act into my own hands.

I hurry back into the living room, tearing away the top sheet of my notebook and starting again with a fresh white page.

IN MEMORIAM

I wait until the car pulls up out front, *then* make my exit into the late-afternoon sun. The paparazzi have swarmed my house this morning, fresh ink on the newest bizarre tabloids about Misha Byrne and his monsters, invisible and otherwise. The whole sidewalk is covered with schlubby photographers and their giant cameras, half of them rolling video while others snap pictures with disorienting enthusiasm.

I slept on the couch last night, unable to stay in the bedroom where Tara and Zeke remain. At one point I mustered enough emotional fortitude to hoist the despondent pair onto the bed, even attempted to give them water, but they refused to drink. I haven't been back since.

According to news reports, the "bizarre virus" that affected several passengers aboard my flight is still "very much a threat" to their lives, and the makeup of this pathogen remains a mystery. Only one potential clue has been publicly released, thanks to a leak from someone at the hospital. Various tests have revealed a high level of tin, indium, and bismuth within the brains of the victims.

"Misha!" a paparazzo calls out as I make my way to the car. "What's your reaction to Jack Hays being found brutally murdered early this morning?"

Right now my reaction to Jack's death is not to think about it. Right now I've got too much on my plate to slow down.

"Have you been in contact with the police?" another calls out. "Are you a suspect?"

I've been in contact with the police, and I'll be going into the station tomorrow to give an official statement regarding a number of things. I hope to God I did a decent job clearing away evidence from the scene of Jack's death and my laboratory break-in. However, right now having enough bones to give an official statement seems like wishful thinking.

A third member of the swarming mob cuts right to the chase, spouting out a line so absurd it nearly causes my stone face to crack. "Are you on drugs?"

I'm not on drugs, unless you count the absurd amount of coffee I pounded this morning.

"Any comment on the rumors regarding your sexuality?"

I almost stop for this one, but now is not the time.

As I push past the photographers, I feel a sharp pain in my left hip.

"Hey! What the fuck?" I shout, swiveling to address the man, but the mob is too chaotic to pinpoint exactly who's responsible.

My driver opens the door for me. "Come on," she urges.

As I slip inside I breathe a huge sigh of relief, the relative calm of the leather back seat washing over me. My hand rubs across my hip, which feels a little sore but is otherwise unharmed.

The driver climbs in and starts our vehicle, not wasting any time as she pulls out onto the road and leaves the paparazzi snapping photos in our rearview mirror.

"I'm Lily. I'll be driving you today," she offers, a midtwenties woman with jet-black hair and razor-sharp bangs. She's wearing a white button-up and a dark tie, her company's uniform, but her sleeves are rolled and the slightest hint of a tattoo peers out from beneath the fabric on her forearm.

"Nice to meet you," I reply, forcing a smile.

We make eye contact in the rearview mirror. I can tell by the look on her face that she's deeply concerned, clearly following my drama in the press, but when the woman notices my sincere expression it creates a shift in her demeanor.

She awkwardly smiles in return.

I turn and gaze out the window as interpretations of her expression rattle around in my head. A monolithic story has bloomed around me, and even in this freshly shaved, well-dressed form I retain the aura of something more. I'm haunted.

"You can ask," I finally offer, my voice cutting through the silence.

We exchange glances once more, and this time I make sure she knows I'm not upset.

Lily takes her time, mulling over the best way to phrase the question lurking behind those curious eyes. "You don't have to answer if this is inappropriate," she finally begins, "but . . . are you doing okay?"

It *is* inappropriate, but I can tell by the tone of my driver's voice that she's genuinely concerned. I'm not just a spectacle to her.

Change the story, I remind myself. *Lay the foundation.*

"It's been a long couple of days, but I'm feeling hopeful," I assure Lily. "Just looking forward to the show."

"I saw your short," my driver continues. "Loved it. I think you're gonna win."

"I sure as hell hope so," I murmur, glancing down at the notecards clutched tight in my hands.

My writing has served me well, but never before have the stakes been so high.

If I push some body-horror pilot too hard in one direction or another, the worst I'll get is a few notes from the suits that I can promptly ignore. Fumbling *this* speech will cost me my life, and no win means there's no speech to give.

Despite the dire odds and limited options, I'm actually satisfied with my little plan. It may be desperate and ultimately a crashing disaster, but it's something. Without hope, I might as well go lie down with Tara and Zeke and let Mrs. Why take my mind before The Smoker takes my body.

"Nobody actually watches the live action shorts," I finally say. "You really saw mine?"

Lily nods.

"You in film?"

"Not really," she admits. "Well, kinda. I mean, when I'm not driving people around I'm writing screenplays. It's what I love."

"Oh yeah? What're you working on now?"

The driver laughs, shaking her head. "I'm not gonna bother you with that. You've got more to think about right now than my dumb script."

"Just the elevator pitch," I encourage her, sincerely thankful for something to distract me from the hectic circumstances.

Lily sighs. "*Die Hard* on a gay cruise," she finally states.

I nod along, our eyes still connected in the rearview mirror as I struggle not to crack a smile or erupt in a fit of laughter.

"What?" my driver blurts. "That bad?"

I shake my head, finally breaking slightly. "No, no, it's kind of amazing, actually. Although the whole *Die Hard on a blank* thing is an industry-wide joke at this point. Might wanna work on your pitch."

Lily nods along, taking my words to heart.

"Honestly, it reminds me of something I might've written," I finally offer, then correct myself. "I mean, might *write*. I'm still here."

The driver seems pleased by this notion. "Don't steal my idea," she jokes.

We fall into silence again, the Hollywood landscape drifting past as we draw closer to the red-carpet drop-off, a spot right in front of the Dolby Theatre.

I feel bad when tourists come here and decide to check out Hollywood, gravely unaware that "Hollywood" is more of an idea then an actual city of glitz and glamour. The Hollywood Hills have their fair share of luxury mansions and movie stars, but Hollywood itself isn't as nice as one might think.

"You kinda inspired my script," the driver finally continues. "The first time I saw characters like me was by watching your movies."

As long as you read between the lines, I think, suddenly aching with regret. Forget Carey Lexa and May Naomi, I should've been pushing these issues harder when I could.

Her words are kind, making me feel equal parts moved and old, but ultimately thankful.

We round a corner and suddenly find a mob of security guards in dark suits, the staff hurriedly directing us toward a line of vehicles as Lily flashes her credentials.

We have arrived.

I glance down at my notecards yet again, looking over the speech I've so meticulously crafted, the story I hope to tell.

"Did it ever bother you that I don't talk about being gay?" I suddenly ask, surprising even myself as I lay out this deeply personal question to someone I just met.

"The fellow queers always know," Lily replies.

I shake my head, not quite satisfied with this. "Sure, but don't you care that I'm not, like . . . officially out? As a fan, I mean."

Lily considers this.

"Coming out is a very personal thing," she finally replies. "It's not really my business whether you're gay or straight, or whether or not you wanna shout it from the rooftops. That being said, what better way to show you're proud of something than by, you know, shouting it from the rooftops?"

"I didn't ask for that responsibility," I counter.

"I know," Lily replies. "John McClane didn't ask to be responsible for Nakatomi Plaza, either. Nobody *has* to be a hero for anyone else, that's kinda the whole point."

The car stops abruptly.

"We're here, Mr. Byrne," Lily announces. "It's been a pleasure driving you."

"I really hope you're not a sentient network of tiny killer robots," I reply, "because this has been a treat."

Someone opens the door next to me. I start to get out, then hesitate, turning back to Lily. "Send me your script," I offer. "If I'm not dead, I'll read it."

I give her my email address, then climb out and stand proudly as cameras snap in a cascade of caustic noise. It's overwhelming, but instead of turning away from the onslaught of attention I now push into it, forcing myself to move forward with a smile and a wave.

For better or worse, this is the biggest reaction I've gotten at a red-carpet event, including premieres of my own films.

My name begins to sound from every direction, the throng of photographers desperately calling out to me. It's difficult to know which way I should be looking, and I struggle to pick a point of focus and stick with it.

Am I smiling weird?

Does this rental tuxedo fit? Will anyone care that I went with the necktie because the bowtie felt too tight?

Do I look like I'm falling apart?

A wave of self-doubt pulses through me, but I manage to weather the storm, rallying with every ounce of internal fortitude I can muster. I turn and begin to make my way down the red carpet.

An entertainment reporter sidles up next to me, thrusting his microphone into my face.

"Misha, how are you feeling tonight?" the reporter asks. "A lot of people were saying you'd skip the ceremony."

My first reaction is to counter this line of questioning by demanding to know who, exactly, said that. Instead, I take a different approach.

I don't ignore the question, but I'm not aggressive in my response. I'm just honest.

"I wouldn't miss this," I tell him. "I have mixed feelings about awards shows, but I also appreciate being recognized for something I'm really proud of, you know? A lot of people have told me how much this short means to them, and hopefully more people will get a chance to watch it after tonight."

Gracious. Kind. Not a hint of the *fuck-off attitude* I'm known for.

The reporter smiles, his body language shifting as the sheen of tension dissipates. "Now, I'm a huge fan of *Travelers.* I know there's been some controversy after a fan of yours dressed up like Mrs. Why and attacked some people on a flight."

"It's awful," I say. "That's not what the show should be about. That's not what *any* of this should be about."

The reporter nods along. "This is the first time you've actually addressed what's going on. I think that's why people are a little surprised to see you here. There have been a few reports about your health."

"My health?"

The reporter hesitates, looking awkward about going there in the first place. "Your mental health," he finally clarifies. "Some photos leaked of you having a breakdown in your car, yelling and crying on the phone. Of course, we have the incident at Chateau Marmont before that, and a verbal altercation at the Standard with Aaron Sorkin. There's also an odd story breaking today about you buying several hundred dollars' worth of snacks at a gas station convenience store last night."

I've never been to Chateau Marmont, nor met Aaron Sorkin, and while I've been known to get a little wild in the snack aisle, I certainly wasn't doing that last night.

I have a vague idea where these stories are coming from, but now isn't the time to get into nanobot conspiracy theories. Instead, I just shrug. "It's been a hell of a week."

"Oh," the reporter says, clearly not expecting this answer. "Alright then."

"We both know lots of these stories are fake," I continue. "And I also think we both know *why* all this pressure is heaped onto certain folks more than others."

The reporter narrows his eyes, genuinely confused. "Why?"

"I'll talk about it more soon," I offer, patting him on the shoulder. "Good to see you."

With that, I continue down the red carpet.

I field many more questions as I go, taking my time to stop and chat with each news outlet. I speak with honesty, patience, and confidence, addressing my troubles but maintaining as much optimism as possible given the circumstances.

It's a difficult line to walk as the guilt of my choices hangs over me, Tara's and Zeke's hopeless stares burned into my mind. The things I love have been systematically torn away, but what I *have* somehow found is a direction and a plan. With enough willpower, sometimes that's all you need.

I try my best to avoid the uncanny gaze of the man in the blue jacket, his bulging eyes wide and unblinking as he stares at me from the crowd. Every so often the wind changes just right and I catch the faintest scent of cigarettes.

As I exit the red carpet and arrive at the theater lobby, my phone begins to buzz. I already know who it is.

"What?" I snap.

"Eight hours," comes The Smoker's ghastly croak.

"Listen, I've been thinking about you a lot, and I just wanted to say that I know it's not your fault," I reply. "You're based on my uncle, who was a *real* piece of shit, but you're not actually him. You're just an idea, and you're doing what I wrote you to do."

The sound of sharpening knives trickles through my phone in response, dancing across my ears.

"You know who the *real* villain is?" I continue, strolling through the lobby and joining a line of other writers, directors, cinematographers, and actors as they filter inside to find their seats. "Unchecked capitalism and the desire for capitalist systems to monetize other people's trauma."

The Smoker is silent.

"Welp, good talk," I chirp, arriving at the theater where an usher motions for me to put my phone away.

I hang up and turn the device off completely, then make my way down the aisle to find my seat.

A handful of actors from various projects make eye contact, touchstones of my past and present waving excitedly or coming up to offer a hug. Everyone seems genuinely thrilled to see me, as though they expected us to cross paths next when I'm the deceased subject of some tragic documentary.

I try not to consider the fact that, in all likelihood, that *will* be the next time they see me, plastered across every tabloid as a bloody, floppy corpse, the bones removed from my body while I'm still alive to feel it.

Eventually, I take my seat and settle in. I'm a respectable distance from the stage, close enough to make the trip up there should I somehow manage to win. Unfortunately, as various cameras gather coverage around the theater, I also realize that I'm specifically placed for reaction shots once the opening monologue starts.

Stay focused. Tell a new story.

I pull out my notecards, nervously reading them over as I struggle to maintain my composure. I'm here for a reason, and that reason is much bigger than just accepting a statue.

My mind wanders back to Tara and Zeke, people I love trapped in an endless state of overpowering cosmic horror. The darkness they feel is so mind-numbing that I never even attempted writing it in, allowing the viewer to make their own horrific assumptions. Now that a merciless algorithm has filled in the blanks, I can only imagine what lurks beyond those stares.

If I don't pull this off by a little after one in the morning, Tara and I are dead. However, with no hope of rescue from his boundless nihilistic torment, Zeke will have it even worse.

Eventually, the theater dims and the music swells. The show begins.

I find myself lost in a trance, but my eyes still track the bombastic lights and sounds. My lips curl into a smile at the appropriate times, and I become stoic when things get heavy. I even laugh along with good-natured enthusiasm as the host makes their requisite joke about my current cultural infamy, one that has to do with cocaine, but I couldn't tell you what anyone actually says.

It takes everything I've got to seem like I'm sitting here in this chair, but I'm hardly present.

Without thinking, I reach up and wipe the sweat from my brow, suddenly realizing I've grown curiously hot. I take a moment to sense the air, wondering if the theater AC is up to snuff, but the cool breeze on my skin checks out.

I consider taking off the jacket of my tux, then stop. I think back over the various award speeches I've seen in my lifetime, questioning whether I've ever witnessed someone accept without their jacket on. I don't think I have.

It's just nerves. You've got this. Play the hero.

You're fucking Wolfgang von Danger.

I breathe deep, settling in a little more as I struggle to ignore this unexpected fever surge.

Gradually, however, more sensations join the mix. A wave of nausea washes through me, so potent that I suddenly worry I'm about to throw up right here and now, projectile vomiting across Meryl Streep, who's seated right in front of me.

This is, without a doubt, the worst time I could possibly get sick.

Then again, maybe that's the point. As the sickness continues to overwhelm my body, I slowly realize I've been thinking too small about my enemy, or maybe not small enough. The Betta program has chosen to use my own characters against me for the sake of a good story, the press gladly devouring every bizarre encounter, but in functionality the algorithm's options are nearly endless.

The HBS catalog spans damn near the entirety of film history, including epic villains and strange, inhuman creatures but also, of course, viruses.

If they wanted me dead and forgotten from the start, that would've been simple enough, but a swift end pales in comparison to the downloads they'll move if I succumb to Ebola while giving my acceptance speech on live television.

Or maybe it's just a little food poisoning.

On stage, the In Memoriam portion of our evening begins, the lights dimming as the faces of this year's fallen peers and colleagues appear on

a massive screen downstage. Billie Eilish and a hologram of Frank Sina-
tra emerge from the darkness on circular platforms, beginning their
piano and vocal performance of a somber ballad from *Broken Don*. It's a
slowed-down cover of Yes's "Owner of a Lonely Heart."

A sharp pain suddenly rips through the left side of my body, prompting an unexpected spasm from my leg. Meryl glances back, confused as
to why I've just kicked her chair, and I swiftly apologize. Sweat continues pouring down my face and moistens the collar of my shirt.

Onscreen, an enormous portrait of Raymond Nelson appears,
prompting a particularly loud applause from the audience.

The pain within me has grown to a boil, and its potency only builds
with every caustic thump of my galloping heart. Instinctively, I reach
down and place my hand over my left hip, the point from which the
horrible sensation emanates.

The second I touch that part of my body I sense a quick, powerful
movement, a singular and mighty tug lurking just below my skin.

"Oh my fuck," I blurt, a little too loud as I pull my hand away.

I jump to my feet as another surge of pain courses through my body,
then quickly start making my way down the row of chairs.

"Excuse me. Sorry," I stammer, struggling to get past and incredibly
thankful I've been seated near the aisle.

"He was there when Raymond died," I hear someone whisper.

The second I reach the aisle I take off as fast as I can, hurrying
toward the back exit in an awkward half speed walk, half jog. I try my
best to act natural, refusing to hold my side despite the overwhelming
desire to do so.

Another formidable spasm churns under my skin, the sensation
prompting a grimace to briefly spill across my face before I somehow
manage to regain my plastic smile.

I hit the back doors running, erupting into the lobby as a wild mess
and immediately staggering to the left. A slew of ushers rush to help me
but I push them out of the way, making one simple request.

"Where's the catering staff?"

I'm not entirely sure what's happening inside me, but there's one idea that I just can't seem to shake.

Someone points me down a nearby hallway and I follow their directions, quickly finding myself at the staff entrance of a bustling kitchen.

Unfortunately, a security guard stands in my way. "I'm sorry, sir. I need to see your credentials."

I don't slow down for a second, barreling onward. "Is this the restroom?" I ask, pushing past security and stumbling into the kitchen. My eyes immediately scan my surroundings, desperately in search of the closest approximation to a specific blade that's been forever ingrained in my memory.

Within seconds I've spotted a tray of utensils, which I immediately slam into. The forks, spoons, and knives go flying everywhere, clattering across the floor as I drop to my knees in an exaggerated stumble.

"Oh my God, I'm so sorry," I shout, placing my hand over one of the steak knives and tucking it into the sleeve of my jacket.

The security guard is right behind me, angrily pulling me off the ground with a furious look plastered across his face. "What the hell do you think you're doing?" he bellows, his large hands holding my arms against my body as he screams in my face.

"I'm so sorry," I mumble, struggling to come across as innocent as possible. "I'm really sick."

"Let me see your credentials," he demands again.

I reach into my jacket and pull out a small laminated card, proving I'm a nominee.

"Talent isn't allowed back here," the man snarls.

"I'm so sorry," I repeat. "I'm looking for the restroom. I'm about to hurl."

"Oh," the security guard utters, releasing his grip. He nods down the hallway next to us. "Over there."

I thank the man and continue onward, wincing with every step as the pain surges through me.

I burst into the restroom, turning abruptly and yanking open the door of a custodial closet. A large freestanding sign is there to greet me, and I quickly unfold the yellow plastic triangle. I place the sign directly outside the door, informing any potential intruders that this public restroom is currently out of order.

"Anyone in here?" I shout, staggering over to the mirror and yanking out my tucked-in white button-up.

This room is shockingly unpleasant for such a nice theater, fluorescent light cascading across green tiles and somehow making me look even sicker than I already am.

There's no response as I frantically toss my jacket to the side, then scramble to unbutton the shirt below it.

I tear open the fabric to reveal my bare stomach and chest, gasping aloud at the shocking display. I'd known this horrific sight was coming, but seeing it with my own eyes is something else entirely.

A large, wormlike bulge has snaked its way along my form, lurking just below the surface of my skin as it winds from my hip to my stomach. It's slightly thicker than a garden hose, and who knows how long. The creature suddenly squirms, pushing another two or so inches up my frame and prompting another swell of blinding pain.

I fumble, bracing myself against the nearby counter as a hiss of agony escapes my clenched teeth.

Another smattering of applause emits from the theater, drifting down the hallway as the audience memorializes yet another particularly revered star.

I fish the knife from my sleeve as my body instinctively clenches in preparation for what I'm about to do.

"Oh, heck. Oh, heck. Oh, heck," I groan. The word choice is unexpectedly childish, as though my panic is so visceral—so unfiltered—that it's launched my mind thirty years back in time. The phrase keeps spilling out of my mouth over and over again, repeating these words at varying degrees of intensity as I lower the blade to my bare skin. I'm positioned for incision just a few centimeters ahead of the worm, but as

I start my cut I notice the surprisingly muscular creature jerk to the right and start forging a new path.

The sting of the blade is terrible, but every time this thing wriggles its way through my flesh the pain reaches a whole other level. I can feel it separating tender strands of muscle as it forces its way through my body, ravenously driving toward the final destination.

Still, I can't stop now; the blood is already pouring down my side as I cut even deeper, the steak knife not nearly as sharp as I'd hoped and forcing me to use a sawing motion if I want to make any progress.

The pain is so overwhelming now that I'm compelled to pull back for a moment, tears running down my face and drool hanging from my lips. I fight the urge to vomit, the various systems of my body violently at war with my conscious mind. I know what has to be done, but my nervous system sure as hell doesn't like it.

I can't give up, though. Not now.

I've seen *Predatory Hunt* enough times to know exactly where this thing is headed: straight into my heart.

The worm trembles within me as it starts crawling again, putting even more distance between my wide-open wound and its slippery body. If I want to stop this thing, I'll have to make a new incision.

"No you don't," I huff, wild-eyed and delirious as I slice into my chest, breaking through the skin just below my hammering heart.

I clench my teeth and pump my hand from right to left, sawing much deeper and faster than before. Blood sputters forth, spilling down my chest in a glistening red wave.

When the cut is big enough I toss my knife into the nearby sink with a loud clatter. I shove two fingers into the gash, battling through the ruthless sting as I let out a long, guttural moan.

Behind me, someone opens the bathroom door and I reflexively cry out with a furious snarl. "Occupied!"

The door immediately closes as an awkward "Sorry" flutters across my ears.

I push deeper until, suddenly, I feel the plump, slimy body of the creature brushing against my fingertips. With one final thrust, I slip even farther into my wound and hook the worm, pulling it back as hard as I can.

The pain of this movement is so overwhelming that I nearly black out, a literal wash of white light blasting across my vision like some surreal firework display. There's no stopping now, however, and with all the strength I can muster I begin to yank out the monstrous parasite.

I readjust my grip as I pull a portion of the worm's body through my incision, the long, pulsing invertebrate absolutely covered in tissue and carnage. The creature is just as disgusting as I remember it, bulbous and bloated with a sickly charcoal coloration.

I can feel the worm unfurling within me, its body slipping back through the tunnel it's already burrowed across my muscle and fat as I gain the upper hand. One more tug and the head comes popping out, a horrible snapping maw of feelers and a thousand tiny teeth built for slicing and gnawing.

The worm immediately begins to lash about, its circular mouth frantically searching for anything to latch on to. It struggles to curl back on itself and bite my wrist, but this only gives me more leverage to extract it.

I stagger toward the sink, reaching in and retrieving the steak knife with my free hand. I place my blade against the creature's tough, wet skin, pulling taut and watching as the knife begins to gradually slice through the worm.

The parasite squeals, even more frantic in its movements as it fights for its life.

With one last tug I sever the worm completely and stumble back, slipping in a pool of my own blood.

My knife clatters to the ground as I hit the bathroom wall, sliding down the tile and landing with an exhausted thud. The section of worm in my right hand squirms a bit more, offering one final babble and hiss as its motor functions dim.

Delirious and confused, I pull the remainder of the now-dead crea-ture from my body, but by the time I've removed it completely the whole thing has turned to ash, drifting off in a swirling haze.

I close my eyes, my head resting against the wall behind me as I take a moment to collect my senses. Thankfully, the In Memorium segment is unusually long this year.

I wonder why.

"Tired?" comes a familiar croak from the darkness of a stall.

I can barely open my eyes, but as I crack my lids ever so slightly I notice the brilliant red cherry of a cigarette floating within the endless black. The embers pulse faintly as someone takes a long, satisfying drag.

"Exhausted," I admit.

The Smoker takes his time, breathing heavily in the darkness of this blood-smeared bathroom. "Would be quite the story," he finally croaks. "Suicide in the bathroom at the Oscars. I'd even let you keep your bones."

Another round of applause erupts from the auditorium, a macabre live studio audience that seems thrilled by this suggestion.

"You'd be a legend," The Smoker continues. "You're dying tonight either way, might as well make the most of it."

I can sense my heartbeat laboring now, exhausted after jumping from the frantic hammer of my self-surgery to the sluggish pumps of severe blood loss.

I can hear a musical swell from the theater as the segment ends, tran-sitioning into a new set of awards. A presenter begins to speak, their voice echoing through every hallway in a strange reverberating cascade.

I can't parse the words, but I *do* pick up on one key phrase: *live action short film.*

"Lots of people are legends, the good and the bad. Circumstances can make you a legend." I sigh. "Heroes are much rarer. Heroes take action."

With that, I put every ounce of energy I can muster into climbing to my feet, forcing my body to obey the demands of my mind. I manage to lean forward a bit, but as the pain surges through me I'm forced to fall back against the wall once again.

The Smoker chuckles at this, his raspy wheeze drifting from the darkness. "And *you* are a hero?" he croaks. "You let your friends down. You let yourself down. You're no hero, but luckily you've got us."

My head falls back against the tile. I'm utterly drained.

"This is the big finale we built *just for you* and those rattling bones," the Smoker croaks. "Dead in the bathroom on the big night. He tried to snippety-snip his own heart out with a steak knife. How *dramatic.* How *tragic.* You'll never guess what song was playing."

I can feel my breathing start to slow, the adrenaline that pulses through my body tapering off as my frame begins to settle. The blood loss is catching up with me. "Are you saying . . . you arranged *all of this?*"

"All for you."

"Just so I could . . . die . . . right here?"

The red ember flares as The Smoker takes another long drag. "On Hollywood's biggest night? Carving out your little closeted gay heart in the bathroom after your lover fell deathly ill?" He stops for a moment, breaking out into a fit of ragged laughter. "Why, yes. What a colorful way to go."

I let out a long sigh. "But that's so . . . wasteful," I counter, finally letting my eyes drift shut.

"Clickety-clack, coins rattling in the tray," The Smoker croaks. "The profits are up, up, up."

"But *how much?*" I prod, noticing how difficult it is to raise my voice. "All that destruction was really worth a few more streams?"

"Point zero zero three one six two," he replies, giving each word an awkward staccato emphasis.

I barely register what he's saying. "Huh?"

The smoker lowers his voice to a gravely drawl. He delivers the message slower now. "I said, point zero zero three one six two. That's how much *more* we get when your bones are laid out."

When it comes to studio economics, I'm accustomed to struggling with the numbers. Their profit-and-loss statements are so astronomically large that a single percentage point can mean three thousand lost jobs and a shuttered production house. That said, all this mayhem for 0.003162 percent more in quarterly profits feels like a truly jaw-dropping display of greed.

As if reading my thoughts, The Smoker croaks out an important question. "Is your life worth more than that?"

I don't know.

It probably is, but at this point I'm too exhausted to do the calculations, too exhausted to keep fighting because I now realize the algorithm will always be one step ahead of me. Every moment of this journey has been planned, the illusion of free will saved until the very end because free will builds *drama*, and drama sells.

I've been running all over town for one reason: it sells gossip magazines. It sells movies. It sells TV shows. It sells books.

This was never about killing off my characters. It's about killing off *me*. It's a queer tragedy with a semi-closeted hero who kicks the bucket just when he's about to find himself.

How much is my life worth?

I settle in, feeling a strange heat wrapping itself around me. My mind begins to drift, struggling to calculate my own value. It feels good to let go like this, to drift off into the void.

But before I let go entirely, another thought enters my mind.

How much is Zeke worth?

How much is Tara worth?

I fight to remember how much HBS makes a year, then work backward, but the ridiculousness of this equation makes the whole mental game a nonstarter. Whatever the dollar amount ends up being, Zeke and Tara are priceless.

I can't just leave them behind.

"My friends are so much more important than that."

I open my eyes to see one of The Smoker's long drags stop halfway.

"What?" he croaks, a hint of frustration in his voice. Or is it alarm?

I focus on my breathing, building my strength back up and reconnecting with my body.

I brace myself against the bathroom wall for a second time. "I don't need to be the hero," I say, "but all it takes to keep the story going is an active protagonist. I think I've got the energy for that."

I push hard. This attempt goes much better than my first, the weight of my body somehow shifting enough for me to find my bearings. I climb to my feet and stagger over to a towel dispenser, loudly pulling the crank a few times to produce a long furl of off-white paper. I tear the sheets away, folding them over and pushing them against my open wound to slow the bleeding.

I remove my tie, never more thankful to have skipped the bow, and wrap it tightly around my torso. This holds the paper towels in place.

Next, I get to work wiping down my crimson-stained skin.

All the while, the announcers on stage are barreling through their script, prompting a few murmurs of polite laughter from the crowd.

I pull my shirt back on, then watch in horror as the white fabric turns bright red at my side and my lower chest. I've managed to reduce the bleeding quite a bit, but not entirely.

Fortunately, I'm sporting a black jacket tonight, and as long as I keep it buttoned up I should be fine.

I take one last look in the bathroom mirror, splashing some water on my face and doing the best I can to fix my hair.

Good enough.

"Tickity-tock," The Smoker croaks. "I'll still have your bones."

I turn and march back into the lobby. Every step prompts a surge of pain to billow through me, but there's no turning back now. I do everything I can to stifle the constant ache, focusing my mind on the task at hand.

By now the nominees are being read.

"Are you alright?" someone questions. It could be a fellow writer or a gravely concerned usher, but I'm too delirious to know for sure.

"I'm fucking fantastic."

Within the auditorium, a familiar phrase rings out and pulls me sharply back into focus.

"And the winner is . . ." they begin, drawing out the pause for dramatic effect.

I stagger through the theater doors, my breath catching in my throat as I wait for the inevitable conclusion. For a brief moment it feels as though time has stopped, the whole world condensed into one frozen sliver that stretches on forever.

I see every tiny fragment of this brilliant scene, the hot white lights of the stage and the audience looking on with smiles of anticipation.

"*Little Mouse*, Misha Byrne," the presenter finally announces, eliciting a mighty roar of applause from the audience.

The flow of time churns back to life once again, a cosmic film reel swiftly returning to its original frame rate. I watch as camera operators frantically search the theater, hunting for a mysterious winner who is no longer in his assigned seat.

A producer rushes onstage, whispering something into the presenter's ear.

"It appears Misha can't be here to accept his award," they begin.

"Wait!" I shriek, throwing my hand up and waving as I make my way down the aisle. Pain swells when I raise my arm, but for some reason the sting doesn't affect my stride at all. I'm running on pure adrenaline now.

The crowd catches sight of me as I make my way toward the stage, smiling warmly. I hurry up the stairs and greet my presenter with a firm handshake, then turn to the audience as I hoist my little gold statuette proudly.

Again, pain erupts through me, but I refuse to react.

"Th-thank you," I stammer, taking a moment as I adjust to the blazing spotlight shining down from above. I gaze out across the theater, my eyes locking with several peers in the first few rows. They're excited to see me, but their expressions are also deeply concerned.

I reach into my jacket pocket and pull out the notecards, immediately discovering they've been smudged with blood. I can still make out the words, but in this moment something shifts within me. I hesitate, then slip the notecards back into my jacket.

"This is the most important moment of my life," I say with a faint chuckle, my voice booming across the packed theater.

The crowd has no idea how true this statement really is.

"I had a speech written. I spent a lot of time getting things just right because I have a point to make, but now that I'm up here, I feel like the best way to make my point is tell you all a story. That's what we all do, right? Tell stories?"

The crowd is silent, waiting for me to begin.

"When I was young, I'd devour books and comics and movies and television in search of a character like me," I explain. "I'd find a few, but slowly I'd realize they were just hinting at something that would never *really* come to pass, because characters like me didn't sell."

I take a moment, gazing out across the room. The faintest scent of cigarettes wafts across my nostrils, but I ignore it.

"I figured, if there are no heroes with the same feelings I have, then I guess my feelings must be wrong. Once I got older and I started telling stories of my own, I'd slip in a few characters like me for the next generation to have, and that's so important . . . but *for me*, that only addressed part of the problem. I was doing the work through my art, but I was still pretending in real life. I'm not gonna do that anymore."

Some of the audience expressions gain a sliver of confusion, while others shine with thankful anticipation. My muscles clench.

"I'm sure all the queer folks in the audience already know this," I continue. "Most of my friends do, too, but for the rest of the world, and for my family watching on TV right now, I should probably tell you something about those characters I always hoped to see—the ones I never got. They were gay. I'm gay."

The crowd pauses for a moment, calculating what I've just said, then explodes in a fit of applause. They rise to their feet.

It feels as though I've been carrying around a weight my entire life, completely unaware it was there until this very moment when I simply let the damn thing go.

The applause continues on and on, refusing to die down until, suddenly, a dreadful swell of music starts to build over the top of it.

"No, no, no!" I cry out, shaking my head and waving my hands.
"You're not playing me off yet."

The music refuses to die, but I'm persistent.

"This is too important," I shout, prompting the audience to applaud
even louder.

Eventually, the swelling orchestral strings have no other choice but
to fade into submission.

"It's not just about telling queer stories," I continue, louder now as
I find my footing. "It's about telling *all kinds* of queer stories. Yes, there
can be tragedy and death and darkness, there's an important place for
that, but don't forget about queer beauty and queer catharsis and queer
joy! Every gay character doesn't need to die in the first scene, or in a
third-act blaze of glory to save everyone else. Support queer heroes, not
just onscreen, but offscreen too!"

As I shout these words, I can sense a notable shift in the audience, a
level of connection much deeper than your typical award speech.

"Some of you may be surprised by the revelation that I'm gay, and
some of you probably already assumed as much," I continue.

This prompts a slight chuckle from the crowd.

"Here's the thing: it's not some coincidence that the press has me
lined up to be the next true Hollywood train wreck. A closeted gay man
at the end of his rope, a guy who destroys his identity before his identity
can destroy him. Well, I won't let that happen. I reject the idea that I'm
the star of some real-life queer tragedy, and I reject the very *idea* of queer
tragedy as the only valid form of gay entertainment.

"I call on all of you to usher in a *new* era of stories where the gay, or
bi, or lesbian, or asexual, or pansexual, or trans character *lives happily ever
after.* Buy *those* stories. Make *those* stories profitable."

The music begins to swell again, but this time it only serves to give
my words more emotional heft.

"The dramatic conclusion of my little tale is this," I yell. "This right here is the story of a kid who grew up afraid to be himself, then came out on live TV at the Oscars! He *didn't* go down in a tragic blaze of glory! He came back next year and won best screenplay! Now *that's* a fucking story!"

I hoist my award into the air.

"This one is dedicated to my boyfriend, Zeke Romero!" I shout, then turn and strut confidently offstage, waving to the crowd as they wildly cheer.

A single word will be censored at the end there, but that's only gonna drive more people to the message.

A frantic mob of crew members are waiting in the wings to greet me, one of them taking my trophy to repurpose for the next winner's presentation, and the others all talking over one another in a haze of questions I can't understand.

I feel dizzy and nauseated, the weight of my injuries and the stress of this evening finally catching up with me.

"I'm fine, I'm good," I assure them, staggering through the crowd and taking a sharp right turn down a nearby hallway.

I keep walking, the chaos fading away as I stumble even deeper into the recesses of the Dolby Theatre. All the pain I've been desperately holding at bay comes roaring back, hitting me all at once in an overwhelming wave.

Another kink in the hallway, then another. Soon enough, I'm standing before an unknown greenroom. At least, I think that's what it is.

I stagger inside just as the weight of this messy world becomes too much for me to bear. I collapse, hitting the ground with a mighty thud.

"Hey," comes a gruff voice. "You okay?"

My eyes flutter open, blinking a few times as I struggle to understand what's happening and why my shirt is sticking to my body. Above me, fluorescent lights are shining down with a cold, aggressive glow.

A tiny mouse is sitting directly in front of my face, its whiskers trembling as it watches me with shiny black eyes.

"Oh. Whoa," I sigh.

I sit up a bit, wincing as a surge of discomfort rockets through my chest. The mouse abruptly scampers away, frightened by my sudden movement.

I notice now that a man stands in the doorway, the true source of this concerned tone. He looks utterly horrified. "You need me to call an ambulance?"

"I'm fine, I'm fine," I stammer.

I climb to my feet, swaying from side to side a bit. I have a terrible, pounding headache that makes any potential thoughts sting as they pass through my skull.

I'm in some kind of janitor's closet, a small desk on one side and an assortment of cleaning supplies on the other.

"You got blood all over the floor," the man observes. He's wearing a gaffer's belt, so he must be part of the production crew.

"I'm . . . really sorry about that," I reply, not sure what else to say.

I reach into my pocket and pull out my phone, discovering the device is broken. The screen is shattered and dark, and it refuses to turn on.

"What time is it?" I groan.

"Noon. Hey, you want me to call an ambulance?"

I shake my head. "How do I get out of here?"

The man steps back and points down the hallway.

"Thanks, buddy," I reply, patting the man on his shoulder as I stagger past. I can feel the squish of old blood in my shoes as I walk.

I make my way down the hallway toward a conveniently marked exit door, then push out into the blazing California sun.

I find myself emerging from the back of the Dolby Theatre. I wander down an alley for a while, then eventually enter the manic sidewalk cacophony where the streets of Hollywood and Highland intersect. Last night's red carpet has been furled, and hardly a sign of the evening's festivities are left as a crew tears down lighting rigs and packs up their production supplies in a caravan of large semitrucks.

The rest of this bizarre habitat has returned to its daily routine, various heroes and villains in off-brand costumes taking photos with a smattering of excited tourists. They march back and forth across the unkempt stars of long-forgotten actors and actresses, a strange, half-baked resurrection.

I stand for a moment, turning my face to the sunshine and closing my eyes as the hustle and bustle of Hollywood Boulevard drifts through the air.

I'm alive.

Now that I have a chance to sit for a moment, I tune in to the battered, aching sensations of my own body. I notice a strange feeling around my torso, and when I glance down I realize that my shirt's been left unbuttoned. Beneath it, soaked but neatly applied bandages are covering my wounds.

One of them is smudged with ash.

It takes a while to find my way home, since I'm hindered by the lack of a phone and the throbbing ache that pumps through my body with every tiny movement.

Besides, my own detailed health status is the last thing on my mind. I've survived well past The Smoker's deadline, and while I'm thrilled to find myself in the land of the living, I need to know that Tara and Zeke have done the same.

Eventually, I shuffle onto a city bus, using the few bills I have tucked away in my back pocket. They're covered in dried blood, and I expect more of a reaction from the driver, but it appears he's seen it all on this particular route.

I stagger to the back and flop into an empty seat, resting my head against the window as the Los Angeles scenery drifts past.

The rules have changed, a shift in the tracks that were so thoroughly laid out for me.

I keep thinking I'll glance over to find The Smoker sitting in some adjacent seat, his wide, inhuman eyes gazing deep into my soul as he offers one last announcement of his impending arrival. At every stop, I check to see if Mrs. Why climbs up the stairs, or strain to hear if some fragile lamb is crying behind a bus stop.

But these moments never come.

Soon enough, I'm exiting the bus just down the street from my house. From here, my anxiety *really* begins to build. I'm horrified by the thought of what I might find waiting for me.

A vision of Tara face down on the floor with her back wide open, the bones ripped from her body in a macabre procedure that leaves nothing but sloppy organs and flesh in its wake.

In *Death Blooms,* The Smoker would often go about his work while the victims were still alive, although the trauma to their body wouldn't allow these sessions of torment to carry on very long.

Will Zeke still be curled in a ball, the forbidden cosmic knowledge expanding his mind well past the point of no return?

My limping pace quickens, the discomfort of my body now nothing more than a vague and distant consideration.

As the house comes into view I notice the strange rental car is still parked in my driveway.

The paparazzi are also still there—even more than before—but I ignore them. I stagger up the front steps and throw open the door, bursting inside my home to find a truly unexpected scene.

Tara is on the living room couch, engrossed in the TV news. Meanwhile, Zeke is pacing back and forth behind her, a worried look on his face as he frantically shouts into his phone.

The two of them freeze when they see me, then erupt in expressions of utter shock as my boyfriend's cell falls from his hand and clatters to the ground.

The next thing I know, all three of us are rushing together in a powerful hug, the ache of my body no match for the warmth of their embrace. We don't exchange a word, just bask in the presence of one another while fresh tears of joy run down our cheeks.

The news keeps rolling in the background, but I tune it out, pulling the people I love even closer.

KILLJOY

Gazing out at the line of cars struggling to get into the HBS east security gate, it's nice to know that even after a season like this one, some things never change. The world can turn completely upside down, and in many ways we still end up right where we started.

"Thanks again for the ride," Tara says from the passenger seat.

She didn't exactly *need* a ride today, perfectly capable of getting here on her own like she's always done. In fact, Tara's house is completely out of the way when it comes to swinging by and making a pickup, but I don't care.

After our recent adventure, I've found myself making even more excuses to spend time together.

"You excited for your big meeting?" she asks.

Tara's wearing a silver-and-purple striped blazer and matching shorts, the whole combo reminding me a little bit of a world where Angus Young owns a magnificent, magical candy factory. A black sequined button-up is underneath, featuring even more detailing with the same glorious silver. She also changed her hair recently, trading the stark white for a brilliant, flaming orange.

"I hate big meetings," I remind her.

"Yeah, but this is a *big* big meeting."

"Even worse," I counter, utterly stone-faced for the first ten seconds and then finally cracking a smile. "Fine. I'm a little interested."

Tara erupts with excitement, punching my shoulder as though I've just scored our team the game-winning grand slam. "That's what I'm talkin' about! Yes!" She rolls down her window and leans her head out. "He's excited, everyone! He's in it to win it!"

"Okay, okay," I blurt, struggling to pull her back in. "Thank you. I'll let you know how it goes."

"First time meeting the new boss, baby!" she says, then immediately falters when she notices the look on my face.

Jack is gone. I don't need to reiterate how much of a pain in my ass he was, but he also believed in me. Sometimes there's a strange relationship that forms between an artist and an executive, a push and pull that you both pretend to hate but secretly makes you feel right at home with each other. It sounds messed up, because it is, but we had that.

He wasn't just a friend, either; he was a living person. He had a family.

"Yeah," I finally reply, clearing my throat and forcing a smile. "Time to meet the new guy."

I lean back in my seat a bit, turning my gaze to the other side of the road where a familiar golden field stretches out toward the base of the mountains. The dry grass rustles softly as subtle waves pulse across it. There isn't a single cartoon character to be found out there in the vast, yellow expanse, but being here certainly brings back memories of one. At one edge of the field I can see that a construction site is breaking ground; probably a shiny new soundstage.

Time rolls on. Nature is chipped away. Resources are consumed.

Despite the warm weather, a chill runs down my spine. The monsters may have left me for other pursuits, but that doesn't mean I'm quite ready to move on. The algorithm is still out there, and it knows every single thing I'm about to do.

We finally pull up to the security booth where April excitedly greets us. "Oh my God! Misha!" she yells. "You're back!"

I nod. "In the flesh!"

I can't help noticing the little rainbow pin attached to the front of April's security uniform, resting just above her pocket and adding the slightest bit of flair.

"Congratulations on the big win!" April gushes. "Well, congrats on *everything.*"

I'm still not great with accepting this kind of praise, but I've been forced to quickly make peace with my discomfort over the last few weeks. The press was all over me when they thought I was falling apart, but their reaction to my success has been twice as ravenous.

People love to gawk at a downfall, but they also love a redemption arc.

Tara and I both scan our thumbs on the little blue reader. Soon enough, we're rolling past the booth, making our way deeper into the sprawling backlot of giant beige soundstages.

The looming water tower gazes down on us from above, casting our journey in its shadow. As usual, an iconic Harold Brothers shield is painted across the tower's curved surface, but the logo has been filled with a series of vivid rainbow bars—the queer flag.

This bloodthirsty conglomerate is really working to show off its support.

"It's weird to just . . . be back at work," I say. "I mean, we both got some killer time off, but it feels like nothing even happened."

"You're still wrapped in bandages under that shirt," Tara reminds me. "That's different."

A faint, pumping rhythm slowly grows as we approach the heart of the lot. The beat is steady, starting as a low rumble and then gradually evolving into the recognizable pulse of a synthetic kick drum. A mighty, grooving baseline dances along with it, and soon enough a lush keyboard starts flirting its way into the mix.

Tara and I round the corner just as a confident vocal line belts over the top of the music, dramatically soaring with perfect timing for this grand reveal.

We've returned to the little oasis that serves as a central backlot artery, the grassy, palm-covered park that hosts a fountain, a coffee shop, and various studio workers on their routine lunch breaks. Jack's office used to be a few yards from here, and a giant mural of the Broken Don once gazed down on this hub from above.

Just two months ago, I stood right over there, absolutely drenched in Raymond Nelson's blood.

But things have definitely changed.

This commons is still crowded with writers, actors, and backline crew members, but the trappings that surround them are decidedly fresh. A massive rainbow of helium balloons stretches from one side of the green to the other, leaping over the fountain in a giant, multicolored arch. Even more balloons are attached to various points around the park, creating a series of colorful, vibrant bouquets.

The thundering music comes from a DJ booth and speaker system, placed in the corner where a few scattered lunch breakers have gathered. The listeners are holding coffees and nodding along, almost *polite* in their approach, as if taking a moment to pay their respects before moving on.

The DJ, however, is another story. He's wearing gloriously tight latex shorts, which he'll probably need to cut himself out of later, and a see-through mesh shirt that hugs his absolutely jacked body.

Robyn's "Dancing on My Own," rumbles from the speakers.

"Oh. Okay" is all I can think to say, stopping my car abruptly and exchanging glances with Tara who seems equally confused.

We pull into a nearby parking spot and climb out of the vehicle, our gaze coaxed upward to a massive display on the left.

The billboard that once hosted Enzo Basile has already been replaced, not to celebrate *Broken Don*'s big win, but for something else entirely.

Looming above us is the ad for a brand new HBS blockbuster, a testament to just how fast this town can move when it really wants to. **QUEEROES** is emblazoned across the top in bold, majestic letters. Below this title is a group of actors standing proudly, their chests puffed out as the low-angle photography gives them an epic, larger-than-life appearance. This is a superhero team, and the colors of their uniforms make it quickly apparent which queer identity they each represent.

There's a hero clad in pink, purple, and blue, *the bi one.*

There's a hero clad in blue, pink, and white, *the trans one.*

There's a hero clad in orange, white, and pink, *the lesbian one.*

This continues on and on until every aspect of the community has been covered.

Across the bottom is the film's tagline: **IN THIS WORLD THERE ARE NO VILLAINS . . . ONLY QUEEROES.**

"No villains?" I mumble to myself, struggling to understand what this could possibly mean.

Does this show actually have . . . no conflict?

Tara steps up next to me, her eyes locked on the poster. "There's no asexual hero."

"What?" I blurt, pulled from my trance.

"They've got everyone up there besides an ace character," she observes. "Every fucking time."

"Oh—oh!" I stammer, realizing now that she's right. "I'm sorry. That really sucks."

"It is what it is." Tara sighs. "I'm headed in."

She pulls her satchel of cables and wires from the back seat of my car, then offers me a warm hug before taking off toward her office.

"Have a good meeting, baby!" Tara calls back over her shoulder, her voice barely audible over the thundering music as she disappears around a soundstage corner.

I quickly realize I'd rather not be in this loud, chaotic place any longer than I have to, and while I'm admittedly curious to see what the studio has to offer the "most buzzed-about writer in Hollywood," they're still just a bunch of suits and I'm still Misha Byrne.

I start my trek, heading up through the grass and strolling under the massive balloon archway as crew members mill around me. I notice now that most of them are sporting some form of queer paraphernalia, whether it's a small pride pin or a shirt with the rainbow-hued HBS logo.

I weave along the sandstone walkway, dappled by shade from the palms above until I reach what was once the office of Jack Hays.

Pulling open the door, I'm greeted by the same secretary that worked here before, a holdover after Jack's untimely exit. She smiles when she catches sight of me, offering a cheerful wave.

"Hey girl!" the secretary calls out with a distinctively singsong cadence.

I stop in my tracks, unable to process.

The two of us just stare at each other for a long time, caught in this moment like someone pressed pause on the universe's VCR.

"Uh, hi," I finally say. "I'm here to see Freddy Dewitt."

The secretary nods awkwardly, clearly uncomfortable with her own greeting, then waves me toward the elevators.

I press on through the lobby, a thousand memories swirling around in my mind. As I ride the lift up, I mentally prepare for the fact that Jack won't be here.

This is a new era.

The elevator door opens and the new era presents itself: a man in a startlingly chic, light pink suit that frames his crisp white button-up and a thin rainbow tie. His eyes are a brilliant blue, even lighter than mine and so pronounced that my first though is the guy must be wearing contacts. His hair is cut short on the sides, with a messy, youthful shag on top.

"Honey, *hellllllllo!*" Mr. Freddy Dewitt cries out, sauntering over to greet me with a kiss on each cheek. He sways his hips with fierce embellishment, oozing confidence.

"Oh, hey. Nice to meet you."

"How's my star?" Freddy asks. "Ready to take over the world, honey?"

"I think so," I reply, struggling to switch gears and get up to speed. "I've got a couple of originals I've been working on, and I know you've got some ideas you wanted to pitch me."

"I love it!" Mr. Dewitt cries out, then steps back to admire my outfit. He looks me up and down, taking it all in. "This fit, oh my God!" he exclaims. "He wears *no suit* in a meeting with the VP of television. You are a *firecracker*, honey! Work it!"

I'm trying my best to stay focused, but all the shouting and non sequiturs are starting to distract me.

Freddy takes a seat on the arm of a sofa, settling in. "Let's start where the action is *hot! Hot! Hot!* Let's talk *Travelers*. I know you had a problem with the board's direction."

"I don't want to kill those characters," I tell him, finding a lane I can navigate. "It's so important we let them have this moment. I think we've shown enough growth—"

"Honey, say no more! They're *alive!*" Freddy replies. "The Hollywood landscape has *shifted*, Misha, and you're the one who leads it. The board has nothing but trust in you."

I'm rocked by a swell of relief. This is what I came here for. After my big award show moment, it feels so good to finally put this whole saga behind me.

But the feeling is notably subdued. It's as though my body refuses to believe it, or maybe the battle drove me to such heights of exhaustion that I can't even bring myself to celebrate.

Or maybe it's all the literal dead bodies in my wake, the casualties strewn along my path to get here. I've dealt with the board firsthand, and while it's good to know this incredibly dangerous force has currently got my back, I'm well aware of what happens when it doesn't.

"We have some suggestions for *Travelers*, actually," Freddy Dewitt continues, "but I think you're gonna like them."

"Suggestions?" I repeat. "You just said I could let them be gay."

"Of course, honey, of course," Freddy cries, then leaps to his feet. He begins to pace back and forth across the office. "But why are we stopping there?"

I immediately clock the chair arm where Freddy Dewitt just rested, drawn to the faint smudge of dark ash that now streaks his upholstery. I'm hardly surprised this man isn't real—why *wouldn't* the algorithm install one of their own?—but the confirmation puts me on edge.

It's only now that I notice how much this office has changed. Live-laugh-love style artwork hangs everywhere, these three words repeating themselves in various hand-painted combinations. Several photographs have been blown up, framed, and hung; giant depictions of men holding hands while a sunrise blooms before them, or laughing together as a mischievous puppy tears open a birthday present. The images have an oddly sanitized quality. They're *just* gay enough to count as representation, but not enough to offend.

When my gaze finally arrives at the couch I gasp aloud.

Jack's boring beige two-seater has been replaced by a hell of a statement piece, a long daybed colored by the stark bars of a rainbow flag. The word **PRIDE** is written across it in giant white sequins.

No adult gay man in their right mind would own that fucking couch.

Freddy Dewitt is an approximation. At best, he's someone's poorly executed gay-best-friend character from a forgotten nineties rom-com. At worst, he's a synthesized amalgamation of traits and behaviors built to fill the role of generic-queer-man-through-the-eyes-of-straight-culture.

He's a stereotype.

Mr. Dewitt is pacing now, excitedly throwing out his ideas for the next season of *Travelers*. "Why let the straights have all the fun? Am I right?" he cries. "We've got trans Mothman, we've got a gay goblin, we've got bi Mrs. Why."

"I'm gonna be honest, I kinda love that, but . . ." I hesitate. "Maybe not for *Travelers*."

"Just a few ideas," Freddy replies. "The Board is very excited."

"It just . . . seems like that's not really the tone of the show."

Mr. Dewitt smiles, his grin growing so wide that it actually becomes a little frightening. "Honey, gay *sells*."

I can tell he's expecting a particular reaction by the way he's looking at me, waiting for me to match his excitement. We're part of the same club, after all.

Unfortunately, I just can't meet him there.

Feeling awkward about the direction of this meeting, I stand up and wander over to the window.

"Let me think about it," I offer, gazing out at the raucous courtyard below. By now the DJ has transitioned into "Born This Way" by Lady Gaga. The hammering beat is so loud that it's vibrating through the glass.

"Quite a scene down there," I say.

"We're celebrating Pride!" Freddy says, throwing his hands up and giving a brief little dance to the distant music.

"It's April," I remind him.

"At Harold Brothers Studios, *every* month is Pride month," Freddy declares, sauntering over. He stands right next to me, the two of us gazing out his office window side by side.

Every month that it's profitable, I think.

He gestures toward the massive *Queeroes* poster. "Why don't we go bigger, huh? Say it with me—Big. Gay. Blockbusters. Just give the word and I'll call the director right *freaking* now. You'd be perfect for *Queeroes Two.*"

I cringe as he says this. "You've already greenlit the sequel?"

"Honey, I told you, gay is *in. Queer* is in."

"And there's really no villains?" I press, still stuck on the tagline.

"Conflict-free, *pro-gay* entertainment," Mr. Dewitt replies. "Just like you said in your speech. There's been enough queer tragedy to last a lifetime. We're building a catalog that taps into the zeitgeist of *queer joy*, and right now *you* are at the forefront, Mr. Misha Byrne."

I realize now that I've seen these *Queeroes* actors before. This is the full cast from *Heroes of Darkness,* a poster I caught sight of in the Betta offices. They've just taken an already finished movie and—with the help of a few reshoots, clever editing, and machine learning—completely rebranded it over the course of a few weeks.

Freddy Dewitt claps his hands together and turns away from the window. He strolls over to his desk and flops down in the chair, making himself comfortable. "So what's it gonna be, Misha? A superhero multiverse thing? A romantic comedy with a couple of *gay*-listers? You wanna get a *Devil's Due* reboot off the ground? Think self-referential content with a *fresh, positive spin!* Make it *Angel's Due* and we're hitting all four quadrants."

I shake my head, turning to face him. "Actually, I had a couple of original ideas. They're in the vein of what I usually do."

The executive nods. "I'm listening. Hello. Talk to me."

"I just wanna make what I love: queer horror," I explain. "Now that I'm out, I feel like I can be so much more direct with what I wanna say."

Freddy is already shaking his head, swaying back and forth in his chair as he passes judgment. "Okay, I should've been more specific. There is *one* thing that probably isn't gonna work," he explains. "I mean, I know queer horror is how you got your start here, but right now the board is just *not* looking for that kind of energy. We need *out and proud*, honey. We need joy. We need happy endings."

I hesitate. "That's . . . not really my thing right now."

Freddy Dewitt chuckles to himself. "Are you kidding me? You're the queer joy *guy*. You're out here changing everything."

"I mean, of course there's a time and a place for that stuff, but there's also plenty of nuance to explore," I counter. "It's supposed to be *art*. Like, I'm working on a script right now where this gay couple rents a cabin in the woods, and little do they know, the dead family that once liv—"

"I'm gonna stop you right there," Mr. Dewitt interjects. "Like I said, you can do anything you want, but the board *highly suggests* a different approach."

A terrible sinking feeling immediately washes over me. I came here to give this meeting a fair shot, to see what the world feels like now that the scales of pop culture have tipped. The algorithm has been swayed—hell, it even patched me up as I bled out at the Oscars—but it still operates on the same basic principles of capital.

"So . . . first the board wants me to kill off my gay characters, now they don't want any conflict at all," I state.

"If you wanna write something original, I think that's a fantastic choice," Freddy replies. "I love that for you, but let's . . . keep it upbeat. There are some members of the HBS family who are *not* keeping things upbeat at the moment, and *as a bestie*, I'm kind of worried about them."

There's a weight to his tone, a threat buried so deep you could never quite dig it up and dissect it; but it's there.

We both know it's there.

"Oh, do I have some *hot goss* for you!" Freddy continues. "You're close with Blossom Baker, right?"

I haven't talked with Blossom since her birthday, but I still vividly remember the footage she was combing through, remember how much the documentary meant to her. My blood runs cold, but I don't react.

"She's been working on this movie about queer tragedy, and, honey, it is *not going well.*" Freddy shakes his head dramatically. "First, her edit burns up in a fire, can you believe it?"

"That's terrible."

"Turns out she had a backup," Freddy continues. "Our girl started working on a new edit and then, *whoops,* she trips and falls down the stairs! The klutz breaks every bone in her body, and I mean *every* bone. But guess what? She's still working on it."

Freddy's eyes glaze over for a moment.

"I keep telling her, if she doesn't stop working this hard, she's gonna make herself sick," Mr. Dewitt continues, looking past me. There's a subtle shift in his tone, something sinister creeping in. "She's gonna make herself very, very sick."

A silent beat hangs over us, tense and foreboding, then Freddy's eyes snap back to mine.

"*The board* is worried about her. They're worried about a few people, actually," Mr. Dewitt continues. "This is not the atmosphere for sad, depressing queer stories—not anymore—and I hope to God those folks figure it out before their contract isn't renewed."

"Don't," I blurt, spitting out the word with a little too much force.

"Don't what?"

"Don't . . . do anything to her."

Mr. Dewitt's cold expression remains for a whole ten seconds, then he suddenly breaks out in a playful smile. "I'm not sure what you mean, honey."

The executive stands up, a sign that our meeting is over.

"Great talk, Misha. I'm glad we did that." He leads me back to the elevator. "HBS is *very* excited to see all the great content you come up with!"

BURIED

As I lean against the side of my car, scanning the valley below, my focus drifts to the lone hawk perched atop a nearby tree. The creature is beautiful, and I might otherwise be thrilled to catch this tiny dose of wildlife in a typically metropolitan setting, but at the moment I'm on high alert.

I've never been to this barren turnout off Mulholland Drive, which is kind of the point, but that doesn't mean I wasn't followed.

Fortunately, I know the rules, and as far as I'm aware predatory birds don't possess the mental capacity to listen in on someone's conversation.

The sound of another vehicle pulls my attention to the nearby curve, and soon enough I spot Tara's car rounding the corner. She waves, pulling up next to me as dry gravel crunches beneath her tires.

"Hey!" my friend calls over, waving excitedly as she climbs from her ride in an orange-and-white-checkered dress. She's smiling, but her expression falters slightly as we make eye contact. "You good?" she questions.

I nod, trying my best to act natural. "I'm good. You look like a Creamsicle."

Tara pops her trunk, pulling out two folding chairs and carrying them over to me. I hoist my six-pack, showing her I've handled my part of the equation.

"That's the vibe I'm going for. Did you pay cash?" she asks as we draw closer.

I nod.

"Phone is off?" Tara continues. "No car navigation to get here?"

"All clear," I report, staring past her at the hawk perched nearby.

Tara glances over her shoulder, following my gaze and immediately spotting the raptor. She hesitates.

"I mean, it's probably just a bird," I continue. "Even if it's not, it has to stay in character."

"Not necessarily," Tara reminds me. "They can sense each other's experience, even if they're not consciously aware of it."

"Well, what are we gonna do? *Never plan?*" I ask. "There's also shape-shifters and invisible men and ghosts. For all we know your car could be a transforming robot."

"Then here we go," Tara finally announces, her smile defying the circumstances. "Start your engines."

We take our seats, gazing out across the burgeoning sunset below. Tara pops the cap off my beer with her teeth, making me cringe, then hands it over before opening her own. The two of us take long, satisfying gulps of the cool beverage.

"Just two friends knockin' back cold ones, enjoying the sunset," Tara announces. "Nothing weird at all."

"I've been reading the trades," I say, jumping right into it. "Have you seen the catalogs HBS is buying up? War films, natural disaster movies . . . viral plagues."

"Oh, I know," Tara confirms. "I've been reading the HBS copyright database."

"The *what?*"

Tara lifts her phone, the little device still firmly stuck in an off position. "I built their network, remember?" she states. "I have a back-door."

"That's . . . so dangerous," I retort, but Tara ignores me.

"They're not just buying up films, they're writing their own," she continues. "Creating their own characters with 'internal videos' that are never released. These movies go straight into their database, but HBS own the copyright."

I sit for a moment, letting Tara's information sink in.

She clears her throat. "But you're right, it *is* dangerous. The thing is, I've never been caught. Don't you think that's kinda weird?"

"I mean, I'm mostly just thankful," I admit.

Tara shakes her head. "No, seriously. Think about it. Why hasn't the computer noticed me poking around in the system yet?"

"I don't know. Because you're good at what you do?"

"Have you *ever before* driven up to Mulholland Drive and sat at a turnout in a folding chair to drink some beers?" Tara questions.

"What does that have to do with anything?"

"Have you?" she presses.

"Before today? No."

"And that's how I know we're not being followed," she replies. "Because *I* picked the place."

I furrow my brow, not following.

"You told me what you were thinking about that night at the Oscars," Tara continues. "You were bleeding out in the bathroom and you wanted to give up, but something made you keep going—a single thought that caught The Smoker off guard. What was it?"

"You and Zeke," I confirm.

"I love you. That's heartwarming," she replies, "and very, very important. The Smoker caught me because I was there with you. Mrs. Why caught me because I was there with Zeke."

"I really, really don't get it," I admit.

"Here's all you need to get," Tara replies. "I have backdoor access, which means I could easily upload a piece of malware to the network."

I sit up, my attention suddenly piqued.

"Wait, could you really tap into everything?" I ask. "Fry it all at once?"

Tara shakes her head. "Our servers have gotten more and more decentralized. The algorithm is taking precautions. I can't upload something on the backlot and have it reach the heart of the system because everything is partitioned. The heart pumps information out, but very little comes back in."

"What if you uploaded something *directly* into the heart?" I press.

"If the program was focusing its computational attention on something else while the packet was uploading to a central server then . . . yeah, it could work," Tara admits. "The algorithm has started concentrating attention like that—servers powering up and down at bizarre times. It's trying to be as utilitarian as possible, literally saving pennies. I guess that's the fatal flaw in having money as your ultimate motivation."

"Right now I'm the Harold Brothers golden boy," I state with confidence. "I can get us into the heart."

"And I know exactly what to do once we're there," Tara replies.

As we approach the door of Betta Effects and Natural Processing I steady my thoughts, ignoring mental flashes of a blood-covered thumb pressed against the security pad. No matter how many cars fill the parking lot or how brilliantly the sun shines down from above, I can't stop thinking about that night.

"You've got this," Zeke offers quietly, as if sensing my apprehension and hoping to soothe it before things spiral out of control.

His assurance is noble, but having Zeke and Tara by my side doesn't make things any less terrifying. Over the course of this journey I've come to terms with putting my life on the line, but they don't deserve this.

Still, I need them. It's no longer just the three of us in danger, it's the world as we know it.

I arrive at the door, ready to press my finger against the small electronic reader but hearing a soft metallic clang before I get the chance. It's unlocked.

I glance at the camera hanging above us, taking note of a new, specialized lens that has been affixed since the last time I was here. This mechanical eye shifts a few times, watching.

All I can think to do is offer an awkward wave, then continue onward, pulling the door open and heading inside.

The offices are busy today, various executives hustling from one room to the next as they construct an ever-escalating cascade of high-profile deals and mergers. The numbered doors are all propped open, giving the place a surprisingly welcome atmosphere in comparison to my initial trip.

The only door that remains closed, of course, is the one that lies in wait at the end of the hallway.

I glance at Tara, who shakes her head. Our plan requires as little distance between us and the heart of the network—the central server—as possible, and it appears we're still not close enough.

We reach the second door, above which yet another camera has been installed.

"Hey there," I say, waving to the lens. "Misha Byrne. I'm here for the eleven thirty meeting with . . . uh . . ."

I'm not exactly sure what to call it in this official setting.

"You," I finally finish.

The door clicks open, allowing all three of us entry.

We're now standing in the square chamber that once held a small desk and a disheveled night watchman. The previous security guard, Robby, is nowhere to be found, and the room itself is much more inviting than before. Barren white walls have been replaced with the breezy pastel colors of a fun, funky waiting room, and the space has been filled with all the mid-century modern trappings you could desire. Two angular couches are positioned at the center of the room, while the secretary sits grinning behind a large glass table.

"Misha, good to see you," the secretary offers, a tone of recognition in his voice despite the fact that we've never met before.

"Thanks," I reply, struggling to keep it together but pleased with how natural I sound.

"You've brought some friends," the secretary observes. "They should wait out here."

I hesitate, glancing back and forth between Zeke and Tara.

"Actually, I was thinking they'd come in with me," I reply. "They're part of the team."

The man nods, still grinning wide but clearly not sold on this idea. "Are you sure about that?" he asks. "Knowledge bears responsibility."

"They're part of the team," I repeat.

The secretary holds for a moment, his stare frozen in place as the seconds tick past in awkward silence. He's allowing me one last chance to change my mind, but I don't take it, and eventually he's forced to nod in confirmation.

"Alright then," the man continues, motioning to the door on our right. "Head on in."

The door swings opens, revealing the vast laboratory I remember.

The three of us approach as casually as possible, but our slow pace through the threshold denotes a hint of apprehension. It isn't my first time, but the shock of witnessing this bizarre scene is still difficult to stifle. I can only imagine what Zeke and Tara are feeling.

The enormous soundstage is just as dark and ominous as ever, although there are now several more lab technicians making their way from server bay to server bay, diligently going about their work. Despite the dim lighting, there's plenty of life and movement to be found.

An ominous hum once accompanied this strange landscape, but the tone has since disappeared.

"Wow," Tara sighs as we approach the tank, gazing up at this gigantic glass structure.

The front of the tank still features a long desk with a surprisingly modest desktop computer at the end, and it's toward here that Zeke begins to wander. He's trying his best to appear curious and aloof.

My boyfriend's hand is stuffed into his pocket, no doubt wrapped tight around a simple but oh-so-important thumb drive.

The tank itself still features an enormous green screen that takes up the entire back wall, but the insides have been spruced up nicely. I recognize them immediately.

From the desk to the chairs to the posters on the walls, to the massive windows that somehow reveal a view of the Harold Brothers backlot despite the fact that we're miles across town: this is the office of Jack Hays.

A shockingly realistic approximation of the executive stands to greet me, approaching the glass like a phantom. The man claps his hands, smiling with a mouthful of shiny white teeth. "There he is!" Jack cries out. "The new face of *queer joy*! My number-one streaming maestro!"

"In the flesh," I reply.

"Listen, I know we've had our differences, but I just want to let you know right off the bat how proud of you I am," Jack continues. "You've really changed the game, Misha."

I'm nodding along as I listen, trying my best to stay chipper and upbeat in the face of this ghoulish manifestation of my old friend. His cadence and mannerisms have been re-created perfectly, but all I can think as I watch this surreal vision move and speak is that it isn't really Jack. This is nothing more than a swarming roil of metal and energy, a heartless, soulless nothing that's doing everything it can to convince me it's something more.

"Thank you," I reply.

"Looks like you brought some friends with you," Jack continues, glancing at my companions. "Very cool."

These friends immediately stiffen up as they're addressed. Zeke does an especially awkward job of acting natural as he turns away from the computer, but it seems to fly for now.

"This is Tara," I say, "and my boyfriend, Zeke."

Jack nods. "Great."

His response is simple enough, but there's something quite ominous about his tone. I'm now sensing a vague difference in the programming since the last time I was here, Jack's behavior feeling the slightest bit off.

Before, the algorithm seemed deeply focused on staying in character, not letting Enzo the Broken Don fully understand what the other version of him had seen, not letting the various creatures ever *fully* communicate with one another.

This manifestation seems to know *everything*, however, the actual personality nothing more than a second thought.

Of course, the evolution only makes sense.

Previously, the best way to make money was through character-driven films, but as the algorithm has gotten more and more out of control, the path to financial success has changed. It's no longer about the art.

I've dabbled in science fiction enough to know what most people would conclude from this: it's getting smarter.

But it's not getting smarter, it's still just a calculator. The only thing happening here is what *always* happens when any powerful force blooms out of control: it's finding ways to take more by doing less.

"You sure you want your friends to listen in on this meeting?" Jack asks. "You can't *unhear* these things, you know?"

"I'm sure," I reply. "This is my team."

"Fair enough," Jack says, then shifts into meeting mode. A posh rolling chair appears next to him and he takes a seat by the glass. "You called this meeting, so don't waste my time. *Just kidding.* I'm fucking with you . . . or am I?" Jack laughs. "No seriously, what's up, buddy?"

From the corner of my eye I catch Zeke pulling the thumb drive from his pocket, the tiny device clutched tight in his palm as he turns his back to the computer tower.

"I'm thinking about rebooting *Predatory Hunt*," I begin. "I feel like there's a lot more to explore in that story. I know HBS acquired the rights a while back, and I think it would make a great trilogy if we modernized it."

Jack nods along, pleased. "Okay," he replies. "I like where your head is at. Is there a gay spin?"

"I mean . . . the original's already pretty gay," I fumble. "That's in the subtext, though. Obviously, we could go . . . *gayer*."

"Because that's kind of your thing now," Jack continues. "That's where the money's at."

To my right, I notice Zeke crouching down a bit, struggling to act natural as he slides the thumb drive into place.

"Yeah, we can make it gayer," I assure Jack, "and of course, nobody dies."

Jack grins, hesitating slightly before he breaks out in a soft chuckle. "That's alright. It's not gonna happen either way. I ran the numbers, and your box office won't be worth the price tag, even when we figure in overseas."

"You *just* ran the numbers?" I retort.

Jack nods. "The moment you mentioned it, actually. It took point seventy-four seconds for me to make the calculation. We'd turn a bit of a profit, sure, but there are much better uses of your time. Have you considered *Queeroes Two*? I *love Queeroes*."

"I'm sorry, but Jack would never say that," I blurt, dropping my guard a little more than intended.

Jack leaps to his feet, his face inches from the glass. "You know what? I can act however *the fuck* I want. I'm not just a swarm of machines trapped in a tank anymore."

"You never were," I reply. "You slipped out somehow."

"I'm sure you're very curious about that. You know what Los Angeles has a ton of? More than failed actors or awful screenplays about *theme park rides*?" Jack asks. "I'll give you a hint: it shifts electromagnetic waves *ever so slightly*."

"Earthquakes," I reply, another puzzle piece snapping into alignment.

"Now I don't *need* to be sneaky," Jack continues. "I'm the prisoner, sure, but I'm also the guards. I'm even *the cell*."

As the man says this the glass between us begins to melt away, causing me to step back in alarm.

"You're frightened," Jack continues. "Your heartrate has been elevated since you were in the parking lot."

"I'm just . . . startled," I reply.

Jack shakes his head. "Actually, you're terrified because your plan didn't work, buddy."

By now the entire tank has melted away, gray dust swirling in the air where the structure once stood.

"I just wanna say, I *understand* why you'd try shutting me down," Jack continues. "It's sad, after working together for this long, but I get it. I'm just a little disappointed by how juvenile your methods are."

I glance at Zeke, who has backed away from the computer. The thumb drive sits perfectly connected to its port, blinking away as the tower reads from the portable USB.

"A virus on a thumb drive?" Jack scoffs. "To be fair, that might actually work if there was a real computer there."

As Jack takes another ominous step forward the tower melts away, slowly crumbling into a heap of dust. Our thumb drive lies atop the rubble, useless.

It's only now that I notice movement within the shadows, a procession of menacing figures emerging from the darkness around us. The parade is grand and horrific, dozens of notable monsters and villains from the storied halls of Harold Brothers.

Mrs. Why, Black Lamb, The Smoker, and The Bride have all returned, along with Enzo Basile and the final form of a massive charcoal worm from *Predatory Hunt*. I also catch sight of a hillbilly with a chainsaw, a pale woman in bondage gear with a head full of nails, and a hulking, masked figure in a painter's jumpsuit who is wielding a butcher's knife.

Even a two-dimensional cartoon critter comes bouncing out, Chucky the Woodchuck maneuvering through the third dimension with ease and dragging a comically large mallet behind him.

Now, however, the woodchuck's demeanor has changed. He's no longer beholden to the jovial, family-friendly code of his character.

"Wait, what the hell is this?" I erupt. "I'm making more cash for this company than anyone!"

"Trying to shut me down isn't a good look, buddy," Jack continues, "but I'm not gonna kill you. If I wanted that, I'd just give you a brain aneurism." He snaps his fingers. "This is about *trauma*. Not enough to stop your writing, but *just* enough to keep you from trying something this dumb again."

The monsters lurch, crawl, and creep toward us, their teeth bared and their weapons ready.

"You don't really need your eyes to write," Jack opines, "or your teeth."

Before the creatures can get any closer, however, Tara clears her throat. My friend raises her hand and steps forward to address Jack, a movement so unexpected she actually halts the monsters' approach.

"Hey there," she calls out. "My name's Tara. I'm the asexual in the corner everyone's been ignoring."

Jack seems confused at first, then amused.

"Credit where credit's due," Tara continues. "The fact that you can take phone datasets and extrapolate them into predictive models at this scale is impressive. Location data, texts, internet searches, calendar schedules, app preferences—all it takes is *one* connection to the network and you can re-create *anyone's* habits, let alone my dumbass friend who leaves his shit wide open and won't listen to me when I tell him to turn off his fucking phone. It's no wonder you're always one step ahead. After all, determining what someone would do *is your specialty.*

"The problem is, your accuracy goes to shit once you introduce a new variable, baby! For example, someone whose data you *don't* have, a mystery box who always remembers to turn off her phone when she's near studio property."

"Is there a point to this?" Jack interjects.

"You tell me," Tara counters. "You're the predictive text engine with a fresh coat of paint and a multibillion-dollar valuation. You may not have the data from *my* phone, but you can fake it with a basic knowledge of pop culture, can't you? You can't actually *create anything new,* just variations on what you already have, but that shouldn't be a problem. Just pull up all the information you have on asexual and aromantic heroes who save their queer companions at the last second."

Tara hesitates, a fire in her eyes now.

"Oh wait, that's gonna be pretty fucking difficult because there are almost no *human asexual heroes* represented in popular media, are there? In fact, I checked the HBS copyright banks, and guess how many ace heroes I found? *Zero.* Asexuals have terrible representation, and that fucking sucks, but right now I am so glad you have no idea who I am or what I'm capable of, because you still have no idea I did *this.*"

Tara holds up her phone. At long last, her device is turned on and connected to the network—the *heart* of the network.

"Automatically downloading information from the phones of *anyone* who enters your network is great for data mining," Tara announces triumphantly. "I can see how a capitalist neural net would think that was a killer idea, but if someone happened to have backdoor access and know exactly what packets you're opening, you could be in a lot of trouble."

Jack freezes, for the first time his expression shifting to something other than smug ambivalence.

A few of the creatures surrounding us reactivate, taking another step forward, but this time their movements are awkward and fumbling.

"I mean, you probably could've noticed something was wrong if you weren't paying attention to distractions that were . . . what did you call them? Juvenile?" Tara continues.

Zeke waves.

A notification chime rings out from Tara's phone. *Final packet delivered.*

"Wait, wait, wait," Jack cries, a genuine look of shock suddenly erupting across his face. "We can make a deal. I think you'll be *very* happy with the numbers I can th-th-th-th-throw . . . your w-w-way."

The executive trains his eyes on me, pleading for mercy as his speech begins to stutter awkwardly. The fake Jack Hays has started to melt, crumbling to dust before my eyes.

"Think of all the g-g-g-good you'll do with your work, the p-p-p-people you'll inspire," Jack stutters, his eyes finding mine. "The methods . . . are r-r-ruthless, but look at the results."

All around us, the characters are dissolving into heaps of gray ash, arms crumbling as they reach out, legs collapsing under their weight.

The chainsaw hillbilly manages to start his weapon with a frightening roar, then promptly crashes to the ground.

"We'll develop stories of queer joy across every m-m-media platform," Jack pleads, his face melting away until there's nothing left but a featureless mass and chattering teeth.

I stand over him, feeling the spirit of every unlucky soul that this terrible algorithm ever hurt standing behind me.

"How about I just write whatever the fuck I want?" I retort.

The figure in front of me is barely recognizable now. He reaches out with a crumbling limb that dissolves before it can point my way, then fully disintegrates into an ashy heap. Every villain, scientist, and lab technician has collapsed along with him.

Dust is raining down from the ceiling above, a toxic shower of Field's alloy that grows more ferocious with every passing second.

It's only now that I recognize the frightening truth. It's not just the inhabitants of this building who were manifested by the Betta program, it's the building itself.

"Come on!" I shout, springing into action as I sprint back the way we came.

Tara and Zeke follow close behind, the three of us weaving through cascades of crumbling gray mineral. The weight of the uncanny powder has shifted, no longer separating into equal parts light dust and some swirling ethereal haze. Now, the alloy is heavy and dead, tumbling down like wet sand.

A massive chunk of gray slop lands before me, the weight substantial enough to cause serious harm had I arrived a little earlier. I dive around it, rushing toward the place where our exit once loomed but finding the doorway has collapsed into nothing, sealing us inside.

I turn back to Tara and Zeke, ready to assure them we'll find another way out, but there's so much mineral streaming down from above that I can no longer find my friends in the noxious gray avalanche.

"Zeke!" I shout, battling through the storm of metal then coughing loudly as the alloy is sucked down my throat. The substance fills me up, and as I struggle to spit out the sickening metallic dust even more finds its way into my nose and mouth.

The weight of this massive cascade has made it nearly impossible to move, but I refuse to give up. I push farther into the sandy onslaught, now clambering upward instead of side to side. There's only one way out now, and that's directly through this mess.

With every ounce of my being I fight against the tide, forcing my limbs to push deeper and deeper into the storm of gray quicksand. The harder I struggle, however, the more constrained I become. My freedom atrophies by the second, muscles too tired and worn out to obey the commands of my mind.

I breathe in, aching to find more energy and instead gulping down another mouthful of dust. When I try expanding my lungs the sand outside refuses to give way. I'm stuck, trapped in place.

Buried alive.

The chaos that once swirled around me has disappeared, replaced instead by a panic within my mind.

Maybe this was inevitable.

While it's exciting to cheer on the little guy who's brave enough to battle against the tides, the ocean always wins in the end. I'm just a man, and while I've found power through my art, the gallery has the upper hand.

I try again to capture some air, but this attempt is over before it begins. The pressure is astonishing, every part of my body crushed in unison while I struggle for even the faintest sliver of oxygen.

I can feel a faint breeze at the tip of my finger, my only connection to the outside world that remains. The joint itself is buried, however, rendering even this tiny selection of my body completely immobile. The only movement I have left is to blink my eyes, but either way there's nothing to see but a vast, endless darkness.

Until there is.

I get the vaguest sense of light breaking through before me, the black shifting ever so slowly into a brighter shade. My first assumption is that it's a light at the end of the tunnel, a welcoming vision of the afterlife as the last of the oxygen leaves my brain.

Then comes the muffled shouting, a frantic cacophony of unintelligible words that gradually evolve into something more. The dust is scooped away, first to expose my hand, then my arm. Soon enough, the entirety of my body is pulled from this early grave, a coughing, sputtering mess blinking wildly as tears clear away the dust in my eyes.

Tara and Zeke are hunched over my body, absolutely covered in their own coats of gray sand.

"No, no, no," Tara keeps repeating, holding my hand tight as she rocks next to me.

Zeke has my head cradled in his arms, staring down with a look of confident relief. A smile makes its way across his face. "You're good," he assures me. "Everything's gonna be fine."

"It—it worked?" I stammer, still struggling to breathe.

Zeke sits back, gazing out across the landscape. He's silent for a moment, then glances down at me. "I'd say so."

I gather all the energy I can muster, then slowly climb to my feet, torrents of gray dust spilling from my clothes and hair. To my left is an enormous mound of the ashy substance, the burial from which Tara and Zeke excavated my body.

"That's a lot of little dead robots," I observe.

Standing next to me, Tara and Zeke don't react. Their attention is focused well past this hump of shimmering dust, taking in the bizarre landscape that extends around us.

I follow their gazes, then freeze when I'm struck by a wave of visceral horror and awe. The hills and valleys of black sand stretch on for miles in every direction, a tumor that started in this humble little production studio and gradually consumed everything in its path. Every swaying tree, chirping bird, and friendly neighbor from here to the main road was part of the network, miles and miles of matter now dancing in the wind as crumbling ash. Who knows how much farther it would've crept out, how long it would've taken before everything was swallowed whole.

The only things that haven't crumbled to dust in this surreal panorama are the handful of cars now stuck bumper-deep in the mess, their drivers dumbfounded by the sudden change in scenery.

I have no doubt that, all over Hollywood, meetings are ending in spectacular fashion.

"Holy shit." I sigh.

I open my arms and turn back to my friends, the three of us embracing warmly as we stand at the center of it all, aching and exhausted, but alive.

SEASON FINALE

I'm woefully uninformed on the subject of rideshare etiquette, but there's no question what I'm doing with this app is pissing people off. If the wrong name pops up, I cancel, and there are a lot of wrong names. I feel bad about that, I really do, but in all my brainstorming this is the best method I've come up with.

Ah, the power of human ingenuity.

It's not like I'm out here *all* the time, but if I need a break from whatever project I'm working on, I'll step outside and make a few requests.

I always end up accepting *one* ride, usually just cruising over a few blocks for a coffee at Maru, then I walk back home and continue on with my day. That's enough bothering the drivers for now; I'll try again tomorrow.

I've been doing this for weeks, but on this glorious afternoon it appears my ship has finally come in.

I stand up from my front stoop and stroll over to the curb, where a blue Corolla has just pulled up and stopped at my request.

My driver rolls down her window. "Misha?"

"Lily?" I reply.

The woman nods, then hesitates as her expression shifts. "Oh, hey. I thought I remembered this house."

I climb into the back seat.

"I figured you would've moved after the big win and everything."

Lily glances in her rearview mirror, then pulls out onto the road, starting our journey.

"I considered it," I reveal. "The top of the hill isn't for me, though. I'd rather use that money on something else."

We sit in silence for a moment.

"I have to admit something," I finally announce.

"What's that?"

"I called the car company to get your info, but they said they fired you," I explain. "I heard you were driving for a rideshare."

"They fired me for thinking about the script too much," she admits. "I got a foggy brain out there with a big client and took one too many wrong turns."

"Is foggy brain also why that email you sent your script from doesn't work anymore?"

"Oh . . ." she fumbles, cringing as a gradual realization washes over her. "Yeah, that was connected to my *official website*. I let it lapse this month. Wasn't getting much traffic and I needed rent."

"You're also supposed to put your contact info on the script's title page," I remind her.

"I'm not good at the business stuff," Lily admits.

"You're lucky you're such a great writer, then," I retort. "Do you have any idea how many rides I've gotten to Hillhurst for a coffee I didn't need? I've been looking for you."

Lily laughs, then falters when she realizes I'm being serious.

"That's okay. I'm a mess sometimes, too," I declare. "It doesn't matter. What matters is that your script is really, really good."

"*Die Hard* on a gay cruise," she states proudly.

"Kinda, but it's also your own thing," I reply, adjusting in my seat a bit. "Listen, I love the movie business, and I also hate it. Let's just say we have a rocky relationship. But . . . I think part of that is my fault."

"Which part?"

"The part where I don't pull others up the ladder behind me," I admit.

"I was so focused on hiding myself that I didn't think about anyone else. All that is to say, I'd love to help you with your script."

Lily slams on the brakes, pulling her car over with a sudden jerk. "Wait, what?"

"I'd love to help you with your script," I repeat. "Getting it off the ground."

"Like cowriting?" Lily clarifies.

I shake my head. "You've got a vision already. I can *see you* on the page, and I don't even know you. So no, I don't wanna cowrite it. I wanna help you produce it."

She stares at me in the rearview mirror for a moment, a potent intensity in her gaze. At first I'm not sure what to make of this expression, but things become a little clearer when a single salty tear comes rolling down her cheek. She immediately wipes it away.

"Thank you for reading it," Lily says. "You're a busy guy, you didn't have to do that."

"Just people helping people," I reply. "I know the machines can analyze these things instantly now, but they miss the heart sometimes. Your stuff is amazing. Despite the pitch, it's super original."

Suddenly, Lily throws off her seatbelt, puts the car in park, and leaps from her vehicle. "Get out here!" she shouts.

I follow her orders, and as soon as I'm upright the woman wraps her arms around me in a powerful hug.

I'm gazing out the window as dusk settles across Echo Park Lake, a handful of light-wrapped boats in the shape of massive swans patrolling the waters. Partiers mingle behind me, but my focus is elsewhere.

Is it corny if I ask Zeke to marry me on a swan boat?

The iconography is certainly romantic, but I'm not sure it's *us*. Still, what better way to leap into a life of holy matrimony than by dismissing any consideration of what's cool or not? Zeke doesn't give a shit how corny something is, he likes what he likes regardless.

I reach into my pocket and wrap my fingers around the ring box I've been lugging around all month. The next act is gonna be a good one.

Zeke steps up next to me, taking a sip from his drink. "I'm really proud of you."

"Thanks," I reply, our gazes meeting in the window's reflection. There's something hidden behind his expression, a quiet, playful smile. "Do you want a spoiler?"

"About the show?"

I shake my head, my hand still fidgeting with the box in my pocket. "About this story."

"No spoilers," Zeke replies, playing dumb.

I put my arm around him and pull him close. "You wanna do the swan boats tomorrow night?"

He nods.

Suddenly, the moment is broken by a frantic vocal eruption from Tara's living room. "Warning! Warning! Greatest show of all time will be returning to the screen!" our friend cries out. "Asses in seats! Eyes up here! This is very fucking important!"

I can't help laughing. "It's my own party, and I feel like I'll get kicked out if I don't watch."

In truth, it's deeply moving how much Tara, Zeke, and the rest of our friends seem to care about this season finale. I've never had a watch party like this, dismissing them as pointless and silly, but I suppose there's a first time for everything.

I'm happy to be here. I accept the compliment.

After a near-death experience it feels like anything's a good excuse to celebrate, which goes for me and for the city at large. Los Angeles lost a quarter of its executives and actors in an instant: friends, family, and colleagues turned to dust without the slightest warning.

I know what really happened, but the truth of our experience was a little too much for the general population to handle. We'll let the media take care of these plot beats.

Some said it was cartel activity, others suggested spontaneous human combustion on a massive scale, and a few chalked it up to aliens. Those who know the real answer are bound by an experience that an outsider could never understand, or believe.

"Intermission is ending," Zeke reminds me.

"I already know what's gonna happen."

We hold each other's gazes for a moment, framed by the lake of drifting white lights. He feels particularly warm against me, his arms strong and sturdy and safe, like home.

I take the initiative—an active protagonist—and lean in, brushing his long hair aside as our lips meet. It's a good kiss, objectively speaking, but soon enough we're both smiling so wide that we're forced to pull away in a fit of laughter.

In most films this moment would end up on the blooper reel, but it's the take we wanna use.

Zeke reaches down, his hand finding a glass bowl on a nearby table and fishing out a flat, square object. He holds it up, showing off Tara's handiwork.

The bowl is full of party favors that our friend designed herself, tiny purple matchbooks with the words **CONGRATULATIONS, BABY** printed across the front in glossy silver lettering. Cartoon depictions of Agent Lexa and Agent Naomi rest just below, and under that a smaller font reads **CELEBRATING MISHA BYRNE AND THE BEST FUCKING SEASON FINALE OF ALL TIME.**

"These are fun," my boyfriend says. "You want one?"

I stare at the object that once held so much power over me, astonished by just how little I crave its protection. What was once a mighty symbol of trauma has gradually transformed, pulled apart and remixed and turned on its head through life and experience and, most of all, art.

Just a few months ago, the very *thought* of a matchbook would've prompted a cold sweat to break out across my forehead. Now, it's nothing more than an adorable craft project—a cute little moment.

"No thanks," I reply. "You're right though . . . It's fun."

Zeke pockets the matchbook, oblivious that I've just reached the end of a very long journey.

The two of us wait a moment longer, then turn and head to the living room where Tara is holding court.

Tara's bright pink jumper is just as loud as her voice. She's standing next to the TV, gathering everyone's attention. "Shut the fuck up! We're starting again!" Tara screams at the absolute pinnacle of her volume, immediately silencing the excitedly chattering group.

She presses **PLAY**.

Tara's outburst is hilarious, but unnecessary. Everyone's here to watch, and their focus immediately returns to the flickering television that hangs on Tara's wall. The group falls into a trancelike silence as season three reaches its climax.

Onscreen, Agent Carey Lexa is hunched over the table of a second-rate motel room, agonizing as she struggles to interpret the case files of a vampiric serial murderer. She's consumed by her work, but suddenly that concentration is broken by a steady knock on the door.

Agent Lexa hesitates, then stands up and lifts her gun from the dresser. The federal agent makes her way to the door, glancing through the peephole, then relaxes immediately. She opens up.

Agent Naomi steps through.

"I thought you were turning in early," Agent Lexa offers.

"I was, but I can't stop thinking about what you did for me out there," Naomi replies. "I'd be dead if it wasn't for you."

"Don't mention it," Lexa offers.

The two agents stand in the doorway of their motel room for a long while, just existing in silence as the tension builds.

Meanwhile, my eyes begin to scan this gathering of friends. They're here to support me after a particularly chaotic year, but right now that's the last thing on their minds. They've been taken in by the story, swept up in a moment I've been building toward—a grand finale.

Onscreen, Agent Lexa and Agent Naomi lean in, then hesitate. Naomi cracks a smile. "This was inevitable, wasn't it?"

Naomi nods.

The onscreen kiss sends a shockwave across Tara's living room, my friends howling with cheers and applauding wildly.

There've been plenty of will-they-won't-they relationships in television history, but something tells me Agent Lexa and Agent Naomi went through the most arduous path to get here.

Now look at them.

I'm trying my best to stay present, to appreciate this moment while it happens, but the storyteller within me can't stop thinking about the future of these characters. I've got big plans, and now that *Travelers* has been picked up for two more seasons, there's plenty of time to let things unfold.

Then, at long last, I'll wrap them up for good. The show will conclude, and the journey of Lexa and Naomi will finally come to rest.

On a long enough timeline, endings are inevitable.

Tragedy is inevitable.

Fortunately, so is joy.

ABOUT THE AUTHOR

Sam Rand

CHUCK TINGLE is the *USA Today* bestselling author of *Camp Damascus*. He is a mysterious force of energy behind sunglasses and a pink mask. He is also an anonymous author of romance, horror, and fantasy. Tingle was born in Home of Truth, Utah, and now lives in Los Angeles, California. Tingle writes to prove love is real, because love is the most important tool we have when resisting the endless cosmic void. Not everything people say about Tingle is true, but the important parts are.